The fiery brillia[...] which you see on the [...] phy." This is the revo[...] ful laser beam records light waves in diamond-like facets so tiny that 9,000,000 fit in a square inch. No print or photograph can match the vibrant colors and radiant glow of a hologram.

So look for the Zebra Hologram Heart whenever you buy a historical romance. It is a shimmering reflection of our guarantee that you'll find consistent quality between the covers!

## LOVE'S MAGIC SPELL

"Do the men of your village tell you how beautiful you are, Summer?" Sebastian asked.

"The sweetness of your words is like honey to trap bees. And this bee stings!" she retorted.

Sebastian chuckled softly, then his hand reached to touch her chin lightly and lift her mouth to his. The chuckle died and his eyes registered shock as the cold blade of a knife was pressed against his throat.

For what seemed an eternity they looked at each other. She did not mean to bend—the prick of the knife told him that—but the dangerous glow in his eyes should have warned her that Sebastian did not mean to bend either.

Slowly he enclosed her wrist in an iron-hard grip that numbed her fingers. Still their gazes held—hers defiant and his warming with a stirring need that was rapidly pushing all other thoughts aside. She felt the heat of her blood pounding through her as the knife slipped from her fingers, and the roar of thunder echoed about them as their eyes continued the silent battle.

His nearness and the desire written plainly on his features made her whisper a word of resistance as his mouth touched hers. [...] she moaned against his mouth.

But her [...] declared yes, and a deep ache began to grow within her [...] that left her trembling and unable to withstand the power of the magic he was weaving about her [...]

## BESTSELLERS BY SYLVIE F. SOMMERFIELD ARE BACK IN STOCK!

B.R.

# Captive Embrace

### SYLVIE F. SOMMERFIELD

**ZEBRA BOOKS**
**KENSINGTON PUBLISHING CORP.**

ZEBRA BOOKS

are published by

Kensington Publishing Corp.
475 Park Avenue South
New York, NY 10016

First printing: April 1986

Printed in the United States of America

*To Leann Shoaf—*
*with thanks for all the hard work*

## Chapter One

*March, 1773 . . . England*

The room was in semidarkness, but enough of the early afternoon sun filtered through the draperies to illuminate the two who writhed together amid the tangled sheets in the huge, four-poster bed. Soft, murmured words and throaty moans accentuated the enjoyment each derived from this pleasant interlude.

The woman's long, slender legs were wrapped about the man's hips. Her hands caressed his broad back and lean waist while her body arched to meet his driving thrusts. A few pale beams of sunlight touched the gold of the man's hair, and through half-closed, passion-filled eyes, the woman looked up into green orbs that blazed with a devil's fire.

She panted softly and wild desire surged through her as his iron hardness drove her beyond any restraint she might have had. Her body throbbed, overcome as it was by the ferocity of his tense, tormenting maleness. He was rough and demanding, but she welcomed the roughness, for it drove her beyond the knowledge that there was a place within this man she could not reach though she strove to gain it with a panic born of desperation.

"Oh . . . God . . . Sebastian . . . please . . ." Her body quivered as it reached completion and once again she was torn by an anguishing sense of loss as he slid from her body and rolled away from her.

They lay in an uncomfortable silence for some time, each not daring to say the words that would shatter the calm.

Slowly his rasping breathing quieted and he moved to a sitting position on the edge of the bed, his back to her.

"Sebastian?" she ventured in a ragged whisper.

Seconds passed before he answered, and his hesitation confirmed her fears.

"Kate," he began. "I have to—"

"Don't," she whispered, then rose quickly to her knees behind him and pressed her cheek to his broad back. He could feel her tears touching his skin. He hated what was happening but was as helpless to stop it as he would have been to prevent the earth from turning. Her arms circled his waist and her hands urged him closer. Gently but firmly he gripped her hands and loosened their hold. Then he rose and walked to a nearby chair to pick up the clothes he had thrown down in his urgency to claim her. She watched him as he slowly began to dress.

She had known from the first that she desired Sebastian Cain. In fact, she had made her conquest a deliberate act. Kate Maxwell was a beauty with her golden hair and her cornflower blue eyes. She was an heiress to a very small fortune in her own right, but she had married Lord Gerald Maxwell—a man nearly old enough to be her grandfather—in order to gain the monumental Maxwell fortune. Kate had known she would be Lord Gerald's only heir.

This role had satisfied her immensely until Sebastian

Cain had walked into her life. She had desired him immediately and had first contrived a meeting, then a deliberate seduction.

Now he had come to her, telling her of his plans and asking her to leave Maxwell and his fortune and come with him to an unknown wilderness. She wanted Seb, but she wanted the Maxwell fortune as well, and she fully intended to have both.

She had no hold on him except that of her body, in which he had taken such pleasure, but she was confident that he was intoxicated by her charms. He had been honest with her from the start, telling her of his insatiable need to find some elusive thing—something that would hold him and something he could hold. He had explained his desire to build his own fortune in America and his equally strong desire that she help him build it. She wanted to tame him, though she knew others had failed. Sebastian Cain was as elusive as the dream he sought and as wild and irrepressible as a tornado. What he wanted he usually got, but it never seemed enough. He would alight briefly, then move on, always leaving behind a void as great as the one inside him that relentlessly drove him toward the unknown.

As she watched him now from under thick lashes, she realized he had the power to make desire spring to life within her again, though it had only been a short time since they had explored the depths of passion together. He was wildly handsome, she mused, with his green eyes that could smolder with a violent sensuality that made her turn weak inside. But she knew those eyes could easily turn as cold as the frozen snows. And experiencing such a look frightened her far more than enduring his anger, for she knew how the coldness of his eyes could devastate.

He dressed slowly as if he were thinking carefully

about what hung unsaid in the silence. She took the time to absorb everything about him. She watched the muscles ripple under his taut, bronzed skin and recognized their power. He was tall and solid, and his rigid musculature was the product of much physical activity. His hair was as gold as the morning sun and his phenomenal eyes were a unique shade of green that could only be described as jade. His face seemed at first rugged, yet there was also a gentleness, as if life hadn't been sure of just how to complete it. His mouth was wide and sensual, and Kate could almost feel the pressure of his lips again where they had conquered hers a short time before. His smile was quick and could melt the coldest heart as easily as it had melted hers several months earlier.

After donning his pants, Sebastian returned to the bed and sat down beside her. Their eyes met, and she read in his what she had dreaded.

"You . . . you really are going, aren't you?" She blinked back the tears she was so adept at bringing into her wide eyes and noticed Sebastian's reaction with satisfaction.

"But Seb," she pleaded. "Listen to me."

"Kate, we talked about this before."

She reached out a hand to touch his cheek. "I thought I could hold you. I love you, Seb. Why can't that be enough for you? Why can't you stay with me?"

"I can't, Kate. I can't. I have to go . . . and you could come with me. I begged you once before. The choice has always been yours. Why don't you just pack tonight? By tomorrow we could be on our way. We could leave everything behind and forget all the gossips and scandal peddlers. It would be so easy, Kate . . . and so good for us."

"You . . . I can't just go. To . . . to that savage place. I've heard such terrible stories. There's . . . there's wild

10

and uncivilized people there. Sebastian, don't be cruel. Stay with me. I can make you happy if you give me the chance."

"Not here, Kate," he replied determinedly. "I'm leaving in the morning and I want you to come with me. But"—he shrugged—"as I said, the choice is yours. I want you as my wife and I can no longer tolerate this sneaking about. You don't love him. Leave him now and come with me."

"It's just so easy for you, isn't it?" she asked in pretend anger.

"Damnit Kate, you weren't exactly forced into this, you know. Being together was your idea. If I'm not mistaken, the offer came from you. I care about you, Kate, but don't make me the villain in this affair. Your husband is a very rich man, but he is twice your age. Are his money and position so necessary to you?"

"No, I guess force isn't your method. You play the game so well, don't you?" She was truly angry now and gave no thought to her nakedness as she rose to face him. "You never really give, do you Sebastian? You just take, and then walk away untouched and uncaring. I owe Gerald more than that. He has been good to me and I can't hurt him. Stay a while longer. One day we'll be able to be together."

"That's foolish, Kate. I care for you. I want you to be with me. I don't think I'm asking too much."

"If you truly cared for me, you wouldn't be so demanding. You would understand. You wouldn't be so terrible to me."

His eyes flashed with cool anger as he moved closer. "And I took advantage of your innocence?" He laughed harshly. "Hardly, Kate. I thought what we shared was good for both of us, but I guess I was wrong. You want to have everything your way." He lowered his voice to a firm and determined level.

11

"Come with me, Kate. I'm asking for the last time. But either way, I'm leaving next Monday."

"You ask everything, Sebastian," she said as she sobbed.

"I guess that's it," he replied. "I want a woman who's willing to share my life and what I do. Maybe . . . maybe we both made a mistake. Maybe all we did share was passion."

She choked on a sob that was half anger, half anguish as she absorbed the blow of his words.

"I'll hate you if you leave me now."

"Will you Kate?" he asked coolly. "Will you really?"

Before she could answer, he was pulling her against his hard chest and binding her firmly to him so she could hardly breathe.

"Let me go, Sebastian."

"Not yet, Kate. Tell me," he whispered in a warm, caressing tone. "Tell me you hate me. Tell me you don't want me to make love to you. Tell me to go."

"I hate you. I . . . I want you to go."

He chuckled as he held her immobile with one powerful arm and stroked her quivering flesh gently with his hand.

"Do you?" he asked softly. She tried to squirm free, but it was useless. Her head turned from his to keep his lips from finding hers, but that too was impossible.

"You don't hate me," he muttered raggedly as his free hand continued to caress her. "And I cannot hate you. Please, Kate. Come with me. We'll be happy."

She fought in desperation, trying to deny the fierce heat that blossomed into an ache she could not control. She wanted to keep Sebastian near until the day she could have both him and her husband's wealth.

His arm was tight about her waist and pressed her to him. Her body arched against his, and even though she pushed one hand against his chest to repel him, the other was caught between their bodies, making the pressure she exerted an ineffectual force.

"I don't want you like this! I won't be with you again until you promise to stay."

"You want me as much as I want you. I can feel the heat of your body, and I can see it in your eyes."

His free hand tangled in her hair and he drew back her head until she was forced to part her lips in protest. Then he kissed her with a ferocity that stormed her senses as his open mouth captured her parted lips and held them open. His tongue ravaged her mouth and called forth a stream of sensations against which she was unable to defend herself.

"Tell me now," he ground out. "Tell me you hate me."

"Sebastian," she sobbed, "you are hateful and cruel." She allowed her tears to suggest a helplessness she did not feel.

Quelling the anger that had overcome him momentarily, he kissed her again, gently, and released her.

"Good-bye, Kate," he said softly. "I'm sorry. If you would just . . ." He turned away.

She collapsed on the bed and wept as he put on the rest of his clothes and left without speaking again.

She stared at the closed door. "I love you, Sebastian," she whispered. "You will change your mind. You will see the truth and stay. We could have the world at our feet. You'll come back Sebastian. You're mine and you will come back."


Sebastian left the house and called for a carriage. Kate had been his mistress for nearly six months, he reflected. He could not understand why she refused to go with him when she claimed she loved him. To Sebastian, the Maxwell money meant nothing. He

13

wanted her, and he had believed they could leave everything behind and have a happy life together. They would have been withdrawing as well from the strict society in which they lived, and he had hoped therefore to keep her from being hurt.

It was as if he were being drawn by some unseen force to a destination of which he had no knowledge. But Kate—his beautiful Kate—would be the center of his life, the mother of his children, and a symbol of English womanhood in the New World. He had always admired her blond, delicate beauty and had dreamed of her residing in his home and creating an atmosphere of gentility in the young country he wanted to make his own.

Wealthy and spoiled, Sebastian had always had whatever he desired. Now it angered him to feel so insecure and moreover, to allow Kate to see it.

He took his mind from her, knowing that if his thoughts dwelled on her any longer, he would weaken and stay, just as she wanted him to. Now he was determined to start his life afresh in the New World and come back for her when he could offer her everything.

He decided to return home for the evening meal with his parents and his younger brother; Nathaniel. Then he would tell them of his purchase of land in America and of his plans to leave within the week. He needed the challenge; he needed to escape from a place and time that seemed to be stifling him.


Dinner proved to be an uneventful affair, and afterward Sebastian found himself surrounded by his family in the drawing room of their elaborate home as he tried to summon the words to tell them of his plans.

Sebastian knew that because he was the eldest of two children, his parents would not look favorably upon his latest decision. His brother, Nathaniel, who was younger than the twenty-seven-year-old Sebastian by three years, profoundly worshiped his older brother, and Sebastian assumed Nathaniel would approve of whatever he chose to do.

"Great God!" his father exclaimed angrily when Sebastian finally revealed his plans. "To a heathen land? What in God's name for? What do you need that you don't have here?"

"Freedom," Sebastian explained gently.

"Freedom from what? Sebastian, you have the very best of everything," his mother declared, a worried frown on her face. "What more do you want?"

Before Sebastian could answer, his father exploded, "No, by God! You will not go! I am tired of your frittering your life away in the pursuit of women and other foolishness. I will not allow you to run off on another excursion that has no purpose. I will not allow it!"

"Father," Sebastian reminded him, "you can't stop me."

"Sebastian"—his father's voice grew calm—"you are my oldest son. You are the heir to a fortune. I do not want you to go."

"It is only for a year or two. There is another fortune to be made—this time, my own. I'm going to do this, Father," he said quietly, "with or without your blessing."

No one had noticed the glow of deep admiration and near worship in Nathaniel's eyes then, but later, as the two stood in the garden and talked, the younger man revealed the plan that he had formulated after hearing his brother's announcement. They had always been close from childhood, and Nathaniel walked in his brother's footsteps whenever he could.

"When do you leave, Sebastian?" Nathaniel inquired casually.

"Next Monday at dawn, on the *Resound,*" Sebastian

replied. "Coming to the dock to see me off?" He laughed shortly. "I don't suppose Father will."

"Neither will I," Nathaniel retorted. Sebastian was quiet, stung by his brother's rejection.

"I'm going with you," Nathaniel announced, grinning.

"Like hell you are!"

"I am. I told Mother a while ago. It's only two years, and I'd rather be with you than anywhere else. Mother understands. Besides, she doesn't want you to go alone."

"I'll talk to her."

"It won't do any good. Sebastian, please. I want to go. It's the most exciting thing I can think of, and I'd like to share it with you. When we come back, we'll have a lot of stories to tell once we settle down and have children. Sebastian, please let me go with you."

Sebastian realized how much more fulfilling this new venture would be if he shared it with his brother. Nathaniel could see the look of acceptance in his eyes and he laughed. Sebastian laughed with him, for the anticipation of adventure gripped him anew.

"Well, I guess we go together," Sebastian said.

"Tell me about it," Nathaniel added quickly.

"There's land to be had, Nathaniel," Sebastian explained excitedly, "large tracts of land just for the taking, available to the first ones who grab the opportunity."

"And you're the one to grab it." Nathaniel chuckled.

Sebastian wasn't sure he appreciated his brother's humor. "That's what opportunities are for," he replied gruffly. "If you don't grab what you can when you want it, someone else will."

"You're right," Nathaniel agreed. "I envy you, Sebastian, and I admire you. I've never seen anything—or anyone—slip through your fingers once you've set your mind to obtaining it. I expect to learn a lot from the old master on this trip. Tell me"—he nudged Sebastian with his elbow—"are there women as pretty as Kate for the taking as well?"

At Sebastian's dark scowl, Nathaniel whistled lightly. "I see Kate didn't like the idea of this venture."

"No," Sebastian said quietly. "She had decided . . . she isn't going." Sebastian's eyes were dark with the pain of his separation from the woman he felt he loved.

"Funny. I thought she cared for you more than that. She refused to go?" Nathaniel questioned, his voice gentle.

"It seems she's afraid," Sebastian replied vaguely.

"Sebastian, why don't you demand that she go, force her to decide?"

Sebastian shook his head. "I have another way," he said determinedly. "One day Kate will go with me."

Nathaniel clapped him on the shoulder as they walked back into the house.


The following Monday a still-angry father and a teary-eyed mother waved good-bye as the *Resound* left the dock. Nathaniel and Sebastian stood together, still laughing over their parents' strict admonitions that Sebastian take care of his brother. Suppressing a grin, their eldest son had told them he had done so for years and would probably continue to do so for the rest of Nathaniel's life.

The two brothers watched as the sails filled and both surrendered to a feeling of euphoria as they contemplated the freedom and adventure awaiting them.

# *Chapter Two*

*May, 1773*

As she ran, fear tugged at her mind. Surrounded by a gray mist, she could not see the threat that hovered near, but she could feel it. It tingled up her spine and lent wings to her feet.

Low-hanging branches reached to brush her skin and thorny brambles tore at her clothes. Sweat slicked her skin and her heart throbbed painfully. She could feel the heat of the tears in her eyes, and her lungs seemed to be aflame as she released her breath in soft, rasping gasps.

She wanted to cry out but could not. Renewed panic filled her as she sensed that whatever was following was drawing nearer and nearer. The power of something dark filled her mind and she knew some deadly evil was slowly closing a trap about her.

Something touched her, tore at her clothes, and she could feel the breath of her pursuers. Pursuers? Why did she feel there was more than one?

Someone or something gripped her and she twisted from its grasp only to find herself slipping. She cried out in anguished despair as she stumbled forward and tumbled over an embankment to crash against the hard ground. Pain tore at her and she cried out again as darkness momentarily overtook her.

She felt the cold, hard earth beneath her and struggled to rise. Then, slowly, she lifted her head to look up at the dark form hovering between her and the grayish sky. Then the swirling mist seemed to dissolve as if it were parting to reveal him.

He stood between her and the gradually lightening sky, his legs braced apart and a smoking gun in his hand. His shoulders were broad; he seemed massive and strong. Light glimmered in bronze gold hair, and his jade eyes seemed to glow with an unearthly gleam as he smiled and reached for her.

Her frightened cry jerked her to startled wakefulness. She sat up in her bunk on the ship *Bethany,* trembling and wet with sweat at the return of a violent dream she had not had for a long, long time. To most people, dreams were unimportant, but to Summer, dreams meant much.

Born of a union between a white man and the beautiful medicine woman, Singing Bells, Summer was blessed—or perhaps cursed, she thought—with a strange gift for prophecy and healing. There were times when this gift frightened her, for she could not seem to control its use. Prophecy came to her in dreams or sudden visions that always overwhelmed or terrified her. The healing power was something she had tried to master and this had caused her innumerable problems. In fact, these very strange powers were the reason she was on her way home now.

She had been fifteen when Clayton Storm had sent her to school in England. He had felt she needed the culture of both societies, though she had lived in the wilderness with him since her birth and had spent much of her time with the Indians in the nearby village from

19

which her mother had come.

Summer rose from the bunk. Clad only in her chemise, she was damp with sweat nevertheless, from both the heat of the small ship's cabin and the nightmare from which she had just awakened. She poured some tepid water onto a cloth and pressed it against her skin to try to cool it. After awhile she gave up and donned her dress so that she could walk on deck. It was quite late and only a skeleton crew manned the ship. The dark sky was sprinkled with diamond-bright stars, and a cool breeze filled the sails and moved the ship along at a brisk rate of speed; yet it was not fast enough for Summer, who longed to see the shore of home. Once again Summer realized how much she had hated the confinement of school and the restricting clothes she had been forced to wear. She missed the soft buckskin tunic that had given her such freedom.

She closed her eyes and, for the first time in nearly five years, she allowed her mind to open—to reach for the place she called home and the people she loved so dearly. She promised herself that once she was home no power on earth could make her return to the miserable situation from which she had just escaped.

To be sure she could not be stopped, she had sent no messages to her family and had not told anyone at the school about her plan. She knew she would not have been aboard the ship now if she had. She remembered well the final confrontation that had made her decide to go home.

Summer had arrived in London a wild, untamed child, and her dark Indian beauty had caused quite a stir. Lord Matthew Gordon and his wife, who were very close friends of her father's, had tried their best to make her comfortable and happy in their home during summer vacations and holidays. But they had not been able to control the envy and bigotry of those with whom Summer had come in contact. As she grew older, her beauty had blossomed like a butterfly emerging from a cocoon, and it had attracted men like bees to honey.

It had taken some time to realize that because of her half-Indian blood, the white men looked at her not as a woman to marry, but one to take as a mistress if they could. They looked at her with eyes of lust and saw only the lure of her beauty. Very slowly a new emotion had begun to grow within her, a sickening distrust of them all—all the white world. This distrust had grown, and her emotional turmoil had led her into an explosive situation just three weeks before.

She had come to the school with deep trepidation but with an equally strong determination to succeed. Her father had wanted her to be educated in the white man's schools and she had vowed to accomplish this because it was his wish. From the time she had arrived in England, almost everyone she met had looked at her with curiosity rather than with understanding. She did not resemble her white father enough to convince them that she was heir to the Storm fortune. She looked more like her Indian mother, and because most had been certain that Clay Storm would never have married an Indian, Summer had been accused of being illegitimate. These cruel people had no way of knowing about the strange gifts her mother had given her, gifts that had allowed her access to their emotions and thoughts, which she had found ugly and condemning. And her rare and innocent beauty had made her the envy of the other girls at school and the prey of every dashing young male.

She had been able to make only a few friends at the school. One of them had been Emily Gill, and their friendship had grown slowly. Emily was a bright, laughing girl who always seemed sure the world was an enchanted place filled with heros and heroines. She had befriended Summer and they had exchanged the confidences young girls often share. Yet it was this very friendship that eventually caused Summer great anguish. . . .

The knock on her door came long after midnight. She opened the door to find Emily's roommate, Heather, shivering in the dim shadows of the hallway and trying not to cry.

"Heather! What's the matter?"

"Oh, Summer, can you come to our room? Emily . . . she . . . she's sick."

"Sick? What's wrong? Why don't you call the headmistress?" Summer whispered, trying not to wake the girl who shared her room.

"She doesn't want me to. Summer, please come. I don't know what to do."

"All right," she agreed. Together they moved down the hallway. When they entered the room, Summer's senses warned her that the situation was much more serious than she had thought.

Emily lay on the bed, and by the light of the candle, Summer could see that her face was a ghastly white.

Summer went to kneel by the bed and rested her cool hand against Emily's fevered brow. Slowly Emily's eyes fluttered open and a half smile touched her pale lips.

"Summer," she whispered.

"Emily, what is wrong? Shall we call a doctor?"

Emily's eyes widened, filling with terror, and her face grew gray.

"No! No! Summer, promise me please . . . no doctors . . . no one . . . no one must know. I shall die of the shame."

"Shame? Why should you be ashamed because you

22

are ill?"

Emily groaned and clutched her abdomen. Tears escaped beneath her closed lids to glisten on her cheeks.

Summer's gaze met Heather's across the bed. Heather's eyes were wet with tears, but she nodded her head gently.

The first emotion to touch Summer was anger. She moved around the bed and gripped Heather's trembling arm and dragged her to a corner.

"Heather . . . is she . . . ?"

"Yes," Heather gasped. "She . . . she has been sneaking out to meet him. When she found out she was pregnant she told him."

"And?"

"He just laughed at her . . . said he couldn't be sure it was his. She tried to . . . oh Summer!" Heather moaned, wringing her hands. "What shall we do? Will she die?"

"No!" Summer said, fury at the conscienceless man broiling within her. "She shall not die!"

Summer had used her healing gifts often, but never in the white man's world. She knew they would never believe or understand them. Forcing a frightened Heather to help her, she uncovered Emily. For a moment she was aghast at the blood draining the life from Emily's body. Then she drew herself together, determined that Emily would not die, and just as determined to inform the man responsible of her near death. Emily was moaning softly now and wet with perspiration. They washed her and padded her with thick towels to staunch the flow of life-draining blood. Heather sobbed softly, fearing Emily's death, but Summer refused to listen. Once Emily was clean and covered warmly to alleviate her shivering, Summer knelt by the bed and laid one hand on Emily's abdomen and gripped one of her hands firmly with the other. She

23

closed her eyes and again drew on the unexplainable power that she possessed.

It swirled about her, this black mist that seemed to draw all her energy and focus it like a chain linking her with the girl on the bed. She felt it surge like a tidal wave through her to Emily. Her eyes closed and she quivered, gripped in the strength of the force she could not control or understand.

Heather had backed herself against the wall, and her eyes were wide with shock and fear. She did not know what was happening, and a startled, muffled scream choked in her throat when she saw that Emily had stopped moaning with the pain and had seemed to relax. Then, slowly, Emily's lips took on a tinge of pink, her pale cheeks returned to their normal color, and her eyes fluttered open.

Summer slumped in utter exhaustion, but her hand still gripped Emily's, who was gazing at her with a wondrous yet frightened look on her face.

All was silent in the semi-dark room as the three gazed at one other, uncertain of what had just happened.

Heather moved toward the door and Summer leapt to her feet to catch her before she could leave. She grasped Heather's arm and drew her out into the hall and shut the door behind them.

"What . . . what did you do?" Heather gasped in awe.

"Heather, you must not tell anyone—*anyone*—what you have seen. I have no answers for it. It is just something that happens. Promise me you will tell no one—no one, do you understand? You must forget what you saw." She gripped Heather's arm until the girl cried out and tears rolled down her cheeks. "Promise me . . . promise me."

"I . . . I won't say anything. Besides, no one would

believe me anyway."

"Heather, you must tell me . . ."

Again Heather tried to draw away, but Summer clung to her relentlessly. "You must tell me."

"What? I don't know anything."

"Don't lie to me. I have the power to heal, and I also can tell when someone lies to me."

It was not exactly the truth, but Summer knew she had achieved the desired result when she saw new fear leap into Heather's eyes.

"Tell me who he is. Who is the father? And who was responsible for killing the baby and almost killing Emily as well? You know . . . and you will tell me."

Summer's eyes blazed with fury and she roughly shook Heather as she spoke. Heather was frightened of both the power she had just witnessed and Summer's anger.

"S . . . Sinclair Masterson," Heather stammered.

"Lord Charles Masterson's son?" Summer questioned in amazement and saw Heather nod. "Who was the other?"

"Before God, Summer, I don't know. I just knew she was upset after his rejection. Then she came home earlier today . . . like this."

"Go to my room, Heather, and try to get some sleep."

"What are you going to do?"

"Stay with Emily for awhile," Summer said grimly. "Then I'll pay Sinclair Masterson and his family a visit."

# Chapter Three

Summer sat by Emily until dawn streaked the sky and she had assured herself that Emily slept a restful, natural sleep. Then she rose and went back to her room. She did not awaken Heather but instead donned her clothes swiftly and went quietly down the stairs and out of the building. She walked for some time, gathering her thoughts. It was difficult for her to believe Sinclair's cruelty in turning Emily away when she had to face such a terrible thing. And to disclaim his own child, to drive Emily to desperation—and nearly to death! she thought angrily. She wanted to look at him when she told him of the tragedy that had nearly happened. She had to see his face, look into his eyes.

After a while she took a carriage and gave the driver the Mastersons' address. It was a long drive and she used the time to try to bring her rage under control.

She stepped down from the carriage in front of the Masterson mansion and stood for a moment looking at it. It was a magnificent edifice, signifying the wealth and position of the Masterson family. She wondered how such cruelty could come from such beauty as she walked to the front door and knocked.

The door was opened by an austere butler.

"Yes, Miss?"

"Is Mr. Masterson in?"

"The elder or the younger, Miss?"

"Mr. Sinclair Masterson."

"Yes, Miss, he is in."

"May I see him please?"

He stepped aside and Summer moved past him, conscious of his curiosity.

"If you come this way, Miss, you can wait in the library. I will inform Mr. Masterson that you are here."

"Thank you."

She waited in the library for over half an hour before the door opened again and Sinclair walked in. It was obvious she had roused him from sleep and that he was still recovering from a late night of drinking. His eyes were puffy and red rimmed and his efforts to appear casual were undermined by his tired face and trembling hands. At the moment, he urgently desired another strong drink to bring his nerves under control.

Sinclair knew Summer, even if she did not know him. He had seen her at several social functions but had been so involved in the seduction of Emily that he had mentally placed Summer on a list of females he would investigate at a later date. She turned to look at him and the smile on his lips faded as he saw the glow of cold anger in her eyes. He was unprepared for it.

"You wanted to see me?"

"Yes."

"Please sit down," he offered as he moved closer to her. He was disconcerted by the way she was studying him. Summer had reached mentally for him, a practice she had tried to control since she had been among white people, and she had felt his thoughts and emotions. They made her feel cold and wary.

"I prefer to stand, thank you."

"What do you want to see me about . . . Summer."

27

"You know who I am?"

"Yes, I have seen you before."

"Then . . . maybe you know why I am here?"

"No, I've no idea," he replied, though his eyes fled from her steady gaze.

"Emily almost died last night," she said in a quiet voice.

Shock registered first in his eyes, then a cold wariness. "I don't understand what this has to do with me. I have only known Emily—"

"Please don't take me for a fool. I know what has been going on," Summer bluffed, watching his eyes narrow and grow even colder.

"I have no idea what you are talking about. If you don't mind, I have not had breakfast and I have a busy day ahead of me."

"Too busy to know that the child she carried is dead?"

"What do you want, Summer?"

"I just wanted to look at you," she said with a calm half smile. "I wanted to see what kind of man would do such a thing."

His cheeks flushed in anger.

"What are you accusing me of, and what proof do you have that I am guilty? I suggest that any woman who finds herself pregnant out of wedlock has herself to blame. And besides, why do you think I am responsible? Emily had others before me and after me. If she's been stupid enough to get herself with child and can find no one to blame for it, it's certainly not my problem."

Summer felt something within her grow hard and cold as she gazed at him in disbelief. He could not know that she perceived the blackness within him like a tangible force. She knew him for what he was—a selfish, cold person—and saw that he did not care at all that his own unborn child was dead and that the woman who had loved him and had conceived the child with him had suffered terribly.

To Summer this was the final straw, and she choked on the taste of his betrayal. There was nothing more she could say to him, or wanted to say to him. In her eyes he had become the supreme example of the cruel white world, and she found she could no longer bear to live within its confines. She would leave, she decided. She would go home as soon as the last few weeks of her schooling were completed.

She was so filled with disgust for the man standing before her that she was left without words to tell him how despicable she thought he was.

"Emily was a fool to think she could trap me into marriage. The Mastersons have a name to protect. I must marry in my own class."

"And Emily is not of your class?" Summer said.

"A merchant's daughter?" he replied arrogantly. Now his eyes narrowed again and he looked at her more closely, as if debating her prospects—and the Storm fortune. It made her physically ill to watch him mentally strip and examine her. She knew he was debating whether or not the Storm fortune would be enough compensation for marrying a half-breed.

"Summer, you must understand," he said smoothly, "that this has happened to many wealthy men. Women can trap them so easily. Fortune hunters will stop at nothing."

"Yes," she said, "I imagine there are some so cold and callous they will stop at nothing to get what pleases them."

"I see"—he smiled—"that you do understand. I suppose with a fortune as vast as the Storms', you have run across that difficulty too. Perhaps we can talk, you and I, and become friends."

29

She swallowed against the bitterness that rose in her throat. Her savage nature was becoming hard to control. She wanted to attack him. She would have liked to have had a sharp knife in her hand, for at that moment, she would have happily castrated him.

"I must go," she said abruptly, knowing that if she stayed in his presence a moment longer she would resort to some type of violence. She walked rapidly to the door, but he was beside her before she could open it. His hand touched her arm and she fought her revulsion.

"Shall I see you out?"

She looked up at his eyes and saw into the very depths of his soul.

"No . . . I can find my way out." She withdrew her arm from his grasp and walked out the door, leaving him gazing after her with a contemplative look in his eyes. He would convince her that he had had nothing to do with Emily. He would charm her until she and her fortune were his. After all, he thought, despite her beauty and wealth, she was still half savage—a half-breed born of illicit love. It would be easy, he thought.

Within two days Emily had physically recovered from her brush with death, but not emotionally. Summer and Heather alternated their time so she would not be alone. They fended off questions by telling everyone that Emily was suffering from influenza. Most kept their distance.

Emily's continued state of silent depression worried Summer. All her senses were aware that Emily's mind dwelt in the deepest darkness. Summer's hatred for Sinclair grew, and her abhorrence of white society grew with it. No man, she thought, would ever bind her, especially a white man.

In the stillness of the early morning hours, she sat in a large chair beside Emily's bed. White moonlight lit the room, making Emily's pale face seem ghastly in its whiteness. Her wide eyes had been on Summer for the past half hour, as Summer dozed lightly, struggling to be conscious enough to hear if Emily should need anything.

"Summer," Emily whispered.

Instantly Summer's eyes opened and she moved to sit on the edge of Emily's bed.

"Are you all right? Do you need anything?"

"Summer"—Emily's voice was faint and tremulous —"you have been so kind to me. I'm sorry I have caused everyone so much trouble. It would have been better if you had let me die."

"Emily, don't talk like that. You're just weak and tired."

"I am tired, Summer," Emily answered, "but I want to talk to you."

"We can talk tomorrow, when you're more rested."

"No!" There was distress in her eyes and her hands moved in agitation. "Now!"

"All right," Summer agreed. "Please don't get so upset."

"Summer . . . what did you do? I felt such a force . . . so much strength. I don't understand."

"You are not alone," Summer replied. "I don't know either."

"You mean—"

"I mean it just happens. I have no more control over it than I do the sunrise. Emily, I hope you won't tell anyone what I can do. The others consider me a freak now. If they knew of this, I can imagine what would be in everyone's mind—witchcraft or some such thing."

31

"Don't worry, Summer"—Emily's voice was calm—"I . . . I won't ever tell anyone. I just wanted to thank you . . . even though it was a mistake."

"Don't talk like that. You have a lot to live for. You're young. You have your whole life ahead of you."

"A lot to live for!" Emily laughed a brittle laugh. "You don't understand. My parents struggled so hard so that I could have a chance to be educated, to marry well. Now . . . now that will never be. I am ruined. No man will have me."

"You can't judge every man by him," Summer answered, but both knew her words lacked conviction. The society in which they both were caught would be quick to condemn and brand Emily for what had happened. It angered Summer to feel so helpless, and again she felt the gnawing desire to return to the peace of the mountains and the wilderness. She yearned for the calm strength and gentle understanding of her father and foster mother. She wanted to hear the laughter of the people of Hawk's village and know the peace his silent presence had always brought. She wanted to go home.

"Summer?"

"What?"

"You've never been happy here, have you?"

"Not really," Summer admitted. "But it's what my father wanted. It will be over soon; then I can go home."

"Yes"—Emily sighed—"we both need to escape."

"Are you going to go home, Emily?"

There was a distant look in Emily's eyes and a half smile on her face.

"Yes. I will escape too."

"You'll see," Summer said. "Everything will be different. You can pick up the pieces and begin again. It will be all right."

"Yes," Emily replied quietly. "Summer . . . could I have some hot tea?"

"Of course. I'll go down and make you some. Will you be all right until I get back?"

"I'll be fine, Summer. Don't worry about me anymore . . . I'll be all right."

"I'll be back in less than half an hour."

Emily nodded. Summer tucked the quilt about her friend, then left the room and closed the door softly behind her. She had taken only one candle from the room and walked slowly because of its dim light. She made her way to the kitchen and, after stirring the embers of the banked fire to life, she put the kettle on. Then she sat before the fire, huddling in her shawl to keep warm until the kettle began to boil.

She was startled by a voice from the doorway behind her.

"What are ye doin' this time a night fussin' around my kitchen?" The voice was stern and angry until Summer spun about.

"Oh, Summer, 'tis you. What's the matter child, homesick again?"

"No, Mrs. Collins, I'm just getting Emily a cup of tea."

Henrietta Collins had been the school's cook for nearly twenty-five years. She knew a great deal about what went on within the school walls. Her astute gaze studied the girl crouching before the fire.

"Is the child feeling any better? You have been a godsend to her, I imagine. This influenza—it's left her weak?"

"Yes, she is a little weak, but I think she will be all right in a few days."

"I hope she appreciates how good you've been to her

33

these past days. None of the other stuck-up fillies have paid her any mind."

"Maybe it's best they haven't. She needs rest the most."

"You're a good-hearted girl, Summer. But I always have the feelin' that you just don't belong among those others. It's like you're about to fly away. I notice you don't cozy up to any of 'em either. It's surprising. A girl pretty as you, with as much money as the Storm family has, usually draws 'em like flies."

Again Summer thought of Sinclair and Emily and her distaste rose, showing plainly in her eyes where it was not missed by Mrs. Collins. "I . . . I guess I don't make friends that easily."

Henrietta made a sharp, disbelieving sound, but before she could speak, Summer saw that her water had come to a boil and she rose to prepare the tea.

"Are you planning to stay up the night?"

"Yes."

"Then we'll make more tea and I'll come and sit with you and keep you company. We can have a nice chat."

"Wonderful. I was wondering how I was going to stay awake." Summer laughed.

They filled two more cups and left the kitchen. Henrietta carried two cups and Summer the third, so it was Summer who reached to open the bedroom door and stepped inside.

She stood paralyzed as the cup of tea crashed to the floor. Her eyes were wide with horror and her senses were awash in a wave of intense blackness.

"Oh, Holy Mother," Henrietta gasped from behind her.

Summer could have wept from the futility and despair she felt. She could not seem to move, transfixed as she was by the scene before her, a scene that would linger in her mind for a long time.

34

The body of Emily Gill swayed slowly back and forth. The stool on which she had stood to hang herself from the wide beams of the high ceiling now lay tipped over on the floor. She looked like a helpless child. Before darkness claimed her, Summer whispered Emily's name. Then she crumpled silently to the floor.

## Chapter Four

After Emily's funeral, Summer had returned to her room, packed her belongings, and departed without a word to anyone. By the time it was discovered that she was missing from the school, the ship was well under way and Summer safely on it.

Now she stood at the ship's rail and tried to erase the horrible memories from her mind. She lifted her face to catch the touch of the cool breeze. It was a warm, star-studded night, and there was just enough wind to fill the canvas sails and push the ship along at a brisk clip.

Try as she might, she could not think of anything but Emily. She had condemned Sinclair, condemned white society, and condemned herself for leaving Emily alone, knowing the state of mind she was in. Now she was running to the only safe harbor she knew—her family.

She was determined to convince her father that she was meant to stay in the wilderness. Then she would go on to the village of her mother's people and speak with its chief, Black Cloud, who was like a grandfather to her. Perhaps, in his wisdom, the old chief could help her find some reason for the tragedy that had occurred. Maybe then she could learn to live with it . . .

Her eyes brightened when the coast of home came into view several days later, and she could barely control the excitement that surged through her. Once she was ashore, she arranged for a young boy to stay with her baggage, then took a carriage to the office of Charles Brewster, one of her father's closest friends.

Brewster was taken completely by surprise when he saw her appear at his office door. As she was ushered in by his secretary, he came around his desk with hands outstretched toward her.

"Summer, my dear child, what a pleasant surprise this is. Your father never told me you were coming home on this ship."

"I'm afraid, Mr. Brewster"—Summer laughed— "that my father didn't know I was coming."

"I don't understand. You sent no word?"

"No . . . there really wasn't much time. I'm afraid I left in rather a hurry."

"Well child, you must come home and have dinner with Mrs. Brewster and me. I will send word to your father and you can stay with us until he arrives."

"You are very kind, Mr. Brewster"—Summer smiled her most charming smile and raised her eyes to him in wide innocence—"but what I would really like to have, if you would be so very kind, is a horse."

"A horse?" he replied, a curious frown on his cherubic face. "What in heaven's name do you want with a horse?"

"I want to go home."

"But my dear," he blustered, "you cannot just . . . just take a horse and go—a woman . . . alone. Why . . . why your father would have my scalp."

"Now, Mr. Brewster," she coaxed, "Father will be so happy to have me home, he won't even ask how I acquired the horse. And," she said, lowering her voice to a secretive whisper, "I'll never tell."

"I . . . I simply cannot let you go alone. I simply cannot."

"Please, Mr. Brewster. You know very well I was taught by the best, my father. I will have no trouble getting home alone. I really want to surprise them all. I beg you, Mr. Brewster, please get a horse for me."

"Summer . . ."

Tears filled the young woman's eyes. "I want to go home, and I can be there in less than two days if you help me. Please?" The tears were effective, as she knew they would be; it had always been so since her childhood. She had been able to move Mr. Brewster from the time she was nine.

A little more coaxing and the horse was offered, along with the agreement that her baggage would be safe at Mr. Brewster's until she could come for it. All she planned to take with her was a pair of buckskin pants, a tunic, and high-laced moccasins. The rest of civilization's trappings she intended to leave behind.

The baggage was sent to Mr. Brewster's house, and two hours later, clad in her Indian garb with her hair parted in the center and caught in a long braid, Summer mounted a fine sorrel mare and soon left the town behind as she headed toward home. She had purchased enough food to last the short time it would take her to get home.

Home! her heart sang. She gloried in everything around her and rode slowly so that she would not miss a thing. She breathed deeply to catch the scent of the trees, then closed her eyes with the almost painful pleasure of it. It was just as she had remembered through many homesick nights.

Her gaze caught a circling hawk and she shaded her eyes to watch its graceful flight.

At midday she stopped long enough to rest her horse and to eat. She had found a grassy spot near a swiftly running stream and she knew the water would be cool and sweet. It eddied into small pools and at one of these she knelt, preparing to reach her cupped hand into the water to drink. She paused as her reflection glistened in the crystal clear water and drew her attention.

Large, jet black eyes gazed back at her. Without vanity, she regarded her face. It was oval shaped, with gold-bronzed skin and high cheekbones inherited from her mother. Her thick black hair was confined in a long braid that hung to her hips. The wide smile she couldn't suppress was a gift from her father. It was open and sincere and showed the same square teeth. She was graceful of movement, and she noted that her body had become ripely rounded in her burgeoning womanhood.

The form in the water wavered, and for one stark moment it was transformed into the bronzed man of her dream. The vision faded as quickly as it had appeared and the sound of her startled gasp was lost on the early morning breeze.

She touched the cool water with her cupped hand, scooped it up to drink, and watched the widening ripples distort her reflection. Suddenly losing the desire to look into the pool, she closed her eyes and rested on her knees. Lifting her head, she inhaled the sweet-smelling air. Oh, how she loved this place! She laughed softly, thinking of those she would soon see. The warmth of love swept over her and made her heart sing.

In her mind's eye, she pictured her father, Clay Storm, and Sabrina, the woman who had come to share their lives and help both Clay and Summer through a difficult time. Sabrina had given Clay two sons before a serious illness had made it impossible for her to have any more children. The eldest, after Summer, was Clay Jr., who was twelve. He was followed by Jason, who was younger by two years. She loved them all intensely and was profoundly grateful that the traumatic fears of her childhood had been put to rest by the security of the love between her father and her stepmother.

It had been a long time since she had been forced by her gift to see anything that might mean serious harm to her family, but now the strange recurring dream troubled her spirit. She had not been able to determine whether or not she should fear this strange golden man, and for the first time in her life, she could not see beyond her vision to any dark threat that might lurk there. She could only see him and feel some blank darkness that came with her fragmented dreams.

"Why?" she whispered softly, as though she expected the rustling breeze to bring her the answer. Summer grew silent, but she was filled with a sudden urge to mount her horse and ride fast. It was as if some strange voice called to her to hurry, telling her that some tremendous new experience awaited her.

Summer rode until the sun began to near the horizon. She was not alarmed, for she was used to being in the wilderness at night. She was capable of making camp and had more than enough food for a good meal. And she was confident she would reach home sometime the next day.

She laughed to herself about the many times she had tried to outmaneuver Hawk here in this territory and pass him without his knowing. She had finally given that up because she had never succeeded. Hawk was much too astute to miss anything that happened on his land.

The sun was low when she decided to stop. She

dismounted and laid her equipment on the ground as she unburdened her horse. She cared for the animal, watering him first, then rubbing him briskly. As did all those who lived on the frontier, Summer knew the value of her horse.

Once she had cared for him, she prepared a fire, sat on a blanket beside it and ate. She was satisfied with what she had brought, but she knew that, if necessary, she could live off the land as her father had taught her.

The sun had almost disappeared. She sat very still and listened to the sounds about her, watching the rare and beautiful glory of the sunset. It was a moment she would enjoy to the limit, for she remembered again the four terrible years she had endured at school. How she had missed this. Now that she had come home, she vowed she would never leave again.

She gave herself up to the one luxury she only enjoyed in solitude. Mentally she reached for those she loved. Peace and contentment filled her as she touched each one and found that all were safe and warm. No discordant notes sounded in her world. She could go home to them. She freed her mind of the gift her mother, Singing Bells, had given her, the gift she did not fully understand. She only knew that at times the strength of the gift left her shaken. And she also surmised that she had not yet realized the extent of the power she held. There were even times when she was a little frightened of it. She had never spoken to her parents or to anyone else of the new abilities she had discovered. She would speak to Black Cloud when she arrived at the village. She had always thought of Chief Black Cloud as a grandfather, even though he was not a blood relative. He was very old now, but she knew he would understand and tell her what to do with these powers. He had always been a source of inner strength and comfort to her.

She was tired and knew she would have to be awake early. And though she loved to see the sun set, she would be just as thrilled to be awake when it rose again. She rose slowly and put more wood on the fire. Then she enclosed the fire in a double ring of stones, which would gather the heat from the fire as it slowly died and retain it until the wee hours of the morning.

After checking her horse to make sure he was securely tethered and could not wander far, she returned to the fire and lay down, rolling her blanket about her. In a few minutes she slept.

Summer was completely unaware that the glow of her fire had attracted the attention of two others who had been camping nearby. They were wary men who had been pursued often enough to be on constant watch for strangers in their vicinity.

They whispered together and, by mutual agreement, they silently moved toward the fire on foot and very slowly, so that they would not be detected. Through the grey mists of early dawn, they stealthily approached the quiet camp.

Sounds of night still echoed softly in the forest, but they did not wake the girl who slept by the low-burning fire. White moonlight bathed the area in a soft glow, but even its beauty did not reach her. She stirred, and a soft sound came from her parted lips. A frown touched her sleeping face and again she uttered a soft moan. She was caught once more in the wild recurring dream that destroyed her peaceful sleep, the dream that had frightened her so many times before.

Summer awakened suddenly without moving. An

instinctive tingle of warning had drawn her up from sleep. Slowly she opened her eyes and scanned the area beyond her fire. She could not see them, but she sensed them and somehow knew there were more than one, though she had no idea how many. She also detected evil.

After a moment, she spotted a fleeting movement. They were between her and the hobbled horse and she realized she could never reach it in time. Her only chance was to leap to her feet, surprise them, and make for the forest. She closed her eyes for one moment, then, drawing in a deep breath, she leapt to her feet and ran. After a few minutes, she could hear their pursuit.

As she ran, fear tugged at her mind. Surrounded by a grey mist, she could not see the threat that hovered near, but she could feel it. It tingled up her spine and lent wings to her feet. Low-hanging branches brushed her skin and thorny brambles tore at her clothes. Sweat slicked her skin and her heart throbbed painfully. *The dream!* her mind cried out. She could feel the heat of tears in her eyes and her lungs seemed to be aflame as she released her breath in soft, rasping gasps. *The dream!*

She wanted to cry aloud but could not seem to get enough air, and panic filled her as she sensed that whatever was following was drawing nearer and nearer.

The power of something dark filled her mind and she knew some deadly evil was following. Something gripped her clothes and tore at her. She could feel the breath of death on her skin.

She twisted from the grasp of clinging brush only to find her feet tangled in vines and clogged roots. She felt herself slipping and cried out in anguished despair as she stumbled forward over the edge of an embankment to crash against the ground. A sharp cry of pain was forced from her before darkness momentarily over-took her.

She felt the cold, hard earth beneath her as she regained consciousness, and from the foggy, blurred distance she heard shots. She struggled to rise, and at a sign of movement above her, she looked up. A form hovered between her and the brightening sky. The swirling mist seemed to dissolve slowly, and she cried out again as he stood before her as clear and true as she had envisioned him so many times before.

# Chapter Five

The two men rode together in the waning sunlight. They rode in silence and their dusty appearance indicated that they had been traveling for many hours. As they crested a hill, they drew their horses to a halt. The larger of the two dismounted and walked about for a few moments, studying the ground.

"Find anything?" the mounted man asked.

"Nothing." The answer came across crisp and firm. "We've lost them."

"No! We're not going to lose them. I'll find them if I have to trail them to hell and back."

"Damnit, Sebastian, we've been trailing these men for three weeks. I don't think you've slept six hours the whole time. We need to rest. There's no sign of rain, so we can pick up their trail in the morning. People who look like that can't get lost. We'll find 'em, but we need some sleep and we need to eat. Let's stop tonight."

Sebastian didn't answer. He stood gazing at the fading horizon as if he hadn't heard.

"Sebastian?"

"Okay, Cole," Sebastian responded reluctantly. "We'll camp tonight, but we ride 'til dark first. I want to see if those woods down there have any sign."

"Good enough for me," Cole answered.

Sebastian remounted and they rode down the hillside to the dense forest that lay below them. Within the depths of the forest they moved slowly as both bent low to study the ground. They searched for signs until the rays of the sun could no longer penetrate the thick foliage above them and it began to grow too dark to see. It was only then that Sebastian decided to stop.

They found a small clearing and after they unburdened their horses and saw to their care, they built a fire. They sat in silence before the flickering flames for some time.

Cole Robbins studied his friend's face and his eyes were filled with sympathy as he thought back on the reason he and Sebastian were here. Had it only been three weeks? God, it felt like a hundred, he thought. Only three weeks had passed since disaster had dealt them a violent blow. He had met Nathaniel and Sebastian on their arrival and had joined them when the three had found themselves in a rapidly developing friendship. They had been working together less than two months when an event occurred that changed their lives drastically.

Nathaniel had been filled with life and laughter, and Cole had watched the responding sparkle in Sebastian. It seemed the brothers had grown even closer during this short period.

They had managed to acquire a large piece of land and build a house on it. Filled with bright plans for a good future, they had sent a message to their parents. Both enjoyed the beauty of this vast new country and wanted their parents to see it as they did. They knew that when their parents came, they would again be a family. But their hopes were never realized.

The three had just begun to settle in for the night when the renegades struck. There had been four men—

46

two white and two Indian. Their faces were now imprinted in Cole's mind as he knew they were in Sebastian's. The confrontation had been violent and had left them stripped of nearly all they possessed. The house had been burned beyond repair, Sebastian and Cole had been wounded, and Nathaniel had died in his brother's arms.

Sebastian had wept; then cursed and shouted an oath of revenge toward the heavens. After burying his brother, he became cold and quiet, and even Cole could not reach him. He pushed himself on, driven by the desire to find the men who had killed his brother. He avoided Indian camps, and Cole felt that Sebastian had begun to hate all Indians for what two had done. Worse, he had the distinct feeling that Sebastian was somehow blaming himself for his brother's death. It was a festering wound of the soul, and Cole did not know how to reach inside to help ease the dark pain he saw in Sebastian's eyes.

They sat thoughtfully before the fire now, chewing on the dried meat they had carried along. Cole watched Sebastian, unsure of the words he might use to break his friend's brooding silence. Sebastian's thoughts were a great distance from where he was physically, and Cole took the moment to study him.

Tanned deeply by the sun, Sebastian might have been taken for an Indian himself had it not been for the burnished gold of his hair and the deep jade green of his eyes. Dark shadows beneath his eyes, and the pinched, hard look about his mouth were evidence to Cole of the sleepless nights and scanty meals they had foraged along the way.

Cole was twenty-six, only a year shy of Sebastian. He was slim yet exhibited a wiry strength. Under normal circumstances the tawny eyes shaded by his dark brown hair were quick and intelligent, but now they were filled with stress over unanswerable questions.

"You ought to get some sleep," Cole said gently.

"In awhile."

"Sebastian?"

There was a long pause, then, "What?"

"I'd . . . I'd kind of like to know your plans."

"Kill them," Sebastian answered grimly. He turned to look at Cole. "And I don't plan on making it easy."

"And after that?" Cole questioned. He hated the emotions that were tearing his friend to pieces. He was afraid they would get beyond Sebastian's control and turn him cold and bitter.

"I'm not thinking about . . . after that," Sebastian replied. America had given him nothing but sorrow, he realized. He could not think of returning home and facing his parents to tell them of Nathaniel's death, so he pushed it all from his mind and refused to look at Cole again. But he couldn't ignore his friend's sigh of frustration.

"Get some sleep, Cole. You can relieve me after a while."

"You'll wake me?"

"Yes, I'll wake you."

Cole had his doubts, but he was exhausted, so he unrolled his blanket near the fire and, after a few minutes, drifted off to sleep.

Sebastian sat watching the flames licking the dry wood. Sleep was a thing he could hardly bear. It brought only the same memories, the same dreams.

"Nathaniel," he whispered softly, folding his arms across his bent knees and resting his head upon them. In the glow of the fire he could see his brother's body, bathed in blood. He could also see the faces of the men responsible—every line of each face, every shadow, every feature. The white men with their maniacal laughter, and the Indians, two of them—would he ever forget the large one with the three red feathers or the other's bloodcurdling shouts?

No, he would never forget, never—until the day he saw them die by his hand. He refused to entertain the possibility that even then he might not be able to forget. He remembered with grim satisfaction the wound he had inflicted on the chest of one of the Indians. It would mark him forever—until Sebastian caught up with him.

Several hours crept by and Sebastian lost himself in thoughts of revenge. Finally Cole stirred and awoke in the wee hours of the morning. Sitting up, he said, "Sebastian, get a little sleep if you can. I'll watch. If you don't you're going to collapse before you can catch up with them, and you'll be too useless to do anything."

Sebastian knew Cole was right. He wrapped himself in his blanket and tried to sleep, but wrenching, hate-filled thoughts swirled in his mind. Finally he lapsed into a restless slumber, only to be awakened suddenly by his dreams. Sweat bathed his body, and he trembled with the vivid memory of his brother's blood covering his hands. He lay still, staring above at the starry night sky. He would not sleep again.

Just before dawn, he moved closer to the dying fire. Cole lay before it, half awake and half asleep. Soon it would be day; soon it would be light enough to track.

A gray mist began to rise, clouding the area. Sebastian was eager to move on, though he knew it was too soon. He rose, lifted his gun, and began to walk. He had to assuage his restlessness.

Ahead of him was a shallow ravine. Across it lay a flat, brush-filled area. He must have seen the movement for some time before he recognized that someone was running across it and that others were in pursuit.

He stood and waited until the single running form grew closer. He was certain of one thing—the pursuers

49

meant business.

He watched the solitary form stumble and fall, then rise and fall again. He has a lot of courage, Sebastian thought to himself. Maybe he deserves a little help.

Reaching the side of the ravine at that moment and not realizing the edge was near, the lone figure cried out as it stumbled and fell over the edge.

Sebastian lifted his gun and took aim at the ones chasing the fallen figure. He fired one shot, another, then a third, and those in pursuit disappeared into the morning mist.

Sebastian started down the edge of the ravine as the figure lifted its head to look up at him. He stopped in complete surprise. It was a woman—a very beautiful woman, whose face registered not fear, but utter shock!

Sebastian hesitated only a moment; then he skittered down the side of the ravine to land at her side.

"Are you all right?" he questioned.

She gazed at him, unable yet to believe just how clearly she had seen him in her dreams. The first rays of the morning sun glinted on his gold hair and the sight left her momentarily speechless. Sebastian repeated his question as he reached down to lift her easily to her feet. When she did not answer the second time, he concluded that she did not understand him, that she did not speak English.

"Where did you come from?"

Shaken and now slightly frightened, Summer again gave no answer.

Sebastian gripped her arm firmly and drew her along with him. A powerful man, he allowed her no chance for freedom. As her mind began to clear, she tried to reach him mentally, but all she could feel was black, intolerable pain and violent anger. It shattered within her mind, making her retreat in anguish from the encounter.

50

He dragged her back to his camp with him, and a surprised Cole rose to his feet when he saw them coming.

"Sebastian . . . what the—"

"Don't ask me who she is," Sebastian replied curtly. "I don't have any idea. I found her being chased by some men. I scared them off for now, but I don't know how many there were. They might be back, so let's get out of here."

"Who are you?" Cole inquired gently of the obviously shaken Summer.

"Forget it, Cole. She doesn't speak English. I tried. Let's get out of here. We'll have time to try to get through to her later. Come on."

Summer watched as they hastily gathered their things. She searched mentally for Cole and found a sensitivity and a gentleness that relieved her, but as she again reached for Sebastian, she recoiled at the violence that prohibited her entry.

Summer found herself mounted before Sebastian as they rode away from the camp. His arm was like steel about her waist, and she could feel the latent strength of his body. She had no intention of staying with them after they had taken her to safety. They were white and men of the civilization she hated. She did not even want to speak to them.

They rode until almost midday; then they stopped to rest their horses. Without speaking, Sebastian offered Summer meat and water to drink, for he was now convinced that she did not understand his language. And the fact that she was an Indian only made him feel less charitable toward her.

"Who do you think she is?" Cole asked. "And where did she come from?"

"Cole, how can I answer your questions when I can't talk to her? Let's give this some logical thought. Do you

51

have any idea if there are any Indian villages near here?"

"I'm not sure. We've been tracking those four for so long that I'm not sure where we are. If I had to give it a rough guess, I'd say Black Cloud's village would be closest."

"Maybe she is one of Black Cloud's people," Sebastian said, "but what's she doing out here alone?"

Sebastian walked to Summer, who looked up at him with a dark, unfathomable gaze. She stared into the depths of his green eyes and he stood motionless as he sensed something reaching inside and touching him. It was like the heat of a sudden bright flame, and it startled him because he was totally unprepared for it.

He pointed to her. "Black Cloud?" he questioned. Slowly he repeated the words and reluctantly Summer nodded. Sebastian's eyes appraised her, and his reluctant smile turned to a frown. She looked down to see the stain of blood on her leg.

"Damn it! Why didn't you let me know you were hurt?" He had attempted to sound hard, but Summer heard the undertone of strain in his voice. He took her hand and led her to a log, and there he motioned for her to sit.

With surprisingly gentle hands he cleaned the ragged cut on her leg. It was not a serious wound, yet he knelt before her intently, denying to himself that he found pleasure in being near her, in touching her. He looked up and found her dark eyes on him, and for a moment he was lost in a deep black pool. He seemed to be sinking into depths he could not measure, and he felt suspicion, distrust, and an intuitive feeling that she could read his thoughts.

"Sebastian," Cole said softly. "It seems we have company."

Sebastian turned. On the edge of the clearing stood

52

the largest Indian he had ever seen.

Hawk had stood watching what was happening for several moments before the two men sensed he was there. He missed no move of the two white men, but his eyes were on Summer. Hawk, blood brother to Summer's father, had been hunting and had come across the three by accident. He had been taken completely by surprise to find Summer here. The last time he had spoken to her father he had been told she would not be returning for many weeks.

Quickly he saw that she was not hurt seriously. He also knew she was not afraid. He started to move forward to speak to Summer and find out what had happened, but he took only one step before he stopped. Summer had risen, and her hands flew in rapid sign, saying, Don't speak the white man's tongue to me. I will talk with you later.

He nodded, then again walked slowly toward the two white men.

"My God, Sebastian," Cole whispered, "that's got to be the biggest damn Indian I've ever seen."

"I wonder if *he* speaks English," Sebastian replied, this time with a touch of his old humor. It had been a very eventful day, and now he felt that nothing more could surprise him. He almost laughed when Hawk came close to him and answered in perfect English.

"I speak your tongue. What are you doing here and what happened to this child?" Hawk demanded.

"Who are you?" Sebastian countered.

"I am Hawk," the Indian replied with a smile.

"Your village is near? Is she one of your women?" Sebastian asked quickly.

"My village is near, and yes, she is one of our most cherished women. She is our medicine woman."

Sebastian nodded. This he understood. He had been in the territory long enough to know the value of a medicine woman. He had saved her life; maybe in return Hawk's people would help him find the trail of the men he followed.

Quickly Sebastian told Hawk who they were, but he did not reveal the reason they were in his territory. "Come to our fire and eat with us," he said to Hawk. "We can talk, and maybe, since you speak our tongue, you will tell us why we found her where we did, and what she was running from."

Hawk cast a quick, troubled look at Summer. Rapidly he spoke to her in their Indian tongue.

"Summer, do they speak true?" he asked.

"Yes, Hawk. I will explain to you later."

"Why do you not speak to them?"

"Hawk, I cannot explain now." Her eyes turned to Sebastian. "I will explain to you when I have an answer I understand. Please do not betray me now. It . . . it is something I must do."

Hawk knew Summer well and sensed the urgency of her request. He again turned to Sebastian.

"Come to our village. You will rest and eat, and we will talk."

"Is it far?"

"Just a day's ride. We will make camp tonight and reach my village tomorrow, before the midday meal."

"I would like to ask you some questions."

"I will answer if I can."

"I am looking for someone," Sebastian said.

Summer gazed at him while he spoke. His anger and a strange darkness seemed to swell inside her. She could feel it pulse within him and she was shaken by a violence she had never felt before.

"Come, let us travel," Hawk said. "When we reach my village we will help you if we can."

Both Sebastian and Cole agreed, for despite the fact

that Hawk was an Indian, both men felt they could trust him. The four of them traveled steadily through the balance of the day, and this time Summer rode behind Hawk.

For some reason, Summer mused, there was a link between her and this golden-haired man, but each time her mind tried to reach his, it was rebuffed by a dark force that left her breathless and confused.

Sebastian was again lost in thoughts of his brother and he allowed the blackness of his reverie to fill his mind. Maybe this man Hawk could help them, he reflected, for he now suspected that he might have lost the trail. With Hawk, they stood a good chance of finding it again. As he considered this Indian who led them, he was again reminded of the dark-eyed girl. In vain he tried to push her from his thoughts. An Indian girl was not part of his plans, for his heart was still with a blue-eyed woman far away. He was angry with himself that thoughts of Summer wouldn't leave his subconscious mind but instead danced tantalizingly before him.

That night they made camp early and shared what food they had. Then they wrapped themselves in their blankets and bedded down to sleep until sunrise. A short time passed and it seemed that two of them were unable to rest. Sebastian rose quietly and went to the fire. He sat before it, unaware that Summer watched him surreptitiously. She allowed her thoughts to open and hot tears burned her eyes as his intense pain reached her. It mingled with sorrow so deep she could hardly bear it.

Again she wondered why this man had come to her in dreams, and why her mind could not feel anything but pain.

Sebastian sensed her eyes on him and turned to look at her. Their eyes met and held for a long, intense moment. Resolutely she tore her eyes from him, wanting no part of the white world, or any white man. She knew them, and the knowledge was like a sickness, a sickness of which she planned to cure herself.

# *Chapter Six*

By the first light of the new day they were again on their way. In less than an hour all three men knew they were being followed, but only Summer felt the same fear of the previous day and sensed that it was the same threat pursuing them now. What she didn't understand was why they had been chasing her and what connection this had with the man who had rescued her. In the very depths of her she knew there had to be some link, but she could not fathom what it was.

As they rode, Cole and Sebastian would occasionally look back over their shoulders, but they saw no one. Sebastian moved up to ride beside Hawk. "Hawk," he said in a low voice. "We're being followed."

Hawk smiled. "They have been on our trail since the sun rose."

"You've seen them?" Sebastian questioned.

"I do not need to see them to know they are there. They are cowards. We must outnumber them; otherwise they would have attacked before this. Why does someone follow you?"

"Me?" Sebastian responded. "I don't think it is Cole and I they're after. We were trailing four men, and they were at least five or six days ahead of us. There were only two yesterday, and they weren't chasing us."

Summer spoke again rapidly in the Indian tongue, and Hawk listened.

"It is the same ones who came for me, Hawk," she said. "But somehow they are connected to this man."

"How?"

"I don't know. There is something strange and dark in his thoughts. I cannot see him. I must wait."

"Do you think he is lying, Summer?"

"I do not understand why he should lie. What reason could he have?"

"Maybe," Hawk said meditatively, "to get closer to you. Maybe he is one of them."

"Then why rescue me at all?"

"I am not sure we should trust him until you can see for certain."

"I must have some time. There is some barrier between his thoughts and mine. Perhaps in a few days he will not be so guarded. Perhaps then I can see."

Before Hawk could answer again, Sebastian spoke. "Does she agree or not? Does she have any idea who was after her?"

"No, she does not know."

"None of this makes any sense."

"Do you carry anything of value?"

"Hawk, what I own I've got with me, and right now it doesn't amount to much. Cole and I were robbed of just about everything."

"Will you go back to your own people now?" Hawk asked the question, but Summer listened intently for the answer.

"No," Sebastian said firmly. Hawk could feel Summer's entire body grow tense. "I have something I have to do, and I won't rest until it is finished."

"Well, you may rest with us for as long as you

choose," Hawk answered. He was certain that Summer knew more about this man than he did, and he wondered what could exist between them when they had never seen each other before this incident.

They continued on to the village, and even though Hawk and the others knew they were still being followed there was nothing they could do but go on. Hawk was determined that Summer be protected.

Well-placed guards spotted them several miles from the village and rode out to meet them. Hawk was quick to tell them—and to instruct them to tell the villagers— that only the Indian tongue was to be spoken to Summer or to the visitors. The white ones were not to know who she was.

The guards rode swiftly ahead to carry out his orders and to tell Black Cloud that his son returned with Summer.

Just before the village was sighted, another rider approached.

"Summer," Hawk said quietly, "Sleeping Wolf comes."

Sebastian and Cole watched as a large, grim-faced warrior rode toward them.

Sleeping Wolf was as surprised to find Summer as Hawk had been—surprised and thankful, for his need of the medicine woman was great.

"Summer, I am grateful that you come."

"You have need of me, Sleeping Wolf?"

"Yes. It is my son. He cries with the fever. He grows weaker every day. Swift Doe is sick with fear. We will sing your name with great joy, Summer, if you can return our son to us. My life will be yours from this day."

"Let us go quickly."

They moved rapidly now, and both Sebastian and Cole were aware of a sense of urgency, though neither had understood the quick exchange of words. They also knew that Summer was the cause of this haste.

Sebastian contemplated the girl who rode behind Hawk. She was an utterly feminine woman of extreme beauty, yet there seemed to be an aura of mystery surrounding her. It stimulated his interest and curiosity. She was an enigma he could not penetrate, and he found it difficult to control his desire to find out what her secret was and why it drew him toward her even though he fought the attraction.

He had revenge to fill his life. It was all he needed, all he wanted now. He would not allow one slim, mysterious young girl to draw him from the path he had plotted night after night.

They entered the village and Hawk gave orders that Sebastian and Cole were to be taken to a tipi and offered food and comfort befitting honored guests.

As Sebastian and Cole were being led away, Sebastian turned to look back at Hawk and Summer. Many were gathered about her, the most noticeable of whom was a weeping woman. Then the group moved toward another tipi and Summer was drawn inside.

Sebastian could hardly contain his curiosity at this strange behavior. He allowed himself to be taken to his tipi, but there he refused offers of food and drink, and finally he and Cole were left alone.

"Sebastian," Cole said, "what's going on here?"

"I'm not sure," Sebastian replied thoughtfully, "but I sure as hell am going to find out. Come on. Let's take a little walk."

"You think we ought to interfere?"

"We're not going to interfere . . . we're just going to take a look."

"They could get mighty fired up if we poke into something that's none of our business."

Sebastian smiled. "Nobody's told us it's none of our

business. Come on. Let's go."

They left their tipi and walked across the clearing to stand outside the dwelling Summer had entered. They stopped, but only for a moment. Then Sebastian bent to push the door flap open and both men entered.

It was a large tipi, and the group of people who stood in a semicircle did not notice their entry. All eyes were riveted on the child who lay on a pallet in the center of the room and the girl who bent over him. It was silent, so silent that Sebastian could hear the beating of his own heart.

Summer was on her knees beside a boy of about twelve. The child lay unnaturally still and his breathing was almost imperceptible. His eyes were closed, and his hair and skin were wet with sweat.

Sebastian's eyes were drawn to Summer as she knelt in silence. Her trembling hand reached out to rest against the boy's chest. Summer made a soft, low, moaning sound, and her body shuddered. It seemed to Sebastian's startled mind that she was drawing something from the child.

Perspiration appeared on her brow and ran in crystal rivulets down her cheeks, but her eyes remained closed. She kept her hand pressed against the child's chest, and with the other she lifted one of his hands and pressed it against her. Slowly, her body began a rhythmic movement. Gently it swayed back and forth. Sebastian was spellbound by something he could hardly believe, much less understand.

Hawk's gaze left the woman and child for a moment to turn toward Sebastian and Cole. He was powerless now to evict them, for he knew what danger could result if he were to break Summer's concentration. He remained silent, but his anger was great.

Sebastian continued to watch in utter awe the strange, unexplainable occurrence being played out

61

before him.

Summer wept and Sebastian was startled at the sudden touch of pain he felt. She suffered, yet he could taste and feel it.

Minutes passed, and the silence was marred only by the sound of Summer's weeping, and the harsh, raspy breathing of the onlookers.

Summer's body shook as if in the grip of a fierce, biting wind. She clung to the child as if a link had been formed between the two. Her body continued its slow, rhythmic movement, back and forth, back and forth, until the silent watchers were mesmerized.

Sebastian felt his mouth go dry and found that his own body was wet with sweat. The quiet suspense grew, and grew, until Sebastian wanted to shout aloud from the tension. Then suddenly there was a ragged, gasping moan from the child and very slowly his eyes fluttered open. They were clear, bright, and devoid of any sign of illness.

At that moment Summer gave a long, deep sigh and collapsed atop him. Hawk was beside her in a moment and lifted her gently in his arms. With a passion that surprised him, Sebastian longed to go to her himself, to hold her in his own arms and carry her to a quiet place to rest. He didn't move, however, and suddenly felt himself the unwelcome intruder when Hawk passed by and glared at him in silent anger.

"Cole," Sebastian spoke quietly, "you were right. We weren't meant to see this. Let's get out of here. We owe them an apology and from what I saw in Hawk's eyes, we'll be giving it very soon."

Cole nodded his agreement and they left quickly, but not before they saw a happy mother and father help a perfectly healthy child to stand.

They walked across the clearing to their tipi in

silence. Inside they stared at each other in absolute disbelief.

"Sebastian . . . what the hell did we just see?"

"I don't know . . . I don't know."

Sebastian turned to watch as Hawk strode through the entrance. The Indian's impassive face gave no sign of his emotional state, but both Sebastian and Cole knew they should not have trespassed and were prepared for Hawk's anger.

"Hawk," Sebastian began, but it was difficult for him to find words with Hawk's dark gaze holding his.

Hawk was having the same difficulty, for Summer had forced a promise from him just moments before. He would neither discuss her, nor show his anger at their curiosity.

"Your anger," she had said calmly, "will only bring more questions."

Hawk had agreed reluctantly and had walked across the clearing slowly so that he could ease the storm broiling within him and face the white men calmly.

"I'm sorry about what just happened, Hawk," Sebastian continued. "We had no business being there."

"Do not speak of it again," Hawk replied with a rigidly controlled smile. "Have you been given food and water?"

Sebastian was taken by surprise. He had seen Hawk's anger, and now the man was acting as if nothing out of the ordinary had happened. He understood also from Hawk's tone that questions would be unwelcome.

"Yes, thank you."

"Good. You said before that you were looking for someone."

"We are. We have been trailing these men for three weeks."

"They have done you harm?" Hawk purposely asked this question, which he knew to be a breach of privacy, in order to make Sebastian feel the frustrated anger he had felt.

"Yes," Sebastian replied, and Hawk sensed the white man's reluctance to continue. He wanted to inquire further, though it went against custom and against his nature to pressure a guest or to force his departure.

"They have killed . . . someone, and I must find them."

Hawk's astute gaze did not miss the glow of what seemed a fanatical desire for vengeance. Were these the conflicting emotions Summer had felt? He wondered just how quickly he could rid the village of these men, for now he began to see them as a threat to Summer.

"Tell me of these men. Maybe I have seen them."

"Two white men and two Indians," Sebastian began and went on to describe the four.

As they talked, food was brought and they sat before a crackling fire companionably.

Hawk listened closely to the descriptions Sebastian gave, but he could think of no one who fit them.

"I will send out men to see if they can find tracks of these strangers."

"Now that the woman is safe, we will go our way. I must make sure . . . I mean . . . this is a thing I must do."

Hawk nodded, then he rose to his feet. At the tipi door he turned to look at the two men. He would have given anything at this moment to have had Summer's vision, to have known if the darkness she had felt from this man might do her harm. But no matter. He would make sure they did not stay any longer than necessary, despite what Summer felt.

"I will send scouts at sunrise. If there are any strangers crossing our land, we will know," Hawk told them and was gone before either man could reply.

"I get the strange feeling"—Cole laughed--"that that man wants us out of this village as soon as possible."

"I think you're right, and I'm certain it has something to do with that girl we found and what we just saw."

"Sebastian, why don't we just get out of this territory before—"

He stopped when he looked into Sebastian's eyes and saw fury flaring into an intense blaze.

"And the ones who murdered my brother would be free to go their way, maybe to kill again? I would never be able to live with myself."

"And can you live with yourself now? Do you eat or sleep? For God's sake Sebastian. It's eating you alive and it's not just those men. It's your stupid guilt."

There was a moment of absolute, cold silence, and Cole found himself regretting his words, for the pain that had sprung into Sebastian's eyes was terrible to behold.

"Sebastian . . . I . . ." Sebastian rose and walked to the door. "Sebastian, I didn't . . ."

But Sebastian was gone. Cole sighed deeply. He fervently wished he had not reopened the wound and hurt his friend. He also prayed that something or someone would bring some light into Sebastian's life and allow him to laugh, or even smile again.


Sebastian walked slowly, inhaling deeply to try to control the shaking rage that was like a thick black cloud in his mind. This anger had been the only thing

65

that had kept him going these past weeks.

He walked through the shade of the trees that stood near the village. Slumping down at the base of a tall pine, he folded his arms across bent knees, and bowed his head wearily. Though his eyes were closed, the nightmare was still vivid in his mind. Nathaniel . . . who had laughed and sang and had been so in love with life and the new land they had adopted. Nathaniel . . . who would have been alive now if not for him. He groaned under the weight of his self-inflicted guilt. Then, in self-defense, his hatred began to blossom. He wanted only to find the men responsible. He wanted only to see them die . . . slowly . . . at his hand. He would make sure they suffered, as his brother had suffered. He could give no thought to what he would do after that.

Summer had lain silently for a while to regain her strength. She always underwent total exhaustion after using her phenomenal healing gift. It frightened her now as it had from the time of her childhood, but she could not stop helping people. She wondered again whether it was a gift or a curse.

Still a little tired, she rose and put more wood on the fire. As she warmed herself beside it, she felt a renewal of the gratitude she always experienced when she had succeeded in defeating the dark bringer of death. And with the thought of her success came a reminder of the man who had been an unsolved mystery to her for so long. Why was his heart and mind the only barrier she could not cross? Why did she feel that the men who had pursued her were in some way connected to him?

Restlessly, she rose to her feet and walked to the door of the tipi. She stood in the entrance for a moment, watching the peaceful movement in the village that was her second home.

Vivid childhood memories brought the touch of a smile to her lips, but in a moment it faded. She felt . . . what? Her mind reached . . . searched . . . and found sorrow—deep, intense sorrow—and anger.

After another few minutes she found the direction from which it came. She saw that Sebastian sat beneath a tree some distance away. Slowly she walked toward him.

Sebastian became aware of Summer when she stopped beside him. He rose and stood close to her. As he gazed down at her, she wondered why she felt a strange touch of sympathy for this man when she harbored only distrust and anger for others of his race.

"I wish you could understand me," he said. "I would like to tell you I'm sorry for the intrusion, yet I'm amazed by what I saw."

Summer wanted to speak to him and was, in fact, surprised that she wanted to comfort him somehow in his great sorrow. Again she wished the perceptions of her gift were something she could halt at will, for she still could not rid herself of the disconcerting thought that he was connected to the men who had pursued her. She had to find out how they were related before she could begin to trust him with her own secrets.

Sebastian had been trapping in the territory since his arrival and, on occasion, he had run across Indians. He had learned the rudiments of the signs they used, at least enough to make them understand he was friendly. Now he made one of those signs to tell that he was a friend.

Summer smiled and her hands flew quickly in response. Laughing, Sebastian caught them between his.

"Whoa!" He laughed. "That's too fast for me."

He touched his head and shook it negatively,

implying that he did not understand her rapid signs.

Summer laughed softly and slowly repeated the sign he had given her: I am a friend.

He liked the sound of her laughter. In fact, just being near her stirred his reluctant emotions and awakened sensations he tried to ignore, though he couldn't quite seem to. Sebastian pointed to himself and slowly pronounced his name, "Se-bas-tian. Sebastian," he repeated, pleased with her quick smile.

"Sebastian," she echoed.

He nodded and pointed to her, and she was quick to reply. "Summer."

"Summer," he repeated. "It's a beautiful name. It suits you. You are a very beautiful woman."

He tried to think of some way to communicate with her. Stretching out the palm of his left hand and using two fingers of his right hand, he made a motion like walking. Then he pointed to the path that ran toward the river. He was quite pleased with himself when again she smiled and nodded. Together they began to walk in the shade of the trees.

From a distance, Hawk watched with a worried frown on his face. Not only was Summer like a daughter to him; she was the most important member of his tribe. He knew she had felt some darkness in this man, a connection to the ones who had pursued her. It took him only a moment to decide to follow them. Like a shadow, he blended into the forest and sought a path that would eventually cross theirs. He knew the forest well and would not be seen unless he chose to reveal himself.

Sebastian and Summer walked in silence. To Sebastian it was a somewhat serene silence. Peace of mind was something he had not enjoyed for a long time.

To Summer it was a moment for mental listening,

and she was again frustrated when she encountered a dark barrier that would not let her in. It seemed that the mystery surrounding this man of her dreams would remain.

Then suddenly a picture rapidly crossed her thoughts and vanished almost as quickly as it had come. There had been another man—golden, as this one was—laughing and walking beside Sebastian. The picture grew in intensity once more and she saw the man fall. There was blood, and weeping, then the picture was gone and there was darkness again.

They stopped walking when the path met the river, and they stood on the bank side by side. Sebastian found himself in a most difficult situation. He had set his course, knew his goal and his ultimate destination, yet he found himself drawn beyond his will to this dark-eyed girl. And he couldn't even communicate in her language! he realized with vexation.

He turned to face her. Their eyes met and for one intense moment his heart seemed to stop and then begin to beat fiercely. He wanted to deny it, this fire that leapt through his veins. He wanted to push her from him but found his rebellious body warming and filling with raw desire.

Summer's wide, fathomless eyes watched him intently, and she was aware of the heat of desire that had sprung into his eyes. She had seen it before and part of her grew angry and tried to resist, though another part of her was mutinous to her will and set her pulse to beating wildly.

She bit back the words that formed on her lips and exerted rigid control over her senses, which were becoming alarmingly aware of him. Had the earth really shook beneath her feet until it had made her whole body tremble? Had the breeze suddenly become so heated that it made her skin seem afire?

She could feel herself quivering with a strange anticipation that left her startled and suddenly vulnerable, and she silently searched for her breath, which seemed caught somewhere in her breast.

Sebastian saw awareness in her eyes and felt the spark of something wild and untamed leap between them. Despite the soundless warning that rang out in his mind, and despite his self-imposed promises, he reached for her.

She stiffened for a moment at his touch, but a liquid warmth coursed through her as he drew her close enough for their bodies to meet.

He felt a longing to taste the soft lips that were so near, to touch the velvet skin. His arm held her while one hand lightly caressed her throat, then lifted her head. He bent and brushed the soft corner of her mouth with a kiss so light she was startled by its gentleness. A soft fluttering sensation seemed to burst to life within her.

No, her mind screamed. He is just another of the white world who deceives! but her body would not listen. Her heart throbbed heavily and she was suffused with a strange combination of pleasure and pain.

Drugged with the sweetness of her, he kissed first one corner of her mouth and then the other. Her body, pressed close to his, seemed a perfect fit, he mused in wonder. Then all at once, he was consumed by a passion so fierce that he was momentarily lost in a dizzying spiral of savage need.

His tongue brushed the fullness of her lower lip; then, catching it between his, he sucked gently and felt her trembling increase.

Now she slowly began to resist, but he possessed her mouth, first gently, then savagely, as if he wanted to draw something from the depths of her soul.

Her mind whirled beyond thought and she clung to

70

him, unable to stop the flood of sensation his actions elicited, or control the feeling that she was melting to fit his need.

In a last, desperate attempt to regain her reason, she gave an agonized groan, pressed her palms against his chest, and reluctantly drew her lips from his.

"No," she whispered frantically. How could she have been so weak, so ignorant of the power he wielded, and so foolish as to have allowed it to overwhelm her senses? She would have spoken then, would have cried out her anger and distrust, but another voice broke the stillness.

"Summer." Hawk's voice was deceptively innocent of what he had seen. It was as if he had come upon them only at that moment.

Both Sebastian and Summer spun about, and though neither realized it, the emotions they had aroused in each other were plainly written on their faces.

When he reached them, Hawk smiled, but Sebastian was aware that the smile traveled only as far as his mouth. His eyes remained cold and unbending.

Hawk spoke quickly in his language as he reached to touch Summer's arm. "Summer, return to the village."

"Hawk . . . I . . ."

"We cannot trust him yet."

"Hawk," Sebastian interrupted, "this is not what you think."

"Is it not?" Hawk replied casually. "I have sent scouts to try to find the trail you seek or word of the men you hunt. In three days you should know. From this day to that, stay away from Summer."

Sebastian was angry with himself and with Hawk. His eyes met Summer's for a moment, then he turned and walked back to the village.

"Hawk—" Summer began again.

"Summer, listen to me . . . listen to your own thoughts. You do not know him yet. You have said yourself that you cannot see him. Maybe it is because his heart is black and he comes here to harm you."

"From what I know of white men, that is possible," she admitted. "But I must know, Hawk. I cannot control my gifts but I must know."

"Even if you do not like what you see?"

"Even then. There is something within him that is hurt. He has turned upon himself for some reason. It is pain and sorrow I feel."

"Perhaps the pain and sorrow of others?"

"Perhaps," she said softly as her eyes followed Sebastian's retreating figure, "it's his own."

"Summer, walk carefully. Remember also what you are to many. Listen and find out more before you speak—before you let him too close. Promise me this much."

"All right, Hawk. I will keep my secret a little longer. I will be careful."

"It is all I ask."

They walked back to the village in silence.

# *Chapter Seven*

Sebastian moved toward the village sorting his thoughts. He told himself that what had just happened had been his method of self-defense against the power Summer seemed to have that enabled her to reach the spot he had guarded so carefully.

Kate was the woman he wanted, and no other woman could take her place, especially an Indian squaw. She would never be the kind of woman who could make his home beautiful or be its capable mistress, as he knew Kate could. She was an Indian, and he had no intention of spending the rest of his life in a tipi with half-naked, half-breed children running about his feet. Selfishly, he never considered that Summer might not want to share her life with a white man.

He vowed he would not let such a thing happen again. He could not allow anyone to turn his mind away from the revenge he sought, revenge that would assuage his guilt.

He stepped inside his tipi and found that Cole was gone. Food had been prepared for him, so he sat down and ate. He had barely finished when Cole returned. Sebastian had no intention of making an issue of what had transpired between them earlier, and to Cole's relief, Sebastian smiled.

"Let's ride out for awhile and see if we can pick up their trail," Sebastian suggested.

Cole readily agreed. He was much too uncomfortable sitting around and doing nothing.

"Sebastian, I've been talking to a few of them. It's amazing how many of the children speak our language. Not well of course, but I can understand them."

"I wonder . . ."

"Wonder what?"

"Why a woman as important as Hawk says she is can't speak our language, especially since Hawk and many of the children do."

"Maybe," Cole offered, "she just doesn't choose to speak it."

Sebastian thought about that for a time, then dismissed the idea. He had looked into her eyes and had seen something unexplainable, but he didn't believe she was a deceptive person. He grinned as his thoughts drifted to how pretty she was, and how full and soft her mouth was, and how sweet it had tasted. Then he asked, "And what other information did you gather?"

"Well, for one thing, there's going to be a celebration tonight. I guess the child's parents are showing their gratitude, both to their gods, and," he added, watching Sebastian's expression, "to Summer . . . the healer."

"Is that what they call her?"

"Among other things. She's an important lady. Part of the celebration is for us, too."

"Us? Why?"

"Because we rescued Summer. From what little I can gather, she wasn't born here. She just sort of . . . comes to them. When I started asking questions about where she came from and who her family is, well"—Cole

74

shrugged—"they just sort of . . . forget how to speak English."

"It gets more mysterious every minute. So we're going to be part of the celebration. When does it start?"

"After the sun sets."

"Well then, let's go. Maybe we can scare up some tracks between now and then. I'd like to get out of here as quickly as we can."

Cole followed after Sebastian, though he harbored severe doubts that they could find tracks when Hawk's warriors had not been able to. And he also wondered why Sebastian was in such a rush to leave the village.

They spent several hours in a vain attempt to find some clue to the whereabouts of the men they had trailed for so long. All traces seemed to have vanished, as if the men had disappeared into thin air.

The sun was nearing the horizon when they rode back into the village. It was soon obvious to them that the villagers had begun preparing for the celebration hours before. The sounds of excitement were in the air and there was a bustle of activity. A large fire burned in the clearing that was the center of the village. Around it seats of honor had been arranged for several who were not yet present.

Sebastian and Cole approached the fire, but they had not walked far before Hawk spotted them and moved forward to greet them.

"I am glad you have returned," Hawk said. "Come and eat and enjoy the celebration with us. Sleeping Wolf and Swift Doe would like to speak to you. They are grateful you were there when Summer needed you."

At Sebastian's questioning look, Hawk smiled. "They are the parents of the child who was sick," he explained.

"The one Summer cured?" Sebastian inquired humbly.

"Yes," Hawk repeated. "The one Summer cured."

"Where is Summer? Will she be here?" Sebastian had tried to make the question sound casual and was surprised at his own impatience for Hawk's answer.

"She is with my father. They will both come soon. My father is very old and Summer is a great comfort to him. When she comes to us, he keeps her with him for as long as he can."

"When she comes to you?" Sebastian queried. "Does she live somewhere near so that she knows when you need her?"

"Summer," Hawk said in a deep, thoughtful voice, "does not have to be near to know."

Before Sebastian could ask any more questions, he was halted by the emotion he saw reflected in Hawk's eyes. Sebastian's gaze followed Hawk's.

From a very large tipi two people emerged, and Sebastian recognized Summer immediately. The other was an old man, whose tanned and weathered skin was wrinkled and taut over his bones. His hair was white and he moved slowly though steadily, with one hand resting on Summer's shoulder. It was obvious from the way Summer held herself that she was showing this man great respect. The two walked slowly to the previously prepared seats and the old chief sat. Summer dropped to her knees at his feet, then rested beside him on the ground.

It was the signal for the festivities to begin.


The celebration had continued for some time before Cole bent near Sebastian to speak in a low whisper. "I wonder if we're going to get to meet the old chief."

"I guess whenever he decides he wants to talk to us."

"Black Cloud has quite a reputation."

"What kind of reputation?"

"He's a strong chief. Takes good care of his people."

"I can believe that. They look like a pretty contented group. I'd like to know more about the connection between them and Summer. You said she wasn't born here?"

"No, but I couldn't find out anything else."

"Well, she had to come from somewhere. Where was she coming from when we found her, and who was she running from?"

Cole looked closely at Sebastian. "What do you care? You saved her, and they're grateful. In a few days we'll be gone. We're on a hunt. What does one woman you hardly know have to do with it?"

"I wish I knew," Sebastian murmured. "I wish I knew."

Black Cloud and Summer had spoken at length in his tipi. She had gone to him as soon as she could, and he had welcomed her with the same pleasure he always felt whenever he saw her. Summer had laughed softly as she had knelt before the old man, and he had smiled and had reached out his hand to touch her hair.

"You are a welcome sight for these old eyes, my child," he had said.

"It's a pleasure to see you again, Grandfather."

"Your father and mother, they are well?"

"I hope so. I need to send a message. My family does not know I am home yet," she had gone on to explain.

The old man had chuckled and had patted her hand. "We will send someone."

Then he bent forward to study her closely.

"Summer, the white one—the one who came to help you—what do you see in him?"

"I wanted to talk to you about him, Grandfather. For the first time, I have not been able to see, and I do not understand."

"Hawk tells me that you choose to keep a secret the fact that you speak his language. What is your reason?"

Summer had tried to explain by recounting the whole situation. After she had revealed her feelings, she had sat quietly, reflecting that this man before her was one of the dearest people in her life, that his wisdom meant a great deal to her, and that she knew he understood her completely. These thoughts had given her comfort.

"If you believe that he is somehow connected to the ones who tried to harm you, then do you believe he could be one of them?"

"I don't trust any of the white men, but I would have some questions answered. I don't know why I cannot see or feel his thoughts as I can others."

"I shall speak with him," Black Cloud had said firmly. Then he had risen to his feet, but his advanced age had made him unsteady. He had rested a hand on Summer's shoulder and they had left the tipi together.

Black Cloud sat regally, with Summer close to him. His gaze missed nothing that was going on about him, yet it was some time before he beckoned for a young boy to come to him. Black Cloud spoke, and in moments the boy was delivering a message to Sebastian and Cole.

"Our chief would speak with you."

"Let's go, Cole." Sebastian smiled. "I'm anxious to hear what the old man has to say."

The words he spoke were not completely true, for he also wanted to be near Summer again. He wanted to see if he was only imagining what he had sensed before, that there was something different—special—about this girl. As they made their way through the crowd,

Cole's eyes were on the old chief and Sebastian's were locked on the dark eyes of the girl who knelt beside him.

Black Cloud was a man who had seen much in his years. He knew and understood people. His experienced eyes examined the two white men as they approached. It took him only moments to sense the force that seemed to be drawing Sebastian to Summer. His eyes never left her, and his unguarded gaze was easily read by the old man.

Questions stormed Black Cloud's mind. Would this be the man who would try to do what Clay Storm had tried with Summer's mother? Would he attempt to take Summer from the people who loved and needed her? Was Sebastian a danger to Summer? Did he come to this place with evil in his heart? Or was he one who would come into Summer's life to share it and give her happiness? And Summer, who felt and saw beyond the normal—why could she not see into this man's heart?

The two sat near Black Cloud. Sebastian had to forcibly tear his eyes from Summer.

"Welcome to our village," Black Cloud said. "We are in your debt for what you have done for Summer. We would do something to show our gratitude. Share this celebration with us and tell us your needs so that we can repay you." Black Cloud motioned toward the seats near him as he spoke, and both men now accepted the seats of honor with pleasure.

Cole sat on Black Cloud's left and Sebastian on his right, with Summer still seated on the ground between him and the old chief.

Sebastian looked down on her dark head and controlled the urge to reach out and gently caress the shiny black tresses that had been left unbraided and cascaded down her back in a flowing silken mass.

He watched the glow of firelight on her skin and was

79

wrenched violently by the sudden surge of desire that tore through him. He would have given anything at that moment to hold her in his arms, to tangle his hands in the softness of her hair and brand her lips with his.

"It is not necessary to give us anything but your friendship. Cole and I are just happy that we were there at the right time. Although," he added as his eyes turned to the woman before him, "I can't imagine why anyone would want to harm anyone like Summer." As he spoke, Summer turned slightly and lifted her eyes to meet his. "Someone as gentle as she," he continued, "certainly could not have done harm to anyone."

As if of its own volition, his voice had softened and had become nearly a caress. Its tenderness caused completely different reactions in those who watched and listened. Cole found it a pleasant surprise. Sebastian had been so dark and moody since his brother's death that Cole welcomed anything that would soothe him in any way. Black Cloud heard it and recognized, with some concern, that Sebastian was thoroughly entangled in the silken web of Summer's mystery.

But for Summer, his voice held more. She felt the touch of something dangerous yet strangely exciting. More from habit than from need, she mentally reached for him, only to be met by the same dark barrier. Again it surprised her. The gentleness of his words and the warmth in his eyes seemed a shield between her and whatever lay in his mind. Yet she felt the force was not directed outward, but inward. He was aiming the darkness at his own heart.

As the celebration continued, there was much laughter and merriment. Everyone seemed to be enjoying the festivities. Sebastian found a great deal of pleasure in simply watching Summer. Emotions flowed across her expressive face, and her eyes sparkled with the joy she always shared with her people. Although born of two worlds, Summer had finally found the path between, and now she could experience both with equal pleasure.

The two white visitors were introduced to many of the tribesmen, but Sebastian and Cole were most impressed with Hawk's wife, Snow Woman, and with Carrie Mackintire, the beautiful white wife of Walking Horse, who was a close friend to Hawk and Summer. They met Snow Woman first, and found her to be a shy, gentle woman with a smile that lit her face like sunshine. She seemed the perfect complement to Hawk's noble strength. But Carrie Mackintire came as a complete surprise to both men, and Sebastian immediately began to wonder how he could talk to her alone long enough to ask some questions.

It was obvious to the visitors that Walking Horse loved his small, auburn-haired wife deeply and was very proud of her beauty. And though they also sensed his reluctance to explain her presence here, Sebastian boldly asked how they had met.

"I am grateful that Carrie was visiting nearby," he told them, "or I might never have seen her."

Walking Horse knew he had made a mistake as soon as the words had left his mouth, and neither Sebastian nor Cole missed the quick frown that Hawk gave him, which silenced him immediately.

"Visiting?" Sebastian questioned. "There are white families near here?"

Grudgingly, Hawk answered. He could not lie to these men, for lying was a practice that was alien to the Indian. "Only one," Hawk said. "They are some distance away."

It was all the information Hawk was prepared to offer, and both men knew it, though they remained extremely curious. But before any more could be said, the throbbing drums called young and old to enjoy the dancing and the Indians' favorite pastime, story telling.

The onlookers cheered as story after story was acted out with dancing and song. This part of the celebration continued until the moon stood high in a star-studded sky. Then slowly the occupants of the village began to drift away to their own tipis.

Summer and Hawk saw to Black Cloud's comfort before they walked slowly to their own tipis. Black Cloud's words were in Summer's mind as they moved through the village. He had not given Summer the answers she needed.

"Summer, my child," Black Cloud had said, "you were given a gift by the gods. It is not for us to question where it leads you. You must feel what is true in your heart . . . then you must follow that path. I cannot believe that after all your life it would lead you into trouble now. I did not see evil in his face—the white one—but I, like you, am not sure what was there."

"I will find out before I speak with him, Grandfather," she had said. "There is something dark that hovers about him. I don't know if it has anything to do with me, but I don't intend to let him get too close until I know. And even then it would still be hard for me to trust a white man."

"Go to your bed, Summer. Sleep. Maybe tomorrow will give you the answers you seek."

"Yes, Grandfather." She had smiled and had touched the old man gently and lovingly. Then she had risen to stand beside Hawk. Together they had wished the old man a good rest and then had departed. Now they walked in silence.

"Summer?"

"Yes, Hawk?"

"Do you not think it would be best if you went home? Do not misunderstand my words," he added hastily. "It is my great love for you that makes me worry. It is hard to believe he was there just in time to help you. Even you say that the evil that tried to harm you in some way touches him."

Summer smiled. "I know you are thinking of my welfare, Hawk, and you need not tell me it is because you love me. I understand well your love for my family." She stopped walking and looked at him. "I . . . I am not afraid. It is the white men who will leave quickly. They are used to much comfort."

"No," he replied in a resigned voice. "You are not afraid." Summer smiled again and turned to continue toward her own tipi. Hawk's eyes watched her until the darkness swallowed her up.

"I am afraid, Summer," he said in a sad whisper. "I am afraid."

As Summer continued to walk, her mind was on Hawk's worry and on the one who had stood at the edge of her thoughts all evening—Sebastian.

She stood in front of her tipi for several moments, knowing she would not find sleep without dreams, and at this moment she could not face what might be the conclusion of the dream that had become reality.

She turned and walked the path she and Sebastian had strolled hours before. She would go to the same spot by the river where they had stood. Perhaps there her thoughts could find him and release her from this strange turmoil she was experiencing.

She knew the path well, for she had walked it from the time of her childhood. Her steps were light and that is why she saw Sebastian before he sensed her presence.

He stood gazing out over the water. Framed by the light of the huge yellow moon, his lean form and broad shoulders stood out before her like the trunk of a huge oak.

At this moment she was unsure and somewhat afraid

83

to reach for him mentally. She feared she would see or feel what she didn't want to see or feel again. She could go now, she realized, as silently as she had come, and he would never know.

Sebastian stood enveloped in his grief. He thought he was alone with it, and he tried once more to wash the guilt from his heart, but it was impossible. His mind continued to cry out that if not for him, Nathaniel—the brother he loved so dearly—would still be alive.

"Sebastian?"

He was not sure he had heard his name until it was repeated.

"Sebastian."

He turned.

The moon was behind him now and he seemed a very large shadow, but Summer was bathed in its glow. The vision she made caused him to draw in his breath sharply.

Her dark hair flowed smoothly to her hips and her slim body, in tawny buckskin, was clearly outlined by the soft light. Her face seemed to him to be aglow with the moonlight, as if it were a radiance emanating from her, and her eyes were wide and as dark as the night.

For a moment neither moved. Sebastian could again feel the strange sensation of being drawn to her. He fought it with all he possessed.

"Summer"—he smiled—"I thought everyone else was asleep by now."

When she did not answer, he chuckled. "I forgot that you can't understand me."

Slowly he walked toward her. When he stood beside her, she could feel the strength of him. His masculine scent, clean and warm, was a heady influence, but firmly she controlled her emotions. He was white, and he was dangerous.

"The moonlight is something you should wear all the

84

time," he said softly. "It suits you." Gentle fingers brushed away a strand of hair from her cheek and lingered to caress it.

"Summer," he murmured. "You're very beautiful. How could I expect you to understand the nightmares I face? What would you know of death . . . of guilt?"

He sighed deeply. "What is it about you? Why do I feel . . . peace?" He added the last word as if he couldn't quite believe it. Then he abruptly turned away, only to quickly spin about and face her again.

"I don't need your peace," he said harshly.

For an instant, Summer closed her eyes and let her mind open to him. She desperately wanted to know why he was here and what was in his thoughts. His angry words had shaken her.

He suddenly took hold of her shoulders and there was a violent collision as his thoughts touched hers. She saw a swirling mist of unexplainable emotions. Below them she sensed a gentleness that he didn't want, a peace that he couldn't face, and a beauty that reached to touch a place he had to guard.

Her soft, vulnerable lips parted in a soundless cry as her thoughts met confusion. Then his head was bending lower as he drew her into his arms and his lips came down upon hers. For a moment she melted into him. Then, stunned by the fact that against all her common sense she actually had been about to trust a man she hardly knew, she stepped back, away from him.

Disbelief was written on both their faces, for the power that had forged them together still tingled through their bodies and the taste of it was still upon their lips. She wanted to step into his arms again, wanted to mold her body against his and feel the brilliant flame that had touched her before, but instead she maintained rigid control. It took all the strength she possessed, for she was certain that if he touched her again she would be lost. She pressed one hand against his chest and slowly shook her head negatively.

"I know you don't understand me," he said gently. "Maybe even I don't understand what drives me. I only know that I want you . . . and I don't want to want you. There is no time for us, Summer, and I would probably hurt you. But I want you—God help me—I want you."

He stepped toward her, but with a soft sound that was almost like a cry of pain, she turned and was swallowed up by the night.

## Chapter Eight

The three warriors whom Hawk had sent to track the men Sebastian had trailed into their territory did not return the next day or the following two. It was a difficult three days for both Summer and Sebastian.

Cole seemed to find the village and its inhabitants a pleasant diversion. The warriors enjoyed teaching him their ways, and he had a great deal of fun trying to acquire their prowess, both with horses and with bows and arrows. Sebastian joined his friend on occasion, and they provided a great source of amusement for the warriors who watched the frustrated visitors attempt to match their skill. The Indians rode like the wind and could do phenomenal tricks from horseback that astounded Cole and Sebastian. And try as they might, they could not duplicate such feats.

But no matter how Sebastian tried to keep his mind on other things, he continually saw Summer crossing his line of vision. He watched her working with the women, laughing with the children, walking with Hawk, or talking with Black Cloud. Often he found himself fighting an unreasonable irritation at the obviously close relationships she shared with these people and the way they all seemed to talk so easily

87

together. He wondered what magic this girl possessed that she held the attention of a man as powerful as Hawk, a man who would one day be Chief.

He knew quite well that Summer was considered different from the other women. Although young, she commanded respect. He wondered at this, but knew she would not allow him to get close enough to ask any questions. He had touched it once, the essence of Summer, and had come away shaken. Now his resolve was firm. Sebastian had death in his heart and he refused to make room for another emotion, one that might be strong enough to dilute the other. Nathaniel could not die in vain. His guilt refused to let it be.

He did not know that Summer too was conscious of every move he made. She watched the sun touch his golden hair and admired his masculine form when he dressed as an Indian, in breechclout and leather leggings, to compete with the warriors. She made it a point to have other things to do at such times, for it annoyed her to hear his deep laughter or see a faraway look in his eyes.

Summer had been taught to explore her senses, her mind, and her being, and now she was helpless to close the channel. Emotions coursed through her like a flowing river, and one emotion grew stronger each day—an uneasy fear of the bond that was slowly growing between her and Sebastian, despite their efforts to avoid each other.

On the third night after the celebration—a star-kissed night of warm breezes that carried the fragrant scents of wild blossoms and pungent pine—the moon hung low and cast a golden glow on the horizon. Summer, restless from her continuing dreams, had risen from her mat to walk in the cool night air. She strolled along a tree-lined path deep in thought, wishing desperately that the gods would answer her questions or give her some hint of what Sebastian's presence might mean.

She was drawn to him in a curious way she had tried to resist, though she still did not know for certain whether he was a friend or an enemy. She could not overcome her concern that there was a force linking her, Sebastian, and the threat she had felt in the forest.

She walked to a fallen tree and sat down. As she gazed at the moon, she tried unsuccessfully to sort out her confused thoughts.

Three Feathers was as much an expert in the wild as the best of Hawk's warriors. Like a shadow he had eluded them and had circled back to remain near enough to the village to watch the comings and goings of its inhabitants. He waited for the moment they would relax their guard, the one moment when Summer might make the mistake of going too far away from the camp. He had seen her clearly the first time, and his desire to have the medicine woman of Hawk's village had been kindled. Now another desire burned within him as well—to kill the golden-haired man who had interfered in his plans to capture Summer.

He had slept in the heat of the afternoon so that in the evening he could prowl the periphery of the village on constant watch. His efforts had not been wasted. A grim smile touched his lips as he saw Summer drift away from the village and out of sight of the guards who protected her. The entire village was now between him and Summer, and slowly he began to circle about it. He moved cautiously and soundlessly, his mind intent on his prey.

Summer was drawn rapidly from her reverie as

darkness exploded in her mind. Its shattering recurrence made her gasp, for she knew it was the same dark thing that had stormed her senses before.

She rose to her feet and realized that it was stalking her. It came from the direction of the village, and this surprised her. She didn't want to face the possibility that it might indeed be Sebastian. She fought this idea with all the strength she possessed, and in the process her mind reached out for Sebastian. Mentally she cried out his name in a silent prayer that he was not the cause of her fear.

She backed away from the direction of the danger. Her eyes searched the darkness, and though there was no sign of movement, she knew that the danger was very real. Her mind cried out: *Sebastian! Sebastian!*


Sebastian suddenly came awake with a severe jolt that startled him. He sat up in his bed, sure that someone had called to him but so disoriented that he couldn't determine the source or location. He looked across the nearly dead fire to see that Cole was still deeply asleep.

Wrinkling his brow in confusion, he shook his head from side to side and laughed at himself. He lay back down, but in seconds, the call came to him again.

*Sebastian!*

It was Summer's voice, and it was touched with panic.

Again he sat up, puzzled that Cole had remained completely undisturbed.

He rose quickly. He had been sleeping naked, as was his custom, and it took him only a moment to slip into buckskin breeches and moccasins. He did not take time to put on his shirt, but grabbed up his gun and went to the tipi door. He stood just outside it, looking about him and trying to determine the direction of the call.

90

He soon realized that the village was totally quiet. Had he truly heard a cry for help?

Like a responding answer, his name echoed clearly in his mind and unmistakably in Summer's voice. It was even clear enough for him to estimate its location.

He set off at a gentle lope in that direction, and after he crossed the village and passed the cleared circle around its outskirts, he entered the wooded area. Just within the shadows he stopped again to listen.


Maneuvering slowly so the guards would not detect his presence, Three Feathers moved in Summer's direction. He stopped suddenly and stood completely still, his attention drawn to the edge of the forest less than five hundred yards away where he had just seen a tall form enter the trees. He muttered angrily, wondering who else could be advancing toward Summer. The form had moved to block him from the girl, but Three Feathers was determined to carry out his abduction. He bent low toward the ground and took one slow step at a time so that no twig would snap and no sound would be heard.

He might have ended everything to his satisfaction if he had not been so preoccupied with catching sight of Summer and monitoring the progress of the shadowed form. In his concentration, he missed detecting the presence of two strategically placed, alert guards. A soft whistled sound told him that he had been spotted.

Again he cursed angrily. Making a quick decision, he moved to escape the guards, leaving Summer for another time.


Summer continued to retreat from the silent threat of danger as she tried to maneuver toward the village.

She moved very slowly, mentally fighting her paralyzing fear and keeping close watch about her for any sign of the danger she knew was somewhere near.

From where she was she could vaguely see the edge of the clearing through the shadow-filled trees. Calculating the distance, she decided to make a run for it. She promised herself that if she made it safely, she would obey Hawk's orders from now on.

Catching her lip between her teeth and gripping her hands into fists, she began to run, only to collide headlong into Sebastian.

He cursed as he caught the whirling form that broke from the darkness, and she cried out in shock as she found herself caught in iron-hard arms and crushed against a broad, naked chest.

She fought wildly and it was all Sebastian could do to hold onto her. Summer was determined that no one would succeed in harming her while she had an ounce of strength left.

Sebastian had fairly had the wind knocked out of him when Summer had collided with him. Now her soft curves filled his arms, but she battled so furiously that he found it necessary to get a good hold on her before he could speak.

"Summer!"

She wanted to scream but controlled the urge as her senses told her that the overwhelming threat was receding. She sagged against Sebastian's chest, and his arms closed about her to hold her close as both surrendered to relief that she was safe.

It was only a moment later that both became aware of much more. Sebastian felt sensation tingling through his veins like warm wine. He was lost in the scent of her hair as soft strands blew against his face and he reveled in the warmth of her soft woman's body that molded itself against his.

Summer also felt awareness, awareness that stirred unwanted memories to life. Once again she was allowing herself to be caught up in the overwhelming masculinity of him, to be swept away by an emotion she had vowed to suppress.

She struggled to escape the arms that held her and forcefully pushed herself away from him. At that moment the two guards appeared.

"Summer, a warrior came this way. He was not of our village. Have you seen anyone?"

Sebastian did not understand the words, but he sensed their meaning. It was obvious now that Summer had been running from an intruder, and that the guards were on his trail.

"It was not this one?" she asked quickly.

"No, it was not a white man. Are you safe?"

"Yes," she answered confidently. "Yes, I am."

"Then we will follow him. Maybe he is one of those whom the white men seek."

"Thank you, Beaver Tail."

As quickly as the two had come, they melted into the forest, and again Summer and Sebastian stood in silence.

The realization that he had heard Summer's call for help and the guards had not was just beginning to register in Sebastian's mind, along with the idea that her powers might be of some use to him. This revelation was another detail to add to the growing list of unaccountable occurrences in his relationship with this beautiful but mysterious woman. But the most difficult problem he had to cope with at the moment was the raging desire that surged through him—that and the fact that he didn't have the ability to talk to her.

"Damn," he muttered. "I wish you could understand me. I wish we could talk. I need your help, Summer, and I've no way of asking you. And I'm certain Hawk

93

will not speak to you on my behalf."

She didn't answer. He sighed and motioned to her to walk with him back to the village. If she could use the strange powers she had to help him find the ones he sought, maybe he and Cole would stand a chance, he mused. But he couldn't talk to her; he couldn't make her understand.

She stood still and he stopped to look at her. "Summer?"

Anger at her own feelings filled her. Why should she care if he needed her help? Why should she help him when she did not trust him, when he was part of the society she hated? If she didn't help him, he would go; then she could push him from her thoughts and maybe the strange dreams would stop.

Having had these thoughts, she couldn't believe it was her own voice she heard speaking. "Sebastian, don't go. Perhaps . . . perhaps I can help."

Absolute shock stopped Sebastian in his tracks. He walked back to face her.

"I'll be damned," he muttered in angry surprise as he approached her. "You've learned to speak English rapidly, haven't you?" he snapped. "What kind of game were you playing?"

"Sebastian, I'm sorry that you are angry with me. It was very important that I did what I did."

"Important to make fools of the white intruders? Did you derive some kind of perverse amusement from it? Did you laugh about it with Hawk, who obviously enjoyed keeping your little secret?"

"Sebastian—"

"Don't waste your words. I'll be leaving in the morning, whether your friends have found a trail or not. I have no time for playing your little games."

"I don't owe you an explanation. But maybe I can help you."

94

"Why did you lie to me?"

Her eyes had begun to glow with an anger that matched his.

"I do not lie! You are the one who decided I could not speak English. I never told you I couldn't."

"No, but you never told me you could, either. Why didn't you just say so?"

"For what reason?" she asked in a quiet voice, trying to contain her anger. "White men have their ways of collecting payment on debts. They usually take advantage." Her simple statement took him unawares.

"What do you know of me?" he snapped. "I need help to find the men who killed my brother. I don't need to be involved with a . . . a child who wants to play games."

Now her anger blossomed. "And what do you know of me? I could have said nothing! I could have just let you go on your futile chase. Like all white men, you can't understand kindness—or any other decent feelings. You judge everything and everybody by your own selves. You want a woman where you think you can walk over her; then you'll take what you please and push her aside." Her anger was now a blank, red rage. "I know what you were thinking. A nice half-breed squaw. Maybe she'll help and be a good bedmate at the same time." She stopped only because she was panting for breath and words failed her.

Sebastian was both angry and fascinated. He saw that her eyes sparkled with her fury and that she was literally trembling with anger.

"I didn't think—"

"I know," she snarled. "Your kind doesn't think."

"Now wait a minute," he exploded. "Don't you think you're being a little unfair? You don't know me, so how can you say 'my kind'?" He moved closer to her and his jade eyes were aglow with more than anger. "Maybe,"

95

he continued, "my kind is more your kind than you bargained for. Maybe . . . you're just a little afraid."

"Afraid?" she nearly shouted. "Afraid of you?"

"No," he said, his voice lowering to a taunting whisper, "afraid of yourself."

The color drained from her face, then returned to flood it crimson. She breathed in sharply, seeing his eyes glint with angry amusement and his mouth quirk in a mocking half smile that taunted her.

Fury raised her hand and aimed it, but strong fingers caught it before it could strike. He laughed softly and jerked her forcibly against him. A hard-muscled arm circled her waist and drew her even closer, pinning one of her arms between them. The other he held in a viselike grip. She glared up at him, more infuriated by her body's reaction than by his boldness. The moist warmth of his breath touched her cheek as he kissed it very gently. She gurgled an angry protest a moment before his mouth found hers and she stiffened when his lips touched hers with a feather-light kiss.

"No!" she groaned as she writhed in his arms. Then suddenly she was released and they stood apart, completely aware of each other. His eyes were filled with a sparkling challenge, a challenge she didn't dare refuse.

"I'm not afraid of anything," she ground out.

"No?" He chuckled. "Easy to say when you have someone like Hawk to stand guard. Easy to say, but you still won't help me." He shrugged. "So, who will ever know the truth of your words"—he lowered his voice to a near whisper—"except you?"

"What do you want of me, Sebastian Cain?" she asked.

"Help me find the ones who killed my brother. I don't know what kind of power you have, but I've seen . . . strange things. Summer," he said urgently, "help me. I need to find these men. I need to—"

"Kill them," she finished.

"Yes."

"Tell me, Sebastian," she said softly, "who's afraid now?"

Before she could understand his intent, she was again caught up in strong arms and held breathless against a chest that to her soft flesh felt like iron.

She lifted surprised eyes to him and saw the glow of anger—and more—in the depths of his jade orbs.

"Fear?" he said in a deceptively soft voice. "Perhaps. But my fear is very different from yours, my love. I fear death . . . but you fear living, feeling, sharing."

She was stung by his casual piercing of her defenses. Yet as he continued to hold her body pressed against his, her hurt diminished and was replaced by fascination that their hearts seemed to be beating as one.

Her feet barely touched the ground as he held her, and from her assaulted senses and from the fiery gleam in his eyes, she could tell that he was fully aroused. Something savage rose up in her and she struggled to be free, but she succeeded only in forcing him to hold her tighter. She glared into his eyes and her breath caught as she read his intent.

# Chapter Nine

She was mesmerized as his head bent slowly and his lips hovered unbearably close to hers.

"You would rape me!" She groaned as if it were the only way to protect herself from something she did not understand.

"Rape?" he questioned with a soft chuckle. "Are you so sure it would be rape? Are you so sure you would not be willing . . . maybe even eager?"

What was he doing to her? she thought wildly. Why could she not spit her anger back at him? Why did her body feel as though it were floating away from her, weightless and drifting, unable to regain solid ground?

Slowly he let her weight slide down his body. She wanted to resist and even squeaked a helpless sound before his open mouth stopped all protest.

It was a brutal kiss. His tongue forced her lips apart and thrust with an overwhelming possession. She could not breathe, nor could she control her wayward body. She could not seem to concentrate on anything but the sensations that stormed her. No longer did she have the strength or the desire to leave his captive embrace. She was hard-pressed to stop her world from spinning into oblivion.

In the pit of her belly, strange fluttering sensations grew until she could not control them. She was aware not only of his throbbing maleness pressing against her, but also of the passion and hot desire that had become a taunting within her own body. That ache grew and grew until she cried out against his demanding mouth.

"I will not take you by force," he whispered against the rapidly beating pulse at her throat. "But you must tell me no . . . you must tell me . . ."

His mouth moved hungrily over her flesh, scalding it with white-hot flame. His lips touched and tasted, returning again and again to her mouth to drink of its sweetness.

Summer's rage had now become a raw, inflamed hunger. Her mouth quivered, warmed, then began a voracious search of its own. She heard his ragged gasp as their lips parted for only a moment before they began to blend again fiercely.

Soon his mouth sought the skin of her neck, and his tongue traced a weaving pattern over her flesh until she whimpered softly in pleasure. He loosened the ties of her tunic and brushed it from her shoulders, and his lips found sensitive spots to torment. The tunic dropped lower, urged by strong hands intent upon revealing her breasts.

Gently he cupped one full globe in his hand. He caressed and caught the soft nipple between his fingers and drew it to a hard peak with his touch. Then he bent his head and she gasped as his lips found the crest and sucked gently. His tongue stroked and teased until sparks of pain and pleasure danced before her eyes and she moaned softly in a throaty purr of ecstasy.

She held his head between her hands and felt the soft, thick texture of his hair between her fingers as he moved from one passion-swollen crest to the other. His hands loosened the skirt she wore and it dropped unheeded at her feet. Then he drew her down to the soft grass. She lay beneath his gaze now, caught in a savage abandon. He saw that her head was thrown back and her eyes were closed. Her soft mouth was parted and she trembled in her primitive need.

His hands first touched lightly upon her slim thighs, then moved up to trace a path across her belly to her waist and up to cup her breasts gently. He teased the peaks into budding response, then bent to capture one again in his mouth. His tongue flicked lightly and she murmured her pleasure.

His hands stroked and caressed her sensitive flesh until her body sought their touch urgently, as if demanding that they release the torment within her. His fingers touched the soft velvet swell of her womanhood, caressing, probing gently until she arched to meet them. She was trembling violently now as his fingers moved deeper, opening her gently and lifting her to a plane of near senseless abandon.

Slowly his lips brushed a path down her heated skin, stopping to taste, to nibble, to tease, until she was ready to shriek with her need for fulfillment. Her skin tasted sweet, but he yearned to taste another sweetness. Then his mouth touched the flaming petals of her passion-moistened core. She gasped and writhed, not to escape him but to urge him to deeper penetration. His tongue probed gently at first, then with fiery swirling thrusts, until she felt she would go mad with raging, pulsing passion.

At last neither could bear the ecstatic torture a moment longer. Lying on his side, Sebastian drew her to him, wanting to hold her when he first entered her.

He drew her leg over him and bound her to him as he pressed his throbbing manhood to the depths of the warm, moist sheath of her body. For a moment she stiffened, and in Sebastian's mind he could feel her pain as if it were his own. Then suddenly it disappeared and their hearts pounded wildly as he thrust within her again, deeper, faster, until they careened beyond the world, beyond time and place.

They were oblivious to all but the flaming glory of their mutual possession. The magnificent force of it carried them to a climax that shattered their universe and left them panting, eyes closed, clinging to each other until the world could right itself again.

Breathing slowed, hearts ceased to pound, blood slowed and mind regained control of senses that had been totally abandoned.

Summer gave a soft, ragged moan of anguish and sat up abruptly, but Sebastian was quick to grab hold of her and draw her down to lie close to him. She fought for a moment, but his show of superior strength convinced her that she would not leave his side unless he freed her.

"Let me go, Sebastian."

"Why Summer? So you can run away and hide? What we just shared was a glorious thing. Why should you run away from what we both want?"

"I do not run away . . . nor do I hide," she replied coldly. He loosened his hold and she rose quickly and began to gather her clothes. If he had said something then—one word to assure her that this had been more than just the sharing of raw passion—she might have altered her thoughts. But he didn't—he couldn't—and in a few moments the chance was lost.

He rose to stand behind her.

"I want to be with you again," he said as he gripped her shoulders. Her back was to him and he pressed his face against the silk of her hair, inhaling the clean scent of it. The thought crossed his mind that having an Indian mistress for a time would not be a bad idea.

She was choked to temporary silence by the rage that filled her. He would take her . . . use her, then toss her aside as nothing when he chose to move on. He was no different from all the others, and the hardest thing to bear was the fact that he had no realization of what he was asking. He still thought of her as nothing more than an Indian squaw.

She tried to blot from her mind the memory of his touch, which had disintegrated every fiber of her being until she had become mindless and wanton in his hands. It would never happen again, and she would prove to him that it would not—could not. Slowly she turned to face him.

"I," she said firmly, her eyes defiantly holding his, "am no man's mistress to be taken so easily. You would have your Indian squaw," she said angrily. "Is this not what you truly want? Tell me, Sebastian, will you stay with me—wed me, so that I will not have to face the disgrace of my people? Or are you so unfeeling as to believe it honors me, and those who love me, that I have been used by the noble white man?"

"You make it sound like I forced you to be with me," Sebastian cried angrily, wounded by the accuracy of her attack. He had meant just that, to let her fill the void until he could bring Kate. "I cannot stay here, Summer. I have to find the men who killed my brother and destroyed my home."

"My words were only to prove to you that such a relationship is impossible. We are worlds apart and what we want is very different. I will not be so weak again, nor am I such a fool as to be caught up in words—words that would take my freedom and leave me without my honor."

He came to her side, standing near enough to touch her, but he did not. His eyes held her as his hands could not. "Are we going to deny what we just shared?" he asked softly.

She vowed to do just that, but her heart betrayed her. She turned away from his penetrating gaze before it stirred emotions within her that she could not afford to rekindle.

"On your terms, Sebastian," she said softly, "there is nothing more for us to share." She hesitated in breathless anticipation, waiting for him to say the words she longed to hear.

Sebastian reached out a hand to stop her but let it drop when he realized he could not offer her what she wanted. He would find Nathaniel's killers, he would rebuild his house and then he would seek Kate, the woman who would make his home everything he desired. He could not envision Summer—a half-wild medicine woman—presiding over a home and servants. That he and Summer had shared something magical he could not deny, but he was also convinced that he would find as much when Kate came to him.

"Summer," he said quietly, but he spoke to the emptiness about him, for Summer had already gone.

Blinded by tears she had refused to shed in Sebastian's presence, Summer ran toward the village. She wanted only to be alone in her own tipi before she gave way to the pain. Her despair was agonizing, for she had surrendered despite her determination to resist his magnetism.

So involved was she in regaining her mental equilibrium that she did not see Cole until she bumped into him. He caught her before she could fall.

"Summer?" he said in surprise as he steadied her. "Have you seen Sebastian? Sebastian," he repeated, still unaware that she could speak his language.

"Yes, Cole," she answered. "He is down by the river."

Cole blinked and dropped his hand from her arm in total surprise.

"Summer, you—"

"Yes, I speak your language."

Even in the dim light of the moon, he could see the tears streaked on her cheeks. He immediately sensed their origin and cursed Sebastian silently for his ability to be so stubborn and sometimes cruel.

"I guess I don't have to ask if he is responsible for the tears," Cole said gently. "Damnit, I'm sorry, Summer."

She felt so vulnerable and helpless against his kindness that she choked back her sobs.

"What has he said that has upset you so?"

"It is nothing of importance," she replied. Brushing the tears from her cheeks she lifted her eyes defiantly to his.

"Nothing of importance?" Cole queried gently. "You do not strike me as a woman who weeps over nothing. Can I help?"

Summer realized he was sincere in wanting to help her. And because he knew Sebastian better than anyone else, he might be able to answer her questions.

They began to walk slowly back toward the village.

"Sebastian," she began hesitantly, "does not seem to have a high regard for my people."

Cole sighed. "He is blinded by so many things. Sometimes I wish he were not so strong. Then maybe someone could push a little reason into him."

"Why, Cole?" Summer whispered. "Why?"

"I don't want to say words that will hurt you."

"I need the truth," she said.

"The truth," he repeated. "Sometimes I'm not too sure of what is and what isn't."

"Cole . . . please tell me what you know."

There were several moments of silence as Cole made his decision. He did not want to see Summer hurt and he felt that if Sebastian stayed on the course he now followed, it would be impossible to prevent it.

"There is . . . someone else in Sebastian's mind . . . someone else . . . he wants."

"She is white?" Summer asked softly.

"He is a fool, Summer," Cole replied angrily. "He cannot see that she refused to give up anything for him. Her chance to inherit a fortune meant so much more to her than he did. Yet he still sees her as the gracious lady who will preside over this . . . this dynasty he seems so determined to create."

Again Summer was torn, but this time by another emotion, one she tried in vain to quell.

"Is she beautiful?"

"From what Nathaniel told me, very. Kate has golden hair and blue eyes and a pedigree that makes her. . . ." He shrugged.

"What Sebastian wants," Summer completed.

"It's a combination of things. It was Indians who killed his brother. The wound is still too fresh, and he can't trust. He's . . . sort of like a wounded animal, thrashing about and hurting others in his own pain."

"He is hurting only himself," Summer replied, and Cole silently agreed. If Sebastian could not see the woman Summer was because he was blinded by a hollow beauty, then he did not deserve Summer's care.

"I know," Cole replied aloud.

Summer wondered if Sebastian would be the same as other whites. Would he turn from Kate to her if he knew she was the daughter of Clayton Storm, whose wealth and name were known and envied throughout England. Would he be appeased by her wealth, or would he still need the golden-haired, blue-eyed woman whose appearance bespoke her bloodlines.

She would never tell him who she was. She would never let him know that there was also great wealth and

105

a powerful name behind her. If Sebastian ever turned to her, it would be because he wanted only her, Summer, not the daughter of Clayton Storm.

Summer knew it would be impossible for her to deny Sebastian's plea for help. Her power possessed her; she did not possess it. She knew it would drive her to help him, but it would be Summer the medicine woman and half-breed who aided him, not Summer Storm.

They had reached Summer's tipi and now she turned to smile up at him.

"Summer," Cole said gently, "don't judge Sebastian too harshly. He is confused about what he wants. He needs help to find his brother's killers. He won't be able to see clearly or make any kind of commitment until he does. I don't know if he spoke to you about it, but I believe, even if he doesn't, that you can help. I've seen your strange powers at work. Maybe . . . maybe you could find a trace of these men."

Cole had no way of knowing what had transpired between Sebastian and Summer, and therefore no way of realizing he was asking Summer to make the way easy for Sebastian to rush into the arms of another woman.

"If Sebastian would tell me of his brother, and of the men who killed him, I might be able to sense them. Then we could search. If they were near us, I would know."

Cole was hopeful. "Then maybe . . ." he began.

"I . . . I do not think Sebastian will speak to me of . . . anything in his past. He would prefer to walk his own trail."

"It's the wrong trail."

"It is his trail . . . his choice."

"I suppose you are right, but I wish you would think about it. You are, from everything I've heard about you, a woman of strength and vision. The people of your village have great love and respect for you. Surely you would not withhold your powers if you could help?"

She wanted to shout at him that she didn't want to help, that she would not be used. But she knew Cole would not understand, and she respected his bond of friendship with Sebastian.

"I will give your words some thought, Cole. Maybe I will help . . . if Sebastian will let me."

He smiled down into her dark eyes. "You are a very beautiful woman, Summer—not just your physical self, but inside. I wish . . ."

"Wish what?"

"Never mind. It's not important."

"What do you see when you look at me, Cole?"

"What?"

"Do you see Summer . . . or a half-breed woman who could be of some help to you?"

It suddenly became very clear to Cole just what she was talking about, and answers tumbled into place about where and how he had run into her and their proximity to Sebastian. He could have bitten his tongue; then he felt the senseless urge to find Sebastian and beat some sense into him.

"Summer," he said gently, "I see a beautiful and sensitive woman whom I would like to call friend. Anyone who does not see this is foolish and very, very stupid." She laughed softly and his chuckle joined hers. "And," he added, "I don't often talk about my friends that way."

"I shall think about what you have said, Cole. Maybe Sebastian and I can reach an agreement. If he wants me to help him find these men, I will . . . but it will not bring him satisfaction."

"I know that. Neither will the other plans he has in mind, but he has to find that out for himself."

107

"Yes," she whispered softly, "he has to find out and decide for himself." She looked up at Cole and smiled again. "Good night, Cole."

"Good night, Summer." Cole touched her arm lightly, then turned and walked away.

Summer went into her tipi and as she lay on the far mat near the fire, her tumultuous thoughts burned through her mind.

She closed her eyes as the memory of Sebastian's caresses stirred her. She became angry with herself for letting him reach inside her and touch emotions she was once more unable to harness.

She groaned as she rolled on her side and gazed into the fire. Slowly, determinedly, she brought herself under control. There could be no truth between her and Sebastian. Only by her secrecy could he choose freely.

She promised herself she would keep silent about her past and would not question his. But she vowed also that she would never again allow herself to weaken in the face of his desire, for desire was all it was.

She nursed her anger carefully, building it into a wall that she would use as a defense. Tomorrow she would talk to him, tell him that she would willingly use her powers to help him find his brother's killers.

Now her thoughts drifted against her will to the woman that Sebastian had chosen. Cole felt that Sebastian was blind to her true nature, but was he?

Despite everything she could do to prevent it, the vision of Sebastian with a beautiful, golden-haired woman in his arms brought a soft sound of agonized despair to her lips.

Why, she asked herself, why did the gods who controlled her power send her dreams of this man when he was not to be part of her future? Why did the fact that she was half white, half Indian always cause such turmoil in her life? And why, she thought angrily, must

108

she be drawn to a man who had no room in his heart for anything but his own selfish desires.

Well, let him have his lady, she decided. Let him put his values where he wanted them. She didn't care. She would do her best to help him; then he would leave her life forever . . . and she would forget him.

She began to think of the young warrior Hawk had sent to tell her father of her return from school. She wondered just how angry her father would be at her leaving school and how much angrier he would be when he found out that she had left the village with two strange white men. She would have to convince Sebastian to wait a few more days before he resumed his search.

If she could keep her own identity a secret, she would like to have Sebastian meet her father. She would like to know what her father might see in Sebastian.

As she drifted off to sleep, she was again forced to defend her thoughts from Sebastian's invasion. She moaned softly as she imagined a hard mouth brushing tenderly against hers and gentle hands stirring her blood.

After awhile Summer surrendered to her dreams and only then did she experience the joy of giving without consequence and without questions. Every touch was relived without the doubts and the anger. Only the pleasure—the sheer, unparalleled pleasure—remained.

# *Chapter Ten*

Inside the tipi the darkness was broken only by the dim glimmer of a nearly dead fire. The soft glow of the dying embers touched the faces of the two who sat nearby, causing their features to appear half in shadow, half in amber light. They spoke in whispers.

Sebastian held a stick in his hand and was drawing a rough map on the earth floor. "If we split up," Sebastian was saying as he drew a triangle in the dirt, "we can meet here by the river. Maybe one of us will come up with some sign."

Cole nodded, but his eyes were watching Sebastian closely. It was obvious that Sebastian planned to leave the village very early.

"None of Hawk's warriors have returned with any word," Cole commented. "Maybe we should wait until they do."

"No," Sebastian replied. "It's time we leave here and get on with what needs to be done. If we linger much longer, we might never find them."

"Sebastian, have you told Hawk we're leaving? If his men do find something, he should know where to seek us."

"I've told Hawk," Sebastian responded, and by his tone Cole could tell that Sebastian had not told anyone else but Hawk about his departure.

"But," Cole inquired softly, "you've told . . . no one else?"

"No!" Again Sebastian answered crisply. "This concerns no one else."

"Sebastian—"

"Cole," Sebastian interrupted firmly, "I'm leaving within the hour. If you choose to stay here, I'll understand . . . but I'm leaving."

Cole wondered if it was leaving, or running. But he didn't ask. "You know damn well I'm going with you," Cole answered. But in his mind he knew he was going in order to protect Sebastian more than for any other reason. After Sebastian found the men he sought and took his revenge, he would need Cole there to help him put his life back together.

"We'd best pack up and get moving." Sebastian put his words into action by rising and gathering together his equipment. Cole sighed but began gathering his things as well.

The sky was still dark and only a thin band of light was bordering the horizon when Sebastian and Cole rode from the village. Hawk stood in the dim light, a tall shadow watching them ride away. He was satisfied to see that the threat to Summer and to his village was departing.

He had been a polite host when Sebastian had told him they would be leaving, but he had said no words to urge them to stay. Now he felt relief as he watched the two riders disappear in the shadows. He was also quite pleased in his assumption that they would be long gone before Summer heard news of their departure. But Hawk did not consider Summer's penchant for rising early.

Summer stirred into wakefulness with a restless feeling, as if something had subtly nudged her from her dreams.

It was just growing light enough to see when she rose from the warmth of her blankets. Her first thoughts were of Sebastian and the hard words they had thrown at each other. This was a new day, and it would give her the opportunity to talk with him again.

She wanted to tell him about herself and the gift she possessed, which had given her the ability to see him long before he had come into her life. And deep inside she felt she had to prove that she was not afraid of anything, especially him.

Dressing quickly, she left her tipi and walked across the village to the one that had been allotted to Sebastian and Cole. Kneeling in front of it was the old woman who had cooked the meals for the two men. Summer smiled as the old woman looked up at her.

"Wind Song," Summer said, "have our visitors awakened yet?"

"They have awakened and have eaten, Summer," Wind Song replied.

"I would speak to them."

"But they left."

"Left? To go to the river to bathe?"

"No. They packed their things and took their horses. They are gone, and I do not think they are planning to return."

Summer was at first shocked, but then she realized that Sebastian was again caught up in his quest and was running from anything that might stand in his way. She still remembered his cold eyes, but she had seen beyond them to the pain and guilt he was trying to hide. The decision came quickly and clearly. She turned and strode first to Hawk's tipi. There she called out to him. By the sound of her voice, Hawk knew instantly why she was there. Reluctantly, he went to the entrance flap.

"Good morning, Summer. You rise early." He tried to be nonchalant.

"Hawk, did you know our visitors had gone?"

"Yes, I knew," he answered honestly.

"You are pleased he is gone?"

"Summer . . . it is better so. He is trouble. He would hurt you."

"Hawk," she replied slowly, "our life circles are not ours to form; they are formed by the gods. Nothing must interfere."

She was angry, yet she loved this tall, dark man as if he were her father. She knew that what he had done he had done for love of her. She could see the warring emotions in the depths of his ebony eyes. He was afraid also, and fear was something a man of his strength and courage could not tolerate. He had fought back in the only way he knew, by ridding himself of the threat that touched his life and the life of the one he loved. Summer stepped closer and put her hand on his arm.

"Do you think I would do anything foolish that might hurt those who have cared for and loved me for so long?" she asked gently. "I have always come when you needed me, Hawk, have I not?"

Reluctantly he agreed, but she could still feel the resistance within him.

"I must follow the gift that drives me, Hawk," she explained patiently. "He is wounded and I must help him. Can you not understand that?"

"It is not his wounds that worry me. It is the wounds

113

he might give you that fill my heart with anger."

"We cannot run and hide from what the gods have planned. We must face it. I will not be hurt, for I can do as I did when I was a child. I can run to my foster father, Hawk." She smiled and he smiled in return. Against her very gentle, stubborn logic, he had no defense.

"Speak to my father before you decide to do anything," Hawk suggested, hoping the old chief would have the words to keep Summer from trying to go to Sebastian. If enough time passed, maybe she would see the impossibilities of following him.

Summer agreed. She knew what was in Hawk's thoughts, but she chose not to exchange what she thought would be useless words. Her mind had already chosen the path she would take. She would find Sebastian and she would use all her powers to help him, but she would also try with every ounce of her strength to make him see the futility of his chosen course. She would try to turn his heart away from death and back to living.

Within Black Cloud's tipi Summer sat cross-legged at the feet of the old man. Though she considered him the wisest of men, she was determined not even his disapproval would dissuade her from the path she knew she had to follow.

For the first time in her life, Black Cloud had disagreed with her choices. He had warned her of the threat that had touched her twice, reminding her of the fact that even she had admitted that the danger had somehow been connected to Sebastian. And he had concluded that following Sebastian might lead her to pain and disaster.

As she rose to leave, she knew in her heart that despite the words of Hawk and Black Cloud she would do what she felt was right. In silence, she went to her tipi and closed the flap behind her.

Hawk waited several hours before going to her. He had wanted to give her time to recover her emotions and perhaps examine her thoughts enough to realize that he and his father had been right.

In front of her tipi he called out to her, but she did not answer. Hawk waited, thinking she might be sleeping, then he called out to her again. It was only when she didn't answer his second call that his heart began to pound. He prayed he was wrong as he pushed the flap aside and saw an empty tipi. Summer was gone.

He cursed as he raced across the village to where the horses were being cared for by a young boy.

"Little Bear, did Summer take her horse?"

"Yes," the wide-eyed boy answered quickly. He stood in trembling awe of the huge warrior. Hawk could sense his fear, and he smiled and controlled the anger in his voice.

"How long has she been gone?"

"Many hours. Since after the morning meal."

"Make my horse ready," Hawk commanded. Swiftly he returned to his tipi. There he quickly explained to Snow Woman what had happened while he prepared a bundle for traveling.

"Hawk," Snow Woman said softly, "perhaps you should let her go. Summer must feel she is doing the right thing. It it not often you question what she does."

"This time she is blinded," he said. "And she is riding toward disaster. I cannot let it happen."

"Maybe this is not in your power to stop," she suggested.

He turned to look at her. "You think it is selfishness

that tells me to go and find her? It is not, Snow Woman. I think of her father, who is my blood brother. I think of the ones from which she ran, both in her dreams and later, when he found her. I feel she is in danger, and I would protect her."

"I only worry about the reasons you use. Do you protect her . . . or do you feel anger because she cares for the white man you do not trust?"

"I am not sure of that. I will find her . . . and when I know she is safe, then I will think of reasons."

Before she could speak again, he brushed a light kiss across her lips and was gone. She walked to the tipi flap and watched him ride away.

Summer had gathered a few things for travel; then, taking her knife, she had cut a long slit in the back of her tipi and had slipped out. She made her way rapidly to the horses. Smiling at the boy who cared for them, she took her horse and rode away. She did not caution him to keep silent for she knew he could never lie to Hawk. She wanted only time—time before Hawk discovered her departure.

It took her only a short time to find Sebastian's trail. She followed as swiftly as she could. She knew it would be at least nightfall before she caught up with him, for she had to travel slowly in order to keep his tracks in sight.

Three Feathers had been asleep, but he rose when the sun struck his eyes. He had kept a close watch on the village until late into the night; then he had slept. His patience was unlimited; he would wait until he could accomplish his goal, even if it took weeks. His mind dwelt on the slim curves of the girl he had almost captured. Since that aborted attempt, he had seen much of her, and she had inflamed his desire. His mind turned to thoughts of possessing her. He would have her, and he would kill the man who had stepped between her and what he had wanted.

He stood and stretched, then went to the brush to relieve himself. He would eat, then again find a safe place from which to watch. He laughed at the ease with which he had eluded Hawk's warriors. In his mind, no warrior lived that was better than he in the wilds.

He was about to hunt for something to eat when a movement on the distant horizon caught his eye. His heart leapt, for even at this distance he recognized the woman who rode the trail—Summer. With a grim smile on his face, he prepared to travel. This night he would have his desire. He licked his lips as if he could taste her capture already, then he mounted and cautiously began to follow.


Sebastian moved slowly. Still unused to tracking, he found it nerve-wracking to move at a snail's pace with his eyes glued to the ground. To keep impatience from overcoming him, he turned his mind to the reasons he was here. He allowed himself to dwell on his hatred until it fueled his actions and created a new surge of determination. It had never occurred to him that he would still be outnumbered if he were to come across the ones he sought. That he was unrealistic and driven had also not entered his mind; and neither had the realization that he didn't care if he lost his life. It was almost as if he unconsciously searched for oblivion in order to release himself from his unbearable guilt.

He stopped only for a short time when the sun reached its zenith, mostly to rest his horse, for he did not feel like eating. By the time the sun neared the

117

horizon, he was both mentally and physically exhausted.

He prepared to make camp reluctantly, for if it had not been too dark to track, he would have driven himself until he dropped. He also knew it was going to be difficult for him to sleep, for he was haunted by thoughts of revenge, and thoughts of the dark-eyed girl who had almost succeeded in making him face himself. He had deliberately refused to think of her while he traveled, but could he do the same when he slept, when he dreamed?

He made a fire, tended to his horse, and prepared a small amount of food and forced himself to eat it. Then he faced the interminable hours between sleep and wakefulness, during which he might again relive scenes he wanted to forget.

The night grew dark as a cluster of rain-filled clouds skittered across the moon, and a slight breeze began to rise. Still he sat by the fire, reluctant to wrap himself in his blanket and try for sleep. He could have wept with frustration as he tried to ward off the face of his brother as it had been when last he held the blood-soaked body in his arms. Then the image began to fade and another formed. He fought it, but it refused to go. He saw the wide, dark, and too understanding eyes of Summer.

"Damn you, Summer," he murmured. "Go away. Leave me be. I don't need you. Once I find them, I will rebuild. Kate will wash away your memory. I don't need you."

A movement beyond the periphery of his firelight drew his attention. Someone moved in the darkness. Slowly he drew his gun and waited. He was completely unprepared for the vision that appeared before him.

He sat in stunned silence, unable to accept the fact that she had stepped from his thoughts into reality.

"Summer," he said in a quiet, disbelieving voice.

"Sebastian, can I warm myself by your fire?" She spoke softly, with a hesitant half smile on her face.

It was only when she spoke that the reality of her presence finally jolted his mind.

"What the hell are you doing here?" he demanded in an angry voice.

"I followed you," she answered truthfully.

He rose to his feet and went to her. Taking her shoulders in a rough grip, he shook her slightly. "Damnit, it's dangerous for you to be traveling alone out here. What's the matter with Hawk? Why would he let you go like this, with no one to travel with you?"

"Hawk did not know that I left. I suppose he has found out by now, but he can do nothing about it."

"Of all the stupid . . . Summer, you are the most tenacious, stubborn, stupid female . . ." He paused in the face of her smile, but his anger continued to grow.

"Why? Why did you come here? Don't you have any idea of the danger you could be in?"

"Did you not . . . ask for my help? Did you not challenge me by saying I was afraid to help you? I am not afraid of you or any man . . . especially white men." She smiled. "I have already faced danger in the village. Why would I be in more danger here?" Her eyes spoke eloquently of her answering challenge.

He stepped back from her, finding it difficult to refrain from taking her in his arms. His desire did more to bring him under control than anything else. She was a threat he had to fight, and the best way to do so was to keep her at a distance until he could send her back.

"You leave here tomorrow morning, first thing. I have no intention of letting you travel with me. When I asked for your help, I didn't think it would be just the two of us. It's too dangerous. Besides, I don't need any

119

help, especially from you."

"Why . . . especially from me? Do you think it might prove that I was right and you were wrong? I can tell you of the gifts I possess . . . they might help you."

He chose to disregard her offer. "I told you once, what I have to do, I will do myself. Tomorrow," he said with finality, "you go back."

# *Chapter Eleven*

Sebastian turned his back to her and walked toward the fire, aware of her eyes on him, and of the turbulent emotions she awoke within him to war with his reason. He knelt and stirred the fire to brighter life, then turned to look at her.

"Have you eaten? Are you hungry?"

"Yes, I am hungry. I did not take much, for I could not get to any food without questions being asked."

"You mean you haven't eaten all day?"

"No."

"Sit down by the fire and get warm. You look cold," he said in exasperation. "I'll get you something to eat."

She sat across the fire from him, watching as he moved about preparing what he had left of the rabbit he had killed for his supper. He handed it to her, and she bit into it, keeping her eyes on him. It was disconcerting for him, for he was having difficulty ignoring the lovely picture she made with the firelight touching her face.

"Summer," he said gently. "This is impossible and you know it. What made you do such a thing?"

"I took your challenge," she replied, and his face echoed his surprise. "It was a challenge, was it not? I would help you."

"Do you think you can? If Hawk's warriors cannot find a trace of the ones I seek, how can you be successful?"

"Sebastian . . . it is so difficult to explain unless you try to understand."

"All right, I'm listening."

"I must tell you of my mother first, so you will know the full story. It is a strange and sometimes unbelievable thing, but believe me, it is true. Sometimes even I am afraid of this thing that touches me, yet I cannot fight it. It is stronger than I and I know it is good . . . and I know I must use it when the time comes to do so."

Summer went on to tell Sebastian about her mother, and her death when she was born. She explained that her father had chosen to educate her in the white schools, but she omitted the fact that her father was a very wealthy and important man in the white world.

She spoke in a quiet voice as she told of the powers her mother had possessed and the way they were developing in her. She told of the times when even she had been astounded by her ability to heal. She spoke of her ability to see what she sometimes did not want to see. Then she told of her seeing him so often in her dreams, and the shock of seeing him the morning he had found her. Quietly she added that she understood the battle he was fighting. She read the look in his eyes and knew he was having a hard time believing all she had said.

"I wish you had the power to raise the dead," he said bitterly. "Nathaniel is dead, and I am to blame. I am as dead as he is, and I can't . . . maybe I don't want to let it go. I want to kill them. That is all I want now. It is all I live for."

"And after you have killed?" she questioned quietly.

122

"Will you seek life then?"

"I don't know," he replied tiredly. "I can't live with what I have done, and I can't undo it. Maybe revenge will give me some release."

She felt his pain; it was like a weight on her heart. Without a word, she rose and went to him. She dropped to her knees in front of him and he was surprised to see tears in her eyes. "Can you speak to me of him? Can you tell me what happened?"

"Why?" he rasped. "Why do you want me to speak of what I cannot face?"

"I would know him . . . I would feel his death. And even though you do not believe this, I would feel the men who killed him. If there is a way I can reach for them, then perhaps your way will be easier. I would walk this path with you."

For a moment thought was suspended as he gazed into her compassionate eyes. It was as if she had touched him somewhere within the depths of his soul, and he found it almost impossible to break the spell he felt swirling about him.

Quietly he began to talk, to tell her of thoughts and emotions he had hidden even from himself. The renewed pain of it washed through him like a flood he could no longer control. When he described the men who had attacked them, his voice was hard and bitter.

She felt them, knew them with her heart, and knew that if she were near them she would know. She also knew that if he killed in the state he was now in, the act would never cleanse his guilt or give him peace. First he would have to face himself. He would have to realize he was not guilty of his brother's death, that it had been the will of the gods. He would have to absolve himself of the guilt and create a new path to follow. She knew this as surely as she knew she would help, whether he believed in her or not. Her power gave her no choice.

Summer was about to speak, but before she could do so the shock of a dark presence struck her, drawing from her a strangled sound. Sebastian lifted his head to look into her eyes and found them wide with fear and surprise.

"Summer?"

"It is here again," she whispered.

"What?"

"Sebastian . . . someone's here . . . something . . . he is near us. It's the same evil I felt before. It's out there . . . close."

Before Sebastian could reply, the soft whinny of disturbed horses told him that Summer spoke the truth. Someone lurked in the shadows outside their camp. If Summer was right, and he no longer doubted it, it was the same influence she had felt when she had been threatened the night in the village.

Slowly Sebastian sat up and drew Summer up with him. He moved casually, as if there was nothing unusual in their movements. He went to his pack and unrolled a blanket, which he spread on the ground. It appeared that he was making a bed for them to share.

"Summer, come over here . . . slowly. We don't want to alarm our visitor." She did what he told her. "Good. Now sit down."

"Sebastian?"

"Do as I tell you," he said curtly, but he kissed her lightly and smiled to soften the words. "I want you to stay here and act as if nothing is wrong. In fact, if you can keep his attention, I'd be grateful."

"What are you going to do?"

"Pretend I'm going to the horse, then circle around and surprise our friend."

"No . . . please . . ." Her words were silenced by his fingers touching her lips.

"Summer, we can't let him take us by surprise. We

124

know he's there, and he doesn't know we know, so he won't be prepared. Trust me and stay still."

It took all the nerve she had, feeling the blackness she felt, to watch Sebastian slowly move toward the horses, which were just beyond the range of the firelight. Once he reached them, he stood by them and calmed them, then he slipped away from the light and began to work his way around the camp, watching for the intruder.


Three Feathers had followed Summer from far enough away to make sure she did not sense his presence. He was certain she would somehow know he was near. It was growing dark and still she traveled, and he was concerned that he might lose her in the darkness.

It was then that he saw the glow of a fire in the distance and knew Summer's destination. He let her get far ahead of him, for he was now sure of where to find her. Because he could not judge how many were in the camp, he used a great deal of caution.

The sight before him, when he finally crept close enough to see, pleased him immensely. A man would find it difficult, he thought, to have his mind on protection when he was in Summer's arms. He smiled to himself, planning the exact moment he would strike, the moment when the man's thoughts and attention would be centered on Summer.

He watched as the man rose and identified him with another surge of pleasure. He would have both the ones he sought, the one who had ruined his plans before, and Summer.

The man was preparing a bed for them to share, and Three Feathers could have laughed, for he would share that bed with Summer while the white one would be forced to watch. The thought excited him, and he remained still while the man went to calm the horses, which had sensed his presence. Then his eyes returned to Summer. He could see her clearly and was completely captivated. He had to have her. So intent was he on observing Summer that he did not notice that the man was no longer by the horses. He watched as Summer unbraided her hair and ran her fingers through it. Her sensuous actions whetted his appetite and his eyes remained riveted on her.

Sebastian moved slowly and with caution. His eyes scanned the area, but he saw no one. Slowly he moved in a circle about the camp. Three Feathers was so well hidden that Sebastian almost missed his dark form as he knelt in the shadows watching the fire and the girl before it. Sebastian's eyes went over the brave's head to Summer.

Aware that she was being observed, Summer did all she could to keep the attention of the silent watcher. She rose and untied the tunic top she wore, drew it over her head, and threw it aside. She was convincingly acting the part of a woman readying herself for her man.

Sebastian smiled, for he hadn't missed the beauty of her copper-gold skin in the glow of the fire. Stealthily he moved toward the crouching figure. He was close enough now to hear the intruder's shallow breathing; then suddenly a shaft of moonlight exposed the man's face.

Sebastian was filled with rage—a black, uncontrollable rage. It nearly choked him with its violence. Emitting an animal snarl of fury, he threw himself on the crouching shadow.

Three Feathers spun about but remained off balance because of his position. He could only ward off the attack, and he fell back as Sebastian landed upon him. But Three Feathers was a powerful man and in moments Sebastian was fighting for his life. The thrashing figures rolled upon the ground, each trying to gain the upper hand.

Summer heard them struggling and, grabbing up a long piece of burning wood, she made her way to the scene. She cried out when she saw the two locked in battle, for though Sebastian was large and strong, Three Feathers seemed just as powerful.

The two fought on amid much panting, grunting, and cursing. Finally, Three Feather's hand closed on a rock and he struck Sebastian a glancing blow to the head, stunning him momentarily. That moment was all Three Feathers needed to turn on Summer. She thrust the burning wood toward him, and he knew she was intent on defending herself. Sebastian's groan told him he would soon be ready to fight again, and Three Feathers was not sure he could overcome the two of them. With a snarl of defeat, he faded into the shadows and was gone.

Summer ran to Sebastian's side as he groaned and sat up. "Sebastian! Are you all right?"

"I'm all right," he replied. "Damnit it! He got away."

"He was the one who was chasing me," Summer said quickly.

Sebastian looked up at her in surprise, then he spoke grimly. "Now I know why the evil you felt was connected to Cole and me."

"Why?"

"He is one of the ones responsible for Nathaniel's death. Now at least I know they're still somewhere in this area."

He staggered to his feet and tentatively touched the wound on his head, from which blood was flowing freely.

"We've got to get out of here. He knows we're only two. He'll be back, probably with reinforcements."

"I know a cave. It's not too far. Let me help you."

As quickly as they could, they gathered their things. Summer could see that Sebastian was hurt more severely than he would admit, but she held her tongue. She was confident that once they were in the cave they would be relatively safe, and she would be able to tend his wound with her healing power.

# Chapter Twelve

It was a tedious and very uncomfortable ride to the cave. They walked their horses down a stream to hide their tracks and used every maneuver the two of them knew to keep from being followed. By the time they approached their destination, Sebastian had a resounding headache. It nauseated him and made him dizzy, and he found he was having trouble staying upright in the saddle. He slid off his horse gratefully when Summer announced that they had reached the cave.

Summer insisted on caring for the horses, and Sebastian was too weak to protest. He entered the cave, and she followed several minutes later.

"The horses are safe. Lie down, and I will help you."

Unsure of what she meant, Sebastian lay on the blanket she had spread on the hard-packed dirt floor of the cave. He closed his eyes and heard her moving about as she made a small, smokeless fire. Then she brought Sebastian's water sack from his saddlebag.

After a few minutes, he felt a cool, wet cloth being placed gently across his head. He groaned and opened his eyes to see a shadowy face above him that swirled nauseatingly in and out of focus. He heard her voice softly whispering, and if he had not been so sick, he would have sworn she was chanting some kind of prayer.

The cloth was removed, and he felt her cool hand on his forehead. His whole being reacted suddenly as a strange current of strength began flowing from her hand to him. He blinked his eyes open and saw Summer kneeling beside him. He didn't believe it—it didn't seem possible—yet it was so. The pain and dizziness melted from his body, and with it went the nausea and blurred sight. Her eyes were closed, and he was reminded of her experience with the child on the mat in the village. It was as if she were drawing the pain out of him, and the effect astounded him.

He stared at her as if he had never seen her before, and for the first time he truly understood the phenomenal power she possessed. It frightened him, and yet it amazed him.

She took her hand from his head as soon as she saw the clearness of his eyes, then she moved to the other side of the fire.

"You feel no more pain?"

"No," he answered in an incredulous tone. "What did you do?"

She shrugged and laughed hesitantly. "I do not know. It is a thing that just happens. I no longer question; for I must accept it . . . no matter how I feel."

"And it frightens you, doesn't it?"

"Sometimes."

He smiled. "Have you always been such a stubborn and determined creature?"

For a moment she thought he was laughing at her and her eyes grew cold.

"I do not ask you to understand," she said in a remote tone. "It is not a choice I have to make. I must do what I know is right"—she turned her impervious gaze on him—"just as I choose to help you, even though I know that what I am falls short of your high standards."

"Summer, I didn't mean to ridicule you," he said gently. "And as far as my standards are concerned, you jumped to that conclusion. I don't know why you are so bitter toward white men."

"I do not judge you," she argued. "And I know all of the white ways I care to know."

"How Summer?"

"What?"

"How do you know? A young Indian girl, raised here in this wilderness—how could you know? Or do you just believe the tales others tell?"

The firelight was reflected in her ebony eyes as she gazed at him across the fire. Unwelcome and traumatic memories flooded back unbidden. The challenge Sebastian had offered had been clear to her and she had accepted it. Her power had taken command as it always did when someone was hurt or needed help as Sebastian had. Now she found she was wishing she had listened to the warnings she had given herself. Her defenses rose, and she drew her battle lines. She would not allow him to use his charm to defeat her. And she certainly would not answer his baited question.

"I think," he said easily, "that you are filled with false ideas . . . about a lot of things. Tell me, Summer, what of the men in your tribe? Have they been foolish enough to overlook your . . . obvious charms, or"—he chuckled—"do you consider all men the same?"

"They are honorable men who know our customs. They would not do—"

"Do what?" he urged, realizing she was thinking of another time . . . and another man. He wondered who this man was who had stirred such animosity. He was irritated at the thought and annoyed at her refusal to

131

answer him.

Outside, black clouds had obscured the light of the moon and the stars could no longer be seen. A breeze slowly grew until it bent the trees and sent a rustling sound through the darkness. Bright flashes of lightning and a low rumble of thunder announced a sudden summer storm. The lightning brightened the entrance of the cave and startled its occupants, who looked toward the opening to see a steady rain beginning to fall.

"Well," Sebastian said, "I don't think our night visitor will be trailing any tracks now."

"No," Summer whispered. "It's safe now. He cannot track us in this."

Sebastian turned to her and her eyes lifted to his.

He watched the brilliance of the lightning touch her face quickly, then dissolve to reveal the subtler glow of the fire. His body quickened with a desire that jolted him. He watched the softness of her mouth and the dreamy haze of her eyes as she stared into the fire, lost in thought. He was startled by his own thoughts, for he desperately wanted her—and wanted her to want him. It was the first time he had felt this way about any woman.

He rose to go to her and dropped down on one knee beside her. Her chin lifted in defiance, as if she were daring him in some way, and she seemed ready to do battle.

"Do the men of your village tell you how beautiful you are, Summer?" he asked softly. "Or how your skin glows in firelight like melted gold? Do they tell you that your sweet mouth was meant for tasting?"

"The sweetness of your words is like honey to trap bees. Do not speak to me so, Sebastian Cain. This bee stings."

He chuckled softly, then his hand reached to touch

her chin lightly and lift her mouth to his. The chuckle died and his eyes registered shock as the cold blade of a knife was pressed against his throat.

For what seemed an eternity they looked at each other. She did not mean to bend—the prick of the knife told him that—but the dangerous glow in his eyes should have warned her that Sebastian did not mean to bend either.

"You are a healer . . . a medicine woman. You have used your powers to heal me because it's in you to heal. You won't kill—you can't," he said in a voice of velvet-coated steel.

For a moment he continued to stare into her wide, dark eyes. He could see the challenge in them. Slowly he enclosed her wrist in an iron-hard grip that numbed her fingers. Still their gazes held, hers defiant and his warming with a stirring need that was rapidly pushing all other thoughts aside.

She felt the heat of her blood pounding through her then and desperately tried to control the mounting passion that was sending tingling sparks of desire to every nerve. The knife slipped from her fingers as a clap of thunder echoed about them, but still their eyes continued the silent battle.

His nearness and the desire written plainly on his features made her whisper a word of resistance as his mouth touched hers tenderly.

"No," she moaned against his mouth.

He caught her head between his hands and his mouth, hard and passionate now, closed firmly over hers. His tongue thrust deep, tasting her sweetness and setting her head spinning.

She pressed both hands against his chest in a futile attempt to stop his overwhelming masculine assault, which was devouring her resistance and stirring a volcano within her that shot its flames through every inch of her body.

A deep ache began to build inside her, an ache that blossomed into a surging heat that left her trembling and helpless in the magical web he was weaving about her.

The kiss grew deeper and his tongue more daring, as it caressed her mouth sensuously, and her mind refused to focus on anything but the sensations he was so skillfully creating.

They were alone in a cataclysmic universe, sheltered from all but the emotions neither of them could deny. A deafening crash of thunder split the silence about them as their lips met and their bodies came together.

The feel of her quivering body pressed close to his, molding to fit his as if she were part of him, was enough to ignite a flame that threatened to consume them both.

Need flowed through her like a golden stream of fire and she welcomed it—savored it—and sought more. Her traitorous body was awakened to a desire that turned her insides into a hot cauldron. His hands were warm and sure as they explored the softness of her flesh and she quivered under the sensuous magic of his caress.

His hand slipped to the ties of her tunic and deftly untied it, then he pushed it aside with fingertips that brushed her skin and sent flames rushing through her.

She was a tawny gold in the light of the fire, and his senses eagerly soaked up her beauty. Gently he slid his hands from her shoulders to the taut crests of her breasts and captured them in his hands. He moved his thumbs in a circular motion over the hard-peaked tips, then bent his head to capture one in his mouth. His tongue swirled against it, then he sucked gently, creating pinpoints of pleasure that made her gasp and close her eyes in rapture.

An ecstatic hunger gripped her and its exquisite

power set her body on fire and awakened savage instincts that had lain dormant until this moment. They were barely touching, yet both were brilliantly aware of the tremendous force that seemed to be drawing them together.

He put his arms about her and pulled her against him. The touch of her cool skin on his nearly caused him to gasp. Unable to stop the demand of his burning need, he brought his mouth down to capture hers once more.

Every part of Summer's being reached to enfold Sebastian and she opened herself to him completely. Sebastian felt as if she had entered within him and had filled him with a blinding hunger that only she could appease.

Sebastian's hands stroked her skin and left tingling currents in their wake that caused her to shiver and move even more urgently against him. His hands were hard yet gentle on her flesh, leaving her quivering and aching for more.

In the flickering light of the fire their shadows writhed against the rough stone wall and their twining, seeking bodies enacted a strange and sensual dance in the pale gold light.

Soft moans of pleasure broke the stillness and heralded Summer's surrender to the passion Sebastian no longer had to control.

Now his lips replaced his hands in a fiery search of her flesh. His teeth nibbled lightly as his mouth journeyed from her soft lips to the warmth of her skin. Taut, hard nipples stood erect for his assault and he found one, then the other, to savor and tease. His lips blazed a path down the softness of her body, tasting each vulnerable, sensitive spot until Summer could hardly contain her cries of ecstasy.

The flat plain of her belly quivered under the

tormenting touch of his mouth, and she gasped and cried out his name as his mouth moved to the soft flesh of her thighs. The taste of her golden skin was so very sweet that it roused his passion until nothing else existed for him.

Now his hands held her twisting, sweat-sheened body, and she could not escape the questing lips that found the center of her need and inflamed it until she felt she could no longer bear such exquisite torment.

His tongue flicked first in gentle probing, then sought deeper and deeper penetration. He lifted her touch by touch, taste by taste, and moment by glorious moment until he knew she was standing on the brink of fulfillment. But he was not yet ready for her to touch that height.

His lips left her, and their withdrawal drew an agonized groan from Summer. Then he brushed the soft skin of her thighs and nibbled gently at the quivering flesh, forcing the flame within her higher and higher until she could no longer bear it. Her body writhed beneath him and her hands tried to seek out the source of this torment and satisfy the flaming hunger that she could not contain. She cried out her need to him unknowingly, but Sebastian heard her plea and was filled with triumphant pleasure.

He rose above her and allowed his swollen and pulsing manhood to touch the entrance of her warm, passion-moistened sheath. His lips, still damp with her sweetness, claimed hers in an almost brutal kiss. It was in that moment, that earth-shattering moment, that he pressed himself within her with one fierce thrust and began to move in slow yet forceful strokes. He drew from her all she possessed and was filled with the joy of her total response when she began to arch against him more and more fiercely until their bodies moved together with a force that neither could control.

The vibrant sharing of their love was reflected in a wild and joyous dance upon the cave wall. Their shadows leapt and whirled like the fiery emotions that possessed them. Up they climbed, together. Her legs twined about him and her body surged up to meet his every thrust. In a magnificent blending, they drew from each other every ounce of passionate pleasure each could give. Her hands caressed and clung to his hard, muscular body, urging him to deeper and deeper conquest, and the conqueror and the conquered became one as together they reached a shattering climax and tumbled into momentary oblivion.

Afterward, Sebastian caressed her quivering flesh soothingly while he held her close to him. Gently he kissed her closed eyes and tear-dampened cheeks for a moment, then his lips pressed against hers in a seal of possession that was mutual and real. Within each of them some part of the other remained, claiming a place more permanent than either knew.

# *Chapter Thirteen*

Summer looked up into Sebastian's eyes, which seemed to glow like blazing emeralds in the firelight. She wanted so desperately to see unconditional love for her reflected there, but what she thought she saw was satisfaction. Again she had weakened at his touch. Again she had let him lead her into passion he had willingly shared only for the moment.

She sat up abruptly and turned her face from him. It would have been so easy to go to him, to tell him the truth, to tell him that love is built on so much more than wealth and position. But she could not. She would not beg! She would not give him choices. If he ever offered love, it would have to be because he wanted her and her alone. Her pride would not allow anything less. She was Summer Storm, and she would be second to no one, especially the golden-haired woman that lingered in Sebastian's mind.

Sebastian sat up behind her and rested both hands on her shoulders. He was both surprised and unprepared for the fact that he had felt a sudden, startling emptiness when she had left his side so quickly. His obstinate mind refused to listen to his heart, for it had been trained too long on revenge and rebelled at sudden changes. He told himself that she meant nothing more to him than passion fulfilled. She was an Indian and he needed her and her strange power to help him find the men of her race who had wounded him so deeply. He refused to accept the fact that Summer had touched a place within him that had never been awakened before. He could not feel . . . love? The word leapt into his mind and with angry determination he pushed it aside. It would be an impossible alliance— impossible! She would never fit into his plans. It was Kate he wanted; his mind told him so. But a yearning he could not quell made him reach for Summer to draw her back against him.

"Don't," she whispered raggedly as she moved away from him. "Don't touch me, Sebastian."

Though she resisted this new assault, it took very little effort for a man of Sebastian's strength to capture her and hold her close. "Why," he whispered against her hair, "do you insist on denying what we share?"

She struggled but could not free herself from his arms. Desperately she fought, for she felt, as he did, the fire that leapt between them. She knew she had to free herself or be caught forever, unable to escape until the day came when his dream was fulfilled and he no longer wanted or needed her.

"Why," she snarled like a trapped animal, "do you insist on taking when your heart lies elsewhere? Why don't you go to your precious Kate?"

There was an enveloping stillness and both could hear the falling rain and their own breathing. Sebastian dropped his hands and Summer rose and grabbed up the blanket to cover her nakedness. Her eyes locked with his across the fire.

"Summer, who—"

"Who told me about your dream woman?"

"Cole! Damnit Summer . . ."

"Cole had no idea about us. He told me innocently. He's your friend, Sebastian. Maybe more than you deserve."

"I didn't mean for you to hear of her from anyone else but me. He shouldn't have told you."

"And when would you have told me, Sebastian? When it was time to say good-bye?" She laughed harshly. "Was I so wrong about white men, Sebastian? Was I?"

Sebastian was shaken by the look in her eyes. It was not one of anger, nor was it vengeful. What he saw was hurt, and he felt the hurt as if she had struck him. For the first time in a long time Kate slipped from his memory.

He wanted to hold Summer, to erase the pain he saw in her eyes, to caress her and to tell her that he didn't understand what he really felt or wanted. But her eyes and her posture warned him that she had no intention of listening to or believing anything he might say. He meant to tell her they needed to talk, but even that came out wrong.

"Summer . . . I need—"

"I know your needs, Sebastian," she answered coldly. "I will help you. You will find the men you search for. You can kill them and go back to your lady. I hope she is all you need to make you happy."

"Summer, for Heaven's sake. Sit by the fire with me. We need to talk."

She shook her head negatively, moved to her bedroll, and began to make her bed. He watched her in silence, knowing that if he went to her she would only fight what she thought was his casual lust, and, after awhile, he made his own bed.

The fire flickered and its light began to dim. The still steadily falling rain beat a tattoo on the rocks outside the cave and the noise served to muffle Summer's sobs.

140

Sleep did not come easily to either of them.

When Sebastian opened his eyes, it was nearing dawn. The cave had been brightened by a new fire and Summer was already moving about packing her things.

She did not turn to look at him, and her voice was even and cool. "There is a stream nearby where you can wash. I have made some food. If you hurry, we can be on our way by the time the sun is up."

She could not see the look Sebastian gave her. If she had, some of her anger might have cooled. He looked at her straight, slim back and thought, How proud she is . . . and how beautiful. He had noted her beauty before, but only on the surface. It might have been the first time he truly saw Summer.

He rose and left the cave with Summer's dark eyes following him. When he had gone, she began to pack his belongings. This done, she sat by the fire.

It was some time before Sebastian returned, his hair still wet with sparkling drops of water. Summer caught her breath at the picture he made. This man she had seen so often in her dreams had forced her into a nightmare, for his mere presence made her body tingle with awareness. He was so large and so very masculine as he stood before her that her heart skipped a beat. Her body ached to be held in those strong arms, and her lips could taste the desire on his.

But she could not surrender to passion. There had to be more for her. She would not allow it to be otherwise.

Sebastian sat opposite her and began to eat. There was a wall slowly building between them, and he couldn't find the words to break it.

He sighed deeply. Maybe it was better this way. At least when this was over he could go back. His mind reasoned it all out, but a force beyond his will

141

demanded that he ease what was between them. He suddenly discovered that it was of the utmost importance that Summer understand.

"Summer," he said gently and was surprised at the sensations that flowed through him when she raised her questioning eyes to his. He was no longer sure how to go on. "You're so like this country," he continued. "You're wild and beautiful . . . and you demand so much of a man."

"I demand nothing," she replied, "of you or of anyone else. Only honesty . . . and honor. I am as I am, and all I ask is that you see me as I am and respect me. But I would not expect you to understand this."

Stung, he replied shortly, "Why do you say that, Summer? Is it so dishonest to say I want you?"

"As always"—she half smiled—"you want everything your way . . . on your terms." She sighed. "I said I would help you, Sebastian. Anything my powers can do I will do. But I will not be a small part of the dreams you've chosen. When I choose a man, it will be because he loves me . . . and accepts me as I am."

"Maybe you lie to yourself. What happened between us was something you shared completely. You wanted me just as badly as I wanted you. Do you think I didn't know that your response was complete?"

"There is much more to me than my body," she replied. "But you have your eyes set on a dream. I have no place in that dream, Sebastian, and I will not stand on the edge of it."

She rose before he could answer and began to move around the cave. As he watched her, he was annoyed with himself that he could not control the emotions he felt. He began to wonder about the part of Summer he couldn't reach. Something stirred to new life within him as he began to realize that he really didn't know much about Summer at all. He had looked at her from only one direction and now he saw that she had many facets. The thought intrigued him.

He rose and threw dirt on the fire and followed her to where she was packing the last of their things.

"Where do we meet Cole?" she questioned when he joined her.

Sebastian motioned to her as he knelt on the ground. She came and stood beside him. Quickly he sketched the river and where they were at the moment in conjunction with the village and where he thought Cole would be.

"Less than two days," he explained as he rose.

They stood close. Summer looked up into his eyes and a breathless expectancy seemed to hold them both immobile. He could read nothing in her gaze and it disturbed him that he wanted to see himself reflected there. He sensed that she was emotionally doing her best to cut him away from her, and he became irritated, for even though he told himself over and over that their relationship was impossible, he couldn't bear the thought that she might never fill his arms again. Why was the idea so difficult for him? he wondered. When he had left Kate he had not felt this strange tearing of his spirit.

Summer would have given her world if, at that moment, Sebastian had taken her in his arms and told her that nothing else in the world mattered except them, that nothing was more important than the love they could share, and that it did not matter who or what either of them were if they were together. If he had spoken such words, she would have come to his arms with no reservations.

They stood, eyes locked, for a heart-stopping moment. The words hovered unsaid between them, and then the moment was shattered.

Summer turned away, not wanting him to see the

telltale moisture in her eyes. Sebastian turned away, though his senses screamed, Take her! Hold her! She is the elusive thing for which you have been searching. He had been stricken by the truth, a truth he had no way of showing her, for he knew she would not listen—would not believe. In fact, he was unsure he believed it himself.

Both mounted their horses in thoughtful silence and they had ridden side by side for some time before Sebastian spoke. "You told me that you had been educated in a white school. Was it a missionary school?"

"No," she answered hesitantly. "My father sent me to England."

"England. Were you there long?"

"Four years."

"You never told me anything about your father except that he is white. Does he live in England now?"

Summer was reluctant to answer his questions. She did not want her father's position to influence Sebastian. She reined in her horse and he stopped abruptly, looking at her questioningly.

"Why should my father be of any interest to you, Sebastian? He is white and he is a trapper . . . now. That makes me a half-breed."

"Summer," he said gently, "I asked because I wanted to know a little more about you and hoped to get you to talk to me."

"I do not see," she said firmly, "that we have much more to talk about."

"We don't need to be enemies, Summer," he replied patiently. "You are a lot more than just a 'half-breed,' and you have taken a great risk to help me. At least we can be friends."

Friends, she thought. How can we be just friends when I want your love so badly? The words hovered on

144

her tongue, but she could not speak them. Instead, she shrugged as if it no longer mattered to her. It wrenched her heart when she saw the smile fade from his eyes to be replaced by a hurt he would never voice.

"We can be friends for as long as you choose to stay," she added quickly, then she nudged her horse into motion.

They rode in silence until the sun was high and both riders and mounts were thirsty. Summer stopped reluctantly. As long as they were moving, she did not have to face his questions and his nearness.

Summer was not hungry and refused the food Sebastian offered. She drank from the water sac and then took her blanket and walked some distance away. She sat on it and closed her eyes, letting her mind search the area about them. The threat against them was a mutual one and she knew she would sense the danger if it were close.

Sebastian watched her. A ray of sun glinted on her dark hair and turned it to a deep amber fire. Despite her angry words and her defiance, she looked so vulnerable to him.

What was the best way past those barriers she had built between them? he wondered. How could he reach her to tell her what he felt?

Sebastian had not realized that it had been some time since thoughts of Kate or dark violence had been in his mind. For the past twenty or so hours he had concentrated solely on the dark-eyed girl who had closed herself off from him.

By the time he had finished his meal, Summer had risen and was walking back to him.

"There is no one close," she said, "but we had best be on our way. Now that the rain has softened the ground, our tracks will be easy to follow." She was already mounting her horse and Sebastian had no choice but to follow. Within minutes they were again on their way.

From time to time Sebastian observed Summer's thoughtful expression and would have been happily shocked had he known what was going through her mind.

Summer was keenly aware of Sebastian as he rode beside her. She had kept away from him when they had stopped because of the effect he always seemed to have on her. Slowly she was drawing herself under control and forming a shield she knew she would need, for they would have to camp alone another night in the wilderness before they met Cole. She had succumbed to his touch so easily before and knew he could still set fire to her emotions if she allowed him too near.

She closed her eyes momentarily against the stirring of her body. She could still taste his kiss on her lips and feel the sweetness of his touch, a touch that could destroy her tenuous control. Fighting these unwanted memories, she willed herself to consider how he was using her. Sebastian could see the tightness about her mouth and noted the straight back and rigid shoulders, but he could not see the battle that went on within for her eyes remained fixed on the trail ahead.


The sun was nearly gone and the sky was already beginning to darken. Red streaks brushed across the horizon, and the shadows about them grew longer and longer until they blended. Sebastian was about to say that they must soon make camp when Summer brought her horse to a halt.

Wordlessly she slid from her mount and led him to a grassy spot where she unsaddled and tethered him so he could graze.

Sebastian did the same, watching Summer from the corner of his eye. She moved efficiently as if well accustomed to such procedures. Soon they had a fire going and were warming what food they had left.

Summer spread both blankets, one very obviously on the opposite side of the fire from the other. Then they sat down and ate in silence.

Sebastian desperately searched for words to breach her defenses. His only problem was the intangible thing Summer seemed to want. What does she think behind those dark, unreadable eyes? he wondered. What words would melt that cold wall that stood between them? He knew he had to get her to talk to him and was willing to risk her anger in order to release them both from this uncomfortable silence.

He was no novice with women and understood the significance of the tiny pulse beating rapidly at the hollow of her throat. He wanted to kiss her there, to press his lips against the smooth flesh of her throat and caress the soft breasts that jutted firmly against the buckskin tunic she wore.

God, how much I want her, he thought. The excitement tingled through him when he remembered her smooth, curved body beneath his, and his body responded violently to his need. He held himself in check with the severest effort of will as he spoke to her.

"Summer, I was told that you do not really live in Hawk's village."

"No."

"Where do you live? Are your parents living somewhere near the village?"

"Yes . . . not too far. Why do you ask?"

"I guess"—he shrugged—"I'm curious about them." Because her nerves were frayed by Sebastian's nearness, Summer took immediate offense.

"Why? Are you interested in seeing the kind of man who would marry an Indian squaw and live in the wilderness? Are you expecting some kind of a misfit

147

that only an Indian girl would take as a husband?"

"For Christ's sake, why must you twist everything I say?" Sebastian snapped angrily. "Why must you think every word I say is an attack?"

Her words had been purely defensive and she knew it, for something deep inside was sending warnings echoing through her: Don't look into his eyes! Don't let him touch you! You will not be able to fight the flames of desire he can stir within you. He brings to life a part of you that cannot fight him!

Her eyes fled from his and she spoke softly. "I'm sorry. I suppose I am tired. Maybe it would be best if we slept."

She would have said more, but Sebastian rose and walked around the fire to kneel beside her.

He had lost the battle, for he had promised himself he would not touch her again unless she wanted him. But Lord, how he wanted her! he raged inwardly. And as he raged, he was struck by the shattering realization that it was not just her body he wanted but the Summer who lived behind those dark eyes. Why? he asked himself. He had had many women before her. Why did he feel the need to have her respond with not just physical desire, but with her heart and soul.

He lay his hand against her cheek and looked deep into her eyes, searching for . . . he knew not what. He only knew that he wanted her as he had wanted no other in his life. What had suddenly happened? What had changed?

She was physically exhausted and mentally unprepared to handle this attack on her senses. She knew that if he touched her again or kissed her she would be lost, and this time it would be total surrender. Once enveloped in the smoldering heat of passion, she would never be able to retrieve herself. She would follow him until he wanted her no more. She could not allow this to happen, for he would then have the power to take her whenever he chose.

She pushed his hand away and rose quickly to her feet. Sebastian, still on his knees, looked up at her. He felt it rise within him, this deep, burning need, and it left him momentarily speechless. It occurred to him then that he could take her whether she willed it or not. He was much stronger, and he knew she was very nearly defenseless against the passion that could carry them away. But he also sensed that if he did so, she would be lost to him in a way he couldn't consciously comprehend as yet.

He wanted her, and he wanted her to want him, but at that moment he didn't know how to get past the barrier of her unspoken condemnation without destroying any chance for understanding they might have.

Why can't he see, she thought frantically, that it would only take words, just words, to bring her into his arms. But they were words he would not say, for he would not put aside other influences. She wanted to hear, "I love you, Summer, and that is all we need. It doesn't matter who we are or where we are as long as we are together." But he wouldn't—he couldn't, she believed.

Sebastian's only intention was to go to her and find some way to communicate his feelings. He moved to her side, but his eyes belied his intent. They were filled with her, and with the desire he was trying to leash. For a moment that felt like eternity he looked into the depths of her dark orbs.

Summer was torn apart by an aching desire to step into his arms and surrender to the fulfilling passion she knew she would find there. Only her will kept her immobile.

Sebastian felt the intangible force of this will and

149

sensed it was a bridge he could not cross. "I don't know what you're thinking, Summer. I can't get past those eyes. I only know that I don't want to hurt you. You're beautiful and gentle and you have given much to help me. I'm grateful to you. Can we at least try to find some safe ground on which to stand so that we are not at war with each other?"

Had he seen fear flickering across her features? The look disappeared as quickly as it had come and Sebastian would never know that it was fear of her own nearly overpowering desire that had almost weakened all her defenses and sent her into his embrace.

"We can try, Summer," he said softly. "Come by the fire. You need to eat, and I know you're tired."

His gentleness was frustrating. She had been prepared for both verbal and physical battle, but now he confused her with kindness and understanding.

She seemed to Sebastian like a wild bird about to take flight at any moment. To ease the tension, he backed away a few steps and smiled as he waved toward the blankets.

"We can keep the fire between us."

Again her chin tilted up and her eyes sparked.

Sebastian laughed and held up both hands, palms outward. "I only meant that I'll stay on my side—not that you were afraid of me. Truce?" he questioned.

She nodded and returned to her blanket as he returned to his. They ate and Sebastian, trying to keep the atmosphere light, told her of his childhood and his newly built home that had been burned by the renegades. He assured her that one day he would rebuild it.

He did not say anything about future plans and Summer did not question him. She did not want to know.

After awhile, Sebastian suggested they sleep, for

there would be a day of hard riding ahead of them if they were to find Cole by nightfall.

Summer lay on her blanket and drifted off to sleep, but for Sebastian it was not so easy. He watched her as she slept and again had to control the urge to lie beside her and take her in his arms.

He felt a strange hollowness too, as if part of him were missing. And before he succumbed to his drowsiness, the vague thought swept over him that such an emptiness could be filled if only he had—what? The answer remained elusive and sleep claimed him before he could search his mind further.

# Chapter Fourteen

Sabrina Storm closed the door and turned to smile at her newly arrived guests.

"Patrick, I'm so glad you've all come," she said, "but Clay has taken the boys hunting. You'll stay, won't you? Clay should be back tomorrow night."

"Darlin"—Patrick Flynn laughed—"sure and I'd be more than pleased to stay. Your company is enough for me. Clay could stay hunting for a week if he likes."

Patrick Flynn, a happy-go-lucky Irishman, had been a friend of Clay Storm's for over ten years. He had teasingly made it clear to both Sabrina and Clay that he was in love with Sabrina. He had laughingly told Clay he would steal Sabrina from him if she ever gave him the opportunity, to which Sabrina had responded that there would never be such opportunity. They had become sincere and close friends from that day on.

He was a tall, slender man with flame-colored hair, green eyes, and an infectious smile, all of which indicated his Irish ancestry. His wife had died after the birth of his daughter, Kylie, and he had raised his two sons, Simon and James, and his daughter by himself.

In the years since she and Clay had known Patrick, Sabrina had often responded to his flirting by

152

threatening to call his bluff. She had told him that he wanted to remain single so he could charm all the ladies in the territory.

His oldest son, Simon, was twenty-three. He was a tall, handsome boy, dark of hair and eyes and quiet and thoughtful by nature. There was no one in either family that did not know that Simon had given his heart to Summer a long time ago.

The second boy, James, was twenty-one and as opposite from Simon as day from night. He was a carefree boy, solid and squarely built, with the same hair and eyes of his father.

But in Kylie the boisterousness and vibrant color had been muted and subdued. She was fair skinned, with wide, crystal green eyes and hair the color of dark wine. She was very small of build, which was a constant source of wonder to the father of two huge boys.

"In truth"—Patrick grinned—"I promised Kylie she could spend a little time with you and Summer. She misses womenfolk about the house."

"I would love to stay until Summer comes home. Isn't she due to finish school soon?" Kylie asked.

"It should only be a few weeks until school is over. From her last letter, I know Summer is anxious to get home."

"I don't think the child really wanted to leave," Patrick added. "I suspect she only did so because her father wanted it."

"It was good for her, Patrick," Sabrina said. "Whether she agrees or not she is many things. I know she is Singing Bells's daughter and very important to Hawk and his people, but she is Clay's daughter too, and she owes him her loyalty. The Storm name is important, and one day Summer will have to, or want to, marry. Clay wants to make sure she can make comparisons and marry well."

"Wealthy?"

"Not necessarily . . . just happily." Sabrina smiled.

"I wanted Pa to take me to the village for a short visit. I have some things for Swift Doe. The last time I went to town I bought some sewing material, and I'd like to give it to her." Kylie turned from Sabrina to Patrick. "Can't Simon take me for awhile, Pa? We could be back in a week, and then I could stay and visit with Sabrina until Summer gets home."

"Pa?" James added quickly, "could I go with Kylie? Running Wolf has some ponies he was breaking a while back. I'd like to test 'em out a little."

"Well," Patrick said thoughtfully, "maybe you three can go for a time. When Clay returns we'll come and fetch you home."

"Thanks, Pa," James responded, grinning his effervescent, infectious grin.

"Well, at least you'll have to stay and eat before you go," insisted Ellen, who had been housekeeper and companion to the Storm family for years. "I made fresh pie this morning, and I'm sure the boys would like a piece before they go."

"Have you ever seen either of them when they weren't hungry, or when they've refused a piece of your pies or cakes, Ellen?" Kylie laughed. "They're the second most important thing that draws Simon here. The first is still Summer."

"At least Summer can talk about something besides pretty dresses and dances," Simon retorted.

Kylie's eyes danced merrily. The brothers and sister loved one another deeply and enjoyed the banter that usually flowed among them.

"Summer could talk about anything and you'd enjoy it. I'll bet when she gets back you won't even remember what she talks about as long as she talks to you."

154

Again Simon chuckled, but he refused to be baited twice.

"We'd be delighted to sample your pie, Ellen," Patrick told her. "I've a hollow spot needs stuffing, and I know for certain that James and Simon always need filling." He turned his amused glance toward Kylie. "And you leave your brother alone, my girl, and quit your teasing. One day you could be getting it back."

"Pa!" Kylie laughed. "I won't be looking for any boy with moon eyes for a long time. I'm having too much fun."

"That's the truth," James offered. "You've flirted with every boy for a hundred miles around."

Kylie laughed again, a soft, bubbly laugh. "I'm going to be very careful when I choose a husband." She looked up at her father. "I want to catch a man like Pa; then I'd be willing to settle down."

Patrick roared with laughter and swung Kylie up in his arms and gave her a resounding kiss. "You're like your ma, girl. Sweet and smart. I pity the man you set your eyes on if he doesn't fall under your spell right quick. You have enough blarney to catch the smartest man walking."

There was laughter as there always was with the Flynn family present. Ellen served pie and tea, after which Patrick sent Simon, James, and Kylie on their way.

"Be careful camping tonight," he warned the boys. "And take good care of Kylie."

Patrick, Ellen, and Sabrina sat in friendly conversation before the crisply burning fire. For both women it was an opportunity for a little gossip and a chance to find out the news in the surrounding area through which Patrick had just passed. Outside, the sunlight

155

slowly paled from the days red-gold to a shadowy gray. Within, the orange flame of the fire also faded to glowing embers.

After a time, Ellen sought her bed and Sabrina and Patrick remained in companionable silence.

"My dear," Patrick said softly, "why don't you go and get some sleep?"

Sabrina yawned and stretched, which played havoc with Patrick's iron control. If Sabrina were his, he thought, he wouldn't have been able to leave her.

Sabrina rose from her chair. In the faded light she could hardly see Patrick's face.

"I think I shall. Will you be comfortable, Patrick? Would you like another blanket?"

"No, I'm fine," he replied.

"Good night then."

"Good night, Sabrina. Sleep well."

Sabrina's door had barely closed when the sound of an approaching horse was heard. It stopped before the porch and then soft footfalls told Patrick the visitor was an Indian wearing moccasins. Then there was a quick knock on the door.

Patrick rose and Sabrina's door opened at the same time. They exchanged glances. "I'll get it," Patrick said. He walked to the door and opened it to find a tall, young Indian boy, whom both he and Sabrina recognized.

"Walks Tall," Sabrina said in surprise as she walked to the door. "How nice to see you again. Come in."

The young warrior was awed by Sabrina's golden-haired beauty and the fact that she was the woman of Clay Storm. And being in an alien atmosphere inside a house made him self-conscious as well, despite his attempts to hide it.

"Is all well in the village?" Sabrina questioned.

"All is well," he said. "Hawk sends word to Clay

156

Storm and his woman."

Sabrina's lips twitched in a half smile, but she only replied quietly, "Clay is not here. I would listen to Hawk's words and tell Clay when he returns."

"Hawk says to give you word that Summer is in our village."

Sabrina's eyes widened in surprise. "Summer . . . in the village? I don't understand. Why is she out of school so soon, and . . . why is she in the village and not at home?"

For these questions Walks Tall had no answers. He had been cautioned by Hawk to keep his silence about the man who had been with Summer when she came to them, at least until Hawk could speak to Clay about him.

"Now Sabrina, don't get excited," Patrick insisted. "It's obvious she's all right or Hawk would have sent word. And she must have had a reason to come home so soon and to be at the village. It can't be serious, or Hawk would have come himself."

"I hope you're right, Patrick," Sabrina said worriedly. "But it seems strange that she went to the village before coming home. I have a feeling there's more to this than we know."

Patrick kept his silence, as did a very astute Walks Tall.


Clay Storm was, as usual, awake very early. He lay still, enjoying the cool morning air and the beauty about him. He looked across the now dead fire at his two sons, who still lay tangled in their blankets, sound asleep. It always stirred him when he looked at them. He considered himself the luckiest man in the world to possess Sabrina and felt doubly blessed with the two sons she had given him.

157

He watched the sun rim the horizon and was filled with the urge to hurry home. The trip had been more than successful, not only in the hunting, but in his camaraderie with the boys. Now he felt the drawing sensation that he always felt when he had been away from his home too long.

He rose and walked to where the boys slept. Gently shaking one and then the other, he brought them awake.

"Come on boys, it's time to get moving. I'd like to be home before midday and I wouldn't be surprised if Ellen has cooked us up something special. I don't know about you, but I could use a good meal."

Young Clay laughed. "Papa, I don't want to say anything about your cooking until I'm out of reach, but it sure isn't Ellen's."

"I have to agree with you there, son. Let's go home."

They broke their camp and packed everything carefully. The day was still young when they mounted and rode for home. Clay listened to the playful banter between the boys with less than his full attention, for his thoughts kept returning to the golden-haired woman who was calling him home.

It was well before midday that they crested the hill and started down the grade that led to the house. The boys raced ahead and Clay's eyes soon brightened when he saw Sabrina step out on the porch. He was pleased also to see his good friend, Patrick, close behind her.

His smile wavered when he saw another form appear behind the Irishman's, and he wondered if there was anything wrong in Hawk's village that might have brought Walks Tall to his home.

He dismounted and took Sabrina in his arms and kissed her soundly, concentrating for the moment only on the pleasure that holding her always gave him. He kept one arm about her waist as he turned to Patrick and Walks Tall.

"Patrick, it's good to see you again, my friend. What brings you out here, and where's the rest of your family?"

"They've gone to the village. Kylie had some things for Swift Doe. I"—he chuckled—"decided to stay here and try to convince your wife that she married the wrong man."

"Patrick!" Sabrina cried, blushing.

Clay laughed. "Don't worry about him, love. He's a harmless bloke."

"Am I now, laddie? If the lady weren't so blind in love with you, I'd take her right out from under your nose."

They laughed together and Clay turned to the young warrior who waited silently nearby.

"Walks Tall, it is good to see you also. Welcome to my home."

Walks Tall nodded his pleasure at the greeting.

"Are Hawk and his family well?"

"Hawk is well . . . he has sent me."

"Clay," Sabrina said quickly, "Summer is home . . . I mean," she added at his pleased look, "She is in Hawk's village."

Clay's expression grew puzzled. "In Hawk's village? Why did you let her go before I got home?"

"She never came here. Walks Tall just brought word. I didn't know she was home either."

Clay looked at Walks Tall with a questioning look in his blue eyes.

"Hawk said to tell you that Summer is well and is in our village. He says to tell Clay Storm that his daughter is safe and they wait for you to come so they can celebrate her return."

Walks Tall had said what he had been told to say, but

Clay sensed there was much more behind his words.

"Well," he said firmly, "I think it would be a good idea if we gathered our things and went to the village." His eyes caught Patrick's. "We don't want to miss a celebration, do we? Besides, it's been a long time since I've seen my daughter's pretty face."

Patrick's gaze told Clay he wasn't too sure everything was all right either.

The entire family made rapid preparations and by early afternoon they were on their way.

Hawk had followed Summer and Sebastian until the dark clouds of the building storm had driven him to cover. With a heavy heart he had watched the steadily pouring rain, knowing that any tracks they had left had been washed away.

There was no way for him to find them now, and he muttered a prayer to the gods that Summer knew what she was doing, and that she would not let herself be deceived by Sebastian.

He rode back to the village slowly. His heart beat heavily as he saw the group of people who watched his approach. How could he explain to Clay and Sabrina that he had let a strange white man enter their village and lure away the most valuable person in their lives?

After he finished explaining the situation to an upset Sabrina and a very angry Clay, both men turned their eyes westward. In both their hearts was the same question: when they found Summer, would she be all right? If not, Sebastian would pay a much higher price than any he had bargained for.

# Chapter Fifteen

Kate Maxwell stood before the flower-shrouded grave, dabbing delicately at her tear-filled eyes with a white lace handkerchief. The black veil that hid most of her face from the other mourners concealed her pleased smile.

The man who stood next to her squeezed her arm and she looked up into his eyes. He bent close to whisper, "Black becomes you, Kate, but be careful about overacting. It's hard to believe you miss the old man that much."

"Shut up, Richard," Kate hissed and was rewarded by another squeeze followed by his hand brushing the curve of her breast. She cast a quick, angry glance his way and then went on with her performance as the grieving widow of George Maxwell, who had died two days before.

Once the funeral was over, Richard Devale escorted Kate back to her carriage. He joined her inside and they rode back to the Maxwell estate.

They were silent during the ride back, for they did not want the driver to overhear their words. But once inside the house and closed away from prying eyes, Kate came into Richard's arms with a light laugh.

After a deep and prolonged kiss, she moved away from him. "You must be more careful, Richard. Your nasty remark could have proven dangerous. What if someone had heard you?"

Richard laughed. "No one heard. Everyone thought I was the grieving nephew consoling the widow of his beloved uncle—the very beautiful and oh-so-distressed widow," Richard mocked.

Kate drew off her veiled hat and gloves and threw them on a nearby couch. Richard gazed at her with admiring eyes, for the black dress was most flattering to her fair skin, blue eyes and intricately coiffed, gold-colored hair. She was a beauty who had drawn the attention of many men, even at the funeral.

"I don't see why it should take so long for his solicitors to read the will," she said coldly.

"Worried darling?" Richard asked casually as he poured himself a brandy.

"Richard, don't be a bore, and pour me a drink too."

"Of course." He chuckled as he poured the drink and brought it to her.

"What did you mean by worried?" she demanded. "I've nothing to worry about. George loved me. He left everything to me."

"You're so sure of that?" he taunted.

She smiled. "I'm sure. He pawed me enough and slobbered over me enough for me to be very sure."

"Well"—Richard sighed—"tomorrow we'll know what the old man left you. By tomorrow night you just might be very, very rich."

"Yes," Kate said softly, "tomorrow night."

Richard put his brandy glass aside and came to her. He took her roughly into his arms and kissed her almost violently, but she responded to his satisfaction. When he released her, she moved away from him.

"You had better go, Richard," she said softly. "We

don't want people to talk, do we?"

"No, I imagine we don't. But they don't need to know."

"Servants gossip, Richard. Go now. After the will has been read and we are free, we won't have to care anymore. Go now. We'll have plenty of time."

He agreed reluctantly, kissed her again, and left. Kate watched from a lace-draped window until his carriage had driven away. Then she laughed softly.

She turned from the window and went to ring for a servant. A young maid appeared so rapidly that Kate wondered just how close she had been.

"Anna," Kate said frigidly, "go upstairs and get Jennie. I want all my clothes packed and on board the ship by tonight."

"Yes, ma'am," Anna replied and left as rapidly as she had come.

Kate picked up her brandy glass and sipped. A soft chuckle formed into a full-throated laugh as she threw back her head and gave vent to the victory for which she had worked so long.

"Sebastian," she murmured softly, "now we can have it all."


The lawyer's office was very quiet as all present watched Gregory Franklin unfold the will. He did this slowly, so slowly that it set Kate's teeth on edge and she wanted to shout at him. Finally, he cleared his throat and began to read. Kate gripped her handkerchief in her sweaty palms and tried to control her nerves as he read on and on for interminable minutes until all the petty grants had been made. Then Kate drew in her breath.

". . . And to my beloved wife Kate I leave the balance of my fortune. May she enjoy years of happiness for all the love she has given me."

Kate could have screamed out her joy, but she remained silent. She had told Sebastian it would all be worth it. Now she could go to him with a fortune in her hands and they could be happy for the rest of their lives.

She had no intention of going back to the house. The lawyer would be given orders to sell it and send her the money as soon as she sent an address. She would not bother to tell Richard, who would be waiting there for her, that she was sailing into Sebastian's arms.

She left the lawyer's office and walked down the stone steps to her waiting carriage. After giving the driver orders to take her to the dock, she sat back on the seat and smiled to herself. She would go to Sebastian and together they would have enough wealth to last a lifetime, even with Kate's extravagant taste. She would have everything she had ever wanted.

The carriage came to a halt and the driver helped her down. She looked up at the tall masts of the ship that would take her away from the degrading life she had lived, first with George and then with Richard, who had been useful in helping her finally dispose of her husband. And she had placed money in strategic hands in order to make sure Richard never found out where she had gone.

Once on board, she felt deliciously free as she watched the sails unfurl and felt the ship ease away from the dock and head toward new shores and the man who could make her pulses leap and her blood grow warm. Sebastian, she thought, we'll have the world . . . the whole, entire world!

Kate stood at the rail and watched the shoreline slowly fade. She was so engrossed in her thoughts that she did not hear anyone approach until a voice came from behind her, deep and masculine.

"It's a stirring sight, isn't it?"

Kate spun around to look up into the face of a ruggedly handsome man.

"Oh, Captain Sutter, I didn't hear you."

"I know. You were watching the shoreline. It really is an extraordinary view."

He was looking at her, not the shoreline. She knew it, and she was stirred by it.

Luke Sutter was a virile and forceful man who had a strong taste for a pretty female, and this one seemed to him a very tasty morsel indeed. It was a long trip and he much preferred soft company to an empty bed.

Kate smiled invitingly into his eyes. It was a long trip, and Kate was never one to be alone for long. Until she reached Sebastian, she thought, Luke Sutter would be an amusing distraction and would certainly make the trip more interesting.

"I've never given you a tour of my ship," he said in a warm, caressing tone.

Kate widened her blue eyes as she rested her hand on his arm. Her invitation was obvious and she watched his appreciative eyes appraise her body.

"Are there any . . . particular places you would like to show me?" she inquired seductively.

"I thought we might start with my cabin. I have some brandy, and since the air is so crisp for one as delicate as you, you might find it . . . warmer there."

"Captain Sutter . . ."

"Luke."

"Luke," she whispered as she tucked her hand through his arm. "I believe your cabin and a glass of brandy would be the very best place in the world to start."

He smiled, pressed her hand against him, and slowly led her toward his quarters.

Once there, Luke closed the door behind them. He

165

knew there would be no one disturbing him for hours, for he had given his orders before he had approached Kate. He knew women well and wanted the time to savor this one. She was fine and delicate, but Luke was not fooled. Because he was a predator himself, he could easily recognize those qualities in another.

He poured two glasses of brandy while he watched her as she looked at the sea through the porthole. Then, picking up the two glasses, he strode to her side. She turned and he handed her one. As she sipped, she mused that the liquid matched the warmth of her blood. And when his eyes raked over her, she felt an excitement stir deep within her.

"The brandy is excellent," she murmured.

"To drink?" Luke questioned.

"What else?" she inquired.

"Oh, my pretty," Luke said as he set his glass aside and took hers from her hand to place next to his, "there are things one can do with brandy that are most exciting. Shall I show you?" he asked softly as he moved closer. Kate felt the stir of the same urgent hunger that always drove her to reach for what she wanted. And at the moment she wanted Luke Sutter.

"Yes," she responded huskily, "show me."

His hands spanned her slim waist easily and he held her captive as he slowly bent his head to cover her mouth with his. It was a long, deep kiss and his tongue teased and tasted her parted lips, then thrust vigorously and caressed her tongue until a quiver of hot passion swirled through her.

Suddenly he released her lips and his hands moved to the buttons of her dress to loosen one, then another.

She waited breathlessly while he leisurely undressed her, and she saw the heat glowing in his eyes as he raked them over her flesh.

He bent and lifted her in his arms and carried her to

his bed. There he laid her down and she watched through half-closed eyes as he undressed. He was a magnificent male, she thought to herself, and felt a flood of moisture between her thighs as her body urged her to seek fulfillment.

Luke took the two glasses of brandy, carried them to the bed, and placed them on the stand beside it. Then he lay down and she reached for him, but he grasped both of her wrists and held them over her head with one hand. With the other he lifted a glass of brandy and began to dribble it down her body. It ran in little rivulets over the tips of her breasts and down her belly to the soft golden hair between her thighs. Then she moaned rapturously as his lips started at the source and began a journey that would torment her until she cried out and begged him to take her.

His tongue flicked against her heated skin, tasting her flesh and the brandy. His mouth closed over first one mound, then the other, sucking, teasing, his teeth nibbling just enough to make her stir beneath him. The soft tips hardened and grew firm and his mouth became more demanding, sucking harder and harder until she cried out.

Now she squirmed and writhed, but to no avail. His mouth was following the rivulets of brandy, his teeth grazing her flesh, and his tongue tracing a line of fire down, down.

One hand stroked her thighs gently, slowly, teasingly, moving her legs apart until his fingers found her warm, moist, sensitive core. He moved his fingers in a tormenting caress, sliding within her, then away, over and over until she gasped and arched her hips to meet him.

Before she could find release, he moved downward. Following the brandy's path, his lips sought her heated, throbbing apex and found it. He gripped her buttocks

167

and lifted her to meet his seeking tongue. She moaned and tried to escape the torment, but he held her, teasing, nibbling, and thrusting until she was wild and beyond reason.

Now his mouth became almost brutal, and she gasped and moaned. Her hands pressed against his broad shoulders, but he was immovable. He tormented her and drew from her every trembling ounce of passion.

Now he rose above her, knowing she was beyond controlling her urgent need for him. But he would make her suffer first. He put his hard, throbbing manhood to her pulsing, moist entrance, but he did not move.

"Luke . . . please," she panted. Her hips arched to meet him, but he kept himself just out of reach, remaining close enough only to touch and to tease.

"You want me," he gasped raggedly. "Tell me . . . tell me."

She squirmed, pressed upward, but he would give her nothing.

"Luke," she groaned. "Luke, please . . . love me . . . take me now . . . now . . . please."

He pushed himself only partially inside her and withdrew again and again until she wept and begged for release. When he could see that she was far beyond reality, when she had cried out and begged for him, his mouth came crashing down on hers. At the same time he thrust himself within her. He heard her anguished groan and it was half pleasure, half agony, for he was a large and very strong man and he had driven himself to the very hilt of her. Harder and harder he thrust, until her body was quivering like a leaf in a hurricane and she clung to him, a rudderless ship in a storm.

Her world was out of control, for she had never before been victim to such unbridled, brutal possession. She was taken to the heights, flung to the depths, and raised again to fly beyond reason. She had never felt so exultant or so frightened in her life.

Her eyes were still closed when Luke rose to pour them both another brandy. She opened them lazily as he carried the glasses over and sat on the edge of the bed. She accepted one with a trembling hand and took a sip, letting the warmth rejuvenate her. Luke smiled and touched his glass to hers with a soft tinkle.

"To a long"—he paused—"and very exciting trip."

"Yes," she whispered. "To a long . . . and very pleasant interlude."

Luke's lovemaking had been thrilling and exciting, she mused, but he was no Sebastian. She had found a brutality within Luke that had both titillated and frightened her. She would enjoy him for the trip, but once in the colonies, she would forget that Luke Sutter had ever existed. There she would have Sebastian— gentle, sensitive Sebastian—who gave love instead of taking it, who had been able to make her feel wanted, who had made her feel so gloriously weak and wonderfully complete.

Luke bent to kiss her again and she closed her eyes. For this trip she would have Luke, and then . . . she would forget him.


The ship slipped alongside the dock gracefully and was soon made secure. Kate stood by the rail and watched the gangplank slide into place. On a paper in her reticule were written a name and an address where she could find help in securing what she would need to get settled as well as obtain information about where Sebastian had gone. The name was Elenora Gregory. Luke appeared beside her and she could feel herself tremble. Their shared passion had enlightened Kate to

169

forms of lovemaking that she had never heard of or dreamed of before. Luke was a violent and possessive man, and no matter what mood she had been in, he had been able to set her aflame. He had done it with a deliberation that had shaken her to the core. He had tormented her senses and had carried her to heights of wild abandon, from which only he had been able to release her. Then he had completed his mastery of her by making her beg for the ecstasy to which she had become addicted.

"So, where do you go from here? Where will you be staying? I'll be here for about a month; then I'll be gone for six."

She was silent for a moment, having realized that he assumed their affair would go on as long as he desired. She knew him now, and she knew she would have to be very careful.

"You say you'll be here for a month?"

"Yes."

"I'll send you a message to tell you where I'll be staying. I have to see an attorney here and make some arrangements. It won't be long. I'll send you a note within a day or two."

His amused gaze was not on her but on the activity on the dock. "All right. Send me word soon." His voice lowered to a seductive whisper. "I don't want to do without you too long. I'll miss you."

"Yes," she answered hesitantly. "I . . . I'll miss you too, Luke. I'll send word as soon as possible."

She turned to look up at him. He smiled and she felt certain that he had no suspicion of her plans. And by the time he realized her deceit, she would be gone and he would be forced to sail.

"Good-bye . . . for now, Luke."

"Good-bye, sweet."

She left his side and walked down the gangplank.

Luke watched her with the glow of amusement still in his eyes. Then he beckoned to one of his men, who moved hastily to his side.

"Follow her. Let me know where she goes and who she meets. Don't let her know you're there, Tag."

"Aye, sir." The man grinned. "I'll be like a shadow. She'll never know old Tag's on her trail."

After Kate left the ship, her first stop was the office of an attorney. She presented him with letters and papers that would enable him to have her money transferred.

"Mr. Michaels"—Kate smiled her sweetest smile—"you are so kind to help me. I'm so helpless in matters such as this. I was told that you were by far the best man for this type of undertaking."

Joseph Michaels swelled with arrogant pride and it took great effort on Kate's part to contain her laughter.

"I must discover where my fiancé bought his land and then I must arrange transportation there. It is a surprise." She managed to blush demurely. "We are to be married soon."

"But of course, my child. And you will have an extended amount of credit guaranteed by my own hand until your affairs are settled."

"I . . . ah . . . must also find the residence of a Miss Elenora Gregory. I will be staying there as her guest until I can find my future husband and our marriage can be arranged."

"Certainly, my dear. I know Miss Gregory quite well. Her home is not far from here. If you like, I shall arrange transportation there."

"If you please, Mr. Michaels, I would like to do a little shopping first. Can you arrange the transportation for late this afternoon?"

"I most certainly can."

"I shall be most grateful." Kate smiled as she bent toward him and touched his hand. It was amusing to see his eyes light with pleasure. "I . . . if you don't mind seeing to my finances, I should like to buy some . . . ah . . . personal items." She blushed again and Joseph Michaels became her slave.

"My dear child, I shall see to it immediately. You need only go to the shops and choose what you want."

"Thank you so very much." Kate smiled her warmest, most intimate smile. "I shall be on my way then, and return to your office . . . let us say . . . ah, five-thirty?"

"Delightful."

"Perhaps," she inquired demurely, "we could share dinner before the drive to Miss Gregory's?"

He flushed with pleasure at her sweet smile and at the opportunity to dine with such a beautiful woman and nodded.

Kate rose and was escorted to the door, from which Joseph Michaels watched the enticing sway of her slim hips as she walked away.

Kate did visit every shop and ordered all the items she wanted. She bought some very seductive things, which she hoped would please Sebastian.

She could not wait to see his face, to tell him she had come to be with him forever and had brought with her all that they could ever want.

She wondered if he had succeeded in building the house he had wanted, and she shivered with delicious anticipation at the thought of sharing his life and of living with him in the house she knew he had built for her.

She returned at five-thirty to find Joseph ready to escort her to dinner. It was an enjoyable meal, and she took the opportunity to question him to some extent, but he knew very little about where Sebastian's land was, or, in fact, about Sebastian at all.

After dinner, he led her to a carriage that would deliver her to the home of Elenora Gregory, and after a short ride, she saw her destination through the carriage window.

It was a very large and very elaborate house. Kate was quite impressed, for it was obvious that it had taken great wealth to build such a home.

She was most curious about the lady who lived in it, for she had heard a great deal about Elenora Gregory. And from what she had heard, she had decided that Elenora would make a good contact. Now she would see if her decision had been correct.

# Chapter Sixteen

Elenora Gregory stood by a huge window in the drawing room of her mansion. The light that filtered in was a brilliant compliment to her loveliness. She was considered an exceptional beauty, unflawed, at least on the surface. Her skin was smooth and white as porcelain, and her dark almond eyes were wide and fringed by lashes that matched her ebony hair. Her voluptuous curves would make desire race in any man's blood, any man, that is, except the one she had always wanted—Clay Storm.

For years now she had been filled with a burning hatred for the man who had chosen another, and with raging jealousy for the women—Sabrina, Clay's wife, and Summer, his daughter—to whom Clay Storm had given his love.

Today she had chosen to wear a pale blue gown that dipped enticingly low off her shoulders. Her unbound hair fell in artful disarray and created an inviting quality, which she had planned very carefully. Elenora was a shrewd woman who judiciously considered every move she made.

Miles Chandler rose from his seat and walked across the room to stand behind Elenora. His arm reached out to encircle her waist and he drew her back against him, then bent his head to kiss one smooth shoulder. Elenora smiled, convinced that she had completely ensnared him. She closed her eyes and allowed Miles a few minutes of freedom. It would be enough, she knew, to arouse his desire for her. Slowly she turned in the warmth of his circling arm, and lifted her lips to meet his. Molding her body against him, she caressed the hard muscles of his shoulders with gentle hands.

She felt the heat of his body and the surge of intensity as his arms tightened about her. When she knew he was nearing uncontrolled passion, she eased out of his arms and backed away, understanding fully the situation she was deliberately creating.

She moistened her lips delicately and moved sensuously toward the wine decanter that rested on a nearby table. Slowly she poured a glass of wine, walked back to Miles, and handed it to him. He could clearly read temptation in her smoldering eyes.

"This is just a promise of . . . what we can share," she said provocatively.

Miles smiled. "I can wait." His eyes hardened. "Just know I will claim what is promised. Don't tease me, Elenora. It might prove upsetting to you . . . and to your plans."

Elenora would never allow her plans to be upset, and she was willing to go to any lengths to have her revenge.

The trouble had started with the coming of Sabrina McNeil and Clay's subsequent rejection of Elenora. She blamed Sabrina—she hated Sabrina—and for years had planned her revenge, waiting only for the right opportunity. It had come in the form of a wealthy land investor named Miles Chandler.

She had arranged a meeting at a social gathering, using friends who had either known or done business with Miles. Once she had met him, she deliberately set

175

out to seduce him. It was not long before Miles was in her bed and reasonably under her control.

"Miles," she said, breaking free of her reverie, "I've been looking at the map. It seems we have acquired a great deal of land."

Miles chuckled. "Yes, we have, one way or another. When the government opens that whole area for settlers, we will have a large chunk to sell to the highest bidder."

"Some of your influential backers in Washington should be pleased."

Miles came to her again. His hands spanned her waist and he drew her close to him. "And you?" he asked softly. "You should be well pleased. Since your father died, I have been able to make you a very wealthy woman."

Again Elenora moved away from him, and he looked at her with a puzzled, almost angry frown on his face.

"Elenora?"

"Well, I would be pleased . . . except . . ."

"Except what?"

"In the area we own—right in the center—is a large block of land that should be ours."

"You're talking about the Storm property. You might not be aware of it, but there is another piece quite near—I think it borders the Storm's—that has been sold out from under us."

"I am aware of it. Do you know who has bought it?"

"I've heard several names and I'm not too sure, but the name Cain comes up often."

"Yes, I too have heard that Mr. Cain has purchased the property, which is an interesting coincidence."

"Coincidence? What is?"

"I expect a visitor one day soon—a Kate Maxwell. I received a letter from a mutual friend who felt I could be of some help to her. Anyway, she's on her way here.

176

It seems this Sebastian Cain is her fiancé. She's looking for him."

"Why did you invite her to come here?"

"Because of that land Cain has supposedly purchased, which is very close to the Storm's. I might have need of some friends out there. I want the Storm land, and, who knows? She might be of some help to me."

Miles watched her closely and after a few minutes he smiled. "I believe you are after more than land. If I am not mistaken, you seek a little revenge as well."

Elenora turned away so his penetrating gaze would not read her thoughts. Elenora did not want Miles to know that she still harbored desire for Clay. It would be disastrous to her plans if Miles became difficult because of jealousy. She had to let him believe she was after the entire Storm family.

"Yes," she eventually admitted, "I want revenge on the Storms—all of them. Clay should be the last, so he will know what it means to suffer."

"What happened?" Miles questioned.

"It is in the past and I do not care to speak of it. Are you going to help me?"

"What is it you want from me?"

"Miles, I know you better than anyone. I know about all your . . . deals. I know that you have made more than one young woman disappear and have profited handsomely from it. Would it be so difficult to have another vanish?" She paused, then added, "I want Sabrina Storm and, if possible, that half-breed daughter of Clay's to be . . . taken care of. It would not be difficult for you, and they are both quite pretty. You could make a sizable sum."

Miles smiled confidently. "And if I do rid you of these minor nuisances, what are you bargaining with? What do you have to offer to make it worth my effort?"

With a secretive half smile on her face, she moved

with slow, sensuous grace toward him, stopping only when their bodies touched. Her eyes languorously lifted to his. Gently she reached a finger to trace his lips, then rose on tiptoe and lightly touched her lips to his. Slowly she deepened the kiss as she slid her arms about his waist.

She heard the soft groan that escaped him and felt his desire as his arms bound her to him. He began to ravage her mouth with a wild, desperate possessiveness.

"You are a witch," he whispered when their lips parted.

Elenora laughed softly. "But a witch that pleases you, am I not?"

"Oh yes," he breathed. "You please me . . . very much. You are well worth what you are asking, and I shall be pleased to give you what you want. I will get Storm and those about him. We will have what we want and Storm will never know what happened."

Elenora chuckled and offered Miles her warm, moist lips again, but her cold and hungry heart did not accompany them.

As Miles continued to make love to her, she promised herself that soon her revenge would be complete.

She knew much more of Miles's sordid past and dark endeavors than any other human being. When the time came, she would reveal to society the places where he had sold women, as well as the details of many other nefarious schemes in which he was involved. It would be more than enough to sweep him from her life.

Used to the craftiness of women, Miles suspected that Elenora was keeping something from him and had no intention of letting her use him. Instead, he intended to use her, first for physical pleasure because she was far more skilled than any other woman he had known, and second because she could unknowingly aid him in his unscrupulous schemes.

Each wanted something from the other, and each was not only prepared to give, but to betray when the time came to do so.

Elenora slept late the following morning and was awakened by a young maid who told her that Miles had requested her presence downstairs in the library. She rose, pulled her robe about her, and went to meet him. She was astonished to find two other men present, dark, shadowy men who made her skin crawl with their hot, lascivious looks. She assumed they were creatures from the dark side of Miles's life. For once Elenora sat in a high-backed chair and spoke as little as possible. She could not understand why Miles had asked her to join him while he gave orders to these men.

She did not realize that she would now be identified with and involved in what these men were about to do. In their minds, Miles was painting Elenora the same shade of black as himself.

"Elenora, this is Carl Mackin and Toby Cinch," Miles said suavely, introducing his companions. He smiled coldly, pleased with himself. "They are going to take care of that little chore we discussed yesterday."

Both men nodded without speaking, but their eyes missed nothing about Elenora. She shivered, grateful that she was not the one they were after. The thought of being alone in the wilderness with either of these men was repugnant. Yet she had no compunctions about turning the two loose on a young girl like Summer or on her mother, Sabrina.

"Are two men enough?" Elenora asked.

"No, they have two Indian friends who will meet them after they leave here. Two will be enough to take care of Summer Storm and two will handle Sabrina. Once they are out of the territory, no one will ever know what happened to them."

Elenora nodded and listened to the rest of the conversation in silence.

"When are you meeting the others?" Miles inquired.

"In a week," Carl replied. He was a tall, extremely thin man whose cadaverous face was pale and cold. His black eyes, round and icy, darted quickly from one thing to another, missing nothing.

"They's travelin' down from up north aways. We'll meet 'em at Harbor Crossin'," Toby added. He spoke quietly, but his eyes never left the soft white flesh exposed above Elenora's low-cut robe. His face was dark, as were his hair and eyes. Shorter than Carl, he was the same height as Elenora, who suspected him of being a half-breed.

"While you meet them, I will go on to the Storm place and make them an offer for their land," Miles explained. "That way I will find out who is there and what your best opportunities will be. You will wait for me nearby, and I will return to tell you what to do."

Both men nodded again in silent agreement.

"Well," Miles growled, "get along. I'll meet you later."

"You pay us half now," Carl said quickly. "We'll collect the other half when we get back from selling the women."

Miles took a wad of money from his pocket and peeled some bills from it slowly. He smiled as he saw them lick their lips and noted the glow in their avaricious eyes. They turned to leave after grabbing the money.

"Wait!" Elenora called. They turned to face her, and she smiled and rose from her chair. Slowly she walked to the shorter of the two. She watched the effect she had

180

on him as the scent of her perfume reached him. He was an animal, she thought, exactly the right kind of man to suit her purposes.

"These two women . . ." she said softly, "we are not particular about what . . . ah . . . condition they are in when you get rid of them. I'm sure your buyers will accept . . . ah . . . damaged material, will they not?"

"They'll sell for less," the man replied, but Elenora could see that the idea pleased him.

"I don't care what price you get. I just think you ought to share the rewards. Consider it a little gift from me and"—she laughed softly—"enjoy yourselves for as long as you like before you sell them."

Both men looked from Elenora to Miles, who smiled and shrugged eloquently, indicating that he did not care about the fate of the women as long as he did not have to see them.

The door closed behind the two, and Miles turned to Elenora. He smiled as he reached for her, letting the gesture mask the fact that he fully recognized her cold and vicious streak and realized that she didn't trust him.

Miles left that afternoon. He, Carl, and Toby traveled for almost three days before reaching the Storm home, but as they finally crested the hill above it, they were just in time to see Clay, his family, and Patrick ride off.

"They's headed for Hawk's village," Toby said.

"How do you know?" Miles asked.

"That be the only thing out there. Storm's blood brother to Hawk, and his first wife was their medicine woman."

"You know a lot about them."

"I knows them women is sure pretty. I'd like to get hold of that yeller-haired wife of his or that kid he and his first wife had. They be some women."

181

"You've never tried before?"

Toby laughed harshly. "No one man—maybe no bunch of men—is gonna come in and take Clay Storm's woman, much less one of Hawk's."

"But you're going along with us now?"

"We gonna have Three Feathers and one of his braves. If anyone could whip Clay Storm, it just might be Three Feathers. Besides, I want to watch the fight when it come off."

"And"—Carl laughed—"you wouldn't mind a taste of his womenfolk if somebody else makes it possible."

"You're sure right. First time I seed his pretty wife I thought about how it would be to mount her and have her moanin' and groanin' under me. I might teach her a thing or two about men. The one she got is too gentle with 'er. Them uppity kind have to be taught who's the boss."

"Well, when we get them, you can have first chance." Miles laughed. "Until then, you two go and meet your friends. Make camp at Devil's Elbow. We can watch the village and everything that comes and goes from there."

Carl nodded and they turned their horses to ride northward. After less than an hour they stopped in a clearing and prepared to wait, but it was not long before two riders entered the clearing and rode toward them.

Carl watched as they approached. No matter how many times he rode with these two, he would never get used to them. Their presence could still make the hairs on the back of his neck rise and his palms grow sweaty.

The two newcomers stopped near them and slowly dismounted. No smiles touched their faces, and no light of friendship lit their obsidian eyes. They were cold, merciless men.

"Three Feathers," Carl said. "Welcome."

"I come," Three Feathers stated harshly, "because you have promised much."

"I have promised, and I keep my promises to Three Feathers . . . always."

A fleeting glimmer of amusement lit Three Feathers's eyes, but it disappeared quickly. He knew as well as all the others present that no one would even consider not keeping a promise to him. Three Feathers stood tall, just over six feet, and was heavily yet sleekly muscled. His face was all sharp angles, with high cheekbones and a hawklike nose. His mouth was wide and rarely formed a smile. In his thick black hair, which hung loose to his shoulders, he wore three red feathers. They were attached to a band of leather about his brow. He wore only a breechclout and moccasins, which indicated that he had ridden light and far. A long-bladed dangerous-looking knife was in a sheath at his waist, and he carried a white man's gun.

The silent man who stood next to him was only an inch or two shorter and several pounds lighter. He was dressed the same. A new, puckered scar ran from his left shoulder across his bare chest to his waist.

"Let me tell you what we must do," Carl said, "and what has been promised."

The four stood talking for some time. After a few minutes they turned their horses in the same direction Clay and his family had taken, keeping far enough behind them that they would not know they were being followed.

# Chapter Seventeen

It was a gray and misty morning. Sebastian awoke just before dawn. He lay quietly with his eyes turned toward Summer, who still slept soundly. He did not want to awaken her yet. Awake, there was still the unspoken thing between them that Sebastian could not defeat. She talked with him easily and they traveled the same trail together, but there was something about her he could not touch.

The sun began to rise slowly and its light touched Summer's face gently. Sebastian watched her as she slept. The soft rays caressed her skin, turning it to mellow gold. Her thick lashes lay on peach-blush cheeks, and her lips were slightly parted as she breathed slowly, relaxed. The lips . . . so tempting, he mused. He wanted to be able to take her in his arms and awaken her with a kiss. But he knew he would see that look in her eyes again—expectant, as if there were something she was waiting for him to say or do, something that eluded him. He would watch her eyes sadden then, and she would turn from him.

Slowly Sebastian rose. Without a sound, he moved close to her. A very gentle hand reached to touch the soft, thick braid of hair that lay against the blanket. It stirred him, the soft silklike touch of it. If he could only stay here in this wilderness with Summer. But he couldn't. He had other people to think of too.

He caught his breath as Summer stirred and slowly opened her dark eyes. A soft smile, a warm look of pleasure, lit her features briefly then they were gone as quickly as they had come and Summer turned away. Again he felt the same hollow feeling, as if something valuable was being taken from him and he couldn't seem to stop it from happening. He also couldn't seem to stop the bright flame of desire that sprang to life unbidden at the sight of her.

She rose quickly, not wanting to stay close to Sebastian any longer than necessary. It was entirely too destructive to her peace of mind.

Both moved about and soon a small fire had been made and they were eating the remains of the previous night's supper. There was a tension in the air that fairly sparked between them.

Identical thoughts were being subdued by equally strong wills. Summer refused to surrender to the desire to go to him, brush a soft kiss against his firm mouth, and press her body close to his to feel the safety of his arms.

Sebastian refused to force her to surrender to him despite the urge that cried out for him to do just that. He knew he could and would have if he hadn't believed it would bring tears to her eyes and force her to turn away from him.

Their conversation was short and only covered what was necessary for the completion of their tasks. By the time the sun was clearing the horizon, they were again on their way.

Their last stop would be at midday, and by the time the sun was again nearing the horizon, they would find Cole's camp.

The ground began to swell, rising in ridges that required more and more effort from their horses. In some spots it became necessary to lead their mounts over the gully-filled terrain. Both horses had strained to crest the particularly rugged ridge of a grass-covered mound when something unknown frightened Summer's horse. It jerked, pranced, whinnied, then rose on hind legs as if terrified. Taken by surprise, Summer found it impossible to control her horse, even though she was an excellent rider. It bucked in terror and then suddenly both it and Summer were tumbling into the ravine.

Summer screamed once as she and the horse crashed to the ground. Sebastian leapt from his horse with Summer's name on his lips and raced down the edge of the ravine after them. He came to a thumping halt at the bottom.

The horse tried to stagger to its feet, but it was impossible. Its foreleg had been broken. Fear struck Sebastian, not because of the horse, but because Summer lay very still on the ground.

He raced to her side, murmuring her name as he dropped to his knees beside her. He could have wept with relief when he saw she was breathing. But her eyes were closed.

Gently he checked her, his hands moving over her body and down each arm and leg. He was relieved to find that no bones were broken, but it frightened him to think that something might be damaged within. There was a bruise on her temple that was dark and ugly.

Very gently he gathered her into his arms and carried her to the only flat place close by. Beneath a particularly ragged tree, he laid her on a small patch of grass-covered earth.

Her breathing was even and slow, but his own heart was pumping rapidly. His trembling hand brushed away the dirt from her face, then held hers as he whispered her name.

"Summer . . . Summer."

She groaned once, then her eyes fluttered open. Sebastian shook with relief, for they seemed to be clear and to know who he was.

The notion sprang into his mind that he would much rather have taken the fall himself, for he could hardly bear the thought that she might have been killed.

"Sebastian," she groaned in a ragged whisper. "What happened?"

"You took one hell of a fall."

She tried to rise, but he took her by the shoulders and held her firmly.

"Don't even try it. That was a nasty fall. We're camping right here until I'm sure you are all right."

"But . . . we must—"

"We must do nothing until I'm sure you're all right. You scared a year of my life out of me." He laughed shakily. "You owe it to me to keep still until I get my heart beating normally again."

She was about to speak again when her horse whinnied in pain and fear.

"My horse," she cried.

"Lie still. I'll take care of it." Sebastian was sure of what he would find and knew the animal would have to be put out of its misery.

Summer closed her eyes as the shot echoed through the canyons. Tears stung her lids and she remained quiet when Sebastian returned, drawing his horse behind him, and set about making camp.

By the time he had cared for his horse, built a fire, and made Summer comfortable with her blanket under her and his folded beneath her head, she was already feeling better. Even the slight headache she had experienced was disappearing.

"Sebastian, I am all right. We can go on."

"We're not going anywhere until tomorrow morning," he said firmly. "That fall was rough. You need to get some rest."

"But Cole—"

"Will wait until I get there." His eyes grew serious. "Summer, relax. I . . . I don't want anything to happen to you. I'd never forgive myself. Besides"—he smiled to relieve the tension of his words—"if Hawk found out that you got hurt and that I pushed you, he would get mighty upset with me. I, for one, don't want to be responsible for anything happening to you. And I know Hawk's not too happy with me right now as it is."

Summer smiled and Sebastian was pleased. She was in no pain. Because of her youth and good health, she seemed to have survived the fall well. Now he had to keep her still for awhile to make sure.

He sat down beside her.

"Hungry?"

She shook her head negatively.

"Thirsty?"

Again he saw a negative shake. He watched her closely and realized that the shock of what had happened was just beginning to register on her nerves. She began to shiver as if she had suddenly become very cold.

He had nothing left to cover her with. Despite the fact that he knew she was going to resist, he moved closer, easing himself down beside her. He gathered her close to him and, wrapping his arms about her, he cuddled her close. Her body stiffened in sudden resistance.

"Shh, be still. You need to be warm, and there're no more blankets. Lie still. I'm just going to keep you warm. Summer," he whispered softly against her hair, "just let me hold you. Relax. It will be all right . . .

don't be afraid." His voice softened even more as he realized he was weak with relief and at the same time filled with joy that he was holding her close and she was not hurt.

Very slowly her shivering ceased and he could feel her body relax against his. Her breathing grew slower and more steady and he knew she slept. Her head rested against his chest and he held her, feeling a new kind of peace.

He lay still and let her sleep, enjoying the feel of her in his arms. How well her slight body fit to his, he thought, as if she had been meant to be a part of him.

He tried to resurrect Kate from his memory and was shaken to find that he couldn't. He reached in desperation for all the well-laid plans he had made and found a void that seemed to be waiting to be filled with something new and much more lasting than anything he had planned before.

It was long past midday when Summer began to stir. She opened her eyes to find herself resting against Sebastian. She could hear the solid beat of his heart. He was very still and she didn't know if he slept or not, but she felt so warm and so secure that she didn't want to move.

She liked the feel of his hard, muscular body as it pressed against the length of hers. She would have this time, she told herself, and when he left her for his blue-eyed Kate and his beautiful home, she would have something to remember.

They lay together in silence, both wrapped in their own silent thoughts. It was some time before each became aware that the other was no longer asleep.

Slowly she tilted her head up and their eyes met.

Hope surged through her, a desperate kind of hope. Now he would tell her he loved her and that what they could share could be bigger and stronger than all the

189

illusions he had had.

She wanted him . . . and he knew it.

She couldn't seem to draw her gaze from his. His jade eyes seemed to burn into hers, mesmerizing her, holding her captive as he slowly bent his head to touch her lips with his.

She moaned from the depths of her desire like a primitive animal. He took her mouth with a gentleness that caused a stir of something hot and savage in the very depths of her soul. It was a lingering, melting kiss that seemed to stop her heart.

All logic told her not to succumb again, that her weakness for him was deadly. But her body would not listen to logic. It was burning now for him to take her, to lift her to that plane of pleasure to which only he could carry her.

He saw the war in her eyes, but he knew that he would not, could not, release her. He wanted her surrender, her willing surrender. He wanted her to know and share with him the power and exhilaration they had experienced together before.

He heard her whimper as his lips released hers. His breathing was harsh in her ear and matched her own rapid panting.

She grew dizzy with the flood of rapture that swept through her as he touched her cheeks and closed her eyes with gentle kisses. She was powerless to stop it, this flaming desire that grew into a blinding tempest. His kisses were tearing from her all resistance. The path of his seeking mouth led him down the slim column of her throat to linger tantalizingly on her harshly beating pulse.

Her heart hammered frantically against her ribs like a caged bird seeking escape as his tongue parted her lips to explore the warm hollows of her mouth, then left it to seek more sensitive areas of her warming flesh.

"Summer . . . Summer," he whispered as she slid her fingers through his thick burnished gold hair and drew his mouth to hers again.

His hands pushed aside the soft buckskin and she helped him to remove the rest of her clothes. Then he reached out to touch her soft flesh and neither could contain a murmur of pleasure at the naked contact.

His hands were hot against her body, and she gasped as they sought and rediscovered every inch of her. They stroked until she quivered, until rippling tides of rapture carried her higher and higher.

His mouth was like molten fire as it seared her flesh, capturing its softness between his teeth with savage gentleness.

"Sebastian," she moaned, "love me." It was a plaintive cry.

"I do," he whispered. "I do."

He was within her then, and it was a savage yet glorious possession. She wanted him with all that she was or ever would be, and she took him within her body, moving with his, seeking and accepting with a fury that consumed them both.

She cried out against this giving of her body without the promise of more. She cried out against it, but she could not control it.

Suddenly the universe seemed to burst within her in a cataclysmic explosion that sent brilliant streaks of ecstasy through her body and left her clinging to Sebastian as he was clinging to her.

Neither spoke; neither had the ability. They lay still until their pounding pulses slowed and their breathing returned to normal.

Had she begged for him to love her, he wondered in silence, or had it been something he had wished to hear.

Had he told her that he loved her? her mind cried out. Had he said words of passion as he had possessed her or was her mind inventing things she had not heard at all?

He held her close, his one arm about her and the other gently stroking her still-trembling flesh. He was savoring the feeling of sweet euphoria he felt each time he made love to her. It was then he perceived a new and very startling fact. He had never felt this way with any other woman, even Kate. The aftermath of loving her had been empty. With Summer it was fulfilling, precious.

He felt tears against his skin and knew she wept. He knew the barrier of Kate stood between them—Kate and Summer's belief that he was only using her as a surrogate until he could bring Kate here to share the rest of his life with her.

Sebastian also knew that Summer fought her feelings for him, would deny them until he could show her he cared. The only way he could do that was to abandon this quest and take Summer to his land. He would rebuild his house and ask her to stay with him.

He wondered how his parents would feel if he married an Indian princess. And he knew it would be a long, hard journey from realization to convincing Summer. As long as the threat of Kate stood between them, it would be hard to make Summer believe he cared for her more than as just a quick tumble. There was only one way, for words would never do it. She had denied his words before and would do so again, just as she had tried her best to deny the fact that they were caught in a magic neither knew how to—or really wanted to—escape.

He sighed deeply. They would have to go on the way they had been until they reached Cole. Then he would take her back to the village and ask her to come and see the land where he had left the shell of his home. Then he would ask her if she could ever be happy living in a white man's house, away from her people—and with him. Everything would then depend on her answer.

Summer heard his sigh and wondered if his thoughts had already left her and fled to the always hovering ghost of Kate. The idea twisted within her, but her determination began to grow. Why should she weep? He was in her arms, not his precious Kate's. He was here, and maybe his heart would change; maybe, if she chose, she could erase the memory of Kate. But was it just that? Could Sebastian accept the fact of her Indian ancestry? She was sure that if she told him who she really was, there would be no question, but she didn't want it that way.

She had to admit she wanted him, that he could set her world ablaze with passion and master her senses, but it was not enough. Her hunger for him went deeper. Would she ever be able to reach within his heart and find a place that was only hers?

Summer sat up and Sebastian did the same immediately. Her head was lowered and he couldn't see her face. One hand cupped her chin and lifted her head. With his other hand he gently brushed the tears from her cheeks.

"Tears, Summer?" he said softly. "I never mean to make you cry. Why does it always seem to end in tears?"

"Perhaps," she replied, "because it does end, and we have to face reality. Because we both know that this time cannot last forever. We must both return to our own worlds—separate worlds—in which there is no room for the other."

"Why must it end? Why can't it stay like this between

us? We share something very special and I don't want to let go of it."

He was speaking of the future, of making a new life together and working out their difficulties. That was why he was so startled when her eyes grew angry and she drew away from him sharply.

In her mind he was asking her to be his mistress, to share what they had for as long as they could. She did not hear an offer of love; that he seemed to be saving for the woman who always lingered on the edge of his mind. He was offering her the crumbs from the table after he had shared the feast with another.

With a cry that was half anger, half pain, she moved away from him. Her eyes sparkled with a smoldering anger that took Sebastian by surprise.

"I told you once before, Sebastian, I am no man's mistress."

"Summer," he began, "you're twisting my words again."

But Summer's defenses had risen once more. He would lie to her, she assumed, and she would not be foolish enough to believe the lies. He wanted her—that she knew. And she also knew that the heat of his desire could completely destroy her will.

She longed for the words that would change everything, and again the thought intruded into her mind that Sebastian could be hers if she fought for him.

Sebastian reached out and pulled her into his arms. When he chose to hold her this way there was no way to fight him, so she remained still. But her gaze soundlessly spoke volumes and he did not misunderstand any of its meaning.

"Why do we continually have to fight, Summer? Unless you lie, and I don't think you do, you feel what I feel when we touch. Look at me now and tell me it's not the same for you, that you don't share what I feel, that you don't want me as much as I desire you."

She was suddenly blinded by rage. Her mind screamed, Want you . . . desire you . . . you want me—is that all you can say to me?

She twisted in his arms, pressing her hands against his chest. "Always the same words!" she cried aloud. "Wants and desires! It means nothing to me— nothing!"

"Nothing?" he ground out roughly as his arms tightened about her. "Are you telling me that this has all been nothing? I don't believe it, and neither do you. Why do you try to deceive both of us?"

"I deceive no one," she argued as she tried to free herself from his grip. "I do not try to convince myself that you feel any more than lust and the need to bed someone who is convenient when you cannot have the one you truly want."

"That is the largest of all deceptions, Summer," he said softly. "And it is your deception alone. I want you, that is true, but not in place of anyone else." His voice grew mild and soft, which meant, though she could not know it, that Sebastian's temper was rising.

"You have forced me to your will."

"Another deception!" he retorted. He drew her even tighter to him and his eyes blazed with a wicked glow. "What force exists between us is a mutual force. It draws me the same as it does you."

"No," she whispered in vain.

His lips very gently brushed hers. "Yes," he breathed against her mouth, "yes. And there is no way for either of us to fight it." Again his lips were gentle against her cheek. "Summer"—he whispered her name as his lips burned against the soft velvet skin of her throat—"you will never accept what I truly want to say. There is only one way and that is to prove to you with my own method that what is between us is very rare and very precious. And I don't intend to lose you. What I want to prove I will prove, in time. Until then, you will admit to me and to yourself that you want me just as I want you."

"No," she gasped, aware that her breath was quickening and the same nerve-shattering heat was building within her.

"Sebastian, please . . . let me go. Can't you try to understand?"

"Oh, but I do, my sweet, maybe for the first time in a long time. I just don't think you do. But I promise you it won't be long until you know and accept the truth for what it is—that you belong to me."

"It cannot be this way, Sebastian. This can prove nothing."

He smiled into her eyes. Holding her with one strong arm, he gently brushed a wayward strand of hair from her cheek.

"You are still a very stubborn and determined woman. But you most surely are one of a kind."

"I would not doubt that you have said the same words to your blue-eyed woman," she snapped.

"You seem to know an awful lot about Kate." He chuckled and amusement glittered in his eyes. "I will be the first to admit that Kate is one of a kind too. But doesn't that sound a little like jealousy on your part, Summer?"

"She can have you," Summer stormed. "You are arrogant, self-centered, and conceited. You think all you need do is smile and every woman within a mile will desire you."

"Maybe so," he whispered. He still held her bound and, despite her struggles, he deliberately took her mouth in a deep, penetrating kiss.

196

She fought, uselessly, and felt herself slipping into the net of his passion. A rough moan escaped her. As abruptly as the kiss had begun, he released her and stood up. She looked up at him in absolute surprise.

"No force, Summer," he said softly. "But I will tell you this. One day soon you will come to me."

"Not on your terms, Sebastian—never!"

## Chapter Eighteen

Cole had separated from Sebastian and had begun to track slowly, watching for any signs of old camps or of riders who did not belong to Hawk's village.

It would be several days until he met Sebastian at their arranged rendezvous by the river.

He wasn't too sure whether he wanted to find any signs or not. He sighed deeply, wondering if time could ease Sebastian's guilt and make him change his plans. Cole would have liked to have seen Sebastian go back and rebuild his home and make a new start.

Cole's life had been so insecure and unstable that he had admired and adapted to Sebastian and Nathaniel's close relationship quickly. Born in this wildneress to a trapper and his young wife who had died at Cole's birth, Cole had been left with a strange sense of guilt himself and the inability to find a place to set down roots.

His father, grief stricken at the loss of his wife, had been a silent ghost of a man who had cared for his young son in an absent and rather careless way. Warm, close relationships had never been part of Cole's formative years, and he had been filled with a hunger for something for which he had no name.

Hired as a guide by Sebastian and Nathaniel, he had been more than pleased. The relationship had begun to grow, and they had encouraged him to settle down, offering him a small piece of their own land since his finances had not allowed him to buy property for himself.

He had felt the blow of Nathaniel's death almost as deeply as Sebastian, but he had known he would have to keep some control. Mostly it was because he was afraid for Sebastian, who had become the closest thing to a brother he had ever had.

Used to being alone, Cole often kept up a dialogue with himself. In his youth, it had been an outlet in the wilderness, for his father had left him alone much of the time and had been silent when they were together except when he was teaching Cole the rudiments of survival.

"I sure as hell wish something could come along to change Sebastian's way of thinking," he mused aloud. He reached down and patted his horse's neck, convincing himself that the horse was listening attentively and that he was not really talking to himself.

"I don't know if I got the stomach for killin', even if we do find them . . . and to tell the truth, I don't think Sebastian can kill in cold blood either."

His thoughts went to Summer. If Sebastian could only see that she was something utterly different, that she was more a part of this land he loved than was the woman who had refused to come with Sebastian.

Nathaniel had told Cole much about Kate, enough for Cole to know that, if she did come, there would be no place on Sebastian's land for him. Kate had struck him as a greedy woman who wanted everything for herself alone and no one else.

"That kind of woman could kill everything in Sebastian that was worth a grain of salt. Why in the hell

199

don't he look at Summer without that Kate standin' between them? Maybe we'd be able to get off this wretched trail. I know it's gonna be hard for Sebastian to accept Nathaniel's death, but there's a time for grievin' and a time for livin'. Nathaniel would be the last one to want Sebastian all tied in knots like he's been. He was a kid who enjoyed life, and he'd be the one to tell Sebastian to find another way."

Still contemplating the situation, Cole made a stop for a midday meal so that he could rest for a short while. Then he was on his way again, eyes glued to the ground and the area about him for any small sign.

That night he made his first camp. Whistling lightly to himself, he unpacked, built a fire, and made a bed from his saddle and blanket. He ate and settled back, hands clasped behind his head, to admire the star-filled night sky.

They twinkled as dark clouds skittered across them. In the far distance, just past the horizon, he saw flashes of lightning.

"Somebody somewhere is gettin' a hell of a storm," he said aloud. "Sure glad it's there and not here. I'm in no mood to be soaked."

He rolled in his blanket and the soft rumble of distant thunder was the last sound he heard as he drifted off to sleep.

The dawn found him again on the move. He knew this land, had traveled it often with his father. He could name every hill, stream, and river in the territory, and often by their Indian names. He loved the country. He wished fervently that Sebastian would find his way so they could build something fine in this wild and beautiful place.

He thought it interesting that he could envision Sebastian and Summer building here, but he could not see the woman Nathaniel had described being part of this vast, free wilderness, for none of the pleasures he found here could be purchased with money. Never having had more than a few dollars to his name at any given time, Cole had found his pleasures in the people and the land. He could not imagine the extravagances he had been told Kate would demand.

The midday stop was again short. He guessed there would not be much of any importance to tell Sebastian except that wherever the men were, they were not anywhere along the trail Cole followed.

He prayed Sebastian would not run across them either. He wasn't too sure Sebastian would not attack all four of them single-handed. In fact, it worried Cole that Sebastian might expect the two of them to attack the four when they found them.

If Sebastian were to ask his advice—and Cole was pretty sure he wouldn't—he would tell him to leave justice to the ones who held this territory—the Indians. He was sure Hawk would do what needed to be done, since renegades had penetrated his area and killed there.

Not missing the beauty surrounding him, Cole watched sharply for any remote sign, but there was nothing.

He moved at a slow and steady pace for the balance of that day, made camp again that night beneath the branches of a tree, and was up early to resume his search.

He had traveled for almost the entire day when he came to a large outcropping of rock the Indians had always called the Devil's Elbow. It was difficult terrain to cross, so he skirted it, wondering why the hairs on the back of his neck prickled and he felt the strange sensation of something akin to the spiritual presence the Indians always spoke of.

The close of the day found him at the rendezvous

point where he would again join with Sebastian. He supposed, since they had traveled within a somewhat triangular area with the river as a base, they would now begin to crisscross the area until they turned up something concrete. He felt tired just thinking about it.

When he reached the bend in the river that he had marked on the small map Sebastian had given him, he prepared another camp. If his calculations were correct, Sebastian would be along in a very short time.

The sun set, and Cole was mildly surprised that Sebastian had not yet arrived. The moon rose and stars began to appear one after another in a rapidly blackening sky.

Where was Sebastian? He knew Sebastian would most likely be traveling more slowly since he did not know the area as well. He would be patient. If Sebastian were making camp now, it would be the next day before he arrived. Realizing this, Cole drifted off into comfortable sleep.

When he rose again, he found he would have to do some hunting if he wanted anything to eat for the day. Besides, he didn't like the idea of just sitting around and doing nothing. He left all his gear at the camp so Sebastian would know he was around if he were to come when Cole was gone. Taking his gun, he mounted his horse and headed toward the Devil's Elbow. He assumed he would easily find game there since it was an area seldom frequented. The Indians were superstitious about the legends that it was an evil place, and the white man was so scarce in the territory that few knew much about it.

As Cole rode, the ground began to rise. The thought crossed his mind that the Devil's Elbow would be a good place for a running man to hide. The land rose into a double-peaked area, each peak being flat on the top, and there was a plateau in the center several miles

202

wide that was shallow and grassy, with large stands of trees.

He moved his horse very slowly so he would not frighten any game he might see. He had left his horse unshod as the Indians did, and it moved on nearly silent feet. It might have been the reason Cole saw the fine wisps of a smokeless fire before anyone noticed his presence.

He stopped and dismounted. A smokeless fire told him one thing for certain—whoever it was, there were Indians among them. Very few white men knew what to burn that would give off very little smoke.

Slowly, cautiously, and on expertly silent feet, Cole edged his way toward the area from which the smoke was rising. It was just over the next small hill, so he went down on hands and knees and crept silently to the top to peer over. When he did, he was shocked by what he saw.

It was the same four men. There was not one drop of doubt in his mind. Their faces had been so thoroughly etched in his mind that he could not have forgotten even if he had tried. Two Indians, two whites—the same four that had tried to kill him and Sebastian and had killed Nathaniel.

There was no doubt also that they had begun to break camp. He wanted to know if it was a permanent break or whether they returned here often.

As he watched, they extinguished the fire and mounted already-loaded horses. Each man led another pack horse behind. They were moving away permanently. If they had not been, they would have built a temporary enclosure for the pack horses and left some of their gear behind.

Cole watched them as they rode out of sight, then soundlessly he moved down into the now vacant camp.

After a much closer examination, he could tell that

they had returned more than once to this area. But he had no way of telling if they planned on returning again soon. He stood in the center of the camp and contemplated his dilemma.

He had recognized them, the Indian with the three red feathers in his hair and the two villainous-looking whites. But should he tell Sebastian? Could he keep this to himself and hope that time would ease Sebastian's pain and set him on a new course?

If he told Sebastian, then he would have to bring him here and the hunt would be intensified. He walked back to his horse deep in thought and rode back to his camp.

Expecting to see Sebastian already there, he was surprised to find it still empty. Now he began to worry. Had Sebastian run across some kind of trouble? Was he lost?

Cole knew that if he tried to find Sebastian they might cross each other's path and they might not. In this vast country, the chances were they would miss each other. There was no other way but to wait a while longer.

After he tethered his horse, he lay down beneath the shade of a tree. Hands clasped behind his head, he turned his thoughts to what he would say to Sebastian when he arrived.


Sebastian refused to move from their camp until the next morning. He insisted that Summer rest and regain her strength. She argued with him, but he would just grin irritatingly and say that since it was his horse they would have to ride, he would tell her when they would go.

By the time dawn came, Summer was already awake and had their belongings packed. She had discarded much of what she had brought because Sebastian's horse would be weighed down enough carrying both of them. This thought had driven her to another very distracting one. She would have to ride double with him, the last thing in the world she really wanted to do. Sebastian seemed amused by the idea, which annoyed her even more.

Once all their equipment was seen to, Sebastian mounted his horse. Then he leaned down and extended his hand to her. There was a glint of humor in his eyes as he asked, "Do you want to ride in front or in back?"

Both possibilities were upsetting to her. She would have to cling to him if she rode behind, and he would have his arm about her if she rode in front.

"In back," she snapped and heard his soft chuckle as she gripped his hand and placed her foot in the stirrup while he effortlessly swung her up behind him.

Her arms encircled his waist and she could feel the hard, rigid muscle of his back as she pressed against him.

He kicked his horse into motion and her arms tightened reflexively as they jolted forward. To Summer the ride seemed interminable. Riding behind Sebastian was most uncomfortable, but what annoyed her the most was that she thought Sebastian knew it and was doing nothing to make the ride easier.

By the time they stopped, the sun was high and hot. Summer's flesh was moist with perspiration and she could happily have struck him with a sharp blade when she saw the suspicion of a smile in his eyes as he let her slide to the ground.

She refused to eat and sat stubbornly while he took his time doing so. But when he finally decided he was ready to go, she groaned inwardly at the thought of getting up behind him again.

Sebastian mounted, but before Summer could swing

up behind him, he reached down and scooped her up in his arms to settle her before him. She refused to give him the satisfaction of fighting him, for she knew he could hold her and, she thought, it was certainly much more comfortable.

Without a word, Sebastian again urged the horse forward.

His arm about her was strong and comfortable and after a short while she relaxed completely against him.

Soon she grew drowsy and her head dropped to his chest. Sebastian smiled and drew her close. He chuckled to himself, musing that it was much better to hold her when she slept and was not so obstinate.

He looked down on her serene face. "Summer," he whispered as he brushed a light kiss against her hair, "will you ever believe? Will you ever understand that I plan to give up a lot to have you?"

She stirred restlessly and he eased her into a more comfortable position. He smiled to himself. *If she knew how good she felt in my arms and how much I would like to make love to her right now, she would be spitting fire and brimstone.* It was going to be some job, he reflected, trying to convince her that the house he wanted to build would be a good place for a girl who was raised in a tipi.

He wondered about her past, about the trapper father who had tried to turn a young, fiery Indian girl into a lady. He expected that one day he would meet him, but he hoped by the time he did Summer would have become somewhat more agreeable.

He knew he would have to get past the barrier of her distrust of men, white ones in particular. Also, he would have to get through her resistance to him. He did not relish the idea of having to do battle every time he wanted her. Besides, he mused, it would be even more exciting if he could convince her to come to him.

He thought about his own determination during these past weeks. He thought of Nathaniel. Cole had been right. Hawk and his warriors were the best ones to find his killers. He would still see that they paid for what had happened, but he would try to concentrate now on building something from the ashes of what the two of them had begun.

It was only then that his thoughts turned to Kate. For the first time he began to compare Kate to Summer. The discovery he made was so profound that he couldn't quite believe it.

Kate, around whom he had built his dreams, had not wanted to leave the luxury and wealth she had been promised. But Summer had given even when her mind had told her she could get hurt; she had had enough compassion to help him attain his goals and had even sacrificed her own pride to see him have what she thought he truly wanted.

He tightened his arm about her at the thought, and Summer stirred awake. She immediately stiffened and pulled herself erect.

Ah well, he sighed to himself, the war begins again. But at least this time he had more ammunition with which to fight. As far as he was concerned, Summer was about to enter into the most difficult battle she had ever fought. And he would win, he thought with a laugh, because he couldn't afford not to. There was too much at stake.

Cole had begun to worry, for there was still no sign of Sebastian when the sun began to go down. He was a day overdue now. He knew Sebastian was a capable man, and that he, Cole, just couldn't go off running about a territory as big as this and expect to find him.

He went to his fire and dropped down on one knee to

stir it to life. He certainly couldn't sleep, and he figured the brighter the fire the more likely Sebastian would be to see it.

"Damnit, Sebastian," he grunted as he rose to his feet and dusted off his hands. He gazed about him. Shadows were lengthening and the sun was almost below the horizon.

He returned to his blanket and sat down with an exasperated groan. His patience was growing very thin.

The sun disappeared and the darkness closed about the pale light of his fire.

It was then that the sound of an approaching horse brought him to his feet. He watched the outer circle of darkness and soon a darker shadow formed from the darkness.

"Sebastian?"

"Yes, it's me."

"Well, damnit man, it's about time you got here. Where the hell have you been anyhow? I been worried out of ten years."

He would have said a lot more, but at that moment Sebastian's horse entered the circle of firelight.

Cole stared in amazement. This was such a total surprise that he could not speak. Summer!

Questions on the tip of his tongue were stifled, for he realized he should get Sebastian aside to ask him to relate how this strange turn of events had occurred.

"Cole"—Sebastian laughed, knowing just how eaten with curiosity Cole was—"I hope you have something to eat. Summer and I haven't eaten since the sun was high."

"Yes," Cole replied in a stunned voice. "I've been hunting today. There's some fresh meat."

Summer smiled gratefully and walked past Cole toward the fire. Cole glared at Sebastian and dropped his voice to an angry whisper.

"Are you crazy! Where did she come from? I thought you left the village alone. Good God, Hawk will skin you alive for this."

"Don't get so excited, Cole. I didn't take her from the village. She followed me."

"Don't grin so cocky," Cole argued. "I sure as hell bet it wasn't your charm got her to do that. And your charm sure isn't going to work on Hawk."

"I don't think so either," Sebastian replied. "And if you stop getting so worked up I'll tell you about our change of plans."

"Our?"

"Well . . . mine anyhow."

"Just what kind of a 'change of plans'?" Cole asked suspiciously.

"We're going back, Cole," Sebastian said gently.

"Going back?"

"Back to rebuild . . . to start over."

Cole found that what he was hearing was just too good to believe. "And . . . ?"

"And we'll get Hawk and his men to help find the renegades and bring them to some kind of justice."

"This is about the best thing I've heard for a long time."

"I'm . . . I'm taking Summer to my land first. I want her to see it."

"I don't understand any of this, Sebastian. But I kind of get the idea that you and Summer are not exactly seeing eye to eye."

"Hardly," Sebastian answered dryly.

"Tell me"—Cole laughed—"what do you think you're going to do when Hawk gets hold of you?"

"Try to explain before he gets a chance to run his war lance through me."

"Explain what?"

"Explain that there is nothing he can do about me

209

and Summer."

"I didn't know there was a you and Summer."

"I think"—Sebastian laughed—"that I'm the only one who knows there is, but give me time, my friend. First I have to convince her . . . then Hawk . . . then her elusive family."

"Is that all?"

"I've skirted barriers before. I'll get around this one. One way or another."

"Friend," Cole replied, "when you climb mountains, you really climb mountains, don't you?"

Sebastian was about to answer when his eyes were drawn to Summer, who was illuminated by the firelight as she prepared her blanket for sleeping.

Sebastian watched Summer, and Cole kept his eyes on Sebastian. Cole smiled, and there was no doubt left in his mind that Kate Maxwell and revenge had left Sebastian's thoughts and heart and that Summer had filled both.

When they returned to the fire, it became just as obvious that Summer's feelings did not, at the moment, run along the same path as Sebastian's.

Cole listened as Summer told him that she had decided to help, that she had felt her powers could sense when the renegades were near. He knew for certain as she spoke that Sebastian had not yet told her any of his new plans.

He watched the spark of something wild and strong leap between them. To Cole, it seemed that Summer had built some kind of wall around herself and was refusing Sebastian entrance until she was able to control her emotions. Cole was also amused that Sebastian had suddenly developed a cautious patience, as if he were setting himself up for some kind of violent confrontation.

When Summer and Sebastian had rolled in their

blankets to sleep, Cole again sat by the fire deep in thought.

It would be something to watch, he told himself. Sebastian had met his match in Summer. It should be, he thought, an interesting time . . . a very interesting time.

# Chapter Nineteen

Kate Maxwell and Elenora Gregory were kindred spirits. They knew it as instinctively as the tides of the ocean knew the magnetic pull of the moon.

Kate had arrived and had been made welcome by Elenora and in the week that she had been there, she and Elenora had conversed extensively. It had not taken either long to understand the other.

The ruthless knew their own kind, and both women were feline predators that would go to any extent to get what they wanted. For Elenora it was Clay Storm, and for Kate it was Sebastian Cain. What they did not know at this time was that their desires had a common denominator—Summer.

It was nearing the noon hour when each rose. Both were late sleepers and refused to be disturbed until long after the sun had reached its heights. Now they sat together over breakfast and talked of their plans.

"You have heard nothing from Sebastian since he was so foolish as to leave you and all that money?" Elenora questioned.

"No, nothing. But I do know what his plans were. He was bound to build his fortune in the new country. His family has some wealth, but not nearly as much as

George so conveniently left me. I have to let Sebastian know that all his struggles are unnecessary. I have a great deal of money now, enough for both of us to live very well. All I need to do is find out exactly where his land is and go there."

"Miles will have your answers when he gets here this afternoon," Elenora said, then her eyes narrowed. "If you couldn't keep him in England, how do you suppose to hold him now? Surely he does not intend to go back?"

Kate smiled a knowing smile. "Sebastian," she said softly, "is in love with me. As far as he was concerned, it was only George, my husband, who stood between us. He begged me to go with him, but I had worked too hard to get all that money to let it slip through my fingers. George is dead now, and I am free. Once I am with him, I can get Sebastian to do what I want. In time we will return to the society in which people of our wealth and position belong."

"You're very sure." Elenora smiled.

Kate laughed lightly. "I pleased him before and I will please him again. Once he is back in my bed, I shall never let him escape."

"It seems you enjoyed him as much as he did you. Is he worth all this effort? There are many men."

Kate's eyes half closed in remembered passion. She pressed one hand gently on the flesh of her throat and let it drift slowly down to the soft skin above the low-cut morning gown she wore. It was a gesture that bespoke the heated memories she carried.

"There is no man like Sebastian," she explained breathlessly. "I want him, have wanted him for a long time. I have even committed . . . I have done what I have had to do to get him. I will have him and nothing will stand in my way. Nothing . . . and nobody."

This fierce passion was something Elenora under-

213

stood quite well. Although Miles was in her life for expediency, it was Clay Storm for whom she had always yearned. She could taste the success she would have when Sabrina was gone. She and Clay would renew what they once had shared. And this time she would not let him go.

"We are two of a kind, you and I," Elenora whispered. "We know what we want and we are not afraid to go out and get it. I do not see why we cannot be a great help to each other."

"It is a very stupid and cowardly person who does not take what he wants from the world. I have no sympathy for the mealymouthed do-gooders who allow the things they want to slip through their fingers because someone might get hurt," Kate replied.

Elenora laughed and was about to agree with her when the door opened and Miles came in. She held out a hand to Miles with a seductive smile. "Miles, come and join us for breakfast."

"Breakfast?" He chuckled. "Sorry, I've already eaten both breakfast and lunch. In fact, I have been about the business of finding out about your friend, Mr. Cain." He spoke the words to Kate, but his eyes were still on Elenora. "It seems the Cain property you are interested in is about three day's ride from here. Quite a distance for a woman to travel. Would you like me to tell Mr. Cain you are here? I'm sure I can send someone with the message."

"No. I want to surprise him. I want someone to take me there. Can you?"

"Why yes, of course I can, but are you quite sure? It's pretty rugged country out there. Besides"—his eyes turned again to Elenora—"it seems your land borders on the land of a friend of Elenora's."

"Oh really? Well then, Sebastian and I will have neighbors."

Both Elenora and Miles laughed. "Hardly," Miles explained. "I said the properties had a mutual border; that is so. But the distance between . . . Clay Storm's home"—he winked at Elenora—"and Sebastian Cain's is almost three day's journey. There is no such thing as close neighbors out there."

"Ah, well"—Kate laughed—"I should like to have Sebastian all to myself for awhile anyway. How soon can we make some arrangements to go? I'm so excited to be able to find him so easily."

"All right. If you still want to go, I must have a day or so to get a wagon and supplies together. We can leave . . . say . . . day after tomorrow. But," he added with a smile, "it will have to be early in the morning. One does not travel about this country at night. He might run across some not-too-friendly natives."

"Indians—" Elenora translated to a wide-eyed Kate, "most of whom are quite friendly."

Kate gulped. "You mean there are some who are not?"

"Mostly west of Black Cloud's village," Elenora answered.

"You needn't worry," Miles broke in. "I have a few well-chosen men, and I"—he lowered his voice to a smooth warmth—"shall be delighted to be with you and protect you from . . . whatever dangers might frighten you."

Kate smiled, Miles absorbed it with pleasure, and Elenora's eyes smoldered as her mind schemed. Kate could not go unaccompanied into the wilderness, but Miles would not go without Elenora, who was no man's fool. She thought to herself that Miles would have to be carefully watched, and she intended to do just that.

"That is a very good idea, Miles," Elenora said sweetly as she tucked an arm through his and pressed

215

her ample breasts close. "I do believe I shall go with you. We can stop and introduce Kate to the Storms. I would like to see Clay . . . and his pretty wife again."

Miles said nothing to either woman, but he laughed to himself. Elenora was a bitch, a jealous and greedy bitch, he mused, and she would require very careful watching.

"I'll make preparations. Pack as little as possible. A wagon will not carry much since we have to have room to sleep in it. I'll be here to pick you up the day after tomorrow."

He kissed Kate's hand and lightly brushed his tongue across her knuckles. She knew the look in his eye quite well. He was handsome and she would not have been adverse to spending a night or so alone with him in the wilderness.

"You needn't worry about how early it is," Elenora supplied. "I will be going with you and I will see that everything is ready when you get here."

"Why, Elenora," Miles said with a smile that irritated her, "You are very considerate."

"Thank you, Miles," Elenora dripped sweetly. "I wouldn't miss this reunion for anything."

The retort on Miles's lips was left unsaid, but Elenora, to her pleasure, could read it in his eyes as he turned to leave.

Elenora turned back to Kate.

"Come, let us see what we can pack. I'm sure you want a few . . . alluring things for this reunion."

They were both laughing as they climbed the stairs together.


The wagon left town just after daybreak. It held the two women and a driver, and Miles and another man rode alongside it.

The wagon moved slowly and Elenora and Kate

216

were given a lot of time to look about them, but the beauty of the area was lost on both women, who preferred more expensive trappings to the quiet splendor displayed about them.

Miles knew exactly where Sebastian's home was located, and he had studied the maps so well that he had no problem in traveling in a very nearly straight line, which did not bring him close enough to Clay's home to see it.

They were in for a complete surprise when they came upon the spot where Sebastian's home should have stood.

The wagon was still, drawn to a halt at Miles's command. He rode close to the wagon to talk to the two shocked women.

Below them sat the shell of a house. The roof was completely gone as were several sections of walls. The rest was blackened by the fire that had so obviously destroyed it.

"Sebastian!" Kate cried. "My God, what has happened?"

"Fairly obvious," Elenora said. "Those savages have burned his house."

Miles smiled. It was not necessarily savages, he thought to himself.

It was then that they noticed movement within the blackened walls.

"There's someone there," Kate cried.

"Wait here." Miles spoke quickly. He motioned to the rider beside him. The two rode ahead very slowly to make sure the movement within the house was not hostile.

They approached the house and minutes before they could reach it a man stepped out with a rifle in his hand.

"You fellas lookin' fer somebody?" he drawled.

"Yes," Miles said. "We are looking for Sebastian Cain."

"Well . . . you're at the right place . . . but he ain't here."

"May I ask who you are?"

"Yep," the man grinned. "You kin ask."

"Well," Miles said impatiently, "who are you and what are you doing here?"

"Name's Bean, Jake Bean. I'm a friend who's house sittin' until Sebastian gets back. I was gonna work for him and his brother, but the plans kind of got changed."

Miles sighed in exasperation and motioned for those in the wagon to join him. When they did, Kate was the first one to speak.

"Where's Sebastian . . . and who is this?"

"His name is Jake Bean. He says he was to work for Mr. Cain, but he isn't here."

"Where is he . . . and where's his brother, Nathaniel?"

Jake looked at her closely with sad eyes. "Well," he said gently, "if you're lookin' for his brother . . . he's out back."

"Well, why didn't you say that before?" Kate demanded. She spun about and was joined by the others as she walked around the house. Jake followed behind slowly.

When they reached the rear of the house, they stopped and looked about.

"Where is he?" Kate demanded of Jake.

"Well ma'am," Jake said softly as he pointed across a flat, grassy area to a tree that stood near its edge, "he be right over there."

It was then that they noticed the wooden cross that stood over earth that was still mounded from recent digging.

They walked slowly toward it and stood before the grave, the wooden marker of which read: Nathaniel

Cain, age 24.

Kate spun about. "Where is Sebastian?" she shouted. "Is he dead too? Where is he?"

"Well, if you'll let me explain, I'll tell you where he is."

They gathered about Jake, who explained what had occurred and why Sebastian had left. When he finished, Miles turned to Kate.

"I guess you'll have to stay with Elenora until he comes back."

Kate was silent for several minutes, standing very still and gazing about her. Then she turned back to Elenora and Miles.

"I am going to rebuild the house," she stated firmly. "I've more than enough money. I'm sure"—she smiled at Elenora—"that Sebastian would be very appreciative. Miles, you can see to it that I get all the men I need, can't you?"

"Yes . . . but—"

"There is enough material on this land to build a mansion, and a mansion is what I intend to build. All we need are men and the things the land won't provide. Well Miles, will you help me?"

"Of course I'll help you. It's your money."

"Yes," she replied, "it's my money. And this time it's going to buy me what I want. How soon can we get started?"

"Two days to get back and time to get the men and material. We could have the place rebuilt in a little less than a month."

"Good!" Kate laughed. "Then let's get going."

They started to walk back to the wagon and Jake watched them go, silently shaking his head. He'd known the Cain brothers for a short time, but he didn't think Sebastian would take kindly to this woman's walking in, taking over the building of his house, and making it to suit her.

Kate and Elenora walked together. "So"—Elenora laughed—"fate seems to have provided you with exactly what you needed."

"Sebastian will be grateful"—Kate smiled—"and a grateful man will be very . . . susceptible to any future plans I might have. Can you imagine how he will feel when he comes back and finds his house not only rebuilt but better than the original—and furnished?"

"And occupied." Elenora laughed again.

"Of course." Kate shrugged. "At least for awhile. I doubt very much that I'll want to live here any length of time. But I'm not worried. Sebastian will be very . . . cooperative. I'm sure he won't always want to remain in a place as dull and boring as this."

"Even if he does," Elenora replied, "I'm sure you can find some way to change his mind."

They laughed together.

After awhile, Jake stood alone, watching the disappearing wagon and wishing Sebastian would come back—soon.


Over a week passed before Jake saw the returning wagon. It was followed by three others. On the first Jake could clearly see Kate. He suspected that her two friends would be somewhere on the other wagons.

He sighed as he walked out to meet them. He hoped Sebastian would understand that he had no way of stopping what was happening. He could have driven them off for awhile, but he was sure it wouldn't have been for long. The light-haired woman had said she was Sebastian's woman; who was he to call her a liar? And besides, he argued with himself, maybe they were doing Sebastian a good turn by rebuilding his place.

He watched as they stopped before him. There were

now several additional men led by Miles. As he had thought, both women were present, and it did not take Kate long to take command and tell the workmen exactly what she wanted.

First she decided that the house, which had consisted of three rooms downstairs and two large bedrooms upstairs, was to be made larger. She insisted on another huge room downstairs and another on the second floor.

The men exchanged disbelieving glances, but they remained silent and set about their work. In this territory, the kind of house Kate was trying to create was not only out of proportion but unwieldy for the daily life of a wilderness family.

But Kate could not be told. She could only see Sebastian's gratitude and envision the nights they would spend here before she convinced him to sell the house and come with her to a much more glamorous environment.

Luke contemplated the glass of brandy sitting before him. It brought thoughts of Kate and the pleasure she had so freely offered on the journey from England. He twirled the glass gently, watching the amber liquid shimmer in the glass.

He was impatient for word of Kate. Lifting the glass, he drank and returned it to the table none too gently.

No woman walked away from Luke until he was ready to let her go, and he was not yet ready to release Kate Maxwell. He was curious, very curious about his elusive Kate.

Luke was an opportunist who was entirely too clever to let anything valuable slip from his fingers, and he suspected that Kate had value he couldn't yet measure.

He knew she must be quite wealthy and wondered if

there might be a way of sharing that wealth.

Since it was not possible for him to leave port until his cargo was unloaded and another was brought on board, he would have time to see what his beautiful Kate was up to.

At that moment there was a sharp knock on the door.

"Come in."

The opening door revealed the seaman Luke had sent to follow Kate.

"Ah, Tag. It's about time you got back. Where is she now?"

"She's staying in a home owned by a lady named Elenora Gregory."

"Did you find out about both of them?"

"Aye sir." Tag went on to explain all his eyes and ears had discovered, which was a great deal.

When Tag left, Luke knew as much about Kate and Elenora as was possible to learn. Tag had listened closely to gossip and had asked clever questions. He had even turned up the name Miles Chandler.

"So," Luke murmured thoughtfully, "what a trio we have here. Maybe, Luke my friend"—he chuckled—"there's more profit here than you imagined." He lifted the brandy glass and drained its contents.


The open-mouthed workman looked at Kate in utter disbelief. "Glass windows!" he exclaimed. "Ma'am, they just ain't practical out here. They have to be shipped in and they'd cost an arm and a leg."

"Mr. Monroe," Kate said coldly, "you have fought me every inch of the way about this house. Now I'll make it clear to you. Whether you like it or not, this house will be built the way I want it. Do I make myself clear?"

222

"But Ma'am . . ." he protested.

"No buts, Mr. Monroe. I am paying you, and you will do as I say. I want glass windows."

"Yes Ma'am," Caleb Monroe replied. He spat tobacco juice violently as he watched Kate walk away, then heard a muffled chuckle from behind him. He turned to find Jake there.

"Some woman, ain't she?" Jake remarked.

"Damn bitch," Caleb replied. "She's tryin' to build some kind of . . ." he shrugged, "I don't know. It sure don't have any place out here. If your friend is marryin' that woman, I sure as hell feel sorry for him."

"I kinda agree with you. Sebastian doesn't know she's here yet. She don't strike me as the kind of woman he'd marry. But I guess there's been stranger marriages."

"You helped him build in the first place?"

"Yep. I guess when he gets back, I'll sort of mosey on my way. I don't think I could stay around someone like her without gettin' mad enough to smack her one. I got hopes that Sebastian will be kinda shocked when he gets here. I like that boy, and I sure hate to see him tangled up with her. She'll drag him away from here before he gets a chance to put down any roots."

"Drag him away? If she wants to go, why is she building this?" He waved his hand toward something he found hard to name.

"Been fishin' lately?"

"Huh?" Caleb replied, caught unprepared by the change of subject.

"Been fishin' lately?" Jake repeated.

"Sure, why?"

"Well, I reckon if you want to catch a nice big fish, you use the best bait you can get. The better the bait and the craftier the fisherman, the more likely he is to get the fish he wants."

Caleb shook his head and Jake laughed. "I'm just hopin' Sebastian is like that crafty old granddaddy I been fishin' for."

"How's that?"

"He just slips my bait off the hook, swallows it, and swims off laughin' at me."

"Well, in this case"—Caleb grinned—"I sure hope the fish gets away."

They laughed together and went on about their work.

The house grew in proportion to the amazement and disgust of the men who worked on it. Kate was looked at from under furrowed brows, and there was not a worker present who did not dread the sound of her voice or the footsteps that told of her approach.

By the end of the month, the house was nearing completion and Kate, to the relief of everyone, returned to town to buy furniture. She would be gone while the workmen finished the last details of the house, and planned to return just in time to put the furnishings in place.

Kate found great pleasure in spending money, and she ordered the furniture to be made with a great deal of care. She also took the time to see what she could find in the way of hired help, for she had no inclination toward manual labor.

When she arrived at the newly finished house again, she had a promise that all the furnishings would follow soon, and she had in tow a young black girl and two men. The black girl had been bought as a housemaid, and the two men had been indentured to her as hands to do miscellaneous work. She enthroned herself in the house and, in a burst of enthusiasm, even invited Jake to have a room of his own until Sebastian arrived.

Jake refused. His dislike and distrust of Kate had grown with each passing day, and he was sure he could never tolerate living within the same walls as this nasty woman.

Still he did not want to leave until Sebastian returned. The remains of the house had been entrusted to him, and he felt an obligation to explain to Sebastian that none of this had been done with his consent.

Kate felt safe and secure when everything had been completed. She had the house she had wanted, despite the terrible place in which it was located. But, she believed, that would change as soon as Sebastian returned.

Kate also knew she would be quite bored, so she returned to town again to have some days of fun shopping with Elenora, and some nights of pleasure as well. She was pleased with all that was happening and felt she had everything she wanted almost in her grasp.

When she returned to the house again, she was completely unaware of the two who followed her. They camped where they could keep the house under constant watch and settled in to wait and observe Kate's comings and goings.

Luke wanted answers. He wanted to know where Kate was and why she was there. He especially wanted to know about the man with whom she was planning to share her life.

He had, of course, found out a great deal about Kate. Servants had a way of hearing what transpired in a home, and Elenora's were well informed. For Luke, it had been a matter of making friends, then spreading about a little money, enough to grease tongues. And, of course, he was having her followed.

He had also discovered the amount of the enormous fortune Kate had inherited from her husband. His

225

imagination worked on the possibilities until he came up with a satisfactory solution. Kate and Sebastian had been lovers who had been waiting for her husband to die so they could share his fortune and be together. But to Luke, it seemed only reasonable that anyone who could snare Kate and her fortune should have both. And he did not intend for that someone to Sebastian Cain.

## *Chapter Twenty*

As Cole sipped his hot coffee, he held the cup between his hands to warm them. The early morning air was chilly, though he knew that as soon as the sun rose it would be a very warm day. But for now, the cool night air still clung to the earth.

He had quietly stirred the fire and had rebuilt it until it burned crisply. Then he had made the strong coffee.

He wondered what this new day would bring. The night before they had sat around the fire, talking about everything except the situation in which they were involved.

He had sensed from the moment they had arrived that there was some conflict lingering between Sebastian and Summer, but he could not put his finger on its origin. They were speaking to each other he knew, but their tones had been too civil, too polite, as if they had been strangers.

He had watched Sebastian's face throughout the evening, and there had been no doubt in his mind that Sebastian had been emotionally redeemed. But he could not see behind the mask that Summer seemed to be wearing.

Both began to stir. Sebastian rose and stretched,

then left the area of the fire for the brush. After a few minutes, he returned and knelt by the fire to pour himself some of Cole's very strong coffee. He took a sip and grimaced.

"Good God! This is strong enough to melt the hinges of hell!"

Cole chuckled. "It's good for you. Builds your stomach muscles."

"Or destroys them," Sebastian quipped.

"Which way do we move today, Sebastian?"

"Toward my place," Sebastian answered quickly.

"You still haven't told Summer that?"

"Not yet. When the time comes, I will. She thinks we're still looking for tracks. She is still reaching with that strange power of hers, but I guess there's no one close enough for us to be worried about."

Cole kept silent. If the four he had seen leaving Devil's Elbow were far enough away that Summer couldn't feel them, then he did not intend to upset everything that was going so well by telling Sebastian of their presence.

He was about to speak again when his attention was drawn to Summer. She sat upon her blanket and had loosened her hair to run her fingers through it and free it from tangles; then she would rebraid it. It was an utterly sensuous gesture and Cole was caught by it.

Following Cole's gaze, Sebastian turned slightly and was captivated as well.

What a pretty thing she is, Cole thought. He turned to Sebastian with the same words on his lips, but they were left unspoken when he saw the look in Sebastian's eyes.

Sebastian's heart pounded heavily as he absorbed Summer. Unaware that he was watching, she casually untangled her hair and began to braid it. Sebastian could actually feel the silky strands between his fingers.

228

He could see her slim body as it arched to lift her hair. It was as if he could feel her cool flesh next to his. He felt the remembered flame of her touch sing through his body and knew that if it hadn't been for Cole's presence, he would have gone to her and tried to breach the void that hung between them. He wanted her with near desperation, yet he knew he would never again force her to share the blazing passion that he could rouse. He would never again use her own body's needs against her. It would be no good. It would destroy what he really wanted before he got a chance to build it into what he knew could be.

But he could not erase the hunger from his eyes as they raked over her body. Cole read Sebastian's need easily, as did Summer when she lifted her head and Sebastian's eyes met and held hers.

The warmth of his gaze and the open desire in his eyes penetrated her being and almost made her gasp with the sudden, fierce heat of it.

For several moments Cole had the distinct feeling that neither Sebastian nor Summer knew he was there. He could almost feel the current that seemed to flow between them.

It was Summer who turned her face from them. She rose and left the area, carrying her blanket with her.

Summer walked some distance away before she stopped. She closed her eyes, fighting the urge to return. It would be wrong for her, she thought. He did not love her, not in a way that was necessary for her. Surely he could claim her body, set it afire, but that was not enough. She breathed deeply, struggling for control. She would have to return, for they would be leaving soon, but first she would have to regain her self-possession.

She spread her blanket and sat upon it. She had always had an inner strength and now she drew on it for control.

How she wanted to go to him, to walk into the circle of those strong arms and feel the touch of his lips against her flesh. But his terms were more than she could accept: unconditional surrender on her part, a fleeting passion, always standing second to another woman, a woman who stood like a ghost—pale, golden, and very beautiful—between them.

Summer could almost draw up a vision of her, and with anguish she realized she hated this stranger and that she desired Sebastian with her whole heart.

As if she had conjured him up from a dream, Summer opened her eyes and saw Sebastian standing before her. He stood between her and the rising sun so that he was more dark shadow than real, yet she could feel his eyes penetrating her, drawing her, until it took all the effort she could muster to remain still and not fly into his arms.

"Summer," he said gently and extended his hand to her to help her rise, "we are ready to leave."

She put her hand in his and he drew her up, very nearly into his arms.

They stood, touching but not touching, breathing in each other's scents, each willing the other to say the words or cross the barrier that stood between them.

Very slowly his arm circled her waist and drew her to him. Their lips hovered close. He wanted to drown in the depths of her eyes. He wanted to ravage the soft, half-parted lips. And with an urgency that was very nearly pain, he wanted to feel her pressed to him, part of him. He wanted her completely, but he did not move a muscle.

Summer could hear her heart beating and wondered why Sebastian did not feel it, because it thundered so violently. Her body trembled and she used every ounce of strength she possessed to step away from him.

230

Soundlessly she picked up the blanket, turned, and slowly walked away. Sebastian watched her go and the ache within him grew.

Somehow he had to bring back the warm look of love into her eyes. He had to find a way to reach past the dark thoughts she held, the false thoughts she felt were so real. She had lifted him from a well of black and now he did not seem to have the means to get back the look in her eyes he needed to see.


Summer rode before Sebastian and his arm held her securely. She was doing her best to keep herself from resting against him. It seemed interminable hours before the sun was high in the sky and they finally stopped to rest and eat.

Summer used Cole as a shield against Sebastian. She seemed eager to converse with him, if only to drown the unspoken words between her and Sebastian.

While they took time to eat, Cole began to question Summer about her childhood. Without saying anything about her father, she told Cole of childhood escapades in Black Cloud's village.

Sebastian listened to their laughter and found it annoying. But what started out as annoyance slowly began to grow into frustration and poorly controlled jealousy. And Cole absolutely enjoyed rousing emotions that put Sebastian's mind where Cole thought it ought to be—on the dark-eyed girl that rode with them.

"So your mother was medicine woman before you, Summer?" Cole inquired.

"Yes. Her name was Singing Bells. She died when I was born, so I really knew very little of her except for the wonderful things that were told to me."

"It must have been interesting for you as a child to be so . . ."

"Different?" Summer supplied and Cole flushed slightly. "Don't be upset, Cole." She laughed. "I was different. But sometimes it was fun. I always won at games . . . and I could always find lost articles or children who had slipped away from their mothers."

"I'll bet you were a pretty little girl. You've sure grown into a beautiful woman."

"I was very thin and I had long legs like a newborn colt. I was just as clumsy, too."

"Funny, I can't see you as clumsy . . . and"—he chuckled—"your long legs have developed nicely."

Again Summer laughed and Cole laughed with her. He enjoyed the camaraderie that flowed easily between them. If Sebastian had thought that Kate would make the better wife, Cole thought, he had been mistaken. Despite the fact that Summer was Indian and had not had Kate's finery and delicate upbringing, she was still a delightful companion who sparkled with good humor.

Sebastian scowled darkly and rose. "We'd best get going. We're not accomplishing anything just sitting around here talking." Both looked at him in surprise at his sharp words, but they rose and prepared to leave.

Sebastian mounted and again extended a hand to Summer, kicking his foot from the stirrup so she could mount before him. In an effortless, fluid motion he swung her up and settled her comfortably against him.

The three rode carefully, keeping close watch. They wanted to make sure they would not be taken by surprise.

"There's water a few miles on," Cole said at one point. "It's a long way, but if we push a little we can make it by night. It's only a small stream usually, but at least we can water the horses and have a place to wash."

Sebastian and Summer nodded their agreement. It would be a strong push, since she and Sebastian were

232

riding double. It would mean they would have to stop occasionally to let their horse rest.

At each stop Sebastian became more and more irritated, for Summer seemed to have turned completely from him to Cole. He resented the way she laughed and talked easily with Cole, for he did not realize that Cole presented no threat to her and that she could be relaxed with him. If he had thought about it without the intrusion of his jealousy, he would have seen that Cole could not stir her emotions and that she was treating him as a friend. But jealousy hung tenaciously on his mind, a mind that was set on having Summer.

They found the stream as Cole had promised. Summer was delighted, for when she walked along it, she found a small pool where she could bathe. It was not deep, but it was crystal clear and cool, and very inviting.

They had made a fire and Cole was moving about, gathering what little they had left to make a meal.

Summer walked away and Sebastian knew she was going to the stream to bathe while it was still light enough to see.

Sebastian turned to Cole. "Maybe," he said, "you should hunt for some meat."

Cole was surprised. If they were careful, they would have enough food for the next day and it would be easier to hunt then. He was about to say so when he realized Sebastian's attention was on the path that Summer had taken. There was no doubt Sebastian wanted some time alone with Summer, so Cole kept his smile to himself and picked up his gun.

"I'll run across something. I'll be back in an hour—an hour, Sebastian," he repeated.

Sebastian nodded and Cole vanished into the trees. Sebastian sat still for some time. His intention was to wait until Summer returned and then tell her how he felt and where they were heading. At least that's how his intention began. But his mind could envision Summer's golden form wet with cool water. His senses could very nearly smell the sweet scent of her and taste the even sweeter taste of her soft mouth. He wanted to let her know that his need extended far beyond the temporary possession they had known to a much fuller relationship.

His need to see her lifted him to his feet and carried him down the path toward the stream. She was kneeling in the water, her slim, straight back toward him. The water swirled about her hips and she was humming lightly to herself as she cupped her hands and lifted the water to rinse her skin.

In the soft evening light, her skin glowed and little rivulets of water slowly ran down her flesh to return to the stream. For a few minutes he was content to watch. His body remembered all too well the feel of her skin next to his, and he took pleasure in her lack of awareness as she loosened her hair and ran her fingers through it.

She was so breathtakingly beautiful that he had to use absolute iron control to keep from going to her, lifting her soft, sleek body into his arms, and making love to her as his raging desire demanded.

Her wet hands caressed her body, and Sebastian could have groaned aloud at the effect on his senses.

How easy it would be. He could go to her, take her in his arms, and with time and determination he could make her body respond to him. But, he realized dejectedly, that was all that would respond. She would shut him away from her heart and her mind and one day she would be gone forever.

Suddenly Summer became aware she was not alone.

234

She turned slowly and Sebastian's breath seemed to be drawn from his body.

The dying sun bathed her in a red-gold glow, and the crystals of water glistened on her skin like tiny diamonds.

It was passion that had brought him to her, and Summer knew it, just as she knew she had to fight the brilliant touch of desire that now set her nerves tingling.

She reached for her tunic and, in the waning light, Sebastian was treated to a rare and exciting view of her tawny body as it disappeared beneath the buckskin dress.

He sighed. It was better for his control that she had dressed, but his body was putting up a great deal of resistance to the idea.

She stepped from the water to stand beside him, and her eyes were wary and told him she was prepared to do battle. He almost laughed, for her small body was no match for his.

Again the small voice within him told him, Take her, make her yours. But still he knew the elusive thing that was Summer would never really be his. Use force, his instincts told him, and you will open your eyes to find her gone from your world.

"Cole . . ." Summer began, angry at her own weakness in feeling that she needed some defense against Sebastian, who was doing nothing at the moment but regarding her seriously.

"He's gone to see if he can find some meat. He should be back in an hour or so."

She had to fight this sensation of panic, she thought. Why did his presence so alarm her senses that it set her teeth on edge and left her weak?

He walked closer and it took effort on her part to

235

remain still. But he could read nothing in her eyes as she watched him approach.

He wanted to hold her even if it were only for a moment, but he knew his will did not extend quite that far. If he took her in his arms, there would be no way he would release her until he had fulfilled his desire and had possessed her completely. Instead, he came within touching distance and stopped.

"I want to talk to you, Summer. It's important."

"Then talk," she said.

"Let's sit down here, beneath the tree."

This is dangerous, her mind told her, but she sat down in the grass beside him.

"What do you want to say to me, Sebastian?"

"You've been . . . listening with your . . . power?"

"Yes, but I feel nothing. They must be some distance away. I will keep trying every day."

"I . . . I had thought of another possibility."

"What?"

He hoped she couldn't see through his words to the thoughts behind them.

"I thought we might go back, back to my home. It's just as they left it, and since everything began there, you might be able to pick up a stronger feel for them. It might make everything easier."

Summer watched him intently, and in that instant the truth struck her. She could not read Sebastian—she would never be able to touch his mind and know what he thought and planned. The realization shook her for a moment, then she pushed it aside. It did not matter any longer. Once he had found the ones he sought, he would go back to pick up his past and continue with his plans—plans in which she had no permanent part.

She drew up her knees and wrapped her arms about them as she gazed meditatively at the last red glow of

236

the setting sun.

"Perhaps," she said, "it would be better to go there. If I get a true feel for them, I might be able to follow."

Sebastian remained silent, hoping her decision was final. Then he spoke to try to influence her thoughts.

"Where I built my home is very beautiful," he said. "The house is small, but it would have been comfortable. It's the land about it that is so wonderful. I'd really like you to see it."

She turned her head to look at him. "Why . . . why do you want me to see it?"

Cautiously he chose his words. "Summer, you have done a lot to help me. What is so wrong in my wanting you to see what I had, what was destroyed, and what set me on this path?"

She contemplated his words. "Again you might be right. It is possible I can do more if we start where it all began."

He was quite pleased with himself. Once he had her there, he would tell her that he needed her to be part of his life and that together they could rebuild what had been so ruthlessly destroyed. He would tell her that even though their cultures were very different, they could adapt to each other and create a life for themselves.

He would tell her his plans then—that his murderous obsession had vanished and he wanted to build something permanent so that Nathaniel's death would not have been in vain. Through Hawk and his people they would someday find the guilty ones and bring them to justice. He would have to make her see that all he wanted was a future with her.

He would tell her all these things, but not now. Now she did not trust him, and the idea of Kate and another future he had planned still lingered in her mind.

If he took her in his arms now, as he truly wanted to do, and told her that he loved her and needed her to share the rest of her life with him, she would never believe it. She would again think that he was trying to use her love until it could be replaced by a more permanent one. He resolved to tell her as soon as they reached his home.

Summer's thoughts were not so different, nor were they any easier for her to voice. Like Sebastian, she held them within. Neither guessed that if the words had been spoken—if the thoughts had been unlocked and shared—all the problems between them would have been most pleasantly solved.

Summer sighed as she forced away the words that formed on her lips. Stern control kept her from turning to him and opening her arms to embrace him. It kept her from begging him to tell her only once that he loved her and wanted her—not as mistress but as a wife—a mother to his children. She felt a slow ache begin to grow within her, an ache she knew only Sebastian could soothe with the touch of his mouth on hers and the sanctuary of his strong arms to hold her.

Each held at bay the desire that sent its warmth through them.

It was growing dark, and Sebastian could just barely make out Summer's features. They had softened as she had let her mind drift. He would have given anything to have been able to share her thoughts.

It was in that instant of Sebastian's yearning that she turned her face toward him again. Her eyes were luminous and caught the last pale rays of light.

Her beauty struck at the core of his being, and he could not resist one touch to carry with him until the time came to prove to her that his love was enough for them to build a life on.

238

Slowly he bent his head and his lips touched hers in the gentlest of kisses. He gave her no time to resist. He stood up. He knew that if he stayed beside her a moment longer, nothing could stop him from seeking more.

"We'd better go back. Cole"—he laughed—"has probably eaten all the supper."

She rose and they walked together toward camp. It was a time Sebastian would cherish, for it was a quiet moment when he felt she had finally begun to relax in his presence and become more aware of their ability to touch each other's hearts.

Once they returned to the camp, they found that Cole had returned as well and that the meal was ready to be eaten.

Cole was also pleased with the turn of events. He remained quiet too, but he enjoyed the apparent relaxation of hostilities.

They rolled in their blankets and prepared for the night's sleep, but the night's dreams were to destroy all that had been accomplished.

Summer's awareness of a new facet of her relationship with Sebastian was growing within her and she could not sleep. She lay awake, silently contemplating the stars and her future. That was why she heard the soft, whispered sounds and knew Sebastian was caught in a dream. She turned to look at him.

Sebastian's dream was confusing and he fought his way through a mist toward someone he knew he really wanted but could not see. She stood some distance from him and he could barely make out her form through the mist.

Then she became clear as she slowly floated out of the fog. There was a warm and welcoming smile on her face and her arms were outstretched toward him. It was Summer.

But he couldn't seem to move. It was as if he were caught in something that held him. He tried, desperately he tried.

Then he saw the other form. It was shadowed and dark, and it moved toward Summer.

He didn't know why or how, but he knew the shadow's intention. It was to hurt, to kill Summer!

He worked with fury to release himself. He had to get to her. He had to save her. Still it held him . . . and then the shadowed figure became clear. It had hatred in its heart and death on its mind. It wielded a long, sharp blade that was pointed toward Summer's heart. The attacker was clear, too clear. It was Kate!

He cried out in desperation, and a stricken Summer listened as tears stained her cheeks.

"Kate," Sebastian moaned. "Kate."

The words died on Sebastian's lips, but they burned deep into Summer's heart. She muffled her tears and turned away from him. A long, sleepless night lay before her.

Summer was very quiet the next morning as she helped pack the equipment. Both Sebastian and Cole were so involved with saddling the horses and packing their things that her mood was not noticed until the moment they were prepared to leave.

Both Sebastian and Cole mounted. Sebastian slipped his foot from the stirrup and extended his hand to Summer.

For a moment she stood and looked up at him. She had not believed that he was capable of such lies. But his own cry for his beloved Kate had finally proven she was wrong.

"I," she said in a firm yet quiet voice, "will ride with

240

Cole today."

She turned and strode from a surprised Sebastian to an even more surprised Cole. She reached up her hand to Cole, who had no choice but to help her up before him.

Summer and Cole moved forward, and in a few minutes Sebastian followed.

# Chapter Twenty-one

Sebastian was stunned; in fact, he was utterly speechless. What had happened from last night's near acceptance to today's total fury? He could tell from her rigid body and the cold look in her eyes that something was wrong, but he did not have the slightest idea what it could be.

He rode just a little behind Summer and Cole, trying to figure out what he could have said or done to have brought on her renewed anger.

Cole was just as puzzled. Summer was silent, and he tried to think of a way to start a conversation in which she might expose the reason. But it was useless. She answered his efforts in sharp, one-word answers that told him his conversational attempts were unwelcome.

Summer's outer shell was cold and formidable, but within she could still feel the bitterness in her heart. In fact, she could still hear Sebastian's mumbled call for Kate. It burned within her until she could have shrieked with the fury she felt.

She did not wonder at her own anger. She did not ask herself why it should matter to her, when she had felt all along that Sebastian would leave her. She did not question the sting of jealousy for she refused to recognize it as what it was.

When they stopped for a quick midday meal and to rest the horses, Summer walked some distance from them.

"What's wrong with Summer?" Cole questioned. "She sure is different this morning."

"I don't know. I had the feeling last night we were heading toward some safe ground where we could at least talk. I just don't know what happened between then and now."

Cole was certain Sebastian must have done or said something to hurt Summer, and his face must have been reflecting his thoughts, for Sebastian scowled.

"I had nothing to do with it, Cole. It must be that she is just caught up in mental searching and needs to be away from us."

He didn't believe his own words, and he was pretty sure, though he was silent, that Cole didn't believe them either.

That afternoon Summer again chose to ride with Cole, and Sebastian bit back words he wanted to say in a denial of her rejection of him. When they stopped for the night, he would find out why she was angry. He had no intention of forsaking his goals because of her misplaced anger. They were only two or three days away from his home, and he was sure if he didn't settle whatever it was before they arrived, he would never be able to settle it.

By the time they found a place to camp for the night, all three were tired, all three were hungry, and all three were drawn taut by the tension that could almost be tasted.

They went about their preparations for the night with emotions that were held in check only by the determined wills of all three.

Sebastian waited very patiently for the opportunity

to talk to Summer. It came about as she led his horse away from camp.

Very particular about the treatment of horses, as all Indians were, Summer planned to give him water, lead him to a good place to graze, and rub him down very carefully.

She was preparing to do so when Sebastian joined her. She sensed that he stood behind her, but she did not acknowledge him. Briskly she rubbed the horse, but as she did, she pressed her lips together, determined not to turn around.

"Summer," Sebastian said, half angry now, "stop pretending that I don't exist. If you're upset about something, for God's sake turn around and tell me what it is."

She spun around and glared at him, her own nerves frayed.

"Leave me alone, Sebastian . . . just leave me alone. What you wanted from me you have already gotten. Now leave me be!"

She spun about and started to walk away, but Sebastian was growing angry too. He didn't know what was on her mind, but he intended to find out.

He caught up with her just within the shadows of a nearby stand of trees. She was walking rapidly, and he nearly had to run the last few steps to catch up to her. When he did, he grabbed her arm and jerked her around to face him.

Her eyes blazed belligerently and her cheeks were pink with rage.

"Stop running and talk to me," he said furiously. He would have said more, but the words were cut off as her hand struck sharply. His cheek reddened from the force of her hand and his eyes blinked in surprise.

Before he realized it, she had spun about and was gone again. Her figure was a fleeting shadow between

244

the trees. With a sound of fury low in his throat, he charged after her.

Again he ran to catch up with her. They were well away from the camp by now and deep in the dark shadows of the trees.

This time he grabbed her arm and pulled her around so violently that she slammed into him. He caught her in his arms.

Furiously, she pushed his arms away. "Let go of me! Go back to camp. There is nothing we have to talk about."

Though her anger had control of her, his was even more consuming. He was determined now that she would give him reasons.

"I can think of several things we can talk about. One is what the hell has made you so angry at me!"

She was so furious that her eyes filled with tears. There was no way for her to say what was wrong, for truthfully she couldn't find a way to put into words what roiled so violently within her.

She tried to gather her thoughts, for they had twisted within her all day. She inhaled and released her breath in a deep sigh. With effort she controlled her voice.

"Sebastian," she said, her voice smooth, "it just doesn't matter now."

"Doesn't matter?" His voice was tense. "Summer," he said, "it matters to me."

She caught her breath, feeling as though he had struck her. She closed her eyes and said the next words weakly. "Oh, Sebastian, it's not necessary to lie to me to get what you want. I have agreed to help you. Let's let it go at that. Don't say things to me that you and I both know are untrue."

"I swear, Summer, I don't know what you're talking about. Last night . . . well . . . I thought we had some kind of"—he shrugged—"I don't know, just a space

245

. . . a place where we could meet halfway."

"Last night," she repeated, "was . . . was something I was foolish enough to believe. It won't happen again. It was a lie like all the rest."

Sebastian had reached both the end of his patience and the end of his self-control. He did not know what she was talking about, his face still stung slightly from her slap, he was tired, he was hungry, and he wanted her to be warm and giving in his arms. All of this was enough to ignite an action he never anticipated. He reached out and took her in his arms. Then he capped his mistake with another. He thought he could force her to listen.

She struggled and he held her tighter.

Her anger rose, and so did his desire. Warmth blossomed within her, a warmth she fiercely resisted.

A strange kind of fury took control of Sebastian. He could feel the length of her body pressed to his; her mouth was inches below his, and he took it.

He heard her muffled anger as his mouth captured hers and drank deeply. He forced her lips apart and tasted the sweet recesses of her soft mouth. His mind echoed hers in a cry for him to stop, but his senses were beyond its control.

Her hands, caught between them, were ineffectual as they pressed against his chest. Her body was taut and resisted his with all the force his binding arms would permit.

The kiss was deep and very nearly violent. When he released her, both were panting. It was only then that the realization of what he was doing exploded in his mind. He was doing exactly what he told her he would never do again! He was forcing her body to respond to his will without caring for her thoughts. He could see the combination of fear, anger, and barely controlled passion on her face, and an anguished regret filled him.

In one moment he had proven to her that the words he had vowed had been lies. How would he make her believe again—ever?

He released her and watched as she regained control. Her breathing was ragged and her eyes smoldered with such conflicting emotions that he was left unsure of which one to defend himself against. And he knew it would soon be a matter of defense as he watched rage win out over all the others.

"Summer, I'm sorry. I never meant to do that. We were both angry. Why can't we stop letting anger stand between us and what is important to both of us?"

"I didn't know there was anything that important between us," she snapped angrily.

"What do you mean there is nothing important between us? We've shared so much."

"Shared!" she cried. "Sharing takes mutual giving. You've given nothing but lies!"

"I've never lied to you!"

"You've never told me the truth either. Tell me, Sebastian, is this house and all that goes with it so important to you?"

"Of course it is. It's my whole future. It's where I want to live and raise my family."

She could have wept at his reference to Kate and his future—a future without her. To him, she thought, she was still an Indian who had no place in the world he wanted to create, still a half-breed who was convenient. He spoke of sharing as if her body were his for whenever he chose.

In her silence, Sebastian thought she had finally understood that he meant for them to build something together.

"Summer, you said you would come with me."

He had meant for good, but Summer thought he had meant to renew their search.

"Yes . . . I will." She knew her need to help him in his search would drive her unless she did. "That I have no choice in."

Totally misunderstanding her meaning, Sebastian was relieved. He felt she meant no choice in whether or not she loved him. He moved to take her in his arms again, but she backed away. She was confused and just a little afraid that his touch could start a fire she would never be able to extinguish.

"We are tired, both of us," she said. "We cannot talk rationally about anything. We will go to your home. Once we are there . . . we can speak of what is best to do—for both of us."

He nodded, and again their thoughts were miles apart. But he was satisfied that at least she understood that their arrival at his home would be the beginning for both of them.

"Walk back to camp with me," he said quietly.

"No, Sebastian. I think I will sleep here. I want to be alone with my thoughts for awhile."

He was reluctant to leave her, but he knew she would be safe where she was. Of all the people in the world, Summer would be the safest in this wilderness.

He wanted to touch her, but everything about her— her posture, the shuttered look that again appeared in her eyes—told him this was not the time.

"Good night, Summer."

She watched him turn and walk away. Her emotions were in a violent turmoil. She had to find a way to work this problem out in her mind. She would go to Sebastian's house, for maybe the trail could be found from there. But after she had found it, she was going to find a way to get word to Hawk. From then on, the warriors from the village could help Sebastian find the renegades.

Summer went back to retrieve her blanket. She took

it and spread it beneath the trees in a soft, grassy spot. She lay upon it and tried to sort out her feelings.

The gift she possessed had never caused her such pain and trouble before. It was not really very often that she wished she had never had it, but this moment was one of those times. This brought her thoughts back to Sebastian, for against him she had very little protection, even in her mind. She knew that no power on earth could stop the way he could enter her thoughts and set her body aflame.

"Damn you, Sebastian," she whispered to herself. "Why can I not free myself from you? I must find a way . . . I must."

Finally, she drifted off to sleep.


For Sebastian, sleep was not so easy. He lay wide awake. The moon was white and low, standing just over the tops of the trees. It bathed the area in its soft, white glow and penetrated the branches of the trees with thin beams of light.

His mind wandered and eventually drifted to the spot beneath the trees where Summer lay asleep. He clearly could envision her in his mind, and the vision grew until it encompassed every moment he had spent with her.

He could feel the cool, soft texture of her skin on his fingertips and all his senses seemed to be more alive than they had ever been. To stay in one place was agony, so he rose silently. Despite the control he tried to maintain, his feet took him to the path that led to the object of his need.

He walked purposefully and stopped by the tree beneath which Summer slept.

She lay relaxed and breathing deeply in slumber. He stood very still, admiring her slim form bathed in beams of white moonlight. A strong and vital love for her washed through him like a burning-hot flood. He wanted so desperately to hold her and feel her touch that it brought a stinging moisture to his eyes. There was no reluctance any longer. He knelt beside her.

Summer was deep in a dream, and she dreamed of Sebastian. In dreams all wishes can be found and all barriers can be surmounted. She laughed softly as she reached for him and heard his answering laugh as his arms lifted her against him. The magic was theirs and theirs alone, and she felt his lips brush her cheek and the gentle touch of his hands. The feeling was real . . . so very real.

Slowly Summer's eyes opened. The warmth of the dream filled her and the poignant look of need in Sebastian's eyes as he bent near her brooked all the resistance she had.

She lifted her arms to him and with a low moan of pleasure he filled them, drawing her to him, rocking her against him, and holding her as if he would never let her go.

It was a time predestined by all the gods they believed in; it was a time of soaring passions as brilliant as lightning in a stormy sky or as furious as an uncontrollable hurricane. And those passions swept away all but the naked and consuming hunger that drove them.

They kissed frantically, unendingly, drawing life from each other. He tore down every wall of resistance she had formed as he pressed heated kisses along her cheeks and over the soft texture of her throat. He traced a molten path downward until the neck of her tunic forbade him the soft, enticing flesh beneath.

His hands gently removed the tunic and tenderly brushed the soft curves of her breasts, drawing her nerve taut and making her shiver with expectancy.

Then his mouth took hers again gently, hesitantly, then deeply, with soul-fulfilling rapture.

Words became inarticulate gasps that were drawn from the very depths of their mutual need. Flames shot to life within both as they clung to each other. Their bodies entwined and Summer moaned in exultant pleasure as she opened herself to him, drawing him within her, enfolding and accepting his hard body as he drove to reach the center of her.

Her body arched to meet his and her hand caressed the length of his muscular back and felt the rippling muscle as he moved.

He filled her and the heat of him drove her to a pinnacle of ecstasy that shattered within her like a million stars. She felt his urgency and answered it, and together they whirled in a vortex of wild, almost unbearable euphoria.

He could see her face in the pale moonlight. Her eyes were closed and her head was thrown back in abandon and absolute surrender. She was his! And he would hold her forever—he would find a way. Whatever it took, he would never let her go.

Summer lay still and breathless against him. The flaming glory of their passion had left them silent in its aftermath. It was a long, deep silence, for neither could put words to the blissful experience they had just shared. No matter what barriers had been erected, the force that had drawn the two together had overcome them once again.

He lay beside her, his face buried in the softness of her hair. One hand rested gently yet possessively on her curved hip. Her cheek was resting against his chest and she could hear his heart slowly return to its normal beat.

Could they hold this moment, each wondered. Could they capture this time and preserve it until the dawn?

It was a warm and mystical cocoon that held them in its silent folds. One word might fracture it, might allow the entrance of reality, and neither was ready to face that possibility or wanted to let go of the delicious warmth that enclosed them. The night was young, and the lovers were secure for the moment.

Their lips blended again in a tender kiss. Tongues caressed and tasted as they sought to experience all that was the other.

He tangled his hands in her silken mane and brushed delicate kisses against her brow, her closed eyes, her cheeks. He knew the fullest joy when he realized how complete her giving had been. When he felt her lips seek his flesh too, when he felt her hands begin to learn the feel of him, Sebastian could barely contain his delight.

For the first time in his life Sebastian was without words, without control. He wanted to kiss her forever, to join her body to his and hold this very rare and beautiful moment until eternity. He knew that Summer and this night would be forever etched in his heart.

They were fulfilled, but they could not bear to leave each other yet. Her eyes were heavy with passion and she ached for more. His body began to throb again with renewed desire. His hands were gentle as they explored and hers were just as seeking. Each wanted to memorize every part of the other. This night was to be theirs, separate from the machinations of the world that surrounded them, an island where nothing could intrude.

And this was Summer, Sebastian thought. Summer, yielding and soft; Summer, teasing and tempting, her body a fire that filled his blood and would never again release him. His cheek felt the softness of her hair and he inhaled the clean scent of it.

Summer was alive with such sensations that she did not know if she could bear them any longer. She felt them sing along every nerve and fiber of her being. Her skin was so sensitive to his touch that she quivered and gasped with the branding flame of his love.

The night grew deeper, and after awhile they lay together in timeless contentment.

Summer was still in his arms and Sebastian could not bring himself to speak, for he feared that words might wedge themselves between them and sever their delicate bond.

Very slowly he rose on one elbow and looked down into the dark pools of her eyes. He lowered his head and let his lips play gently upon her own for one more precious moment before he spoke.

Her face, touched with moonlight, was still and calm, yet her dark eyes were warm and intense.

"Summer"—he smiled—"I have disturbed your dreams. But it is only a small revenge for how much you have disturbed not only my dreams but my waking hours as well."

Her hand reached up to caress his cheek. She spoke with wonder in her voice, as if she could not quite believe what they had just shared.

"But," she whispered, "you were part of my dream . . . so much a part that I am still not sure I did not create you. I cannot say when you left the dream and became real."

He turned his face to her palm and pressed his lips to it.

"Tomorrow—" he began.

"I do not want to think of tomorrow," she replied as she pressed her fingers against his lips to seal them. "I do not want tomorrow to come."

"But I look forward to tomorrow. For after it comes the night . . . and with the night comes all that I need to make living worthwhile."

"Sebastian?"

"Yes?"

"I cannot face all the tomorrows yet. I still do not understand myself and why I cannot withstand this strange thing between us."

"What are you afraid of, Summer?" he questioned gently.

"Of myself . . . of deception . . . of giving my love when I am not sure what I will receive in return."

"I can only convince you in one way, my love," he replied.

"How?"

"Come with me to the end of my journey. Come with me to my home. Once we are there, I will be able to convince you of all that you mean to me."

"And what will happen there?"

"Wait and see." He grinned. "You will find it a very different life for both of us."

"Different? How?"

"You will see. There will be changes, but I'm sure, as adaptable as you are, you will adjust to what I have in mind."

"But—"

"Shh, love," Sebastian whispered as he again tasted her soft lips. "We will make all our decisions once we get to my home. We have a lot of time to talk about choices and many other things. Why can't we just take this time to get to know each other?"

She would have spoken again, but her words were stopped by the pressure of his mouth against hers.

Surely this was the truth, she thought wildly. Surely this spell he was weaving about her could not be a lie. She must believe! It simply couldn't be possible that this night of wondrous love was a deception.

She would go with him. She would give him this

opportunity to prove that all her beliefs were false, that there was a place in his life for her, and that what he had thought about her heritage was no longer important.

"You'll forget all your false ideas, Summer. You'll forget," he whispered against her hair. His arms tightened about her.

Summer closed her eyes and rested against him, silently hoping his words were true, for she could not see past his words and she wanted so desperately to believe.

In less than two days they would reach Sebastian's home and he was content in the conviction that it would be the beginning of a bright and happy life with Summer at his side.

And she was keeping at bay the thought that this was only another dream, a dream that could turn into the most horrible of nightmares.

# *Chapter Twenty-two*

Cole could have whooped with delight when he woke early the next morning to find the camp empty. Wherever they were, they were together, and that suited him fine. He set about making some food with a soft whistle on his lips and a much lighter heart.

The sun was well above the horizon when he saw Sebastian and Summer walking from the edge of the trees. Sebastian's arm was about Summer's waist and they were talking together.

He breathed a deep sigh of relief and thanked whatever gods had been responsible. The two belonged together, he thought, no matter what. He just hoped it would stay that way.

He hoped also that Summer and Sebastian could find a neutral territory. He wasn't quite sure how they would live; after all, Sebastian had been born and raised with wealth, had access to all the wealthy homes in England, and had obtained an excellent education to go along with all of this. But even though Summer was just an Indian girl, Cole felt she could make Sebastian happy, despite their differences.

He was also glad Sebastian had been led from the path he had been on and, if he ever found the opportunity, he would thank Summer for this.

"Good morning!" Summer smiled at Cole and he returned it brightly as she added, "It's going to be a very nice day."

"It sure is," Cole replied quickly. His eyes sparkled with the obvious pleasure he felt, and the look was not missed by Sebastian, who chuckled softly.

"Let's get on our way as fast as possible, Cole. I'd like to get home by tomorrow morning."

"Home!" Cole said. "That word sure sounds good to me."

"Me too," Sebastian answered quietly as his gaze moved to Summer, who had been occupied bringing Sebastian's horse close to the dying fire to pack it with a small amount of equipment.

"Sebastian," Cole said softly while Summer was still out of range of his voice, "I don't know what happened, but I sure am glad to see you two are happy with each other again. I hope you're smart enough to make it permanent."

"Right now I'm walking carefully. We'll take one step at a time. I've talked her into coming home with me. Once I get her there, I'll find some way of keeping her there. One day . . . it will be permanent."

"I hope everything goes well. You deserve a little happiness, too."

"It's going to go well, Cole," Sebastian said with grim determination. "I've got too much at stake to let anything go wrong. It would have been so easy to lose Summer. When I think of it, I get jumpy. Nothing," he repeated firmly, "is going to come between us ever again."

Cole did not answer, for Summer approached and he happily occupied himself with admiring how beautiful she was with the glow of love in her eyes that she was directing at Sebastian.

Though she tried to control this emotion for fear it might turn to quicksand, she could not camouflage it when she looked at Sebastian, and Cole could read it as clearly as the new day and was overjoyed to see it.

They ate a companionable breakfast and in a short time they were ready to depart. Today there was no question as to where Summer would ride, even though Cole ventured a little teasing on the matter.

He mounted his horse a few minutes before Sebastian. "Summer," he called innocently, "come on and ride with me. I've got lots of stories you haven't heard yet."

Sebastian cocked an eyebrow at Cole in a manner that indicated he was not amused by Cole's invitation.

He was startled when Summer laughed softly and began to walk toward Cole. Quickly he mounted and urged his horse forward. With one fluid move he bent, caught Summer up, and placed her firmly in front of him.

She looked up at him with enough mischief in her eyes to make him laugh aloud. It sent a tingle of excitement through him just to see her eyes alight with something other than anger.

"Comfortable?" he questioned. At her nod Sebastian tapped the horse's flanks with his heels and the horse moved forward.

She relaxed against him, feeling the movement of his body as it blended with that of the horse. He shifted her even closer to him and held the reins with one hand while the other arm snaked about her waist. He let his body roll easily and set about enjoying the feel of her within the circle of his arm.

Feeling completely secure, Summer let her head rest against his shoulder. She closed her eyes and let her senses absorb the luxury. She could not reach within his mind, but if she had been able to, she would have been warmed by his thoughts.

The scent of her was intoxicating, and he felt the familiar fire burning in his blood. In fact, he was so conscious of her that he had to keep his thoughts under complete control or risk whisking her from the horse to a more delightful spot where he could savor her delicious presence more deeply. He soon found himself wishing fervently that Cole were anyplace but right beside them. He also reluctantly realized that they had to move on, for he wanted to reach their destination by the next morning.

He had left his house a burned-out shell, but now he was washed clean of the torment that had claimed him then. He was eager to rebuild, to begin again, and to help Summer adjust to his way of life.

He knew it would be difficult for her, for she had been reared differently, and, except for the mistake her father had made in trying to breed the savage from her by sending her to a white school, she had been spending her life in the wild and living in a tipi.

Oh well, he thought with a sigh, it would be a most pleasant pastime, teaching her to control her untamed spirit and become a lady.

To protect himself from the desire that burned through him, he let his imagination wander to visions of Summer in his home, in his bed, as mistress of his house, and one day, if he were fortunate, as the mother of his children.

That thought excited him to the point of disaster, for his body responded with near violence.

They stopped at midday, and the three sat beneath a tree and ate while their horses had a much-needed rest. Both Sebastian and Cole were completely enthralled by Summer's metamorphosis from a cold and angry individual to a bubbling, carefree girl who brightened everything around her.

259

Cole stood up and stretched. "Lord, it feels good to move around. I'm glad we'll be able to get a good night's sleep soon."

"If there's anything left to sleep on at home," Sebastian added. "I . . . I really didn't look too closely before I left."

Summer was watching him intently, and when he noticed, he smiled. "It's all right, Summer. It's nothing that can't be rebuilt." He stood also, then he reached down a hand to draw Summer to her feet. "Let's take a little walk before we mount those beasts again. I want to be close to home by the time we stop tonight."

Cole was wise enough not to accompany them, although the temptation was great. The thing that actually deterred him was a level and very firm look from Sebastian that told him what might be in store for him should he be so foolish as to join them.

Sebastian and Summer walked for a few minutes until they reached an outcropping of rock that effectively hid them from Cole's view. Her laugh was soft and breathless as Sebastian caught her up in his arms and buried his face in the soft flesh of her throat.

His arms tightened about her until she was no longer standing but forced to cling to him for support. Then he kissed her with a passion that drew the breath from her body. His mouth, open and hungry, pillaged hers until she was dizzy and lost in the warm pleasure he created.

The touch of his lips on hers and the way her body was crushed to his lean, hard frame drew an answering desire from her that was enough to set his pulses pounding and the fury of all-consuming desire raging through his body.

He held her a little away from him. Then he captured her face between his hands and gently, so very gently, touched her lips again and again until she was totally

260

captivated by the sweet magic of it.

Then he drew her close and his cheek rested against her hair. She closed her eyes and clung to him.

Tomorrow . . . tomorrow, his mind kept repeating. Tomorrow they would be home.

"We must go back," he said gently. "We must be on our way so that we can be home by morning. I can't wait to have you where you belong . . . Summer . . ." He whispered her name as their lips blended again, this time in a kiss of sweet promise.

He sighed deeply and again set her from his arms with a short laugh. "It is quite difficult to let you go once I have you in my arms, but there will come a time, my love . . . there will come a time."

In less than an hour they were again on their way.

Their progress was slow. Sebastian's horse was tiring with the double burden. Several times they had to lead their horses and walk. By the time the sun neared the horizon, riders and horses were exhausted and they were forced to make camp.

Sebastian hobbled the horses while Cole built a fire. They had not hunted any food, so there was very little to eat except some scraps of dried meat and water.

Summer was too tired to eat and rejected any of Sebastian's arguments. She sank down on her blanket.

Sebastian moved around the fire, sat down beside her, and put his arm about her. Her head sank to his shoulder gratefully. It did not take long for her to fall asleep.

Soon Cole rolled in his blanket and closed his eyes, and Sebastian eased himself down, stretching out and drawing Summer close to him. He took the edge of the blanket and pulled it up about them.

She slept, curled against him with her head resting on his shoulder. He held her close and thought, as he drifted off to sleep, that when they were finally home,

261

after he had rebuilt and settled everything between them, Summer would be spending every night safe in his arms. It was this pleasant thought that lulled him into sleep.

When Sebastian awoke, the first thing he realized was that Summer was no longer with him.

He sat up abruptly and startled Summer, who was kneeling beside a newly built fire. What drew his attention was that she was in the process of cooking meat—fresh meat.

He must have looked totally shocked, because she laughed.

"I was up early, so I thought I would make breakfast."

"Where . . . how . . . ?"

"How did I get the meat?" She laughed again. "There is no problem getting food here. All one has to know is how to catch it. I was taught as a child by Hawk and my father. I could live well here for as long as I chose to."

He shook his head. "You are a continuous surprise to me. I never quite know what to expect." His smile broadened. "Life with you should be exciting and unpredictable at the very least."

She rose and came to him, and dropped on her knees beside him.

"Sebastian," she began, "I . . . I have much to tell you. I—"

"Shh, Summer," he said as he reached up and took her face between his hands. "We will have all the time in the world to talk. We'll be home soon. I know that life is going to be . . . different for you, but—"

"Sebastian, please listen. I have to tell you about me and who I—"

He drew her down across him and kissed her words away.

"When we get home we'll talk," he whispered. She

sighed. It was useless to try to tell him now. But what would happen when he found out who she really was?

She was confused by many things. The fact that she could not enter his thoughts still bothered her; that she was still unsure of sharing his future made her hesitate to give of herself fully; and worse, if his promises were real, if he really loved her, would he understand why she had kept her background a secret?

Sebastian stood up, and at the same time Cole awoke. He pushed himself up, as surprised as Sebastian had been.

"Smells good," Cole said. "Where did the rabbit come from, Sebastian? I didn't hear you shoot."

"I didn't." Sebastian grinned. "Summer's responsible for the fire and the food."

"Doesn't surprise me." Cole laughed. "I had a feeling all along that the little lady could take care of just about anything. I been out here a long time and I've never run across an Indian who didn't have a way of livin' off the land. Summer"—he turned to her—"I bet you could live out here for weeks and never miss a meal."

"I have, quite often. It is not so hard. I have known how since childhood."

"Well," Sebastian interrupted with a pleased laugh, "no matter how we got it, the food smells good. Let's eat. Home is less than half a day away, so let's get going."

They ate, saddled their horses, and with Summer again in the secure circle of Sebastian's arms, they turned their faces toward home.


Kate stood back and looked at the finished house. She was quite satisfied with it and with the furnishings within.

The workmen she had hired had left the moment the

263

house had been completed. They had left shaking their heads and wondering about the man who would have both house and woman.

Jake had utterly refused to step inside it and had made himself as scarce as possible, returning only often enough to find out whether or not Sebastian had returned.

The house seemed to loom up from the ground, as if it knew that its presence should not have been part of this tranquil wilderness. It suggested an elaborate memory that belonged to another place and another time.

But Kate was pleased, for she wanted some reminder of past luxury until such time as she could persuade Sebastian to sell the house and return with her to England, where she felt they both belonged.

Elenora had helped as much as she could, and the two had become very close. It had only been a day since Elenora had returned home, after explaining to Kate that she had some plans of her own and some scores to settle.

Kate had built a small shack near the house to be used by her two workers, and the young black girl was given a small room off the kitchen so that she would be near her work, for Kate demanded that the house be clean and her meals well cooked and graciously served.

Now Kate waited most impatiently for Sebastian's return. Lifting her skirts, she walked up the four steps to the porch. She stood there for a few minutes, her eyes shaded by her hand, and scanned the horizon. There were no signs of anyone. Then she turned and opened the door and walked inside.

"Mandy!"

The young maid came running, and there was a faint touch of fear in her eyes. She had moved too slowly for Kate once before and had been subjected to Kate's vicious temper. Now when Kate called, she appeared as rapidly as possible.

"Yessum, Miz Maxwell?"

"Where have you been, you lazy slut? It's long past lunch and I'm hungry."

"Yessum . . . it be ready, Miz Maxwell."

"Well, bring it to the table."

Kate moved to the table and sat down. In a very few minutes Mandy was serving her meal.

The past few days had been so repetitious for Kate that she was both annoyed and very bored. She wanted Sebastian to return, was angry, in fact, that he had been so foolish as to attempt to hunt down the renegades who had struck him. After all, he had a great deal of money, so rebuilding was no problem. He could buy whatever he wanted. As far as his brother's death . . . well, she mused, it happened all the time, didn't it? Even home in England young men died in duels and accidents. It was just something that happened, and one had to learn to accept the blows and land on one's feet—no matter what.

Oh well, she thought, when Sebastian returned she would certainly change everything. She would soon convince him that her way was the best.

She stood up and walked to the window and looked out. She closed her eyes for a moment, thinking of how wonderful their nights would be. She could remember vividly the touch of his hands on her skin and the hard, very masculine body that had set her aflame.

Lord, how much she wanted him, she realized. It was as if he had touched her only yesterday. Fervently, she wished he were here beside her at that very moment.

Her eyes were on the crest of the hill some distance away, but her thoughts took some time to follow them. She saw the two horses stop and their riders conduct a lengthy exchange. Then they started down the hill toward the house.

Did she recognize the riders? Did the sun glint on gold hair and touch shoulders of such breadth? Was there such a proud form . . . ? Her heart skipped a beat and his name was a soft whisper on her lips.

"Sebastian."

Her eyes narrowed as she saw the two who accompanied him. A man, one she didn't know, and a—she couldn't believe it—an Indian girl.

"Good Lord"—she laughed softly—"Sebastian has taken a filthy little Indian girl to sleep with." Well, she vowed, she would soon take care of that.

Sebastian would already be surprised to see the house whole again, she reflected. He would be surprised and curious. She smiled to herself. She would be the next surprise. She turned from the window to face the door . . . and waited.


Sebastian's excitement began to grow when he started recognizing the terrain about him. He was on his own land and it had never meant as much to him as it did now, for he had his arm about the woman who had taken him from a path of self-destruction and had offered him a new life.

He smiled to himself as he envisioned carrying her over the threshold of what would one day be their home. It led to warmer visions of enticing her into a large, comfortable bed or spending pleasant hours introducing her to a new way of life. He could see their home brightened by laughing-eyed children.

It gave him a turn when he thought of all that he might have missed. The very last thing in his mind was Kate. She had been banished from his heart by the entrance of Summer and would never retrieve her former place in his affections.

266

He bent his head slightly and brushed Summer's cheek with a light kiss. "It won't be long, Summer. We're very nearly home." Summer shared his pleasure with him. This house and the land it was on meant so much to Sebastian. She was eager to see it. But she was also aware of something tense growing within her, some small fear, that was reaching a warning hand to tell her that something awaited her that would not be so pleasant. Was there some danger for her here, or was she only feeling the remnants of what had transpired in the past?

She had the sudden desire to stop, to hold Sebastian here and not continue on, but resolutely she pushed the impulse aside. If Sebastian were ever to be complete, to be whole again, he would have to go back to the past, mend his spirit, and rebuild from there. And against her deepest fears of disaster rose an even stronger determination to be a part of all he did, all he was, and all they could ever hope to find together.

She turned her head to smile up at him, and he took quick advantage by kissing her lingeringly and very thoroughly.

They rode on, across a small, green valley laden with golden wild flowers. Summer could tell by the tenseness in Sebastian that they were very near his home. She knew how hard yet necessary this was, and she said nothing. She could only be beside him as he retraced the tragedy and overcame its horror.

"Just beyond the hill, Summer," he whispered.

They crested the last hill, and in total shock Sebastian and Cole drew their horses to an abrupt halt. They sat in silence for a moment, absorbing the unbelievable scene that lay before them.

"What the hell . . ." Sebastian breathed in awe.

"If I didn't see it with my own eyes, I wouldn't believe it," Cole said in an incredulous voice. "It's . . ." He

267

couldn't quite find a word to describe what he was seeing.

"I thought you said your house was burned," Summer said softly.

"It was."

"I don't understand."

"Neither do I. It looks like someone has taken it upon himself to rebuild."

"Rebuild!" Cole said in disgust. "Sebastian, whoever built that . . . that place has no idea of what life out here is like. It looks like—"

"Like the governor's mansion." Sebastian laughed, but his eyes darkened to display the thoughts within. "I'm just wondering who had the idea of coming on my land and rebuilding my house. I hope it's not someone who has the notion I might be permanently gone and had decided to claim it for his own." His voice was like tempered steel. Summer could feel the cold bite of it. Sebastian was not a man to relinquish what he felt belonged to him without a battle.

"I guess there's only one way to find out," he added.

"I don't see anyone around," Cole said. "No horses, no sign of anybody."

"Someone must be in the house. It has taken some time to rebuild, and it can't have been finished for very long. Someone is there, and I intend to find out who."

He nudged his horse into motion and Cole was beside him instantly.

They rode down the grade slowly to the front of the house. Still there was no sign of life.

"Stay here for a minute, Summer," Sebastian said. "Let Cole and I check it out first."

Summer was reluctant to do that, and just as Sebastian and Cole opened the front door and started inside, she slid down from the horse and walked up to the door Sebastian had just closed behind him.

268

Something within her tingled with a sharp warning. There is danger here for you, Summer, it said. It was wild and dark inside her, but her heart refused to acknowledge danger to herself when Sebastian might already be facing it alone.

She reached for the handle of the door and opened it slowly. Then she stepped inside and closed it just as softly behind her.

The silence was cut by the sound of Sebastian's voice saying a name that had lain cold in Summer's heart for a long time, and it was followed by the soft, breathless laugh of a woman.

She moved to the door from behind which the sounds had come. Her heart was pounding and every instinct she had was sounding an alarm and telling her to run.

Still she turned the handle and swung open the door. The sight that greeted her was more painful than the twisting of a knife in her body.

Sebastian stood with his arms about a golden-haired woman, who was clinging to him and laughing softly between the kisses she was pressing against his cheeks and lips.

The sounds of Summer's shock made them all spin about. Summer could barely see for the sting of hot tears in her eyes. There was no doubt in her mind that Sebastian had returned to his woman—the Kate of his dreams.

# Chapter Twenty-three

Luke contemplated Tag, who stood before his captain with a satisfied smile on his face. Luke remained silent while Tag had revealed Kate's whereabouts and told of the house she had rebuilt. It was puzzling to Luke that a woman with so much wealth and beauty would bury herself in the wilderness and build a house. It raised so many questions in his mind that he quickly decided to find some answers. He felt the best place to start would be Elenora Gregory.

He stood up slowly, reached in his pocket and drew out a coin. It was enough to make Tag's mouth water. Luke flipped it to Tag, who caught it expertly.

"Good work, Tag. Get back to your duties. I'll handle this business from now on."

Tag pushed the coin deep into his pocket, as if he weren't too sure that Luke wouldn't try to retrieve it. Then he quickly left the room.

Luke sat for a time, contemplating Tag's information and the possible reasons behind what Kate was doing. Then he rose to his feet, grabbed his coat, and left the ship. On the dock he called for a carriage and gave the Gregory address.

A short time later he rapped on the front door of the

Gregory mansion and was admitted by a butler who eyed him curiously, wondering what a ship's captain was doing there. Luke smiled arrogantly.

"Tell Miss Gregrory that it's important that I see her as soon as possible."

"May I tell her the nature of your visit . . . sir?" the butler replied coldly.

"Yes. Tell her we have a mutual acquaintance I would like to discuss."

"Yes, sir," came the stiff reply. Luke had told him nothing to appease his curiosity or give him anything to gossip about when the servants met for the evening meal. He was gone for quite some time; then, finally, Elenora swept into the room.

Luke stood immediately. His first thought was, What a beauty she is, and his second was, Caution, Luke. This woman is a friend of Kate's, and water usually finds its own level.

"Miss Gregory, it's nice of you to see me."

"George tells me that you and I have a friend in common?"

"Yes . . . Kate Maxwell."

"Oh?" Elenora said softly. Her eyes narrowed and her interest was piqued. "Kate," she said softly, "has been remiss in not telling me she has such . . . interesting friends. I had thought I was the only acquaintance she had in this country. Obviously I was wrong."

"I am Captain Luke Sutter. Miss Maxwell was a passenger on my ship. There is . . . ah . . . something I must speak to her about, but I cannot seem to locate her."

"Oh, I'm so sorry, Captain Sutter, but Kate has not been here for some time."

"Where has she gone?"

"To tell you the truth, Captain Sutter, I really don't know. She must have found something of interest

271

elsewhere. She left my home quite some time ago."

Luke was wondering if that was as close to the truth as Elenora had ever gotten.

"You mean she left without telling you where she was going?"

"Well, I had given her the use of my house for awhile, since I had someone to visit. She must have decided to leave while I was gone. I'm sure she will send me word. Would you like to leave some message, or should I just tell her you were here asking about her . . . when I see her?"

Luke was about to answer and try to force some real truth from Elenora when the door opened and Miles walked in.

"Miles," Elenora said sweetly. "Let me introduce you to Captain Luke Sutter. Captain, this is Miles Chandler, my . . . business manager."

The two men shook hands while Elenora watched the shielded eyes of both. She wondered anew what a ship's captain and Kate Maxwell had in common, and if it was information she could use for her own purposes.

"Captain Sutter is looking for Kate Maxwell," Elenora explained and saw Miles's eyes become alert. "It seems she was a passenger on his ship, and he has . . . ah . . . some information. . . ." She looked at Luke and made a helpless feminine gesture that nearly made him laugh, for she had struck him as a woman about as helpless as a black widow spider. "It . . . it was some message that brought you here in search of Kate, wasn't it?"

"Yes"—Luke smiled—"but it really wasn't that important. If you two have business to conduct. . . ."

"Oh, no, Captain," Miles replied. "I just stopped for a quick visit. I must be on my way. I will see you for dinner tonight, Elenora?"

"Yes Miles, of course."

"Good. It was nice to meet you, Captain Sutter. But I'm afraid I must be going."

Luke and Elenora watched Miles leave, and for a moment both were engrossed in their private musings. Elenora was pleased with the disruption of what Miles had assumed would be a quiet and rewarding interlude. It would only heighten his amorous craving for her later, and that thought was most titillating.

Luke was wondering why Miles had gone along with Elenora's lie and what the two had in common with Kate. Obviously, Miles was a successful businessman, and Luke wanted to make sure none of Kate's money was about to slip into Miles's hands. That was something he wanted all for himself.

The door closed behind Miles, and Elenora again turned her attention to Luke. He was both handsome and a very dangerous-looking man. These were ingredients that always had the power to intrigue and excite Elenora.

"I am so sorry I cannot be of any help to you, Captain Sutter. Perhaps," she said softly, "if you were to drop by again . . . say the day after tomorrow . . . about nine? I might be able to give you some word of Kate then."

"That," he said in a warm, caressing tone, "is a most delightful suggestion. Even if no word is forthcoming, just seeing you would be reward enough."

"How gallant of you, Captain Sutter," Elenora said as she walked to the door with him. "I do hope I can help you . . . in some way."

"Oh"—he smiled—"I'm sure you can."

"Then I will see you the day after tomorrow?"

"Yes . . . about nine?"

"About nine," she repeated softly.

She closed the door behind Luke and leaned against

it. It was always invigorating to make a new conquest. And, she mused, the excitement would be even greater if it annoyed Miles.

Outside, Luke stood on the steps for a moment, then he laughed softly to himself and started down; but before he reached the bottom, someone called his name. He turned to see a carriage not far away and Miles Chandler seated within. The door of the carriage swung open as Luke turned, and Miles beckoned to him.

"Can I give you a ride, Captain?"

Luke was sure he had not waited for him just to share a ride. It was obvious that Miles had something to say, and Luke was most anxious to hear it.

He strode across the street to the carriage.

"This is very good of you, Mr. Chandler."

Miles sat back in the seat after closing the door. He smiled a benign smile at Luke. "Miles," he corrected. "I have a feeling . . . Luke, that you and I are going to be a great deal of help to each other."

Luke settled down in the seat and remained quiet as the carriage jerked into motion. He was waiting for Miles to make the first overture. He watched Miles's eyes, but they were hooded and unreadable. Luke suddenly felt as if he had run across a deadly, coiled snake and was waiting to see if it would strike.

"So," Miles said mildly, "you are looking for our friend Kate. Tell me, Luke"—he smiled—"does she know you're looking for her?"

"What difference does it make if she knows or not? And what business is it of yours anyway?" Luke returned his cold smile.

"Let me tell you something, my friend. I am quite interested in making myself a considerable fortune. I'm

274

going to make it in the acquisition of land. I think that you are just as interested in making your own fortune."

"Money," Luke said with a chuckle, "has always held a deep fascination for me. I take it that you want to make some kind of offer."

"Direct and to the point." Miles laughed. "I shall try to make my proposition just as clear. Land, my friend, land. It's going to give the first to possess it incalculable power. I have acquired a great deal of it . . . but I have also acquired a few problems. That is where I need your help."

"What's in it for me?" Luke asked in a low, firm voice.

"I have discussed your . . . friend . . . Kate with Elenora in, shall I say, the most discreet manner. She has at her disposal a very large sum of money. If I am not mistaken, you have your eye on it and the lovely Kate as well."

"I'm sure," Luke replied with cool sarcasm, "that you have your eye on something as well. What does all this have to do with me and Kate?"

"Simple, my friend," Miles said in a tone that had softened dangerously. "The man to whom she has run owns land that I want."

"And?" Luke prompted.

"And when she marries this man, this Sebastian Cain, it will belong to her. Then"—he shrugged—"the rest will be simple."

"Simple?"

"Yes. Kate marries Mr. Cain, we rid ourselves of Mr. Cain, you give the land to me, and you can have the woman and her fortune."

"Where does Elenora stand in this?"

"With her help I'm going to arrange for a similar transference of ownership. The land that borders Mr. Cain's belongs to a Clayton Storm. Elenora will follow

275

the same procedure that you will enact with Kate. In the long run everyone will be happy. Kate will have the money and you will have Kate. Storm will be free of his wife and Elenora will have him."

"And you," Luke said softly, "will eventually get both pieces of land."

"Absolutely correct. No one will lose."

"Except Mr. Cain and Mr. Storm."

Miles shrugged again. "In every great conflict there are some casualties. There is much at stake. Both men are expendable."

Luke realized he was looking at a completely cold and ruthless man, a man who would get what he wanted no matter who he had to use. The thought both excited and frightened him. He wanted Kate's money, and once Kate was in his hands with no one to help her, he would have her and the money. He really didn't care what happened with Clayton Storm or Sebastian Cain.

"What has held you back from taking Storm's land?"

"I have been investigating Mr. Storm for a long time. He was married once before and had a daughter by that marriage. The girl has been away at school but is due to return home soon. I believe Mr. Storm would not hesitate to . . . ah . . . cooperate if his wife and daughter were being held by friends of mine. I expect word of her by the next ship. Then, if you are ready, I will set both plans in motion."

Luke studied Miles's face for some time and Miles sat motionless, waiting. Luke bent forward and Miles smiled at the glow in his eyes.

"Tell me what you want me to do," he said. "I'm ready whenever you are."

The carriage continued to roll on as the two discussed the details of their evil schemes.

\*     \*     \*

Elenora sat before her mirror and brushed her hair. She had had all afternoon to think about Luke. Soon after his departure she had sent for the man who was her eyes and ears about the city. She had asked him to obtain certain information for her. The papers that had been placed in her hands several hours later had been both enlightening and enraging.

She took the papers to the fireplace, crumpled them up, and lit them. Then she stood and watched them burn, making sure there was nothing left.

Now she prepared herself for the evening. Miles would be there soon. She laid the brush down and stared at her image in the mirror. She had played her part well for a long, long time and now she was about to see the completion of the drama. Miles was playing into her hands exactly as she had planned. She had known long ago that his greed for land would be useful. It would take care of Sebastian Cain; it would take care of Sabrina Storm. Eventually *she* would take care of Miles. One day it would all be hers.

She thought of Summer Storm. Since Summer's childhood, Elenora had hated the girl, but now . . . now her return would herald the opportunity for her to have everything she had ever wanted. All she had to do was let Miles believe that she knew nothing of his personal plans and that she was unaware of the rendezvous he and Luke had had earlier in the afternoon.

Everything now depended on the return of Summer Storm. Once she was back, all plans could be put into motion. She would have the last laugh on Miles. It would not be long before the message she had sent to Kate would reach her.

She thought of the agreement she and Kate had reached weeks ago, without Miles's knowledge. The Cain land would be hers and, if all her plans were successful, the Storm land would be hers as well. Then she would eliminate Miles from her life. She would be free, and she would be one of the wealthiest women in the country.

Miles's arrival was announced. Elenora smiled and rose from her dressing table.

She had dressed for the occasion in a gown meant to intoxicate any appreciative male, and Miles was indeed appreciative. She walked down the stairs and into the large drawing room where Miles waited for her. He was sipping from a glass of brandy when she appeared in the doorway. The glass stopped on its way to his lips and his eyes widened with the vision that stood framed before him.

She moved across the floor toward him and stopped just inches away. She could see the effect of her appearance in his eyes and it pleased her.

He inhaled the exotic perfume she wore, then he set the brandy glass aside and took her in his arms. She melted against him and used what charms she possessed to lead him to believe she was entirely caught up in his spell and unaware of his deceit.

"Miles?" she whispered much later when they lay together in her huge, four-poster bed.

"What?"

"You have not contacted those men about Sabrina Storm yet."

"They already have their orders. The Storm house is empty. For some reason the entire family has gone to Hawk's village. No man in his right mind would go into that village to try to take one woman. We must wait. They will not be staying there forever. They have to come home soon."

"Your men, they're nearby?" she inquired casually.

"Near enough. When I find out the Storms have

278

returned home, we'll send word to them."

"How are you going to send word? Where are they?"

Miles was too satiated, too relaxed, to realize where her questions were leading.

"They were at Devil's Elbow. Toby and Carl are pretty close to here, near the old McMillan place, the deserted one. It seems their two Indian friends like to roam around, and"—he laughed—"it seems Three Feathers has his eye on a pretty little squaw from Black Cloud's village. I expect he'll grab her one of these days.

"Who is she?"

"What do you mean, who is she?" He was amused. "I have no idea. One Indian is the same as another. A squaw is a squaw."

This time Elenora laughed with him. Then she turned in his embrace and slid her arms about his waist. Her mouth lingered tauntingly and teasingly on his until he pushed aside all other thoughts but her, which was exactly what she wanted. She had gotten the information she had needed. She now knew where Clay and Sabrina were and where Miles's men could be found. As Miles began to make love to her, she gave her scheming mind free rein to develop that information into a plan of her own.

Miles left in the wee hours of the morning. He thought he was leaving Elenora comfortably asleep. She was not. When the door closed behind him, Elenora was already out of the bed and beginning to dress.

She put on a riding skirt and boots and twisted her hair into a knot on top of her head. Then she left her room and went straight to the stables. She saddled her

279

own horse, led it outside, and mounted quickly. Soon the softer night sound were being drowned out by the noise of receding hoofbeats.

Less than half a mile away she stopped in front of a cottage.

"Rafferty!" she called out. Then she waited a few minutes and called again. "Rafferty!"

The door opened and a large, very dark man stepped out.

"Yes ma'am, Miss Gregory?"

"Get your son. I want you to ride with me. I have a message to take and I need protection."

"Yes ma'am," Rafferty answered. He was gone only a few minutes and returned with a younger version of himself. They prepared their horses and joined her on the trail.

They rode until the sun was just beginning to cast a red glow on the horizon. When they finally stopped, they were outside the ramshackle remains of a house that looked completely deserted.

"Toby!" Elenora called. "Toby, come out here. I have a message from Miles."

The door opened slowly and Toby and Carl stepped outside. Toby could still make Elenora's skin crawl, and when she noted the glow of lust in his eyes, she knew she had been right in bringing armed men with her.

"Now how come Miles sent you?" Toby laughed. "He afraid to come out at night by himself. Don't he think a pretty thing like you needs protection?"

"Don't worry about me," Elenora snapped. "Rafferty here is a dead shot . . . and you've been covered since you stepped out that door."

Toby's eyes went to Rafferty and his son, both of whom made a subtle but still obvious show of the guns

280

they carried.

"Well . . . what do you want?"

"Miles has a job he wants you to do. He couldn't come, so he sent me to tell you."

"What job?"

"You're to go and get your two Indian friends. Then you're to go to Black Cloud's village. You'll wait and watch. The Storms are there. When the right opportunity comes, take Sabrina Storm. Take her to the old mine cave and keep her there. I'll bring you word of what to do next. Wait there for me."

Toby didn't answer. He was still captivated by the picture Elenora made in the light of the rising sun.

"Do you understand me?" she snarled.

"Yes," he said angrily. "I understand you. We'll wait for you at the cave as soon as we snatch the Storm woman out of the village."

"Storm's daughter should be returning soon. I'll send a message and you can be at her home when she gets there."

"Yes ma'am," Toby said sarcastically.

Elenora gave him another cold look, spun her horse about, and in a moment she and her two guards were gone. But Toby continued to stand for a few minutes watching her ride away.

"Damn bitch," he muttered. "When this is over I 'spects I'll pay you a visit. You needs a stronger man to handle you than what you got. One of these days you won't have a gun . . . and you won't have any protection. Then we'll see if we can't take some of that bitchin' out of you."

He turned to Carl, who stood grinning beside him.

"You get her"—Carl laughed—"and I wouldn't mind takin' a turn either."

"When I gets through with her," Toby said in a ragged

tone, "she won't be able to handle you. I intends to make her sorry she ever looked down her nose at me." He turned to Carl. "Come on, let's get goin'. Miles wants the Storm woman, so I guess we better go and get her."

"You ain't thinkin' of just goin' into that village, are you?"

"Hell no. You think I'd take on that Hawk? They'll make a mistake one day. They'll make a wrong move. When they do, we'll snatch her. It won't be hard."

"I kinda get the feelin' you have some plans of your own," Carl said suggestively.

"I been thinkin' on a few things," Toby admitted.

"Like what?"

"Like . . . we been workin' for Miles a long time. Seems to me we do all the work and he gets all the gravy."

"What are we gonna do about it?"

"I'm workin' on a plan in my head. When I get it set I'll tell ya. The only thing is, there's a whole lot of money at stake. I gotta find a way to get rid of Miles and get our hands on all those women."

"Might be a good idea we go and meet up again with Three Feathers and Little Elk. Then we'll decide just what we're gonna do."

"We can sell 'em like we did those other women Miles wanted out of the way."

"There ain't that much profit there. I get the feelin' these women and the men they belong to have a lot of money. I think it's time they shared some of it. Yeah, I think those men will pay real high to get 'em back."

"And you're gonna give 'em back?" Carl laughed.

"We get the money and then"—Toby grinned—"we take 'em out and sell 'em."

"So we make a double profit."

"That's right, so let's get goin'. Sooner we collect 'em, the sooner we get rich."

They laughed together and began gathering supplies. By the time they were on their way the sun was high. At nightfall they were nearing the area where Three Feathers roamed.

# Chapter Twenty-four

Clay Storm dismounted stiffly and stood by his horse. He was so tired he was nearing exhaustion. And he was also trying to control several conflicting emotions, the least of which were utter frustration and cold, hard fury.

Several times in the past few hours he had vowed to murder Sebastian Cain the moment he ran across him. This he alternated with the promise that he would forgive Cain anything if only his daughter were found safe and well.

Hawk was in a no less grim and murderous mood. Along with Patrick, Simon, and several other warriors, they had searched for several days. But it seemed as if the earth had swallowed the three they sought.

The only thing that helped to console them was the fact that Sebastian and Cole had not taken Summer; she had decided to follow them on her own. She must have trusted them, Clay thought. He knew Summer's power to read what was in people's minds and he tried to cling to this knowledge when thoughts of where she could be or what could have happened to her made him fearful.

He knew something else for certain. Summer was

capable of surviving in the wild, and if she had chosen to leave them, she could safely return home. But this only led to the obvious—she had not come home. So wherever she was, she was still with the two white men.

It was late evening. The sun was disappearing and shadows grew longer and blended together until the horizon was vague and blurred.

Hawk dismounted and stood beside Clay. "There is no sign anywhere. My warriors have made a large circle and have returned. Neither Summer nor the two whites are within the circle."

"I don't understand this, Hawk. I never thought that anyone could be in this territory without us knowing it, yet there's no sign of them. No whites know this territory that well to be able to hide from us."

"Summer knows," Hawk suggested gently. "If what Black Cloud said is so, Summer went to help them, not to hide from us. There must be something we don't know, and that worries me." Hawk tried to temper his next words so they would not reflect the fear he felt. "Do you think that the two whites have taken her far away and are holding her for some reason so that she cannot send a signal?"

"For their sakes I hope that isn't so," Clay stated grimly. "If my daughter has come to any harm at their hands, they will live to regret it."

"I feel a great guilt, my brother," Hawk confessed. "She came to me and I should have protected her. The blame lies with me."

Clay put his hand on Hawk's shoulder. "My brother speaks like a foolish child. I know my daughter well. She makes her own choices. No one could have stopped her once she had made up her mind to go."

"But I was blind," Hawk lamented. "I should have seen how her thoughts were moving. She felt the white one's tragedy. I should have known."

"I just cannot bring myself to understand why she came home from school so early, why she was where she was when he found her, and why she didn't have them return her to us instead of to the village. There are a lot of unanswered questions."

"The most important of which is," Hawk replied, "where is Summer now, and is she all right."

"Yes. I agree. I hate to return to Sabrina and tell her that it's been another useless day and we've found no trace of her."

"We will search again at first light. We will find her," Hawk said determinedly. Both men were silently adding prayers that this was true.

When Clay returned to the tipi he and Sabrina were occupying, he hesitated outside for a moment. Then, sighing in resignation at what he knew he would have to face when he went inside, he bent and entered.

His youngest son, Jason, was asleep on a dark fur mat. Sabrina and Clay junior sat beside a low-burning fire. Their faces turned to him expectantly when he entered, but their hopeful looks died as they read his expression.

"There is no sign of her, Clay?" Sabrina asked.

"Nothing. I can't understand it."

"Papa"—young Clay spoke hopefully—"maybe Summer helped the white men she went with . . . and maybe then she went home."

Clay and Sabrina exchanged quick glances. "I hadn't thought of that," Clay admitted. "I was so busy looking, I never thought she might return home. We will go first thing in the morning to find out."

"Clay," Sabrina said, "maybe I should take the boys and Patrick and go home. If Summer is there, I can send word. If she's not, it would be better if you were here with Hawk and the others to continue the hunt. At least that way no matter where she came there would be

286

someone to welcome her."

"I just thought of someplace else we might check," Clay announced. "From what I heard, this Sebastian Cain has a place out here somewhere. It might be best if Hawk keeps looking, you and the boys go home, and I go into town to see if I can find out just where the Cain land is."

"Yes," Sabrina agreed. "It sounds like an excellent plan to me."

"Papa?" young Clay questioned.

"Yes son?"

"Can't I please go with you? Mama and Jason will be all right with Patrick. They won't need my protection too."

Both Clay and Sabrina controlled their smiles with effort, for young Clay was quite serious.

"Well Clay, I think that's a good idea. You and I will go into town tomorrow. It should only take us about three or four days. In the meantime Sabrina, you and Patrick take Jason and maybe Simon or James. If Summer is there or comes home soon, send one of them back here. While we're doing that, Hawk can continue his search."

Young Clay was delighted, but he manfully controlled himself. If there were any three people in the world he worshiped, they were his parents and Summer.

"I think it's time you go to bed Clay," his father suggested. "We'll leave at dawn."

Young Clay obeyed immediately. He didn't want his father to have second thoughts about taking him along. Sabrina smiled up at her husband.

"Come on Sabrina," Clay said. "Let's take a walk. It's a pretty night."

Sabrina kissed both boys and left the tipi to walk the dark path to the river hand in hand with Clay.

"Oh Clay, I'm so worried about Summer. I wish I knew the reason she came to Hawk instead of to us. It's early to have left the school. Do you suppose she is in some kind of trouble or . . . or might need us?"

"The thought has been in my mind since I found out she was home. I . . . I wish I knew if she were all right . . . if she needed me . . ."

Sabrina could feel his doubt, and his pain. "Clay, we must have faith in her judgment too. We must remember how strong Summer is." As they walked, she held his arm and smiled up at him. "You have taught her so well, my love . . . and I don't believe Summer would ever deliberately do anything that would hurt you. You must believe that she thought of us when she made her decision."

Clay slid his arm about Sabrina's waist and hugged her close to him. He kissed the top of her head and chuckled.

"You always have the right answers, my dear. I suppose you always will and it's one of the reasons I love you."

Sabrina was content. They enjoyed the night stroll, he with his arm about her and she with hers about him, and prayers in both hearts for Summer.

Three groups left the village the next morning. Patrick, Sabrina, Simon, and James traveled in the direction of Clay's home, Clay and Clay junior headed for the town, and Hawk and three of his warriors resumed their search.


Hawk, Walking Horse, and two other warriors rode in silence and with determination. They searched for even the smallest sign that a stranger had passed. This time they did not mean to return to the village until they were certain there was no one near enough to

288

be found.

They camped very late that night. The moon had risen long before, but none of the other three would speak of stopping until Hawk commanded. And they were not even relieved when he did, though they obeyed without question.

Hawk and Walking Horse remained awake as the moon started its descent. They spoke quietly so they would not disturb the others.

"Hawk, if we find Sebastian . . . shall we punish him for what he has done?"

"How can we punish him, Walking Horse? Summer chose to go with him. I know this is so, for I saw the torn wall of her tipi, and I know he left alone that morning, for I watched him and his friend go."

"Why did you not try to stop him, when you knew what was in Summer's heart?"

"Because I felt they were a danger to Summer. My greatest mistake was not remembering that when Summer chooses to use her powers"—he smiled at Walking Horse, who chuckled in return—"she will do as she wishes, no matter what I might say."

"Hawk?"

"Yes?"

"Do you think it is possible she might still be where we can find her? Or . . . maybe . . ."

"Do not speak the words, Walking Horse. I hope she is here for us to find. If she is not, Clay will track Sebastian Cain to the end of the land if he has to. And once he finds him, I fear for Sebastian Cain, for Clay is not a man whose family can be touched without someone paying. If Summer is hurt in any way"—his eyes held Walking Horse's—"Sebastian Cain will pay with his life, and the payment will be long and devastating."

There was no more to be said. Neither man's

thoughts left Summer, and neither could sleep.

The rising sun found them again on their way—silent, and with deadly resolve.

Patrick and Sabrina rode side by side and Simon and Jason followed behind. Jason kept up a continual stream of chatter, which indicated his nervousness. It had always been thus with the youngest of the Storms. He was a good many years younger than Summer and had looked toward his older half sister with both awe and reverence.

"I hope Hawk is the one to find Summer and Sebastian," Sabrina said to Patrick.

"Why is that, lassie? Don't you think it woud be better if Clay—"

"No, oh no, Patrick. I'm afraid that Clay is in a murderous mood. He might not listen to a word Mr. Cain might say. He . . . he might do something foolish."

"Don't underestimate Clay. As long as Summer is all right—" He stopped abruptly. Both of them were thinking the same thought. Was Summer all right? And if she was, where was she?

Tears stung Sabrina's eyes as she tried to reject the possibility that something might have happened to the stepdaughter she loved so completely. Behind them a thoughtful Simon was trying to answer Jason's multitude of questions, but his mind and his young heart were with Summer. He could not remember a time when he had not loved her. During their childhood days he had kept a silent guard on his heart, for he knew that Summer had not been meant for him. She was Summer, medicine woman to Hawk's village and the daughter of Clay Storm, whose family stood very close to the throne of England. No, Summer was not for a young trapper like him, though he would never stop loving her.

His mind filled with dark and violent thoughts of what he would do to Sebastian Cain if he ever found him. He, like the others involved in the search, was fearful that Summer had made a drastic mistake in trusting this white man who had come into the village asking for help. Why, he thought, did Summer have to have such a kind and understanding heart? Why did she have to be the one on whom so many depended?

But he knew the answers as soon as the questions formed: because Summer was Summer. It was one of the many reasons why he loved her, yet he knew he could love her for her gentleness and unforgettable beauty alone.

They arrived at Clay's home two days later and were greeted by an enthusiastic Ellen, who was hungry for information. Ellen and Sabrina made everyone comfortable and cooked a delicious supper, after which Sabrina sent Jason off to sleep.

It was not long before Simon sought the solitude of his bed to concentrate on his dreams, dreams in which he could claim Summer as he never could while awake.

Patrick and Sabrina sat before the fire long into the night, their minds and hearts reaching out in the darkness to be with Clay, with Summer, and with Sebastian Cain, who had so suddenly changed everyone's lives.


Clay and his son rode into the town four days later. He took a room for both of them at a tavern and they washed away the dirt from the trail. Next they visited the office of his attorney and, as they stepped into his private office, Mr. Brewster came from behind his desk with a wide smile on his face and a hand extended to Clay.

"Clayton, I am so delighted to see you. And you, my boy"—he beamed at young Clay—"have grown three inches since I saw you last. Before long you will be as tall as your father. Come in, come in and sit down." He waved Clay to a chair. "Tell me, Clay, did Summer get home all right?" He laughed. "She has grown into a lovely young lady. I hope you are not angry that I gave her that horse. She insisted, and I know how many years she spent with Hawk and her mother's people. I was sure she would arrive safe and sound."

"She arrived . . . in Hawk's village," Clay answered.

"Hawk's village? But . . . but she said she was going home."

"Somewhere along the way her mind was changed," Clay explained. "Charles, do you know anything about a man by the name of Sebastian Cain?"

"Sebastian Cain," Charles said thoughtfully. "Somehow the name sounds familiar."

Clay went on to explain the entire situation as far as he knew it.

"From what I understand, Charles, this man has purchased some land somewhere in this territory. I wonder if it is possible for you to find out for me just where it is . . . and anything about him you can."

"But of course, Clay. I'll find out whatever I can. Come back this afternoon."

"My son and I will go find ourselves something to eat. If it is all right with you, we'll be back . . . say . . . about three?"

"Three would be fine."

"Good. Now"—Clay smiled—"I think I'd better feed this young man. If he's as hungry as I am, we'll need a kitchenful of food."

"Why not try the Cock's Crow. I dine there myself quite often. The food is excellent."

"Good idea. I'll see you around three." Charles nodded and watched Clay and his son leave. He had a strange suspicion that Clay Storm was a very angry man.

Clay took his son for a hearty meal, after which they decided to spend some time drifting about the town until it was time to return to Charles's office.

"Maybe we can find a nice gift for your mother . . . and one for Summer . . . to welcome her back home."

Young Clay nodded and gulped back the threat of what he considered unmanly tears. He silently prayed that Summer really would be home soon.

They were walking in the direction of the shops when Clay's name was called out. Both of them turned about to see Elenora Gregory walking in their direction.

Clay stiffened, his eyes grew wary, and his son gazed from him to the woman who approached, and he knew immediately that his father disliked, and distrusted, her.

"Clay," Elenora said softly, her eyes glowing with a warm and open invitation. She totally ignored Clay junior. "It's been a long time since you've been to town. It is good to see you again."

"Elenora." Clay acknowledged her, though too many past memories and her unproven involvement in a plot against Sabrina had bred nothing but distrust for her within him. He vividly recalled Sabrina's near loss and the damage done to his family, which had almost been disastrous.

"What brings you to town, Clay?"

"Oh," Clay responded, "just a little gift buying. We want to purchase something for Summer, who's coming home soon."

"So, she has finished her education," Elenora replied in a sugar-coated tone. "I suppose she will be anxious to get back to that village and her mother's people. I

293

wonder if the schools have been successful in eliminating the savage and creating the lady she should be to carry the Storm name."

Clay junior squared his shoulders, and his blue eyes matched his father's in coldness.

"Summer has always brought pride to the Storm name," Clay answered, "and, unlike some, she has always been a lady."

Elenora flushed, but she chose to ignore Clay's subtle reference to her own unladylike behavior.

"When do you expect her home, Clay?"

Before his father could answer, young Clay stepped neatly into Elenora's trap.

"She's already home. She's just been visiting Hawk and Black Cloud."

Clay refused to show any reaction, but he could have shaken his son when he saw Elenora's eyes narrow. No matter how often he came in contact with Elenora, he still came away with the feeling that she was ready to take advantage of any situation if she thought it might do her some good. Although he couldn't connect her to Summer's disappearance, he began to wonder if Elenora knew Sebastian Cain, and if maybe they were together in this. He remembered too well the time that Sabrina had been taken from him. The same cold fear touched him now. There was no way for him to ask her without alerting her to his suspicions. He decided to ask Charles if Sebastian Cain and Elenora either had met socially or had had any business dealings with each other.

"Of course," Elenora said sweetly, "she would run to them first. I suppose, though they must have tried at that school, it is rather difficult to change what's in the blood."

Clay grinned. "You are so right, Elenora," he replied. "Whatever is bred in, is bred in, and there's no changing it. Summer can trace her ancestry back a long, long way, if that's important. But I think it's more important to Summer to be close to people who love her, without concern for pedigree."

Though she smiled Elenora was furious. She would eliminate this half-breed daughter and the wife. Left alone, Clay would soon be grateful for any crumbs she might throw his way.

"We must be going, Elenora," Clay said.

"Would you like me to come with you and help you choose something . . . suitable?"

"No, thank you. I'm sure I can find something they will both like, and Clay will help me." He bowed and turned away. With narrowed eyes, Elenora watched the two go. Clay was in town for a reason other than gifts, and she intended to find out what it was.

Clay and young Clay returned to Charles's office at the appointed time, and Charles was prepared with the information they sought.

"It seems this Cain has bought some land here, Clay," Charles revealed. "The most amazing thing is that it borders yours. Where the gentleman is building is less than two days' ride from your home."

In Clay's mind the right pieces fell into all the wrong places. He was now thoroughly convinced that Sebastian had deliberately lured Summer away from the village. Clay also suspected that he might have been connected to Summer in England and might even have been the cause of her unexpected trip home. He was confused, worried, and totally determined to find Sebastian Cain and get some answers. And if he discovered them together, or saw that Summer had been harmed, he would make sure Sebastian found the price of his offense very hard to pay.

"Can you provide a map to get to his place?"

"Of course. It will only take a few minutes."

True to his word, Charles provided Clay with a small map, and Clay and young Clay left his office quickly. They had not been gone more than half an hour when Charles heard a knock on his door and his secretary came inside.

"Yes, Mr. Preston?"

"Mr. Brewster, there is a Miss Gregory outside. She does not have an appointment, but she would like to know if you could spare her a few moments of your time."

It was obvious that Preston was quite impressed with the woman who wanted to see him. Charles smiled.

"I take it she's a very attractive young lady?"

Preston grinned. "Yes sir, that she is."

"Show her in, Preston; show her in."

"Yes sir."

Preston left, and he soon returned with Elenora. Charles rose from behind his desk. Always appreciative of an attractive woman, he put on his best smile as he escorted Elenora to a chair.

"Miss . . . ah?"

"Gregory."

"Gregory? . . . Are you by any chance William Gregory's daughter?"

"Yes, I am."

"I am delighted to see you, Miss Gregory. I had the privilege of meeting your father a time or two." Charles was now aware that Elenora was a member of an influential and rather wealthy family. "Can I be of some help to you?"

"Oh, I do hope so, Mr. Brewster," Elenora said sweetly, her eyes wide and innocent. "I do believe, as I was coming down the street, that I saw an old friend of our family's and his son leaving the building."

"Clayton Storm and his oldest boy?"

"Why yes, it really was him then. There is no chance

296

that he might be coming back, is there?"

"No, my dear." Charles chuckled. "He only came in to find out about the owner of the property next to his. I'm afraid he won't be back."

"Next to his," Elenora said softly. "Why that must be the Stevens' property."

"No, it belongs to a man named Sebastian Cain."

"Oh, I see. Well, thank you, Mr. Brewster. If Clay should return, please give him my regards."

"I shall be delighted, Miss Gregory."

Elenora stepped out of the building into the sunlight. She stood still for a few minutes as she gathered her thoughts, then a slow smile crossed her lips as she whispered, "Sebastian Cain . . ."

## Chapter Twenty-five

Sebastian had entered the house and had found himself in a small entrance hall. Three doors opened off it and a staircase was directly before him. With Cole behind him, he moved to the first door and opened it.

They were inside with the door closed behind them before they noticed the woman who stood near the window. Her soft laugh made them both turn in her direction.

Sebastian was completely stunned, and Cole, at first taken by surprise at the taut jerk of Sebastian's body, rapidly deduced that the very beautiful woman with the corn-silk hair was the elusive Kate. He had his assumption verified when Sebastian finally found his voice.

"Kate!"

With a soft laugh Kate ran to Sebastian and threw herself into his arms. She murmured his name over and over between the kisses she pressed on his lips and cheeks. Sebastian's arms went around her reflexively and Cole could have groaned aloud, for at that moment the door opened and Summer entered the room.

She did not speak but stood frozen, her dark eyes

wide and locked on the two embracing before her. Sebastian reached both hands up and loosened Kate's hold, then spun away from her to face Summer just as she stepped back from the door and slammed it in his face.

"Summer!" Sebastian called as he jerked open the door, but Summer was already outside. He caught up with her just as she was mounting his horse. In another moment she would have been gone.

He knew she would not be receptive to words and, in fact, would be gone before he could utter them, so he did the next best thing. He ran to her, grabbed her about the waist, and swung her down from the horse. She fought like an enraged animal, but he finally held her close and immobile. Both were breathing heavily.

At that moment Kate and Cole ran out onto the porch. Both Sebastian and Summer looked up at them. With a scornful half smile on her face, Kate declared, "Good heavens, it is fortunate that I have come, Sebastian. If you have been forced to keep such savage company, you must be desperate. Where on earth did you get this little Indian squaw in the first place?"

Something primitive and violent rose up in Summer. All the pride and savagery she had inherited from the generations of majestic chiefs of her tribe flowed hot in her veins like molten lava. Warriors' courage filled her like a cry to battle. It swirled, combined and blended with the courage of her father's people and issued a challenge from which she was unable to retreat.

Sebastian felt her cease her struggles and he released her. She drew herself up and lifted her chin proudly, though inwardly she seethed with barely controlled anger.

"Summer," Sebastian began, "you have to listen to me."

She swung about, glaring at him. "Why do I have to

299

listen to you?" she cried. "You, with your lies and sweet words. Where is your burned house? Why is your white woman here waiting for you? I will tell you. Like all white men, you live on lies!" She turned back to Kate, and full savage vengeance was written on her face. "I am Summer," she announced, smiling a smile so cold that Kate's sneer faded and uncertainty touched her eyes, "and I give you back your lying man, for I would not soil myself with him."

"Now wait just a damn minute!" Sebastian shouted. "Summer, you keep still and listen. I had no idea Kate was here."

"Sebastian, really!" Kate replied in shock. "Why should you explain the presence of your fiancée to some . . . some Indian whore."

Summer gave a yelp of white hot rage and headed in Kate's direction with a determination that both men recognized as violent. Again Sebastian grabbed at Summer only to receive a solid wallop that rattled him, but still he caught her about the waist and held her.

Summer was using rage to fight her pain and she struck out again and again, but her anguish was almost more than she could bear. She tore herself from Sebastian's arms and before either man could stop her, she was atop Sebastian's horse and riding away. Sebastian threw himself onto Cole's horse and charged after her.

Cole turned to face Kate with a smile he had to force to his lips.

"I don't understand what's going on here," Kate said coldly. "If that savage wants to return home, why doesn't he just let her? What does she have to do with us anyway? And . . . what did she mean about giving me back my man? Sebastian has always been mine."

Cole chuckled and bowed slightly toward Kate. "I am Cole Robbins, a good friend of Sebastian's. I take it you are Kate Maxwell. If you would like to invite me in, I might be able to explain a few things to you."

Kate looked at him and was quite certain that she wouldn't like what he was going to say. But she was just as certain that she wasn't going to let some savage come between her and what she wanted.


Summer kicked her heels into her horse's flanks to urge him to greater speed. She could hear the other horse and knew Sebastian was close behind.

Damn him! her mind screamed.

Though Summer was a skilled rider, she could not outdistance Sebastian. Just as they reached a stand of trees, he came abreast of her. She refused to turn and look at him or to reduce her speed. She was unprepared when he leaned toward her and his strong arm came about her waist to lift her from her saddle.

She tried to fight, but he held her so she could not swing her arm freely. He pulled his horse to a halt. Now he was faced with the dilemma of dismounting without releasing her or opening himself to her furious assault. He slid her to the ground and dismounted as fast as he could, but she took off at a run before he could grab her. He caught up with her easily and spun her about.

Both were breathing raggedly and both were caught up in the violence of emotions they couldn't control. Summer swung and her hand connected with his cheek, but before she could strike again he caught her wrist in a viselike grip. He jerked her into his arms and held her so tightly that she could not move. She glared up at him.

"Let me go, Sebastian!"

"Not on your life."

"I will kill you!" she shrieked. "My father and Hawk will see you dead!"

"Maybe," he said firmly, "but you are going to listen to me if I have to tie you up and keep you tied up for a week!"

"I won't listen to you! I do not want to hear another lie, and that is all your words are."

"You will listen!"

"Go away, Sebastian! Go back to your white-skinned woman. Tell her your lies. Maybe she is fool enough to believe them. I am not, and I never will be again!"

She struggled until she was exhausted, and he continued to hold her until she remained still. But now her quieter rage was more frightening than her violent fury.

"Summer?" he said tentatively, "this was as much of a surprise to me as it was to you."

She quivered in his arms as if he had struck her, but her voice was cold and steady.

"Lies," she replied in a cold, flat voice.

"No. No lies. When I left here, my place was a shell. It had been burned. Do you think I lied to you about Nathaniel's death?"

She remained quiet.

"Summer, look at me," he demanded. But her face was turned away and she would not obey him. He knew that if he loosened his hold for a moment she would be gone. He could endure her violent anger more easily than this cold, deliberate shutting herself off from him.

He held her with one arm and gripped her chin with the other hand, lifting her head so he could look into her eyes. What he saw was enough to shake him to the core.

It was blatantly clear in the stiff resistance of her body and the cold anger in her eyes that Summer had closed herself to anything he might say. Nothing was going to reach her. He just couldn't drag her back and tie her up, he cautioned himself; yet he wondered if he wouldn't do just that if necessity forced him to it. He was not going to let Summer go, even if he had to fight her and the entire world.

Her eyes fell from his steady gaze and he gave her head a firm shake. "Look at me!" he repeated.

Her eyes snapped up to meet his, and he felt her fury. If she had had the strength of a man, Sebastian would have had to defend himself to the death. But he had the advantage of strength, the only advantage he had at the moment.

"I'm not going to let you run away from the truth," he said. They were not the best words he could have chosen. He saw flame in the depths of her eyes.

"I do not run from anything! I have proven that to you. But I am not foolish enough to let your lies betray me again."

"Summer, if you will only listen, I can prove—"

"Keep your proof, and your dreams. I want no part of either of them."

"If you won't let me prove it to you, why don't you use your own gift?"

"What?"

"You have been so busy feeling betrayed and being angry with me that it never occurred to you to use your powers to see if Kate was lying—or to learn any truths at all."

"I do not need to do this. Her presence is enough!"

"It sounds more like jealousy than betrayal to me," he challenged. "Are you afraid to find out? Are you afraid you might be wrong?"

"I am not jealous. Kate is what you have always wanted. Now she is here. You can make all the dreams you have had come true. Why do you still choose to lie to me?"

"First of all, you don't seem to have any real idea of

what I want at all, and second"—he smiled smugly—"I think you really are afraid to use your gifts. I think you are afraid you will find out that all I have said is true, and that your anger really is jealousy."

"You are so arrogant, so sure of yourself. Do you believe you can use people for your own ends and that they will simply submit to whatever pleases you? I know your dreams, Sebastian. Do you think I have not heard you call her name in the night?"

Sebastian remembered the dreams he had had so often recently of Summer in danger from Kate, but he was startled by her interpretation. If she knew his dreams—if she could see within him so well—why didn't she know the truth about his feelings? Then it struck him. For some reason Summer could not read him! She did not know what he felt, for she had never been able to see.

"I'm sorry, Summer," he said sincerely, regretting that he had hurt her in some way he didn't understand. "But again I think all of this is something that exists in your mind and nowhere else. Why won't you try? Why won't you let me tell you what is really true? Are you afraid?" he asked in a softened tone, "that what we share is stronger than both of us? And you are afraid to say I love you, Sebastian—or to hear me tell you that I love you?"

"Don't!" she gasped. She was frightened now in a way she had never experienced before. She did not want him to know how vulnerable she was to his gentleness. She had no intention of giving him the weapon of her love to use against her, just as she could not accept hearing him say "I love you" when it was too late.

Sebastian saw the fear in her eyes. "Come back with me," he urged. "Find out if my words are true, that my house was burned. I don't know how it was rebuilt, but

I'm sure Kate can tell us. Come back and let me tell both you and Kate that"—he inhaled deeply—"that I love you and I'm sorry she came this far, but that house and any future we might have had together just cannot be. Summer, please listen. Don't shut me away."

"Sebastian . . . let me go," she requested calmly. He was unsure of what she would do, but slowly he released her, making sure he kept himself between her and the horses, who were grazing contentedly nearby. He watched her closely as she stepped back from him.

A revelation was blossoming within Summer—that Sebastian just might have been telling her the truth and that no matter what she was, he was in love with her. But how would she ever be sure? She could not penetrate his thoughts.

Sebastian misinterpreted her silence as reluctance and changed his strategy. If he couldn't make her come back and learn the truth, maybe he could make her mad enough to want to come back just to spite him.

"Still afraid, Summer?" he chided softly. "I guess when the going gets rough, your courage disappears."

Her chin jutted stubbornly and her eyes flashed a warning. "My courage is not in question here," she snapped. "It's your lack of honesty that seems to be the trouble."

He laughed a soft, teasing laugh. "It's you who's running away."

"Your woman will not be pleased to see me return," she jabbed. "She might ask a lot of questions about you and your . . . squaw."

"Don't say that," Sebastian shouted.

"Why? Does the truth bother you even when it comes from another?"

He reached out and gripped her shoulders, nearly lifting her off the ground.

"I'm damn sick of you telling me that your Indian

305

blood makes a difference. I do my own choosing, and what you are changes nothing. Maybe you're afraid of touching the white world. I have a feeling some white man has hurt you somehow and you're out for revenge against every white man you see."

He could see that his words touched a sensitive spot and he regretted saying them when he sensed her withdrawal.

"Summer, can't we take one step at a time? Come back and I will prove to you that what I said about my home was true—that what happened to Nathaniel and me was true. Come back with me," he said gently, "and see if your gifts do not tell you what the truth really is."

It was a much gentler challenge than the other, but a challenge nevertheless. And from what his eyes told her, he had more faith in her gifts than she had.

He stepped back from her, praying he was doing the right thing.

"I'm not going to try to hold you, Summer. I'm only going to say that since I have known you, I have been able to see much that I've never imagined before. I have seen your gifts work such miracles. I'm only asking you now to let them work again, to set us both free from doubt."

The silence between them was so deep that the breeze sweeping through the trees seemed almost deafening.

"Summer?"

She had to decide, and it was so difficult. Her pride helped her make the decision. She could not—would not—run again. She had done it in reaction to pain and now she could not force herself to do it again.

"I will come," she said softly.

He did not say another word. It was extremely difficult for him to stifle his urge to snatch her up in his arms. He went for the horses and led hers back, then silently handed her the reins. She mounted and they turned their horses toward Sebastian's home.

"I don't believe it!" Kate cried. "It is not true!"

"Sebastian had no way of knowing you were coming, or that your husband had . . . died. Meeting Summer was an accident," Cole explained.

"Summer! A . . . a . . . savage! An Indian! What was Sebastian thinking of? Even if he needed to bed some whore, it certainly wasn't necessary to bring her home with him."

"You don't understand, Kate, and I wouldn't be calling Summer such names. She is a remarkable lady." Cole lowered his voice suggestively. "She has helped him through a very bad time. She's a very strong and proud woman. You might be friends if you tried."

Kate turned away from Cole and walked to the window. Though her mind was spinning with hatred, it was also attempting to conceive a plan that would rid her of Summer.

"It . . . it was such a shock," she said in a weak, strained voice. "I suppose"—the word caught on a sob—"I should have written him. But . . . but I thought. . . ."

"Kate," Cole said, believing her performance completely, "neither Summer nor Sebastian meant to hurt you. It is just something that happened. Sebastian can explain it all to you when they . . . he gets back."

She stiffened but did not turn around. Sebastian planned to keep that woman in the house *she* had built, and to send her back home! she raged silently.

It was fortunate for her that Cole did not see the cold hatred on her face as her mind began to scheme. This was an Indian. What did she know about keeping a man like Sebastian happy, about being mistress of a house and living the kind of social life that Sebastian was used to? How could he ever take her back to meet his parents?

A slow smile touched her lips. Let him bring her back. In a very short time she would prove to Sebastian and Summer that their union was impossible. She would give Sebastian all the evidence he needed to judge Summer inadequate. She would prove to him beyond a doubt that Summer didn't belong, that she was a stupid, ignorant savage. Sebastian was a proud man, but once he saw Summer's shortcomings, he would understand that though a man might bed such a woman, there was certainly no need to marry her. Oh yes! she thought. Given enough time, she would make Summer so miserable that she would be grateful when Sebastian sent her home.

Kate turned from the window. She presented a beautiful picture of a sweet, defenseless woman, with her tear-stained cheeks and trembling lips.

"I'm sorry. I've acted like a fool. Of course Sebastian didn't know I was coming. It . . . it will take a little time to get over the shock."

"Of course," Cole replied sympathetically. "I can understand how difficult it must be for you."

She smiled a tremulous smile and turned back to the window. At that moment Sebastian and Summer arrived.

Kate watched as they stopped before the house and noted Sebastian's gentleness as he reached to help Summer dismount. She saw the lingering touch and a murderous emotion tore at her. But when she turned to meet them, her face was a controlled mask.

Summer stood beside Sebastian and looked across the room at the woman standing in the light of the window. Her heart twisted when she realized that Kate was indeed very beautiful. Kate took a step toward them and Summer gasped softly as a chill touched her flesh. Something stirred to life deep within her, and it was something she had not felt since childhood. She sensed complete evil in this woman as she had in only one other. She remembered well the ball to which her father and stepmother had taken her as a child. There she had met Elenora Gregory. She had had the same feeling then, as if she could see within the woman before her and could find only a deep black void.

Summer tried to control these thoughts, for the ones to follow were even more confusing. Was it just because she was jealous of this woman's place in Sebastian's life? she wondered. Was she deliberately creating visions that were not there because Kate had a claim on Sebastian's heart?

"Sebastian," Kate said softly, her blue eyes moist with tears, "I am sorry I said such cruel things. It was just the shock."

Sebastian was eager to question Kate because he knew how urgent it was for Summer to hear the answers.

"Kate, I had no idea you were coming here. When I left I thought it was definite that you would not come."

"I was so upset . . . so frightened. I made a terrible mistake, Sebastian. When George died I . . . I realized how foolish I had been. That everything I had was not nearly as important."

"How long have you been here?"

"For quite some time. Sebastian, what happened here? When I arrived there was some strange man guarding the burned-out remains of your house. He . . . he took me to Nathaniel's grave. Oh, Sebastian, I found it hard to believe such destruction . . . and you were gone. What happened?"

"I will explain it all to you, Kate, but first"—he waved his hand to encompass everything—"this . . ."

"I rebuilt it for you. I thought you would be pleased."

"I . . . I am pleased at the thought, Kate," Sebastian answered, but he couldn't elaborate on how drastic and inappropriate the changes were. "I owe you a great deal of money."

"The money is not important, Sebastian. We are." Sebastian wanted to say that she had realized that a little too late. Instead he tried to make it easier for both of them.

"We will talk later, Kate."

Kate felt that Sebastian was telling her they would soon be alone, and she smiled.

"Right now everyone is tired and hungry," Sebastian added.

"Mandy is preparing some dinner," Kate said. "If you two men will see to the horses, I will see that there is food on the table."

"Mandy?" Sebastian questioned.

"Why yes," Kate said in surprise. "We need a cook and someone to clean the house while we're here."

Sebastian was silenced by Kate's reference to "we."

"There are also two men to handle the work. They usually stay in the barn, but I have sent them to town for some supplies. The barn is quite clean, and it has plenty of hay."

She was subtly suggesting that Cole and Summer could sleep in the barn, but the harsh look in Sebastian's eyes halted any further comments.

Summer had been watching Kate closely and had decided that she would not sleep this night under the same roof with her. A clean barn was better.

She had heard Kate speak of rebuilding the house and of Nathaniel's death, and she knew Sebastian had not lied about this. But Kate was so beautiful that Summer found the uncomfortable weight of jealousy settling firmly on her shoulders.

It would be very difficult for any man to leave a

woman so beautiful, she reflected, and one in possession of something she knew white men cherished—great wealth.

She looked around her and realized she could never live in such a place. She thought of her family's warm, comfortable cabin and knew that, despite his wealth, her father had chosen to live so. It was not an elaborate home, but Sabrina and Clay had filled it with so much love that she had never felt it lacking.

Cole and Sebastian left the house to care for the horses, and Kate and Summer were left alone to gaze across the room at each other. Summer could feel the darkness roil up in the woman like a dense black fog. Only grim determination kept her from turning and running from such a force.

But another thought filled her heart and created a defense that was impenetrable. She was Summer Storm, and she would never run from this woman again. She felt pride swell within her until it crowded out all sensations of fear.

Kate walked toward Summer, her gaze dripping disdain. "I'm sure," she said sweetly, "that you must have eaten at a table sometime in your life. I do hope you have some manners. Oh, and we wash for supper." She sniffed arrogantly. "You do bathe, don't you—occasionally?"

Summer's eyes glittered dangerously, but her anger was diffused by a touch of mischief.

"Ugh," she snarled in a low, guttural tone that startled Kate and made her step back quickly. "Why should I wash?" she asked roughly. "I took a bath last week. That is enough for awhile."

"Lord," Kate breathed, "you are a savage. Why don't you go back where you belong?"

Summer laughed suggestively. "I'm not going back. My father beats me. I'll stay with Sebastian. He's warm to sleep with and he treats me good. I'll stay." Summer announced these last words firmly.

Kate could have choked on her fury. But before she could slap Summer as she wanted to do, Cole and Sebastian returned.

But Kate wanted some kind of revenge and some proof for Sebastian that he must get rid of Summer. She was pleased with the idea that occured to her.

"Sebastian, I'm sure your . . . friend would like to bathe before dinner. I'll have Mandy fetch some water to my room." She turned her smile on Summer. "There are many dresses in my closet. You may have one if you choose. I'm sure that buckskin is . . . uncomfortable."

Summer saw Kate's game immediately, but Sebastian and Cole were just relieved that Kate was being friendly.

"Come with me. I'll show you where you can bathe and change."

Sebastian gave Summer a grateful smile when he saw she was willing to go. And willing she was, for Summer desired nothing more than a hot bath. But she smiled to herself, for she was about to give Kate and Sebastian a surprise they had not bargained for.

# *Chapter Twenty-six*

Kate had seen to it that Summer had all the comforts, and Summer realized this when she saw the large wooden tub. She had not been in the room long when a small black girl swung open the door to carry in two buckets of steaming hot water. The buckets were entirely too heavy for her slight body and Summer ran to aid her. Mandy blinked in surprise and a small touch of fear lit her eyes. She was used to a smack or a cold remark from Kate.

"Ah kin handle it, Miz," she said quickly. But Summer had already gripped one bucket and was dumping it into the tub. Mandy poured the other in.

"Ah'll go fetch mo'," she said, then backed away with the two empty buckets as if she couldn't quite believe Summer's kindness.

While she was gone, Summer went to the chest that held Kate's clothes. Under any other circumstances she would have refused to touch anything that belonged to Kate, but for this one night she had to prove to both Kate and Sebastian that Summer Storm was not a woman to be taken lightly.

There was such a quantity of dresses that Summer was delighted. Like any young girl, she was excited by pretty clothes. She stood before them a long time, knowing she would have to choose very carefully.

The one she selected was ivory satin with a neckline so low it made Summer wonder if it would reveal all of her. She placed it on the bed and found soft, filmy undergarments to go with it.

By this time Mandy had returned with two more buckets of water. Summer again helped her dump them into the large tub.

"What is your name?" Summer asked.

"Mandy."

"Well, thank you, Mandy. I appreciate your carrying all that water for me. Why don't you stay and talk with me. Maybe you could help me get dressed. I'm sure I'll need some help lacing this up."

Now Mandy was in total shock. The last kind words she had received from any whites had been spoken so long ago that she could barely remember.

"Yessum," she replied softly, but her stiff, almost fearful demeanor had told Summer exactly what Mandy had expected and the kind of treatment she had become used to here.

Summer eased herself down into the water with a sigh of deep contentment. Mandy laughed to herself as she poured some of Kate's very expensive bath oil into the water. She hated Kate with all her heart, and because she did, she had listened carefully so that she knew what was going on in the house.

She liked the dark-eyed woman Sebastian had brought home with him and her heart had filled with secret delight when she saw Kate's jealousy. Summer chatted easily with Mandy and soon Mandy's tongue had been loosened. Summer was given a minute by minute account of everything that had occurred in the house from the day of Mandy's arrival.

"Miz Kate, she get all de men and dey build up dis

house real quick. But dey doan like it. Even Jake, he go camp somewheres else."

"Who's Jake?"

"He be de man Mr. Sebastian leave to care fo' dis place whilst he be gone. Mr. Sebastian, he doan hab no idea Miss Kate she comin'."

"I see."

"Miss Summer?"

"What Mandy?"

"Yo be stayin' fo' awhile? Mr. Sebastian . . . seems he like yo cuz he bring you home like he mean fo' yo to stay."

"I . . . I don't think so, Mandy. This house . . . it has a lot of bad memories and trouble with it. I guess I would always feel it was Kate's house. Besides . . . Sebastian has to make his choices for himself."

"Yessum," Mandy said in a disappointed tone. She couldn't understand why any man would want the yellow-haired witch if he could have the kind-eyed girl before her.

Summer savored the bath to the fullest, and reluctantly rose from the water only when it had finally cooled.

She was drying herself and slipping into a soft, filmy chemise.

"Miss Summer, yo sho' is pretty. Yo cud make dat man want you iffen yo put yo mind to it."

"Mandy, there's more between a man and a woman than that."

"Yessum"—Mandy giggled—"but dat sho' do make it mo' fun."

"Mandy!" Summer laughed.

"I bet dat's sho' what's in Miz Kate's mind."

"Well, that is none of our business, Mandy."

"Yessum."

Summer sat before the large mirror and ran a brush

through her long, dark hair until it shone. It hung well below her hips, and she had planned to leave it that way until Mandy spoke again.

"Miz Summer?"

"Yes."

"Ah kin fix yo hair real pretty if you've a mind to let me."

"Why Mandy, how kind of you. I'd be very pleased. I have not worn my hair in anything but braids since I left England."

Mandy seemed very adept as she brushed Summer's hair, coiled it upon her head in gleaming ropes, and pinned it securely. Fine wisps of hair remained to frame Summer's face and curl against her slender neck. Mandy was quite pleased with herself as she stood back and observed Summer in the mirror. There was no doubt in Mandy's mind that Summer was the most beautiful woman she had ever seen.

Summer looked at herself in the mirror. It had been so long since she had dressed so. Her golden skin above the ivory gown glowed in the candlelight. The bodice barely concealed her body as it dipped gracefully over the soft mounds of her breasts. She stood and watched the fabric flow softly about her. She looked tall, cool, and very slim. To Mandy she seemed a bronze and ivory vision and the serving girl could barely wait to see the expressions on the faces of the people who waited below.


Sebastian and Cole were both a little impatient because they were exceptionally hungry and couldn't imagine what Summer could be doing that would take so much time.

But Kate sat confidently and waited. She was imagining Summer being unable to choose an appropriate gown, and, with her braided hair, still looking like an Indian girl despite her attire. She would appear dressed for a masquerade, in clothes that would make her look foolish and completely out of place.

She could picture Summer, at a table for probably the first time in her life, eating like an animal and disgusting both Cole and Sebastian.

She was enjoying her ruminations, for she saw a Summer who would be incapable of intelligent conversation and left miserably aware of her inability to fit into a life-style that Sebastian would want.

Sebastian stood up for the fifth time and stretched to ease the unaccustomed inactivity and his stiffening muscles.

Kate watched, and desire stirred within her. He was lean and taut, and she could almost feel the rigid muscles of his back and shoulders as they rippled beneath his tight buckskin shirt.

She had visions of what the night would soon bring, and her skin became flushed and sensitive as she imagined lying in Sebastian's arms and reclaiming the passion they had shared so eagerly in the past. She licked her lips in dreamy anticipation of his hard mouth claiming hers again.

Cole had stretched his long legs before him and was solemnly contemplating the needs of his empty stomach and wishing Summer would hurry.

There was a squeak on the stair and soon Mandy appeared. Her face was still, but her inner glee was barely held in check.

"Miz Summer, she comin' right now."

"Well, it's about time," Kate replied. "We have waited long enough."

Kate rose from her chair, as did Cole. Sebastian turned from the window where he had been contemplating the soft moonlight and the glitter of countless stars.

Summer stood framed in the doorway. There was a soft gasp from Kate, Cole gazed in open-mouthed awe, and Sebastian was stricken so fiercely that he could not seem to catch his breath.

Sebastian saw a goddess of gold and ivory who was bathed in the mellow candlelight. Her figure was displayed to the greatest advantage, for the dress, laced tightly about her slim waist, threatened at any moment to spill forth her abundant charms.

"Summer?" he questioned in a ragged whisper, as if he could not quite believe the woman who stood before him was the same wild and untamed beauty he had known.

Kate's face was livid with raw jealousy and it took every effort she could summon not to shriek her fury, and run to Summer, and rip the offending gown from her. Cole was the first to regain some equilibrium and he started toward Summer. But then he paused suddenly and remained still.

Sebastian had begun to move slowly toward Summer. Their eyes held and Cole was again sure that neither of them knew that anyone else was present.

Sebastian's eyes devoured Summer like a starving man eyeing a banquet. He stopped beside Summer and her dark eyes rose to meet his. He drank in her beauty in one breathless gulp as he slowly lifted her hand and pressed a kiss against her wrist where the throbbing pulse beat a wild tattoo.

"You are so very beautiful," he whispered.

She smiled, content with the effect she had created, but determined that it was just the beginning of a long and rewarding evening. Summer's pride had been attacked one time too often. She would not bow like a defeated slave before the woman who glared at her across the room. She would prove to her, to Sebastian, and to herself that she was an adversary such as Kate Maxwell had never faced before.

It had taken her a long time to come to terms with all that had happened since she had first met Sebastian. Her powers had not aided her because she had been frightened and untrusting. She had fought Sebastian's presence, though deep inside she had known all along that he was meant to be part of her life.

She had done as Sebastian had requested and had opened her mind to Kate. She had listened to her words and to Mandy's. She realized now that Sebastian had told her the truth. And even though she still could not enter Sebastian's mind and hear his thoughts, she resolved to trust his words.

She had also discovered the dark side of Kate's nature; she could see it glowing even now in her eyes. In fact, she felt at the moment that she knew a side of Kate that Sebastian didn't know.

"Thank you," Summer replied. She turned to Kate and smiled her sweetest smile. "I am very grateful that you have let me borrow such a beautiful gown." Kate could not manage a reply. "I know everyone must be very hungry. I am also. Shall we eat?"

Three incredulous people followed Summer to the table. There Summer sparkled. She laughed and chattered in animated conversation while Kate glowered, Cole sat spellbound, and Sebastian surrendered all concerns over Summer's origins, birth, blood, family, or anything else. She was Summer, and that was all he needed. Summer—magnetic, untamed, beautiful, and the recipient of every ounce of love he possessed.

"I had no idea you had been educated in England," Kate said in a frigid tone she was trying to control.

"Yes."

"I thought . . . I mean . . ." Kate began. "I didn't

know that . . ."

"That an Indian would be allowed in a white school in England," Summer finished sweetly.

"Well, it isn't usual."

"No, I suppose it isn't. But it seems my father has some friends."

"I thought your father was a trapper." Cole interjected.

"By choice," Summer replied, her eyes turning to Sebastian, who had taken a deep interest in her answer.

"I don't understand, Summer," Sebastian said. "What do you mean by choice?"

She did not intend to tell Sebastian about her family under these circumstances. When she told him, she wanted it to be at a time when she could explain.

"It . . . it's just that I'm sure my father could be anything he chose to be. But anyway, he saved the life of a very important man and, in exchange, the man told him that if he ever needed a favor, he only had to ask. When I was old enough, he asked."

"Tell me," Kate said quickly, "what did you do, where did you live, before you went to school?"

"I spent my days between my father's cabin and Hawk's village."

"Hawk?" Kate laughed softly.

"Hawk is my foster father," Summer explained with eyes steady and chin rigid. "He has been blood brother to my father since before I was born. He is a fine and honorable man. Spending my childhood years in his village taught me much, especially about kindness and generosity. I would not exchange his village for the finest of cities."

Kate's inability to best Summer angered her, and she chose to bring the dinner to a halt. She was impatient now to bring the entire evening to a close, for if she did, it would hasten the moment when she could have

Sebastian in her arms. Once there, he would soon forget his foolish infatuation and turn to her, where he belonged.

She rose from the table and the three joined her as she left the room. Sebastian had been planning to ask Summer to join him for a stroll in the cool air, but Kate quickly intervened.

"Sebastian, I must talk to you for a minute—alone."

Sebastian could only watch helplessly as Cole invited Summer for the very same walk, to which she agreed. He was hardly able to choke back his disappointment when Cole escorted Summer to the door and winked at him as they left.

Cole and Summer walked slowly. The air was cool and the moon hung high and white in the black, cloudless sky. Cole could tell that Summer's mind was still inside the house.

"Summer?"

"Yes Cole?"

"I didn't get a chance earlier to tell you how pretty you are. That gown has sure made some changes in you."

"No, Cole," Summer said softly. "I am still the same, and I will always be the same. The pretty clothes are nice, but whether I like it or not, maybe I don't belong in Sebastian's world."

"You're crazy, Summer," Cole said evenly. "Sebastian is in love with you. Worlds, places, and things don't matter."

"She . . . she's beautiful, Cole, and Sebastian loved her once."

"To tell you the truth, Summer, I really don't believe that. I think he's only discovered what being in love is since meeting you, and he's now realizing that Kate was never the one." Summer was silent. "Summer?"

"What?"

Cole stopped, and Summer turned to look up at him questioningly.

"You really love Sebastian?"

"Yes Cole, I do. I think I have for a long time, but . . . I can't explain it to you very well, Cole. You see, I first saw Sebastian a long, long time ago, when I was a child. I tried to deny the vision I had been given, just as I tried to deny Sebastian when we first met." Summer went on to tell Cole about Emily and her reasons for feeling as she did about white men.

"When I met Sebastian I was angry, and I hated everything white . . . and I fought myself for wanting him when I thought he wanted another . . . and"—she sighed—"I felt that because of my Indian blood Sebastian could not truly want me for a wife but only for a. . . ." She looked away. "And now . . . even though it would be hard to bear . . . I think I would go with him, be with him, no matter what the reasons." She again looked up into Cole's eyes, almost angrily. "But I will never let her insult my family again."

"Don't worry." Cole laughed. "Tonight Kate got her first hard lesson in courtesy."

"The first!" Summer chuckled.

"If I'm not mistaken, Sebastian is about to give Kate a lesson in being a good loser."

Summer giggled softly. "I can't say that I'm not enjoying the idea."

"Me neither."

"But Cole, she rebuilt his house and—"

"He's got enough money to pay her back and better. He'll put an end to all the problems and send Kate back home." He smiled and reached out to take her hand. "Summer, why don't you tell him that you love him and want to stay with him. Why don't you put an end to this

322

needless battle and enjoy each other."

"I have so much to tell him, Cole, but . . ."

"But what?"

"I can't do it here—in her house. I guess that's how I'll always think of it, as her house."

"Well," Cole said gently, "why don't I go back and tell Sebastian that a very beautiful woman is in the barn waiting to talk to him. He can come to you and both of you can be free of this place. I'd say a barn is just as good a place to start, wouldn't you?"

Summer laughed and stood on her toes to kiss him.

"What a friend you are."

"Sebastian has no idea how close he has come to having you snatched away." He laughed. "One more kiss and I might just do it."

"Then I won't tempt you by kissing you again. But I will tell you how much I appreciate your friendship. Thank you, Cole."

"You're welcome, pretty lady. Now, let me go and send your man to you."

"Good night, Cole."

"Good night, Summer."

Summer watched as Cole walked back toward the house. Then she turned and strode toward the newly built barn.

Inside she found it difficult to see, for the only light came from thin beams of moonlight filtering through cracks in the walls. There was an immense supply of fresy hay stacked in a huge pile. She walked to it and sat down to think of what she would say to Sebastian.

Kate spoke Sebastian's name a second time before she drew his attention from the door that had just closed between him and Summer. He turned to look at her.

323

"Kate, what is it you wanted to talk to me about?"

Kate went to Sebastian and threw her arms about his neck, and with a low, seductive laugh, she retorted, "How can you ask such a thing, Sebastian? I have waited all night to be with you. It has been so long."

Sebastian gently but firmly loosened her arms from his neck. She gazed up at him in pretended hurt and surprise.

"Darling . . . ?" she queried.

"Kate, we have to talk about this. You should have written to tell me you were coming. That would have made it a lot easier for both of us."

"Easier? Sebastian, everything is easy now. George is dead and he left everything to me. We can be together now. I have millions, and we can do anything we please."

"I don't think millions have anything to do with it, Kate. Things have . . . well, everything has changed. Me, my values, my whole life, it's different now."

"It's that woman, isn't it? It's that dirty little Indian."

"Leave Summer out of this. I've changed, Kate. Things are just different. I know for sure now that you and I have never really wanted the same things. We're worlds apart, Kate, and there's no middle ground. I'll pay you back for the house, with more for your trouble."

"Just like that! But you told me you loved me, that you wanted me to come with you!"

"But you wouldn't come!" he replied angrily. "You needed your security and your money. You made your own choices, Kate, and now I've made mine. I'm staying in this country, and if she'll have me, I'm building a life with Summer."

"Sebastian," Kate sobbed. Tears filled her eyes and she came to him, lifting her cornflower eyes to his beseechingly. Her arms came around his waist.

"Sebastian, it's just because you have been away from me for so long. I can see how you might have needed her. But I love you, Sebastian."

"I do need her, Kate," Sebastian said gently as again he removed himself from her arms. "I love her and I intend to marry her."

"How can you think of such a thing? A man with your wealth and position must marry a woman who will be part of such a world."

"From what I've seen tonight, Summer can be part of anything she chooses. But understand this, Kate, whatever kind of life Summer and I live will be her decision, because I would live with her in a tipi if that would make her happy."

"You are cruel, Sebastian"—she moved her body against his—"but I can make you forget her," she said huskily. "Come with me, Sebastian, and we can renew what we had. I can make you forget her."

Sebastian's eyes darkened with an emotion close enough to disgust to enrage Kate. She raised her hand to strike him, but Sebastian caught her wrist in an iron grip that made her cry out.

"Don't, Kate," he said in a dangerously cold tone. "Let's not make this any harder than necessary. I will repay you for the house, and as soon as you get your things packed I will take you to town. Kate, let's try to part as friends."

"Friends! Friends! Sebastian, you cannot do this to me! I won't let you. You would be making a fool of yourself and a joke of your name if you gave it to that Indian slut!"

Sebastian grabbed Kate by the shoulders, eliciting a squeak of fear from her, then he gave her several rough shakes.

"Don't say a word against Summer ever again, Kate. It has always been against my nature to strike a woman, but if you insist on calling Summer names, I might just make an exception."

Kate knew she had pushed Sebastian too far. She had to have time, time to rid herself of Summer and time to draw Sebastian back into her bed.

"Oh Sebastian, I'm sorry. I am so mixed up," she sobbed. But this time her tears were wasted on a resolute Sebastian.

"All right," she said softly. "It will take me a day or two to get my things ready. Then, if you still want me to go, I will."

"Kate, don't be so unhappy. You are young and very beautiful. I'm sure there will be many men most anxious to marry you. You need only snap your fingers and they'll come running."

"It has not all been for nothing," Kate whispered to herself.

"What?"

"Nothing. We can talk in the morning. I'm tired. Good night, Sebastian."

"Good night, Kate."

As he watched her walk away, he was unsure of why he felt he hadn't heard the last of Kate. Sebastian stood alone in the room and wondered if he would look unreasonably jealous if he went outside to find Cole and Summer.

He laughed to himself in disbelief. He was caught in an intricate tangle that could only be unraveled by one slim, dark-eyed girl who he wasn't even sure wanted him. It was a mystery beyond his understanding, this falling in love. But in love he was, and he was impatient to see if he could hear the same words from Summer.

At that moment the door opened and Cole walked in.

Sebastian was looking so expectantly toward the door that Cole had to laugh. And soon Sebastian's laughter joined his.

"Where is Summer?"

"Well . . . I don't know if I should tell you. You've been treating that girl badly and she needs a big brother's protection."

"Cole"—Sebastian grinned—"if you want to be capable of walking tomorrow, you had better answer my question tonight. Where's Summer?"

"My friend," Cole said with a very pleased smile, "for some reason Summer has no desire to be around Kate or this house. She's in the barn . . . waiting for you."

"Thanks, Cole," Sebastian said as he passed Cole at a run. Cole's soft laugh followed.

## Chapter Twenty-seven

Kate had closed her bedroom door behind her and had leaned against it for a moment to control the trembling of her body. She had never been so angry, nor so determined to destroy another person. She thought of Summer and Sebastian together and the idea was so infuriating that she refused to accept it.

She paced the floor for a few moments, her hands gripped together, and one scheme pursued another through her mind. How could she rid herself of Summer? . . . How could she thrust Summer from Sebastian's life and retain him for herself?

She walked to the window and held the curtain aside. Then a low, guttural sound of animal anger escaped her as she watched the scene below. After a few minutes, she left the room and moved on silent feet down the stairs.

Summer had risen from the soft, scented hay in nervous anticipation. She had so many things to say to Sebastian, so many things to explain. Would he understand, or would he be angry at her for all the truths she had left untold? She had never deliberately lied to him, but she knew he might feel as though she had, for she had not told him who and what she really was.

She loved him. That was the brightest truth and it gave her courage. She loved him and she wanted him. For the first time, she would ask Sebastian to make love to her.

She could not bear to sit, or to stand, so she went to the door and pushed it open. The cool night air touched her flesh, which felt feverish and so very sensitive.

She watched as the door of the house opened and Sebastian came out. He started toward the barn. The white moonlight etched his tall form in light and shadow. It touched the gold of his hair and made his muscular form seem even broader.

She moved outside and took a few steps in his direction. At that moment Sebastian saw her and stopped. It seemed an endless moment that he waited. He needed her to come to him, to want him, and slowly she came.

She moved gracefully, and the ivory gown shimmered about her, giving her an ethereal look. He felt as if she were a dream, a goddess he had conjured up from the deepest corner of his heart. She was the completion of him, the part of him that had been missing. He could feel the ache of desire grow within him until it was a force he contained by sheer will. He would not take unless she chose to give.

She stopped within inches of him and her wide, fathomless eyes stared into his. The silence seemed filled with a current so swift and so deep that neither had the strength to resist its pull. Yet no words were necessary to breach the gap of misunderstanding that had stood between them.

Sebastian reached out a tentative hand to touch her cheek. His hand brushed lightly against her skin, following the curve of her cheek to the soft flesh of her throat. His hand traced the outline of the fine collarbone and came to rest on the pulse that raced frantically. Then he slid his fingers gently up the soft skin of her throat to lift her chin. Slowly he bent his head to touch his lips to hers.

Her lips trembled beneath the feather-light touch of his, and she closed her eyes against the almost exquisite pleasure that coursed through her like heated wine.

"Oh, Sebastian," she whispered softly against his mouth. "I love you."

He caught his breath, unsure of whether she had said the words or he had wished them. He caught her face between his hands and his eyes searched hers. He saw his own emotions reflected in her dark eyes, he saw the soft, pouting mouth eager for his kisses, and he saw sweet surrender. His joy melted the very bones of his body and drained away all other thoughts until he was hollow then refilled with hot, unbridled desire.

His arms drew her close and their lips met in a kiss that began as a gentle promise and slowly continued to grow. Gently her arms moved up about his neck and her body pressed closer to him.

The kiss was lingering and sweet as he savored the softness of her mouth. When the kiss ended, they held each other breathlessly.

"Tell me again," he whispered.

"I love you."

"And I love you."

"Sebastian—" she began, but he interrupted.

"I guess I've known that inside from the day I found you. I was so busy with hatred and revenge that I didn't see until now."

"I have so much to say to you, Sebastian."

"Must we talk now?" he asked with a quick grin.

"Yes . . . just for a little while. Sebastian, don't you want to know any more about me than you do?"

"No, I don't. I want to know that you trust me, and that you love me. That's enough for now. We can spend the rest of our years talking . . . maybe." He chuckled. "I, for one, have other plans."

"You must at least forgive me, Sebastian."

"For what?"

"For not really knowing. You are the only person whose thoughts I cannot read."

"You don't need to right now," he joked. "I'm sure you know what I'm thinking."

"Sebastian, please listen."

"A few minutes—no longer," he threatened with a gentle kiss.

Summer went on to explain what she had thought all along and why she had believed he was lying. She told him why she had fought so hard and that she had even harbored thoughts of vengeance against him for having the ability to make her want him even when her mind told her it was all deceit.

"You can have all the revenge you want," he teased. "Force me to your will if you want . . . and, my love, take a lifetime to do it, will you?"

"Don't you want to hear of my father, my past?"

"It isn't the part I'm interested in. I don't really care if you were hatched from an egg. Summer, your time is up."

"You are a stubborn man, Sebastian Cain."

"Very."

"You've only one thing on your mind."

"Right."

"You're not going to listen to any more, are you?"

"You," he said softly as he bent to kiss her again, "are a very intelligent girl. Come with me."

"Where? Not in . . . that house?"

"No." He put his arm about her and with her head on his shoulder they walked to the barn. Neither was aware of the shadowed figure that stood on the darkened porch of the house, the one that had been listening very attentively to all that had been said between the two lovers. Kate stood silently, absorbing the information she had heard and trying to think of some way to use it.

She moved toward the door of the house but stopped and remained silent, listening. She had heard a noise. She knew Cole was asleep and that Sebastian was with Summer. Mandy had long since gone to bed. Yet she sensed that someone was standing in the shadows near the corner of the house. It could only be someone bringing new from Elenora.

She took the chance to call out softly. "Who is it?"

"Shhh," came a whispered reply. "Go to the back of the house. Miz Elenora sent a message."

She moved swiftly, hoping for news to help solve the problem of Summer. The man met her in the thick, black shadows.

"What is it? What does Elenora want?"

"She don't want nothing except to do you a favor."

"What favor?"

"She got word that your man brought Clay Storm's daughter home with him. She sent Three Feathers, Little Elk, and me to take her off your hands."

Kate's heart leapt. But then she realized she would have to think of a plan that would keep Sebastian from following Summer's trail. Within minutes she began to smile.

"Listen," she said quickly. "This is what I want the three of you to do." She went on to explain her plan.

He nodded, then cautiously faded into the shadows. With a smile on her face, Kate went to her room.

There she sat at her desk, took out a sheet of paper, and began to write.

Sebastian and Summer stepped into the barn and he pulled the door closed behind them. The almost total darkness disappointed him, because this night he wanted to see Summer's face as he made love to her.

He brushed a soft kiss across her lips and said, "Stand still. Don't move."

Summer could hear him moving about and in a few minutes the barn was brightened by moonlight as Sebastian pushed open the shutters covering the windows.

As the pale, mellow light flooded the barn, Sebastian turned to look at Summer. He saw willingness in her eyes, but a new shyness. For her this was the first time, and she was suddenly unsure.

He went to her side, brushed a kiss across her lips, and took her hand to lead her to the piles of soft, sweet-smelling hay. He sat down and drew her down beside him. One arm went about her and he tipped her chin up with the other hand to look into her eyes.

She was not afraid of him; that he could see. But he suspected she might be a little afraid of herself. Before, it had been a battle, a defeat. Sebastian did not want it to be that way this time.

Their lips met, very gently, just brushing. Lingeringly, almost lethargically, his lips played on hers, nibbling, tasting, capturing her mouth and releasing it until she made a soft sound of slowly growing desire.

Then his mouth became firm and knowing, moving urgently and with growing heat. As if they had a will of their own, her hands crept up his chest to circle his neck.

He had wanted her like this for so long that he

refused to hurry. He lingered with an even deeper kiss while his hands sought the laces of her dress.

It was a delightful shock for him when she not only moved to help him but sought to free him of his own clothes. He felt her touch against his skin and groaned aloud at the sheer pleasure of her fingers skimming lightly at first then restlessly, as if urging him to more. It was as if she had lightly strummed every nerve and had sent fingers of flame throughout his body.

The loosened gown fell away and the sheer chemise revealed her delectable breasts, whose crests had hardened with passion and had risen against the flimsy material as if seeking the source of this pleasure.

He cupped one in his hand and through the fabric he could feel its warmth. His thumb touched the hardened nipple with a slight pressure and a circling motion. It was an erotic sensation and she breathed a whispered moan. She could hardly believe the aching hunger that caused her whole body to tremble.

Slowly his hands slid up her satin skin to touch her hair. Deftly he loosened the pins and watched it tumble about her.

His eyes darkened to an intense green as he absorbed her beauty, drinking it in with a soft sound of appreciation.

She closed her eyes against the heat of his gaze and felt his hands again as he removed the chemise.

She opened her eyes when she felt his hand leave her and watched in utter fascination as he removed his clothing.

His body was sleek and hard. The long, flawless muscles rippled under taut, tanned skin.

How beautiful he is, she thought immediately. Even his large and throbbing manhood held no fear for her; she felt only a tingling expectation.

She wanted to touch him, to know him as he knew

her. She reached out her hand and he suddenly became still. Gently she touched his face, the square chin with a slight stubble of beard, then slipped through the thick, burnished hair, marveling at how soft and smooth it felt.

She slid her hands down to his shoulders and across his broad, fur-matted chest.

How well proportioned, how taut and hard he felt. Her hands skimmed his narrow waist and rested on his hips. Then she raised uncertain eyes to his and felt the warmth of his gaze fill her.

"Touch me, Summer," he whispered urgently and guided her trembling hand to him. She gasped and he echoed the sound when her hand gripped him. She could feel the throbbing beat as the hard shaft surged with life—a strength and life she shamelessly wanted to feel within her.

With a ragged groan his arms came about her and his mouth sought hers in a kiss that exploded the fragile hold either had on reality. His open mouth plundered hers as they sank to the soft bed of hay beneath them. Slowly and almost reluctantly his mouth left the sweetness of hers to travel to her passion-hardened breasts. He caught one, then the other, tasting deeply, his teeth nibbling just enough to draw a gasp of sheer carnal pleasure as the sweet pain of it swept over her. She was startled when his lips left her responsive nipples and began to touch her flesh beneath the curve of her breasts, then moved down to catch lightly the soft flesh of her belly.

An agonized groan of wanton helplessness came from the very center of her as his hands first caressed her thighs gently then separated them. Through half-closed eyes, she watched as he pressed his lips to the soft flesh of her inner thigh. Slowly, slowly, one kiss after another, he searched and then found her acutely sensitive core. The sensation was so wild and erotic that she wasn't sure she could bear it. Her fingers tangled in his thick hair and she cried out without hearing. She twisted and writhed as his tongue sent warm and nerve-tingling sensations through her. She fought, both to resist and to search for more. Her body won over her mind as it arched up to demand more of the exquisite ecstasy his questing tongue gave.

He rose above her and positioned himself so that his throbbing manhood barely touched her pulsing entrance. He looked down into her passion-blinded eyes. He wanted to see her face when they joined; he wanted to know their pleasure was mutual. He was giving her all of himself, and with an intensity he had shown no other.

He watched her eyes glaze with the heat of her passion. She could only feel now, for he was dark above her like a force from beyond their world. Her body arched up to meet his and both became lost in a swirling maelstrom of magnificent sensation that spun them faster and faster, forcing them to cling to each other as they sought the culmination of their rapturous striving.

It exploded within each at the same instant in time and their cries of completion blended and echoed through their hearts.

She welcomed his weight as he collapsed against her. Keeping her eyes closed to hold on to this miraculous moment as long as possible, she stroked his back with one hand while the other tangled in his hair to hold him close.

Both were glazed with perspiration, and their hearts beat with the same erratic rhythm, which was slowly calming.

He rose on one elbow and their eyes met again. He did not want to leave her body, not yet . . . not ever, and he silently vowed that this night would be all that he could make it.

Very slowly he rolled to his side with his hands beneath her buttocks to draw her with him. He rested her atop him, remaining within her. It was no time for words, for words could never touch what they had shared. In that moment they blended more than bodies; they were fusing all that each could ever be to the other.

He caressed her hair, then ran his hand down over her sleek body to caress the curve of her hip and press her closer. With gentleness they touched, kissed, and tasted. Neither had ever experienced such a magical time. And the gentle sharing slowly began to blossom again into flowering passion.

Soon Summer was stirred by a new warmth as she felt him growing hard within her like the beginning of a new life. She became caught up in the thought of how perfect it would be to know that they were truly creating a new life between them. She craved his hardness and the heat of his passion, and she wanted it to plant within her receptive body the seed of their love.

The night deepened, but neither slept. They were both too filled with wonder. They whispered gentle words, explored each other's bodies, and fulfilled their mutual needs until the first pale streak of dawn touched the horizon. It was a night of perfection.

With the dawn, Summer fell asleep against him in exhaustion. He did not sleep but savored these last few minutes before the day.

He looked down at her face. Her lips were swollen from his ardent kisses and her hair was tangled, yet she had never looked so beautiful. A hard lump rose in his throat as her dark eyes opened languorously and shone with trust. He loved her so completely that the feeling was almost overpowering.

She could read the warmth in his jade eyes and she sighed in utter contentment. He smiled at the sound, thinking that he would keep her this way for a lifetime, holding her beside him through the nights and having the pleasure of waking her with a kiss each morning.

He completed this thought by tenderly brushing her lips with his.

"It's morning, love," he whispered. It thrilled him when she nestled closer, burying her face against his shoulder and murmuring, "The night has been too short. I would stay in your arms longer."

He put his arms about her and pressed her close to him.

"And I don't want to let you go," he said. "I love you so much, Summer, that I find it hard to wait until I can have you where you belong—beside me for always. Summer, I know you hate the idea of this house. Where do you suggest we live? I would be happy to give this one to Cole and build another anywhere you choose."

"Sebastian," she replied seriously, "I do not want to take you from the house you love. I know it means a lot to you, but"—she dipped her head so he could not see her eyes—"it . . . it would always remind me of her. I . . . I couldn't live in it. I could not share that bed with you knowing . . . knowing she planned on . . ."

He laughed and squeezed her until she gasped. "This house means exactly nothing to me, and we won't start our life together haunted by old memories. I will pay Kate and send her home and give the house to Cole. We'll make our own beginning." He looked again into her eyes, brushed his hand across her cheek, then bent to slowly and thoroughly kiss her. "I love you, Summer. That is the only sure thing I need to build my world on. I love you."

"Oh, Sebastian," she murmured as her arms pulled him closer, "I have waited so long to hear you say that.

338

It makes everything complete."

Though neither of them could know it, these words were to echo in Sebastian's mind and heart for a long, long time.

Sebastian stood up, and in the soft morning light Summer again admired the almost animal grace of his lean body. She flushed in remembered pleasure and Sebastian did not miss the warm glow in her dark eyes or the soft pink of her cheeks. In shock he realized he would have been quite happy to remain where they were for the rest of the day. He could not quite believe that after the glorious night they had just shared he could be aroused again by something as simple as the glow of happiness in her eyes. He was impatient for the day they would be alone and would no longer have to worry about being discovered.

He reluctantly drew her to her feet and took a leisurely moment to kiss her and run his hand lightly down the curve of her back. He was captivated when she shivered and moved closer.

With much reluctance he gathered up their clothes and handed her the rather disheveled gown. She looked at it bleakly.

"I'm afraid we've totally destroyed this dress. I'm sure Kate will be angry."

"I'll give her enough money for ten gowns," Sebastian replied. "That will interest her more than anything."

He watched as Summer drew the gown over her head, then he went to her, turned her around, and expertly began to tie the laces he had so delightedly untied the night before. When he was finished, he bent to kiss her bare shoulder.

At that moment an approaching horse was heard. Sebastian and Summer exchanged surprised looks.

"Seems we have company," Sebastian said.

He turned again to Summer who was trying to gather her long hair and arrange it. He watched for a moment, controlling his thoughts with effort while she braided it.

"Let's go see who our guest is," Sebastian said as he extended his hand to her. She took it and they walked from the barn together. Outside they looked in the direction of the approaching rider. Then Sebastian chuckled softly. Summer stood relaxed at his side, knowing the rider was someone Sebastian knew well.

The rider came up to them, dismounted, and, with a wide grin, extended his hand to Sebastian. "Your lookin' well, boy," he said gruffly. "I'm glad to see you back. I have a lot of explaining to do to you." It was then he looked more closely at Summer and his eyes widened though he remained silent.

"Jake"—Sebastian grinned when he saw the multitude of questions written so obviously across Jake's wide and open face—"it's good to be back. This is Summer . . . the woman I intend to marry as soon as possible."

"Huh?"

"I said—"

"I heard what you said. I just don't understand. I was told . . ." He waved helplessly at the house, leaving the rest incomplete.

"Well, I guess we do have a lot to explain to you, too." Sebastian laughed.

"You sure do," Jake answered. He turned to look into Summer's smiling face with instant relief. He could see in the quick look she gave Sebastian that she was deeply in love with him. "I'm pleased to meet you, young lady."

"Summer," Sebastian said, "this is Jake Bean. He's been my right arm for a long time."

"Hello, Mr. Bean," Summer said.

"No mister." Jake grinned as he engulfed Summer's small hand in his and added, "The name is Jake."

His open friendliness made Summer feel as if she had suddenly become a part of something very special.

Sebastian slipped his arm about Summer's waist as they conversed with Jake. In a few minutes the door of the house opened and Cole came out. He joined them and extended a hearty welcome to Jake. They all stood before the house while Sebastian informed Jake of the most recent developments.

Above them Kate stood at her window and watched. There was a smile on her face as she gazed at the dark-haired girl whose head rested against Sebastian's shoulder.

## Chapter Twenty-eight

Cole was amused yet held his silence until Sebastian invited Jake into the house to share breakfast with them. Jake agreed and the four started toward the door. It was then that Cole fell into step beside Summer while Jake kept Sebastian's attention with a description of the building of the house.

"I'm glad everything is peaceful between you and Sebastian."

Summer turned a curious glance toward him. He laughed softly and reached to remove a piece of hay from her hair. She blushed and laughed with him as they entered the house.

The first thing Summer wanted to do was to see if she could get Mandy to help her heat enough water to bathe in. She and Mandy carried several buckets to her room. Then she removed the soiled gown and laid it across the bed.

After Summer had bathed, she dressed and went down to help Mandy, who was preparing breakfast.

Sebastian, Jake, and Cole sat about the table talking while Summer and Mandy placed the plates and utensils before them.

It was then that Kate entered and it came as a

surprise to everyone present when she smiled and sat down to eat with everyone.

Sebastian was relieved, for it seemed that Kate had resigned herself to the inevitable and was accepting the situation gracefully. Summer was just as prepared to try to breach the void between them, although every sense she had was sending nearly violent warning signals. She reasoned that this was caused by her knowledge that Kate and Sebastian had been lovers at one time, for this fact still made her heart twist.

Cole was wary of Kate but willing—for Sebastian and Summer's sake—to accept anything that would ease the situation and bring about a peaceful conclusion.

They ate and laughed together and, in the process, Kate acquired a wealth of information about Summer, the most important of which was that she learned of Summer's powers of concentration and her ability to send and receive mental messages. She stored this in her mind and waited for the moment she would put it to use.

"Cole," Sebastian said, "don't get too comfortable."

"Me? Why?"

"I want to ask a favor of you. But before I do—" He interrupted himself and turned to Kate. "Kate, Jake has said he would be willing to take you back to town. If you tell me what all this has cost, I will see you get back everything you spent. I owe you a debt and I'll see it's paid."

"You needn't worry, Sebastian," she said sweetly. "I am sure I will get . . . whatever I need. In the meantime, I want to congratulate you and Summer. I hope you're happy together."

"Why, thank you, Kate," Sebastian said.

At Kate's words, Summer felt tingles of danger along every nerve and a thick blackness seemed to fill her, but

343

again she pushed these feelings aside and she smiled at Kate.

"I hope you'll be happy, Summer," Kate told her. Her eyes met Summer's, who realized that deep within Kate was still harboring a cold anger.

"Thank you, Kate."

"What is it you want me to do, Sebastian?" Cole asked.

Sebastian laughed. "I want you to go back to Hawk's village."

"Oh, I see," Cole said. "If you are trying to get rid of me, why don't you just shoot me?"

At this everyone laughed.

"If I go anywhere near that village without you and Summer, Hawk isn't going to give me time to explain."

"Hawk is a gentle man," Summer said with a grin that looked decidedly wicked to Cole.

"A gentle man," Cole repeated doubtfully. "And he's not going to be interested in the man who just might know where you are and how you got here? And," he added, "he's not going to be mad enough to either beat it out of me or skin me and ask questions while I'm wiggling in my own blood?"

"No Cole." Summer giggled. "Hawk is really not a violent or unreasonable man. Besides, I will send a message, a written message he will know is from me."

"Well, that's a relief. Now all I have to do is get close enough to give him the message," Cole said resignedly.

Summer went to find paper and pen, which Kate, who followed after her, soon provided. As she stood and watched Summer write the message, she stored away another idea that would further her evil scheme.

"If I must go, it is better that I prepare today so I can leave first thing tomorrow," Kate announced for Summer's benefit. Summer did not reply.

She and Kate returned to the men and Summer

handed the folded message to Cole, who put it in his pocket.

"You're absolutely sure, Summer, that Hawk's going to give me a reasonable chance to explain?"

"Of course . . . reasonable." She laughed.

"Well, Sebastian, if I don't lose my hair or my life, what do you want me to tell him?"

"Tell him," Sebastian replied gently as his jade eyes softened and turned to Summer, "that Summer is safe here with me and"—he smiled—"we'd like to have him at our wedding."

Summer returned Sebastian's warm look, and Kate, though she smiled, seethed with a murderous rage, for she felt that Summer had taken what had belonged to her.

Cole had left the house shortly after breakfast. Now he rode along slowly, secure that all the serious problems were in the past. He was not really nervous about Hawk, at least not at the moment, when he was still far enough away not to feel Hawk's rage.

He was pleased with the way the situation had resolved itself. Summer and Sebastian would marry and live . . . where? He thought of the house and knew for certain that Summer would never live there. Oh well, he thought, that is Sebastian's problem. Once Kate is gone, Summer and Sebastian will work everything out between them.

When he camped that night he lay awake planning what he would say to Hawk. He pushed aside the nagging notion that now he was displaced, had no anchor. He didn't want to face the idea of what he was going to do next. It would be a matter of finding someone who needed a guide or, maybe, he thought, he just might decide to settle down and find a permanent place for himself.

He traveled for the next day and a half in the same state of meditation.

The village would not be too far away now, Cole estimated as he sat beneath a tree and ate a small midday meal. A narrow valley lay before him and he was enjoying the scenery in a somewhat preoccupied manner. He relaxed and contemplated the balance of his ride to the village.

It was then that he saw two riders as they raced across the valley floor. He thought at first that they were two Indian boys out for a race. Then he stood up as he realized the rider in the lead was not Indian. And not only was she not Indian, but she was white. Now he was more than curious, for he didn't know if the one behind her was harmless or if he was chasing her. He made his decision quickly, leapt upon his horse, and started down into the valley directly in their path. One way or another he would be in a good position. If she were being chased, the one behind her would see that she had acquired help and maybe he would leave peacefully. If they were racing, he would at least be in a position to congratulate the winner, whoever it might be.

The two riders were unaware of him as he reached the valley floor, and because they were concentrating on their speed and each other, they did not see him in time.

He appeared before the young girl as if by magic, and Cole watched stunned as her horse reared in shock. She cried out once as she tumbled to the ground.

Cole dismounted and started in her direction as the second rider approached. He was completely unprepared for a small, wild, and completely furious redheaded female who attacked him with a charge that would have put a herd of enraged buffalo to shame. He

346

backed up a step in awe as, hands on hips and flaming hair wild about her, she shouted at him.

"What the blazes do you think you are doing? Of all the stupid stunts I've seen, that is the dumbest! You could have killed me!"

She kept shouting until she was close enough; then she attacked with doubled fists. One blow and Cole began to lose his temper too.

"Now wait a minute! I thought you might need help."

"Help? I was winning. Why should I need your help?"

Now he laughed. "I'm sorry. I guess I thought"—he shrugged—"you were being chased."

By now the second rider had joined them. He was a tall and handsome Indian with a flicker of amusement in his dark eyes. He seemed to be enjoying the girl's anger.

"So Kylie, nobody won," he teased.

"I would have beaten you, Raven, if it hadn't been for him."

"I said I'm sorry," Cole repeated. He was grinning now and the girl looked from one to the other.

"You men are so arrogant. I'll race you both and beat you."

"Where do you come from?" Cole asked. "I haven't seen many whites out here, and especially pretty girls."

"I am Raven," the young brave interrupted. "This woman is a guest in our village."

"Your village?" Cole replied. "Is that Hawk's village?"

"It is so," the brave answered proudly.

"That is just where I'm headed. Can I ride back with you?"

"Of course," Raven answered. He turned to Kylie, "If Kylie does not mind. It is she you stopped from

347

winning the race."

Kylie, whose disposition was usually pleasant and whose sense of honor hovered always near the surface, smiled up at Cole as his eyes turned back to her.

He grinned and held up his hands as if he were surrendering. "I've said I'm sorry. Can you have pity on a poor traveler and let him ride along with you?"

"If you were headed for Hawk's village, it would be rude of us to refuse, wouldn't it?"

"I'm grateful," he replied, and he truly was, because he realized he might get a better reception and be able to get closer to Hawk before Hawk could vent his anger on him.

Raven retrieved Kylie's horse and the three started toward the village.

"I have seen you in our village before," Raven said with a puzzled frown.

"Yes, I guess you have," Cole responded reluctantly.

Suddenly Raven reined in his horse. He turned and looked at Cole. Kylie remained motionless and silent. For some reason, she wanted to hear Cole's reply to Raven's next words.

"You are one of the men for whom Hawk searched. You are one of the men who took Summer." Now Kylie was alert.

"No Raven, it wasn't like that. Will you let me explain?"

Raven nodded.

Cole explained all that had happened until the moment he found them.

"Now," he finished, "I'm the one elected to tell Hawk and invite him to the wedding." He looked at the two, who had listened quietly. "You believe me?"

Raven nodded and smiled. "I have known Summer too long not to know she would try to help anyone she felt needed her. Come. Hawk will listen."

Cole turned to Kylie. "And . . . you believe me?"

She nodded and smiled, and Cole found it a very pleasant sensation indeed to look into Kylie Flynn's green eyes.

They rode on into the village. Cole kept his eyes open for any sign of Hawk, but he had barely dismounted before a voice from beside him told him that Hawk had found him first.

After Cole's departure, Sebastian and Summer decided to go for a ride. Jake made himself scarce for two reasons. First, he didn't like the house itself. It gave him a strange, impermanent feeling. And second, he didn't trust Kate. He had seen her reactions in too many situations to believe she had become a meek, docile kitten.

Mandy walked silently through the quiet house. Kate was in her room and Mandy wanted to keep her distance. She, like Jake, didn't believe the new, sweet-natured Kate.

Kate was not packing her clothes. She had no intention of leaving. Instead, she was working on her plan to make sure that Summer would be the one to go, with Sebastian's blessing—and his hatred.

She sat at her desk again, and before her lay a sheet of paper upon which she was composing a letter from Summer to Sebastian, a letter that would crush Sebastian and force him to turn away from Summer forever. Now she looked over what she had written:

Sebastian:

By the time you finish reading this letter, you will find that I have already gone, and that I have found a way to repay all your lies.

I needed to have you say you loved me to complete everything.

Now you are free to enjoy your house and your money, for I want no part of them or of you.

It was all a game, Sebastian, and I learned the rules from you. Did I not learn to play well? You actually believed I love you.

But you lied too many times and I finally realized you are just like all the rest. I cannot share your life of deceit.

Summer

Kate looked at the letter with satisfaction. She had watched Sebastian and Summer ride away and knew they sought a private place, a place where they could be alone. She could envision them lying together in the sunlight, and the urge to go after them and kill Summer was nearly overwhelming. No, she told herself, she would destroy Summer in another way. Dropping the letter on her desk, she went downstairs. Mandy, who had watched her leave her room, moved silently across the hall. If she packed all of Miss Kate's things, she thought, then she would have to leave soon. She entered Kate's room and began to gather clothes. That is when she saw the letter Kate had been writing. She went to the desk and picked up the letter to look at the swirls and figures on the paper. Then, with a sigh, she put it back. It was a shame, she thought, that she never would have the chance to learn to read. The scratches on the paper looked so pretty.

She had begun to put Kate's belongings into the open portmanteau when Kate reentered the room. Kate's eyes went immediately to the letter she had written and back to Mandy before the realization struck her that if Mandy had read it, she would not be

350

so calm.

She moved to the desk and picked up the letter, then watched Mandy moving about the room. She held the paper toward Mandy.

"Have you read my poetry, Mandy?"

Mandy's dark eyes grew frightened. She backed away from the paper.

"Miz Kate, yo all know ah can't read. But I sho' wouldn't read yo' writin' lesson you axed me to. Ah can't read, Miz Kate."

"It's all right, Mandy," Kate replied. "I'm sure you wouldn't read what wasn't yours to read."

"No ma'am." Mandy shook her head vehemently and repeated, "No ma'am."

"Go down and make some lunch, Mandy. I'm sure Mr. Sebastian will be back before long."

"Yessum."

Mandy left. Kate walked to the mirror and smiled at her reflection.

"Tonight, my dear Summer . . . tonight."


The two horses stood contentedly grazing while the low branches of a tree shadowed and cooled the two who lay entwined in each other's arms beneath it.

Sebastian sat with his back braced against the tree and Summer sat between his legs, resting against him. The loving had been exquisite, but Sebastian treasured these moments of silent sharing even more. She rested against his chest in utter contentment. Summer had loosened her dark hair from its confining braids at Sebastian's insistence, and now he gently coiled the silky strands around his fingers.

He rubbed his cheek gently across the top of her head. One arm rested across her shoulders and his fingers slowly caressed her skin.

"Summer?"

"Ummm?"

"I know you don't want to live in that house. Don't you think it's time we made some plans?"

Summer sighed contentedly. "We have a lifetime to make plans. Let's just enjoy now."

"I do enjoy now," he retorted, chuckling softly, "but I want to make sure what we have now is permanent."

"Sebastian . . . I want you to come with me and meet my parents before we make any decisions."

She was nervous now over her concern that Sebastian would be very angry when he found out the truth about her family. She had accused him of lying, and now he could accuse her of the same offense.

"They can come to the wedding," he teased. "That way, if they have any objections, there won't be much time for them to do anything about it. I'll have you tied to me nice and tight before they can talk you out of it."

She turned in his arms and smiled up at him. "There is no changing what I have in mind," she replied.

"And what do you have in mind?" His voice softened as his eyes warmed and his arms drew her closer.

"Many things," she murmured. "I intend to repay you for all the doubts and fears I had, for all the times I wanted to hear you say I love you."

"I do love you."

"I know . . . now . . . but before . . ."

"Let's forget before, Summer. I was blinded by a lot of things before. Now everything is new and it's best that neither of us look back over our shoulders."

"You are right, Sebastian." She smiled as she ran her fingers up his lean ribs to caress for a moment the expanse of his chest before her arms encircled his neck. "Hearing you say I love you is enough," she whispered. Their lips met and they forgot their thoughts and their words—words that would return to haunt them both.

352

It was some time later that they started the ride back to the house.

Kate stood within the dark confines of the barn. She gazed about her, imagining what had occurred here the night before. It fed the bitterness within her.

She was startled at the sound of a rough, whispering voice even though she had expected it.

"You sure this is gonna work?"

Kate turned toward the two who stood behind her and her eyes were cold.

"It will work if you two are not stupid enough to let her make any noise. Remember, you must keep her unconscious."

"I don't understand why."

"You don't have to understand. It is a fact that she has some kind of power. She can call out to him somehow. You have to keep her mind quiet as well as her voice. Don't make a mistake. If you do, Sebastian Cain will be on you in an instant."

"We can kill him."

"Kill him," Kate said, "and you'll be digging your own graves. Now, you go to the house. Make sure Mandy doesn't see or hear you. Go to the upstairs room. Wait there. When she comes, take her. Leave the note so Sebastian can find it. After he reads it"—she smiled—"you can be sure he won't bother to follow. He'll be too mad and too sure she's betrayed him to follow."

Both men nodded and Kate left the barn. As she walked across the wide yard, Mandy stood in the doorway watching her. The thought crossed Mandy's mind that Kate seemed to be very pleased with herself. Maybe, Mandy thought, she had really decided to forgive and forget and go home to leave Sebastian and

353

Summer to find what happiness they could with each other.

When Kate reached the first step of the porch, she looked up to see Mandy standing in the doorway. She was irritated but, consummate actress that she was, she did not show it. Later she would want Mandy to believe that no harm could have come to Summer from her.

"Mandy, have you finished the food?"

"Yessum."

"Is the table set?"

"Yessum."

"Well, I suppose Sebastian and Summer will be back soon. I imagine they will be hungry. Maybe"—she smiled at Mandy, who was completely taken in by the abrupt change in Kate—"we ought to make this a celebration. After all, I imagine they plan to marry soon. Go see if there is any wine in the house."

"Yessum."

Mandy turned to go back into the house and Kate stood on the porch, gazing out across the vast expanse of land surrounding the site on which Sebastian had chosen to live. Then she turned and entered the kitchen.

"Mandy, do you know where Jake is?"

It was important that Jake was not close enough to interfere in Kate's plans.

"Y'all know how he is, Miz Kate. He done gone off fo' awhile. I 'spects he'll be back tomorrow. He jus' comes and goes like he wants."

"But . . . he won't be likely to come home tonight?"

"No'm, I doan think. He know Mr. Sebastian he wants him to take you back. I 'spects he be here when yo is ready to go."

"All right. Did you find the wine?"

"Yessum."

"Excellent."

Kate walked back out on the porch now. She was torn by impatience. Everything would be a matter of timing. Jake would have to be gone, Mandy would have to keep her attention elsewhere, and Sebastian would have to remain unsuspecting until it was too late.

In the distance she could see the two riders approaching. How well she knew them both, and how conflicting her emotions were. She could barely conceal her hatred for Summer or her passion for Sebastian, which was nearly as powerful.

She closed her eyes for a moment, fairly overcome by the strength of raw emotion that tore through her. Kate seethed with furious passion, and Summer felt it.


Summer reined in her horse, sharply, startling both her horse and Sebastian.

"Summer, what's the matter?"

"I . . . I'm not sure. I feel . . . such blackness."

"What?"

"I don't . . ." Summer shook her head. She felt as if some great threat lay ahead, but she didn't know what it could be. She knew how Kate felt, but, she reasoned, what harm could Kate do her when Sebastian was near? She brushed the fear aside, despite the fact that it took a great deal of effort. "It's nothing, Sebastian. I'm sure it's just my imagination."

"Are you sure, Summer? I know you better than that. What do you feel?"

"It was just a momentary thing, as if someone were . . . full of hate."

Sebastian didn't answer, but he was shaken. He had seen and heard too much of Summer's power to doubt it. Now he assumed they were being followed by someone who would have to be quite near.

"It's best we get back to the house, Summer. It's the safest place, especially if someone's out there. My friend with the three feathers might be around somewhere. Come on, let's go home where it's safe."

Summer nodded and they rode slowly toward the house, where the reality of their danger would soon confront them.

## Chapter Twenty=nine

Summer and Sebastian rode up to the house. They dismounted and Sebastian grasped the reins of both horses. "I'll take care of the horses. Why don't you go in and see if Mandy has some food handy." Before Summer could answer, Kate appeared in the doorway. She smiled as pleasantly as she could.

"There is plenty of food. Mandy has made a fine meal, including wine. Summer, I've had Mandy prepare you a bath. After that we can have a nice dinner to celebrate your coming marriage."

"Good idea," Sebastian replied. "Summer, go on up and relax. A warm bath will do you good. I'll see to the horses and then I'll be in."

Summer nodded. She went inside with Kate, and Sebastian, pulling the horses along with him, headed for the barn. There he unsaddled them, rubbed them down, and gave each some fresh hay. Satisfied with his work, he left the barn, crossed the yard, and took the steps two at a time.

Both Kate and Mandy were in the kitchen putting the last touches on the table.

"Sit down, Sebastian," Kate said. "I'm sure Summer will be down shortly."

Sebastian sat, and Kate sat opposite him. A surge of heady excitement threatened to bring words to her lips she didn't want to say, not yet. She stopped herself by clasping her hands together in her lap and clenching them tightly.

Mandy's puttering about the kitchen annoyed her; Sebastian's obvious contentment annoyed her; in fact, just about every waiting second annoyed her. Time ticked by and now Sebastian seemed to be becoming impatient. He cast a slight frown at the doorway then rose and walked to it.

Not yet! Kate's mind screamed. Just a little more time to make sure they have succeeded.

Restless now, Sebastian returned to the table. He noted that Mandy too seemed touched by a vague, uncomfortable feeling.

"Mandy"—Sebastian smiled at her—"run up and see if Miss Summer is ready yet. Tell her she's got a very hungry man down here."

"Yessuh," Mandy replied. She moved swiftly to the door.

"Mandy," Sebastian added quickly.

"Yessuh?"

"Tell her . . ." His voice softened. "Tell her to hurry, will you. It's been much too long for me."

"Yessuh!" Mandy smiled. In a moment she was gone.

"So, what are you and Summer planning, Sebastian?" Kate inquired. "Will you live here?"

"I don't think so." Sebastian was reluctant to discuss a decision with Kate that he and Summer had not yet made.

"But this house, Sebastian . . ." Kate began.

"I think it would be best if I sold the house and a small piece of property to Cole."

"But . . ."

358

"Kate, let's not argue about a house. Before you leave I will give you a letter of credit. Once you are home, you can reclaim what you spent. I want you to add enough to cover your expenses and to make a profit."

"I don't need—"

"I know you don't, Kate." He smiled. "But ease my guilt a little bit, will you, and take it. I'd feel better."

"All right, Sebastian." Kate sighed. "If you like."

"I do. I—"

Before he could speak further, the sound of Mandy rapidly descending the steps brought Sebastian to his feet.

Mandy ran breathlessly into the room, her eyes wide and frightened. She held an envelope in her hand.

"Mandy?" Sebastian questioned.

"She be gone, suh. Dey ain nobody in any room. She be gone. An I foun' dis on de bed."

Sebastian snatched the envelope as he passed her on the way upstairs. As he took the steps by twos and threes, his heart beat a rapid tattoo against his ribs. He slammed open the door of the first room. It was empty, the window was open, and the wooden tub of water lay untouched in the center. He went rapidly from room to room and found each just as empty. He returned to the first room and stared in disbelief. Then he remembered the letter in his hand. He looked down at it and saw his name on the front. Something within him seemed to grow brittle and hard and he didn't want to open it. But his hands did what his mind still refused. The envelope fluttered to the floor as he read.

Summer had never been so happy in her life. She felt warm and contented as she slowly walked up the stairs. She could still feel Sebastian's lips on hers and the gentle touch of his hands. Her body tingled with the memory. Before long they would marry, Sebastian would meet her family, and he would understand. He would! Her mind and heart both agreed hopefully.

She walked across the short hall and opened the door to her room. She had only taken one step inside the door when the blow was struck. It was done quickly and hard enough that she never knew. She did not have time to utter a sound, but sagged toward the floor. Expertly, she was caught and heaved over the man's shoulder. He moved on silent feet to the window. Even with Summer's added weight, he had no difficulty climbing down the rope. Once on the bottom, he gave a quick jerk on the rope and it tumbled down after him.

He lay Summer down long enough to gather the rope and drape it over one shoulder. Then he retrieved Summer's limp form and moved quickly toward the trees, where his companions waited with their horses. Soundlessly he joined them. Three Feathers smiled as he reached out and took Summer in his arms. They walked their horses until they knew the sound wouldn't carry. Then they kicked them into a run.

The reality of the words on the paper fought Sebastian's disbelief. The battle raged for several minutes before reality won. Something within him seemed to shatter into shards of glass and, like shards of glass, they cut deeply and the wounds bled, cooled, and turned into something even Sebastian could not recognize.

Mandy stood in the doorway, and Kate was behind her. With differing emotions, they watched Sebastian's face.

It tumbled about him, the dreams, the future, everything, and the pain of it was almost more than he could bear. It drew a groan of near agony from him.

"No," he whispered, "I don't believe this. She can't . . . she wouldn't . . ."

The letter dropped from his hands and Mandy ran to pick it up. Kate came to her quickly and snatched it from her. Then she pretended to read it.

"It seems," Kate said softly, "that your little savage was not only a cheat but a liar as well."

"Shut up, Kate!" Sebastian demanded.

"But Sebastian, you can see for yourself," Kate taunted, "she was only playing with you. She's a little tramp who was having a bit of fun at your expense."

Sebastian felt the blow of her words and forced them away. But other words, past words that Summer had spoken, forced themselves into his mind. They burned there like lines of flame: "I intend to repay you . . . Sebastian, I have waited so long to hear you say that . . . it makes everything complete . . . there is no changing what I have in mind . . . hearing you say I love you is enough."

What began as a searing agony was slowly growing into cold fury. She had deliberately deceived him and had led him to believe her surrender, only to laugh and walk away. In his mind the echo of her laughter cut like a sharp knife.

His anger grew and grew until the only thing he could think of was gripping her slender throat in his hands and forcing the life from her. Then even that fury burned hotter and was slowly molded into an iron-hard desire to hear the words from her own lips before he found a form of revenge unlike any Summer had ever imagined.

His face registered his thoughts, and Mandy shrank from him as he turned back toward the door.

"Where are you going, Sebastian?" Kate called after him as he left the room. "What are you going to do?

What about me and Mandy?"

Sebastian stopped. Then he turned back slowly to face a shaking Mandy and Kate, who was just beginning the battle to keep him with her.

"Mandy," Sebastian snapped, "go in Miss Kate's room and help her get her things out of this house."

"Sebastian!" Kate cried.

"Kate, this house has brought disaster from the first. Get your things outside . . . unless you want them to burn with it."

"Burn! Sebastian, are you crazy?"

"Maybe just a little. This house has caused me nothing but pain and loss."

He turned and started down the stairs and Kate flew after him. Once in the kitchen again, he flung open the door. Jake had chosen that moment to return to the barn for some things he needed. His plan had been to come and go like a shadow. He wanted no part of Kate or the house he had helped to build. He had ridden in quietly so no one would know, and he was unprepared for Sebastian's call.

"Jake!"

Jake ran from the barn in total surprise, thinking something disastrous had happened. He stopped by Sebastian.

"Sebastian, what's wrong?"

"Get the horses out of the barn. Saddle two, for Kate and yourself. Leave mine saddled and outside. Then come and help Kate take her things from the house."

Jake could see the glow of yellow flame in Sebastian's eyes and had no intention of crossing his path. He was in a rage that would brook no resistance.

"Jake, I want you to take Kate and Mandy to town."

"All right. What's happened, Sebastian? Where are you going?"

"Out to even a score," Sebastian replied as he turned

to reenter the house.

Mandy and Jake carried out Kate's belongings while Kate still waged a battle with Sebastian. "Sebastian, you are mad. Why chase after that little slut? She isn't worth it. Come with me. We can forget all this and be happy. I can make you forget her, Sebastian."

Sebastian turned on Kate so quickly that she gave a yelp of surprise. He gripped her shoulders and jerked her to him. Her eyes grew wide with fear as she looked up into blazing orbs filled with barely controlled violence.

"Kate, I'm tired of you trying to take over my life. I'm tired of you meddling in my affairs. Understand me well, Kate. I want you out of my house and away from here. I never want to see you again. Go home. I'm sure you can find another fool to spend your money on. Get out of my life, Kate—now!"

Kate was suddenly terrified, for Sebastian looked as if he had indeed lost his mind. She shivered as he pushed her away from him. But she was not yet ready to give up.

"Sebastian," she whimpered, "you don't mean that. It's that Indian bitch. She has hurt you. Why do you have to hurt me?"

"I don't want to hurt you, Kate. I just want you to understand. What was between us is gone . . . I'm not even too sure of what it was, but whatever it was, it's over. Go home Kate. Let me alone."

"You're a damn fool!" Kate shouted. "Can't you see the truth?"

"Maybe for the first time I can. I can see that I don't intend to make the same mistakes twice. The house goes . . . and you go . . . and I . . . I will make sure Summer remembers her deceit . . . remembers it well."

Nothing was going as Kate had planned. Sebastian was slipping away. She was desperate.

"Sebastian, don't go," she pleaded, letting tears slide down her cheeks. "I love you! Come with me!"

"But I don't love you, Kate. I don't think I ever did. It was all a very pretty dream. But dreams turn to nightmares. Before you get hurt, get out of here."

"I don't want to go. I want to stay with you."

"That, my dear," said a voice from the open door, "is a foolish request because you are not staying."

Both Sebastian and Kate spun around to see the man standing just inside the door. Their attention was drawn to the gun that was pointed at them.

"Luke!" Kate gasped.

"Hello, Kate." Luke smiled. "Did you think I didn't know where you were? Foolish Kate." He laughed softly. "I've known every move you've made."

"Who the hell are you?" Sebastian demanded.

"Someone who's going to take some of your troubles off your hands. If Kate and her money are something you don't want, I do."

"I'm not going anywhere with you!" Kate screamed.

"Oh yes, you are." Luke grinned evilly. "I'm taking you aboard my ship and we're sailing. By the time we reach port again, you will be very, very tame, my love. And we'll make sure your fortune is . . . ah . . . well handled."

"I can't let you do that," Sebastian argued.

"How are you going to stop me?" Luke asked in amusement. "Let me tell you about Kate, my friend," he continued. He went on to tell Sebastian what Miles had found out about Kate's past. "The trip over on my ship was a pleasure, for Kate shared my bed as she's shared those of many others. But, that is over. From now on, Kate belongs to me."

"You lie!" Kate screamed. But she could read Sebastian's face and knew he believed Luke.

"No Kate, he doesn't believe you. Your game is over.

364

He knows I'm not lying."

"Where are Jake and Mandy?" Sebastian asked worriedly.

"Tied securely in the barn. You can untie them when I'm gone. If your conscience is hurting you, don't let it. Kate isn't worth it. I'm not going to hurt her. I'll only keep her from hurting anyone else. Besides"—Luke grinned again—"she is the best little whore I've ever had in my bed."

"Bastard!" Kate screeched.

"That I am, love—a complement to your bitchery." He turned his head toward Sebastian. "Tie her hands behind her back."

Sebastian reluctantly tore some kitchen cloths and did as Luke demanded. Then Luke reached out and grabbed Kate's arm, jerking her to him.

"My friend," Luke said seriously to Sebastian, "if I were you, I wouldn't let any past lies Kate might have told you change anything. She's a destructive person who always wants to get what pleases her. I can please her, believe me. Mr. Cain, think of this. When Kate tired of you, as she did her husband, she might have found a way to rid herself of you."

Luke drew Kate with him through the open door and in a few minutes Sebastian heard his retreating horse.

He ran to the barn and released Jake and Mandy, then quickly told them what had happened.

"You want to follow them, Sebastian?" Jake questioned.

Sebastian was silent for several minutes, then he replied quietly. "No, let them go. Jake, I want you to take Mandy with you, but instead of to town, I want you to take her to Hawk's village. I want you to tell Cole what has happened. Tell him I have a little score to settle and then I'll join him. Ask him to be ready. After this I'm heading for the mountains. The further

365

away from people I get, the better."

"Sure, Sebastian," Jake said.

"Mr. Sebastian, suh?"

"Yes Mandy?"

"Yo all mad cuz of dat lettar?"

"Can you read, Mandy?" Sebastian asked gently.

"No suh, ah cain't, but Miz Kate, she wrote a lettar yesterday . . . an' I seed it. I doan know fo' sure, but it shore look like dat letter you got."

"Most letters look alike, Mandy. This one was signed with Summer's name." He bent down and scratched Summer in the dirt, and beside it he scratched Kate. "Can you remember which name was on the bottom?"

Mandy studied the two closely, but she couldn't quite remember. Tears filled her eyes as she looked up at Sebastian.

"Ah doan know," she cried. "Ah cain't recollect iffen it was one or the other, but maybe—"

"It doesn't matter, Mandy," Sebastian comforted her. "It just doesn't matter. You go with Jake."

"Ah's scared of Indians," she moaned.

Sebastian laughed. "There's nothing to be scared of. You'll be fed and cared for, and when I come back, I'll take you to town and we'll find a good place for you."

"Yes suh," Mandy said resignedly.

It didn't take long for Mandy to gather her meager belongings. But she was reluctant to leave when she saw the simmering anger in Sebastian. She wanted to let him know that despite the fact that she could not read, the letters had looked exactly the same to her. She was certain Kate had been the one to write the incriminating letter.

Sebastian was the one who lifted her slight body up behind Jake.

"Wait for me in the village, Jake. What I have to do

won't take too long. I'll be there as soon as I can. Tell Cole to be ready."

"I'll do that. Sebastian . . . you goin' to be all right?"

"I'm fine, Jake, just fine."

His voice was calm and Sebastian even managed, for Jake's sake, to smile. But Jake knew him too well. Within him something was roiling and Jake was shaken. He was about to speak again when Sebastian slapped the horse's rump, which made it jump and move rapidly ahead. It was too late for Jake to even try to stop what Sebastian planned.

Sebastian watched them ride away, then he turned again to look at the house.

The site had been a curse to him. It had caused Nathaniel's death and had enticed Kate to stay and rebuild. He wanted to think of anything but Summer. He could not face that yet. He would track her, for she couldn't be too far ahead. When he found her, he would hear the words from her. What he would do then was a dark thing he forced from his mind.

Slowly he walked toward the porch and climbed the steps. He stood in the deserted kitchen for a minute, then walked slowly through the other empty rooms. The darkness within him was beyond anything he had ever known. It grew like a devouring monster until he reached his limits. With slow deliberation he lifted an oil lamp and held it, studying the flicker of the flame. Then he threw it against the wall and smiled with grim satisfaction as it burst into brilliant flames.

He watched them grow, engulfing curtains and eating at the walls. When the heat became intense, he turned and walked outside. There he stood, a silent witness, as the fire slowly consumed the house.

Knowing his horse was tied safely away, he turned to the barn. He wanted nothing left but ashes. He watched with the same tense calmness as the barn was also consumed.

When it was finished, he gave one last look at the smoking debris, then he mounted his horse and began to scrutinize the area for signs of Summer's route. He was mildly surprised when he found the tracks of three horses instead of one, but rational thinking was beyond him now. Mindlessly, he began to follow.

Again he was surprised when the tracks began to lead into a territory in which he had never been. He didn't know where Summer was going, but he knew he was not going to lose the trail. Where Summer went he would follow, and one day he would catch up.

He crested a hill and looked back at the still-smoldering embers of what he had hoped would be the beginning of a dynasty. Now it was the end of a dream.

The strange numbness still held him as he pulled his eyes away and nudged his horse into motion.

He rode slowly, but he was able to follow. Whomever Summer rode with had no idea that someone was trailing them. They were not too careful and he was able to keep the small signs in view.

He stopped for only short periods, more to rest the horse than himself. But the sun was beginning to descend and he knew for certain he would not catch up with them before dark. He would be forced to make camp and the thought was a most unpleasant one. A lonely camp made room for thought, and he didn't want to think. Not yet.

He was finally resigned to stopping after he had lost the trail twice and had had to retrace his own tracks. He made camp, built a fire, and rolled in a blanket, hoping that sleep would come soon and wipe out the memories.

\*      \*      \*

Clay Storm rode at a ground-eating pace. He knew well the territory in which Sebastian Cain had built his house. He expected to find both Sebastian and Summer there, and he was mulling over what he would do if he found Summer hurt in any way.

What he did not expect to see was the still-glowing embers of what had once been a considerably large house and barn.

Dozens of questions filled his mind. How had the house been burned, and why and by whom? Where was Sebastian Cain and, most important of all, where was Summer now?

He walked about the burning wreckage in disbelief.

Clay had been in the territory for years, had lived with or near Hawk and his people long enough to be an expert tracker. He studied the signs and before too long he was on Sebastian's trail.

It was an easy trail to follow since none of the riders had made an effort to hide their tracks. He also knew there were three riders ahead of the one rider who followed. He assumed that the one riding behind could be doing so to protect the three ahead. An ambush was therefore possible and so he remained alert.

After a short time he realized that the single rider was tracking the other three, and not very capably. This made him suspect that the single rider was Sebastian Cain. But if it were, where was Summer? Was she with the three ahead. If she was, why had she left Cain?

He was filled with too many questions and determined to find the answers quickly.

He watched the sun go down, but he did not stop. He could track a much longer time than the one ahead of him. Although he moved warily, he pressed forward relentlessly.

Now the sun was nearly gone and long, dark

shadows made the way difficult. Clay stopped and studied the area about him. Then he nudged his horse forward to the rise of a hill. From there he visually searched the area. It was then he saw the pale glow of a fire in the distance. He reached down to pat his horse's neck.

"It seems Mr. Cain has been foolish enough to build a fire. Thank you, Mr. Cain," he added softly. "Thank you very much."

Again he was on the move, but this time he had a destination.

As he grew nearer, he became more cautious, and when he was close enough that his horse might be heard, he dismounted, tied his horse, and began to move forward on foot as stealthily as an Indian.

The fire's red glow was an easy target, and he moved close until he was just outside the light.

He looked about very carefully and was soon sure that the man rolled in a blanket near the fire was the man he sought.

He held his rifle in his hand and began to creep forward slowly. When he stood just within the circle of light, he pointed the rifle at the sleeping man.

"Cain . . . get up!"

Sebastian reacted almost immediately. He flung the blanket aside and sat up, abruptly trying to search for his rifle.

"Don't," Clay warned coldly. "Leave it alone or I'll be forced to make a very large hole in you, and I want to talk to you first."

Sebastian drew his hand back and watched as the tall, dark man came closer.

"Where is Summer?" Clay said in a clipped, hard tone. "And I'd advise you, Mr. Cain, to answer quickly and honestly. You tell me where she is and maybe, just maybe, I won't kill you."

Sebastian stared at the unwavering gun, then his eyes rose to the cold, hard, blue eyes that were just as steady.

"Who the hell are you?" Sebastian demanded.

"The name is Storm, Clayton Storm, and that's the last question you get. The rest of your words had better be answers."

# Chapter Thirty

When Patrick, Sabrina, Simon, and Jason arrived at Clay's cabin near midday, Ellen was quite excited and her questions followed quickly. Where was Clay, and where was Summer? "It's been too long since I've seen that child. I hope she doesn't dawdle in that village too much longer."

"Ellen, we have to tell you that Summer isn't in the village," Simon explained.

"Isn't in the village? Where . . . ?"

"We don't know yet, Ellen," Sabrina soothed. "Clay is following the trail. He'll find her."

"Following a trail! Find her! Sabrina, what has happened to that child?" Ellen placed her hands on her hips. "Someone had best be telling me the whole story pretty quick."

"Ellen"—Sabrina laughed—"we will tell you every detail, but do you think we might have a bite to eat while we talk. I'm starved, and I know for certain that Patrick and the boys could use some food."

Ellen was distressed, but her maternal instincts wouldn't allow the younger boys to stand about hungry.

"I'll fix something quick," she replied.

"And I'll come to the kitchen to help you," Sabrina offered. "That way I can answer some of your questions."

They went to the kitchen while Patrick and the two boys cared for the animals.

"We hoped maybe we would find Summer here," Sabrina told Ellen as they moved about the kitchen.

"Here, no, I haven't seen a sign of her. I thought she was in the village."

Sabrina began the story from the moment they had heard that Summer was in the village. Ellen remained silent until Sabrina had finished the entire account.

"Who is this Sebastian Cain?" Ellen questioned. "Why would Summer simply follow him into the wilderness? You don't suppose he's hurt her somehow?"

"Ellen, you and I have known Summer from childhood. You know that whatever it is that controls her will lead her to do what she feels is right. I don't believe she would have followed this man if she hadn't trusted him or felt he needed her."

"I only know that the child is too generous and too kind. It only takes one scalawag to take advantage of that."

"Ellen, Summer would see through a man like that in a minute. She never would have gone after him if she had read evil in him as she has in others. No, we have to have faith in her. Wherever they are they are together, and Clay will find them."

"I guess"—Ellen smiled—"there's a little of you that rubbed off on her. Seems to me you trusted Clay like that when everyone else wasn't sure."

Sabrina paused to mull this over and she was struck by a thought that had not occurred to her before. Was Summer in love with Sebastian Cain? . . . Was she blinded by another force stronger than the one within

373

her? She tried to hold on to this more hopeful possibility as she and Ellen set the table and called Patrick and the others to eat.

The meal was strangely quiet, for everyone's minds and hearts were with Summer.

The day stretched into evening. Simon kept himself and Jason busy cutting wood for Ellen; Patrick found several chores that needed his attention; Ellen sewed; and Sabrina silently worried.

It was very late when Ellen set aside her sewing and went to bed. Jason followed soon after, and before long Simon went off as well.

Patrick and Sabrina sat before the low-burning fire in comfortable silence for some time.

"Patrick?"

"Yes."

"I'm grateful that you and Simon are here."

"I know that, lass. I wouldn't be anyplace else right now. As for Simon"—he chuckled—"he would stay no matter what I said. You know he's in love with Summer."

"Yes, I think I've known that since they were very young."

"I wish it were not so."

"Why?"

"Because . . . the boy's going to get hurt. Summer is not the woman for him. I believe she has her own destiny to fulfill."

"Oh, Patrick," Sabrina said softly, "I worry about this Sebastian Cain. I worry about . . . well . . . about Summer being infatuated with him. Maybe that's why she followed him."

"Sabrina," Patrick said firmly, "you stop thinkin' those things. Summer, she's a real good judge of character. And on top of that, she knows what she means to a lot of people. She'll use her head. It's all going to come out all right."

"You really think so?"

"I believe in her," Patrick answered softly. "Sabrina, why don't you get some sleep?"

"What about you?"

"I think I will too."

Patrick rose and stretched and Sabrina had just risen from her chair when a muffled noise was heard on the porch. They looked at each other and waited, but the sound wasn't repeated.

"Only the wind," Patrick said, mentally fighting the touch of uneasiness that brushed through his mind. The door was still unlocked and he started toward it to lock it for the night. He was less than two steps from it when it was thrown open and he stood facing two men, both well armed and both with looks about them that told Patrick they meant business.

"Keep quiet, my friend." Toby grinned. "We don't want to disturb them that's sleepin', do we?"

"Who are you?" Patrick demanded. "What do you want? If it's robbery, there isn't anything to be found here."

"Don't you worry about us findin' what we want," Carl replied as his eyes shifted to a very frightened Sabrina. "There's gold here, all right," he chuckled softly. He waved the gun toward Sabrina. "Come over here, woman."

Patrick started for Carl, but Toby's gun brought him up short. "Leave her alone!" Patrick ground out. "She's Clay Storm's wife. He'll kill you for this."

"Naw," Toby explained. "He ain't gonna kill nobody. He's just gonna listen when we tell him what we want." Toby glanced at Sabrina. "Do what Carl says and get over there . . . or we're gonna kill your friend here."

Wide eyed with fear, Sabrina moved to Carl's side.

He grinned and put his arm about her and pulled her close to him. She struggled and Patrick again started in her direction. This time he had no intention of stopping. As he passed Toby, Toby raised his rifle and brought the butt down hard on Patrick's head. Patrick crumpled to the floor soundlessly.

"Patrick!" Sabrina cried.

"Be quiet, woman," Carl said. "The first person to come in this room is gonna get shot. You yell and someone comes, he'll be dead."

Sabrina choked back her screams and stood trembling in Carl's arms. He smiled triumphantly. "You better tie her, Toby."

"Yeah," Toby answered. He had two rawhide thongs on his belt in preparation for this. He grasped Sabrina's arms, drew them behind her back, and tied them securely.

"Tie him, too, and gag him. It will be morning before anyone knows she's gone."

Toby tied Patrick and stuffed a piece of cloth in his mouth. While he did this, Carl held Sabrina. Her fear thrilled him. He leaned his rifle against the wall and drew her helpless body against his. With one hand he loosened her hair and threaded his fingers through it.

"I always wanted to do that," he said. "Your hair is so pretty."

Sabrina muffled a moan as he ran his hand down her body. If she cried out, Ellen, Simon or—Lord, no!— even Jason might come. She knew these men would ruthlessly kill them.

He was enjoying the feel of her soft body, and she could feel him harden against her. Then he kissed her, his open mouth hard and bruising against hers. She sobbed when he released her lips.

"Quit playin' and come on. Let's get goin'. We have to meet Three Feathers."

"Okay"—Carl laughed smugly—"but she rides with me."

"Come on, let's go."

They left the house and closed the door quietly behind them. Carl mounted his horse and Toby lifted Sabrina up in front of Carl, then mounted himself. She closed her eyes in misery as the horses silently began to move away from the house.

They rode easily for a time, then a soft cry came from Sabrina as Carl reached for the buttons of her dress and began to unbutton them. Toby paid no attention to what was happening. He would get his share of Sabrina when they got paid by Miles.

Carl slipped his hand inside her dress to cup her breast lightly in his hand. His fingers found the soft crest and squeezed until Sabrina cried out. Now he tried to push the material aside so he could see her, but he could not accomplish this. Angrily he ripped the front of her dress open, tearing it until she was totally naked to the waist and the front of the dress hung in ragged shreds.

"There," he said softly, "that's better."

"Please," Sabrina whispered, "leave me alone."

"Now, pretty lady, I can't do that. You're a sweet thing and I intend to have you under me real soon. Just as soon as Chandler gets your husband's land, I get you. Right now I'm just samplin'. Later I'm gonna show you how it feels to be mounted by a man who knows what to do to a pretty thing like you. You're gonna learn to enjoy it."

Sabrina's anger and the strain were getting the best of her.

"Take your hands off me, you filthy pig. You are going to pay for this. I'll kill you if you touch me again."

Carl laughed and Sabrina was shaken by the sound

377

of twisted pleasure in it. He was the kind of man who would enjoy force. He would be pleased if she cried and begged.

She gritted her teeth while he continued to fondle her, and for the moment she was grateful they were on the move. She wouldn't let herself think about what would happen when they stopped.

Luke rode effortlessly and listened to Kate's sobs until he grew tired of them.

"Be quiet, Kate," he said firmly. "You've always been a cat who could land on her feet. Why don't you just make the best of a situation you can't do anything about?"

"Damn you," Kate gritted in utter frustration. "You can't hold me against my will!"

"Can't I?" Luke inquired smoothly. He bent his head close to Kate's and spoke softly. "Before we reach town, I will make sure you are tied securely and covered. I will carry you aboard myself, and once we are under sail you will have two choices. Come to my bed and we'll share what we both have, or . . . I will turn you over to my men for the two-month journey. Two months with that many woman-hungry men and you will no longer care who and what you are. Life with me will not be so difficult, Kate," he whispered, "as long as you behave."

Kate's very alert mind was already working, and Luke knew it. It would not take long to discover the safest and most profitable course for her at the moment. She would find a way to get back at Luke. Her wealth was her own and she would share it with no one. She would find Luke in a weak moment, and when she did she would—

"Forget it, Kate." Luke chuckled. "I don't intend to

turn my back on you for one minute. I know you for what you are and I'll keep careful watch on my back. Why don't you give up, Kate. We could have a pleasant time together."

Kate made her first move.

"I . . . I suppose it would be exciting . . . the captain and his wife sailing the world together."

Now Luke threw back his head and laughed. "Wife? Who said anything about marrying you? As a wife you might find a way to control me and all the money we're going to share. As a mistress, you'll be more . . . ah . . . cooperative and careful—careful that I don't get tired of you. You might find it best to please me, Kate."

"You are a bastard, Luke."

"I couldn't agree with you more. But Kate, we can have anything in the world we want. Don't call me names, Kate. You may find that this bastard is much more interesting than the life you planned."

He reined in his horse and turned Kate around to look at him. "Kate, you and I are alike, and I intend to prove it to you. You are a woman who needs a man who . . . enjoys the same things. You need a man you can't walk on or walk out on. I'm that man."

"Why, Luke? Why didn't you just leave me alone?"

"Because I had had a taste of something I liked, and I'm not through yet. I want more . . . and I intend to have it."

"You want my money!"

"First. And you second. If you try real hard, I might make you first. If you fail"—his eyes became cold even though he still smiled—"I will still have the money."

She gasped as she comprehended his threat. He would find a way to do exactly what he said he would do. Eventually she would have to get him off guard. She was determined to be mistress of her own money and Luke now stood in the way. She began to scheme and Luke smiled, for he was well prepared for whatever Kate might do. For as long as he wanted her, Kate would be the most exciting mistress he had ever had. With complete confidence that he could control her, Luke removed Kate from Sebastian's life.


Patrick groaned as he slowly regained consciousness. His head was spinning and he felt a black wave of nausea that was so severe he groaned again. Slowly he blinked his eyes open only to close them quickly again as the room began whirling dizzily about him.

He lay still until he could open his eyes with less discomfort. He looked about and realized he had been unconscious for some time. The pale grey sky he could see through the open window told him it was nearing dawn.

He tried to move and found that he was unable to do so. His muscles were stiff, for his hands had been bound behind him. He had to get free. He tried to loosen the cloth that bound his mouth, but it was too tight and wouldn't move.

It had been hours since Sabrina had been taken, and all he could do was pray that someone in the house would rise early. That someone turned out to be Simon.

Simon had not slept well. He had tossed and turned with vague dreams that Summer was in some kind of danger. But he kept getting Summer and Sabrina mixed up. He came awake sweating and confused, wondering which woman had really been in his dream.

He rose from his bed and donned his clothes. He would go and talk to his father. Patrick would understand and maybe help relieve his worry. He wasn't too sure his father, or anyone else for that matter, was up yet, but he was hungry, so he opened the door to his room quietly. He intended to make his way to the kitchen as silently as he could and find something to eat.

He stepped outside his door and closed it behind him. Then he started toward the kitchen. As he entered the living room, he saw his father.

"Pa!" Simon shouted as he ran to Patrick's side. First he checked to see if Patrick was alive, then he loosened the gag from his mouth. His fingers fumbled with the ropes that bound Patrick. His invincible father was hurt and Simon was shaken.

"Pa, are you all right?"

"I'm fine, Simon. Help me to my feet."

Simon offered his hand, but Patrick had to cling to him for support. He was weaving on his feet and fighting the nausea.

"Pa, sit down. You're hurt. What happened?"

"Simon, there's no time for me to be sitting around. Sabrina . . . two men. They came last night and took her."

"You're in no condition to do anything. Tell me what you want done, Pa, and I'll do it."

"Simon, I want you to go and get Hawk, Walking Horse, and a few more braves. Bring them back here."

"What about you, Pa?"

"Wake Ellen and tell her to wash this wound and make me some hot coffee."

Simon rushed to do Patrick's bidding. Ellen was horrified. She had gone through Sabrina's first kidnapping and knew what a tragedy that had almost been. Now she was frightened. Patrick explained quickly while Ellen cared for his wound. Once it was bound, Patrick rose to his feet. He was still a little

381

unsteady, but at least some of the nausea had faded and he could control his spinning head somewhat.

"Simon, be on your way, boy."

"Yes, Pa, I'm going."

Simon left within the hour and, minutes after, Patrick prepared to do the same.

"Patrick! What are you doing?" Ellen cried. "You're too weak to go anywhere."

"Ellen, don't shout, and please use your common sense. They're hours ahead. Someone has to follow and leave a trail for Hawk." He went to Ellen. "I saw those two last night. Sabrina is in more danger than she's ever been in before. They're both animals. Clay isn't here and someone's got to follow. You see, Ellen," he said gently, "it doesn't really matter how I feel. I've got to go."

"Yes," Ellen replied tearfully. "I understand. Oh, Patrick, what will happen to her? Why? Why?"

"I don't know, Ellen. I only know that they better not hurt her. If I have to follow them to the ends of the earth, I'll find them . . . and I'll kill them."

"Oh please, find her, Patrick, please. Clay . . . he won't be able to get over losing her. Find her, Patrick."

"I'll try, Ellen. I'll try. When Simon gets back with Hawk, tell him I'm leaving a trail a blind man could follow. Tell him to get on the trail as quickly as he can."

"I will."

Patrick kissed Ellen's cheek, then somewhat unsteadily he walked from the cabin. In a few minutes Ellen heard him ride away.

She sank down slowly into a chair. So many things had happened so suddenly—so many strange things—starting from the time they had discovered that Summer had gone to Hawk instead of coming home. From then on nothing had been right, Ellen reflected miserably. And now this—Sabrina taken away by Lord knew who. Ellen buried her face in her hands and cried.

Sabrina was enraged, but she refused to plead with the man who held her. She suspected that he would derive a great deal of pleasure from her begging, and she had no intention of allowing that.

They rode steadily and Sabrina realized they did not intend to stop before they reached their final destination. She was grateful, for she could not bear the thought of being in the wilderness alone with two such vile creatures.

They rode through the day, stopping only to care for necessities and to eat sparingly. Carl tormented her but did her no real harm, and it became clear that a third party still stood between them. She wondered who it was.

Toby proved the most talkative, but she couldn't get any real answers from him. He was wary of Carl, who was closed mouthed and always seemed to keep an eye on him.

"How long before we can get out of this territory, Carl?" Toby asked.

"Soon as she pays us."

Sabrina became alert at the word "she." If only they would reveal a name, give her some clue as to who was behind this, then maybe she could understand the reason for this madness.

She had been trying to put together threads of facts, when a germ of an idea insidiously planted itself. There was a blacker, deeper plot here that went beyond mere kidnapping, and somehow she was going to try to get the truth from Carl.

Carl was a self-centered man, and he was also quite ignorant. She placed her hopes on both those characteristics.

"Where are you taking me?" she asked quietly.

"Shut up. We ain't answerin' questions."

"I just wondered if he would be with us all the time."

"He?"

"Toby."

"What do you care?"

"I thought maybe you and I would be alone." She could actually hear Carl thinking.

"Well . . . we're goin' to a cave not far from here. 'Course, Toby will be there all the time. But maybe there's a way for us to be alone."

"How?"

"Maybe I can send Toby with a message. Tell her we got you. If the others ain't there already, we'd have the cave to ourselves." He chuckled as his arm tightened about her. "I knew you'd come around. A woman like you will appreciate a good man between your legs. I'll show you a good time. You're gonna love it."

Sabrina could have choked on her anger, but she kept calm.

"You expecting a lot of others? The profits must be small when you divide up between so many."

"They's only three others. Three Feathers, Little Elk, and Stace."

"What's . . . what's going to happen to me?"

"If you play your cards right, I'll keep you with me. Then the others won't touch you. I'll let them know you're my property."

"But there won't be any profit for any of you."

"Now I'll tell ya, little girl"—Carl laughed—"Miz Elenora, she pays good. But I got an idea there's somethin' between her and Miles Chandler. I think she's double-dealin' him. If so, I'm gonna make a profit . . . and keep you besides."

Sabrina's heart froze at the name from the past. *Elenora!* Elenora was behind this! She knew now it was some form of revenge against her. Now she became truly frightened, for she knew that Elenora would do anything to destroy her, and that she would not care what Sabrina suffered in the process.

She remained quiet and Carl felt satisfied. He would have Sabrina for himself. Hadn't she realized what a man he was? Why, she shivered in his arms as if she couldn't wait for him to take her.

By the end of the day Sabrina was exhausted. But she didn't want to say anything about stopping. There was no telling what these depraved animals would do if they were to make camp now.

But they showed no signs of stopping. They pushed on and on until Sabrina was so tired she could barely stay awake.

It was the middle of the night when both horses came to a halt. Sabrina's heart beat frantically. Were they going to stop now? Would it be the end? She knew she would fight to the death before she would surrender to either one.

Both men dismounted and Carl pulled Sabrina down roughly to stand beside him. Then they unsaddled the horses.

It was only then that Sabrina saw the glow of firelight emanating from the depths of a cave. She closed her eyes as Carl dragged her inside.

Once inside, they walked some distance before entering a large cavern. In the center two Indians and a white man sat by a fire. Carl and Toby pulled Sabrina after them and walked closer. Sabrina saw the tallest Indian stand, and Carl spoke.

"Three Feathers."

"She is another pretty one." Three Feathers grinned

at Sabrina. "She will bring much money."

"Another?" Sabrina questioned.

Three Feathers pointed and Sabrina turned to follow his gesture. When she saw the form lying still on the blanket, a groan of shock and pain came from her. She pushed Carl's hand from her arm and ran to turn the slim form over. She gazed down at a still-unconscious Summer.

## Chapter Thirty-one

Hawk's face was a frozen mask behind which Cole could not get. It was forbidding and to Cole it looked as if Hawk had already determined to not make things pleasant for him. He could feel his nerves grow taut.

"Hawk . . ." he began.

"Where is Summer?" Hawk demanded. "What happened to her since you lured her from this village?"

"It wasn't quite what you think, Hawk," Cole replied quickly. "First, we did not lure her from the village. She followed on her own."

"You were here long enough to know her. I believe your friend Sebastian meant for her to follow. He knew she would try to help those she thought needed her."

"No Hawk, it wasn't like that. Sebastian wasn't luring Summer from here . . . he was running. I knew she sensed his trouble, but I didn't know for a long time that she had followed. We traveled separate paths for awhile. When we met again, Summer was already with him."

"Is she well?"

"The last time I saw her she was both well and very happy," Cole replied. But he could still see doubt in Hawk's eyes and realized it was very difficult for Hawk to believe him.

"Where is she now?"

"She's with Sebastian at his home. Hawk, it was Sebastian who sent me back here. He sent me with a message for you."

"A message?"

"Yes." Cole grinned. "As soon as they make plans, they want Hawk to be present at their wedding celebration."

He saw the words register very slowly, and it was not with as much enthusiasm as he had expected. Hawk's face remained dark and unreadable.

"Come to my tipi," Hawk said coldly. "We must talk."

Cole was surprised. He had thought the news would make Hawk happy and forgiving. What it had done, it seemed, was to make him even more formidable.

Raven and Kylie watched a very sober Cole silently follow Hawk to his tipi and disappear inside.

"My chief is very angry," Raven observed.

"So it seems," Kylie answered. "Why is it, Raven, that he doesn't seem to believe Cole."

"It is a long story, Kylie. My parents have spoken of it. It is something that happened between Hawk and Clay Storm many years ago. This seems to be the old story returning to repeat itself. Hawk will be very hard on Cole."

"Tell me the story," Kylie insisted. As they walked along slowly, Raven recounted an incredible tale of Clay, Sabrina, and Hawk.

"But it is such a beautiful story, Raven. Clay and Sabrina must have loved each other so much."

"But you see, Kylie, the real trouble was Summer."

"Summer! But she was just a child."

"Yes, but her powers were strong even then." He went on to tell her how Clay had tried to separate

388

Summer from the village and described the battle that had been fought and finally won over that.

"So," Kylie said softly, "he thinks Sebastian Cain will do what Clay wanted to do. And this time he just might succeed."

"I hope not," Raven replied. "For Sebastian's and Cole's sakes, I hope not."

Kylie walked for a few minutes in silence. Her thoughts were on Cole. He was certainly a very attractive man, she mused. She liked the sparkle of humor that had been in his eyes when they had met. Her curiosity began to grow and she wondered what he was like and what kind of family he had.

She was also very interested in Cole's marital state. A soft smile lit her face. It would not take long for Kylie Flynn to find her answers, and if they pleased her, it would not take long before she began to appease all her curiosity.

Once inside his tipi, Hawk turned to look at Cole. Silently Cole handed him Summer's note. Hawk didn't seem to be too pleased with it either. He read the note over, then read it again. Then his eyes returned to Cole.

"So they have decided to marry."

"Yes."

"Why?"

"What do you mean, why?"

"Does Sebastian think Summer's honor requires this? It does not. Summer would have her honor among us no matter what. Why do you not go back and tell Summer to come home to us, to those who truly love her."

"Hawk, you have the wrong idea about all this. The wedding is not a question of honor. They truly love each other. Summer is not forced to do this. She wants to marry Sebastian, and he wants her more than anything else in the world." Cole couldn't understand Hawk's obviously well-controlled rage.

"Hawk, what is it? I don't understand. Why should it make you so angry that Sebastian and Summer are in love and want to marry?"

"Because I do not think it's because she loves him, or because he loves her. I think they are caught in something in which their honor is threatened."

"No. I'm telling you. I've been with them. They are happy with each other."

"Summer will come here to marry. When she does, her father and I will convince her how unnecessary it is. She will remain with us."

Cole gazed at Hawk in utter amazement, then all at once he understood Hawk's strange behavior.

"Hawk," he said gently, "you cannot tie Summer to you and this village. You cannot do this and neither can her family. She knows, I'm sure, just how important she is, and she would not hurt you. But Hawk, she has a life to live too, and she has a right to be happy. Would you cheat her of that?"

Hawk was silent for several minutes, for Cole had struck at the heart of the problem. He, as Clay had been, was afraid that Summer would go and never return. He was selfish and he knew it.

"I'm sure Sebastian and Summer will come soon. They are going to decide what they want to do. But they will come soon. I'm sure Summer would like her parents to know and to be here. Why can't we all just be happy with them?"

"You are right, my friend. But it is not an easy thing to let go. And if it is hard for me, it will be harder for her father."

Cole grinned. "I'm sure Summer can find a way around that."

Hawk sighed deeply. "Well, I cannot stop what Summer chooses to do."

"But . . . will you try, or will you accept it and share it?"

"You are determined."

"I want to see them happy."

"I will try." Hawk chuckled. "I cannot speak for her family. Her father searches for her even as we speak."

"And he wants Sebastian's scalp!" Cole laughed.

"Let us say he is less than pleased that Summer followed Sebastian. He will have to explain very quickly."

Cole was relieved that Hawk seemed to have made some sort of peace with the idea and was no longer directing his anger at him. Hawk's next words confirmed Cole's thoughts.

"You are welcome to stay here while we wait for them to come. I know you would not miss the wedding."

"Of my best friend?" Cole grinned. "Not likely."

"Then I will see that you are made comfortable and we will wait."

"Thank you." Cole paused. "Hawk?"

"Yes?"

"Who is the pretty girl with the red hair?"

"Kylie Flynn. Her father is a good friend of Clay Storm's, and Kylie is a very close friend to Summer."

Now Cole's grin grew broader. "Well, well. It looks like Kylie Flynn and I have something in common."

Hawk laughed with him and watched as Cole left his tipi.

Once outside, Cole stood and scanned the village, hoping for a glimpse of red hair. He gave a quick, satisfied laugh when he saw her standing with Raven some distance away. It never occurred to Cole that Kylie had coerced Raven into waiting with her until

Cole came out of Hawk's tipi.

Kylie was quite pleased when she saw Cole walking purposefully toward her. As he stopped beside her, she smiled up at him.

"Miss Flynn," Cole said.

"Well, Mr. Robbins"—Kylie laughed—"I see you have come out all right. Hawk growls fiercely but he does not bite often."

"But when he does," Raven interjected, "I am always grateful I am not the prey."

"Well, it seems that I'm not the prey either," Cole replied. "I came only to bring him the good news that Summer and Sebastian are going to be married."

"I don't know your friend Sebastian," Kylie said, "but I am happy for Summer. She is one of the dearest friends I have."

"Well then," Cole said with a smile, "you will be staying here for the wedding?"

"I wouldn't miss it for anything."

"I'm glad."

"Why?"

"Well, since it might be a few days before Sebastian and Summer got here, I thought we might find some time to get to know each other."

"What an interesting thought, Mr. Robbins."

"Cole . . . the name is Cole."

"Cole," Kylie said sweetly. "And I'm Kylie."

"Very pretty name."

"Thank you."

Raven had already drifted away and Kylie and Cole were left to walk slowly to the tipi she shared with a gracious family.

"You've been here before?" Cole questioned.

"Oh yes. Until Summer left for school, she and I stayed with Hawk often. It was always great fun to be here with Summer. I always enjoyed myself."

"Well . . . it kind of makes me regret I didn't run across Hawk's village a long time ago. It's hard to believe I've roamed this territory for so long and never had enough good luck to be here when you were."

Kylie laughed softly and her eyes sparkled up into his. "Why Cole," she breathed, "do you know that with your blarney"—she tucked her arm through his—"you remind me of someone else."

"Who?"

"My father," she replied slowly. "Yes . . . you remind me very much of my father."

The next two days were pleasurable for Kylie and positively enlightening for Cole, who found himself so entangled in Kylie's warm smile and laughing eyes that he let Summer and Sebastian slip from his mind completely.

For the first time in Cole's life he began to think of permanence and security . . . and a home.

The only thing was, he wasn't quite used to women like Kylie. She laughed easily and found so much joy in the activities of the village that Cole couldn't be sure that he wasn't just part of a short period of fun and nothing more.

In addition, it seemed that Kylie could not be caught alone where he could talk to her seriously. She was popular with the young people of the village, both male and female. But after awhile it seemed to Cole that Raven was her favorite. He had no way of knowing that Kylie and Raven had been companions through their growing years and that she was considered a child of the village. Raven had always been like an older brother to her, but because Cole misinterpreted their relationship, he suffered acute jealousy when he observed the relaxed and easy camaraderie Raven and

Kylie shared.

Why, he wondered, could he not be just as easy? He would have given anything to have gotten Kylie alone. But every attempt was frustrated by the appearance of Raven or someone else.

He had invited her to go swimming, and a laughing Raven had brought several others and it had turned into a party. He had invited her to ride with him, and somehow they had been joined by Raven and other riders. Cole was experiencing utter and complete frustration. He had begun to assume that Kylie wasn't taking him any more seriously than she did any of the others. Slowly, one step at a time, Kylie was driving Cole to the brink.

He lay in his tipi now, hands folded behind his head, and he laughed at himself. He felt like a lecher trying to entice an innocent girl into a clandestine meeting, which, he realized, was exactly what he was doing. He laid one plan, discarded it, and devised another. But none of them seemed to be much good.

He rose from his bed and stepped outside. It was just barely dawn. He sighed. It was forbidden to go into her tipi and wake her. And she might not be too pleased with that either. Oh well, he thought, it was a long day. Some opportunity might present itself.

He was about to go back inside when a movement caught his eye. The flap of Kylie's tipi had been pushed aside and she stepped out.

She carried a large water sac and he knew she was on her way to a nearby stream. He gave a surreptitious look around to see that no one else was in sight; then, with a satisfied smile on his face, he followed her.

Kylie walked to the stream, which was some distance from the village. She knelt to fill the sac, then laid the sac aside, cupped water in her hands, and washed her face. Then she removed her shoes and tucked the skirt

394

of her dress into her belt and waded into the cool water. It felt good. She lifted her hands to remove the pins from her hair, then let it tumble about her.

Morning sun touched her hair, setting it aflame with its light. She was at peace with the world and she hummed softly to herself. That was the way Cole found her.

He stopped near the edge of the stream. "Good morning, Kylie," he began. "It's going to be a beautiful day."

Kylie smiled up at him. Then she waded toward him and Cole framed a picture in his mind that he would carry forever. It was the first time he realized what Sebastian felt for Summer. Cole had fallen in love and faced the fact with a severe case of insecurity.

"Hello, Cole. I didn't think anyone else would be up so early."

"I . . . I always get up early."

"So do I. I like mornings, especially out here."

"Kylie?"

"Yes, Cole?"

"I'd like to talk to you."

"I thought we were." She chuckled.

"I mean . . . I have to talk to you about something very important. Can we sit down here?"

"Of course." Kylie walked ahead of Cole to the shade of a tree. There she placed the water sac aside and sat down. She had hoped for this moment for some time. With sheer devilish delight she had played on Cole and had teased him into being aware of her. He had seemed so cool and aloof that she had been certain he was not interested in her any more than he was in the shy and pretty Indian girls who had cast their dark eyes in his direction . . . and she wanted to hold his interest.

"What's so serious?"

"Kylie . . . I . . . I don't suppose you'll be staying in

395

the village too long."

"No, I guess just until Pa gets back."

"You live a long way from here?"

"Four or five days' ride."

"Do you think your Pa would mind if I rode over once in a while?" He turned to stare at her intently. "I want to see you, Kylie . . . a lot."

"Oh, Cole," Kylie said softly, "I've been waiting for days to hear you say something like that."

Cole gazed at her in surprise, then laughed. "You sure could have fooled me. I thought you didn't know I existed."

"I know you exist," she said softly. "I've felt your presence since the day we met."

Cole reached out and took her hand in his. "Listen, Kylie. I don't have much. Hell, I don't have anything. But I can trap and I can build a small place and get something started. If I do"—he looked into her green eyes and she could see into his heart—"will you consider coming to live there?"

He waited without realizing he was holding his breath.

"Yes, Cole . . . I'd consider that."

For a moment he looked as if he hadn't even heard her, then he expelled his breath. "Kylie," he whispered raggedly. He moved to his knees beside her and reached to draw her tenderly into his arms.

Kylie closed her eyes and slowly lifted her lips to meet his.

Cole was lost, totally and absolutely lost. He held her close to him and could do nothing more than feel the exquisite pleasures of her lips parting beneath his and her firm young body setting his on fire.

Neither of them heard Raven call until he had called several times and had come quite close.

Even then Cole's lips left hers reluctantly. They looked at each other for several instants, and both were

396

slightly dazed at their new discovery.

"Cole! Cole! Kylie!" Raven called.

Cole stood up and reached down to draw Kylie up beside him.

"Yes Raven, we're over here."

Cole was going to make some pointed remark until Raven rushed up to them. Raven's face told them both that he was quite serious.

"Raven, what's the matter?"

"Cole, it is best that you come back to the village quickly. There is a man there called Jake who says it is important that he talk to you right away."

"Jake? What's he doing here?"

"I do not know, but he says we must hurry and find you."

"Lord, there must be something wrong," Cole said. He took Kylie's hand and started back toward the village.

Jake stood by his horse and began to talk almost as soon as Cole approached him.

"I don't believe it," Cole stated firmly after Jake had finished. "Summer wouldn't walk out on Sebastian like that. She was in love with him. I'd stake my life on that. What was Sebastian like when you left him?"

"Cold . . . mad," Jake replied quietly. "And lookin' for some answers."

"And looking for Summer like that. I'd bet Kate was behind this somehow."

"Kate's gone too," Jake replied. He continued to tell Cole what had happened.

"I'm going to get my things together, Jake. We'll go back and pick up his trail. We can't let him find Summer like this, not in his state of mind."

"I guess you're right. I had to bring Mandy here. I'll go with you."

"Good." Cole turned to Kylie. "I'll be back as soon as

397

I can. Don't go away, angel, please."

"I'll be here, Cole."

He smiled and brushed her lips with a soft kiss, then he ran to gather his things. He was in the midst of saddling his horse when another horseman rode rapidly into the village.

Cole listened to Simon's story along with Hawk and some of the other warriors, who were enraged that the wife of Clay Storm had been taken.

"Cole," Hawk said, "you must ride with us, for I believe these things are joined together somehow. We must locate the men who have taken Sabrina. I believe we will find that these men have taken Summer as well."

"Hawk," Cole protested, "what if that is not so? What if Summer's gone alone and Sebastian finds her?"

Hawk turned to look at him. His gaze was steady and his eyes were dark and piercing.

"You know your friend. You say that he loved Summer and she loved him. Tell me, do you think he is a violent man? Do you think a man who loves one minute can hate so deeply the next? Do you think he wants to do her harm . . . or to find out for certain what is in her heart?"

Cole was quiet while his mind considered the Sebastian he knew. The questions pounded in his mind. What did he really think?

"Sebastian won't do her any harm," he concluded aloud, "no matter how or where he finds her. I guess you are right about another thing, too. Sebastian just wants to hear Summer tell him that it's over."

"I thought so." Hawk smiled. "Summer is very seldom wrong. She chose him. I do not believe she would hurt him unless she had a reason. If she left him, she should tell him the reasons herself. Then she can

398

come home to us."

"I'll go with you, Hawk. Jake, too. But after we find Sabrina, I intend to make sure Summer and Sebastian are both all right."

"It will be so," Hawk stated. "You are a good friend. Sebastian is very fortunate. He has been fortunate to know Summer also. She will make her own choices. But if she no longer wishes to remain with him, then he must leave this territory. He will not be welcome here."

Cole was silenced by the unmovable firmness of Hawk's voice. What Hawk said, he meant. Inwardly Cole prayed that what had happened between Summer and Sebastian had been only a lovers' argument.

"I think we had better hurry. We have to catch up with Pa," Simon interjected urgently.

"How are we gonna do that?" Cole questioned.

"Pa said he'd leave a trail a blind man could follow. If he said it, he did it. Besides, I don't want Pa to catch up with those men by himself, 'cause he's mad enough to do something about it on his own."

"You are right," Hawk agreed. He turned to the circle of warriors about him and gave swift, clear commands. It did not take long for Hawk, Walking Horse, Jake, Simon, and Cole to mount their horses and join three other warriors Hawk had chosen.

Kylie stood by her tipi and, as Hawk's party was leaving, Cole rode up beside her. He bent down from the saddle and kissed her.

"Wait for me?" he whispered.

"I will, Cole."

"I'll be back as soon as I can."

"Be careful, Cole. We don't know what kind of men they are. They might not be adverse to shooting someone. I don't want it to be you." Cole laughed softly. Suddenly she found herself caught up and seated before him.

"Cole!"

"I love you, Kylie. I just wanted to tell you before I go. I haven't had much in my life and you sure are the brightest spot. I'll be back. You can count on it. But I need something special to take with me."

Kylie looped her arms about Cole's neck. Her parted lips were warm against his, and he crushed her to him as if he would imprint her and carry her with him. The kiss was most satisfactory, but not what they both wanted.

Slowly Cole lowered Kylie to the ground. He smiled, touched her cheek, then rode away.

Kylie stood and watched with tears in her eyes. "You had better come back, Cole Robbins," she whispered. "You'd better come back." She closed her eyes for a moment. "I love you, Cole," she called softly after him. "Please take care of yourself."

Raven, who had been left with several other warriors to guard the village, came up beside her. Childhood friendship had made them close. Cole's jealousy of Raven was unfounded, for he felt toward Kylie like an older brother might. Now he felt her fears. He had seen days ago that Kylie was in love with Cole. He just couldn't understand why it had taken Cole so long to realize the truth.

They stood together and watched the group ride away.

"He is a good man, Kylie. He feels much for his friends and for his honor."

"Yes," Kylie replied, "I know, Raven. I guess I knew that day in the valley when he met us."

"You love him, sister?"

"Yes, I do."

"Do not be afraid, Kylie. He will return."

"How do you know?" Kylie turned to look up at Raven who grinned boyishly.

"Because you are here, and he is a man whose blood is hot."

"Oh, Raven!" Kylie giggled despite her concern.

"It is good that you laugh, Kylie," he said gently. "Keep the laugh until he returns."

"I will. Thank you, Raven . . . thank you."

# Chapter Thirty-two

Sebastian looked up into Clay Storm's cold blue gaze and suddenly felt as if he were standing on the edge of death. Clay and the gun he pointed at Sebastian were enough to bring Sebastian under control.

"So you're Summer's father."

"I am. Where is she?"

"I don't know."

The rifle loomed larger as Clay took a step toward him.

"I'm telling you I don't know. It's something I'm trying to find out for myself."

"She left the village following you!" Clay stated.

"Well, damnit, she isn't here!"

"I can see that. What I want to know is why, and where she is now."

"I don't have any answers to where," Sebastian said, his anger matching Clay's, "but I can tell you why, if you want to know."

"I want to know."

"If you'll put that gun down and sit down here, I'll tell you the whole story."

Clay walked closer and sat down, but the rifle remained centered on Sebastian's heart.

"Now tell me your story."

"It's not just my story; it's the truth."

"I'll judge that better when you tell me."

Sebastian began with the reason Summer had followed him. He told of his brother and the burned house, but he hesitated when he came to the subject of his relationship with Summer.

Clay's gaze never left Sebastian's face and Sebastian could feel the piercing blue eyes like a blade.

"I loved her," he said finally in a more subdued voice. "I loved her . . . but for her it was just some kind of game."

Clay herked his head up and his eyes blazed. "Now that I don't believe."

"Well, it's the truth too. Summer told me so."

"She said that?"

"Not exactly said . . . but a letter is enough."

Sebastian took the letter from beneath his shirt and silently handed it to Clay, who read it slowly. Then he looked up at Sebastian. This time there was a taut smile on his lips.

"Who is lying to whom, Mr. Cain?" Clay asked gently.

"What?"

"I think all you have told me is your own story."

"The letter should be proof enough."

"It would be . . . if Summer had written it."

"I don't understand. It's pretty obvious to me."

"Mr. Cain, my daughter has been away at school for four years. In that time I have received hundreds of letters from her. Could you believe for one minute that I would not recognize her handwriting when I saw it?"

"What?"

"I said, Summer never wrote this letter."

Sebastian's heart leapt and he reached for the letter to scan it again.

"But it must be. Summer is the only one who could know anything about what is written here."

"Are you so sure of that?"

Sebastian began to think back. It was then that Mandy's words came to him. Kate! Kate had written the letter! But then where was Summer? And with whom? He was completely shaken.

"Tell me, Mr. Cain, if you thought Summer had written this—if you felt she no longer loved or wanted you—why would you follow her?"

Sebastian was again silent as he probed his mind for the answer. He knew why. It was just very difficult to admit it to himself. Because he didn't want to lose her; because he would never feel the truth of it unless she said it to him. And there was another reason. He would have begged her if necessary—given her anything she wanted—in order to convince her to stay with him.

He looked up at Clay's eyes and saw his own thoughts reflected there.

"Because I love her, and I shall love her no matter what. I cannot believe unless she says it is so. Even then, I don't know if I would accept it."

"I will tell you one truth, Sebastian Cain," Clay said firmly. "Summer does not lie. She would never write a letter and run away. She would face you, fight if necessary, but she would never offer anything but the truth. It was the way of her mother and her people, and I hope it is the way of her father and his people. She has many gifts. Complete honesty is one of them."

Sebastian remained silent as his mind groped for the words to make Clay understand. But his efforts were unnecessary, for Clay understood all too well. His memories went back to long ago misunderstandings. He knew how much pain it could cause. He saw it etched in the younger man's face.

"Mr. Cain," he began, "why don't we begin again? I

think we have a great deal to say to each other. In the morning we will ride together to find Summer."

Sebastian was more than grateful for this offer. And once he began to talk, he released everything. It was like a bursting dam.

When he finished, Clay began to talk and Sebastian learned everything there was to know about Summer, including the details of the immense wealth and prestigious name behind her.

"And you say she doesn't lie!"

"Did she ever tell you she was not wealthy?"

"No, but—"

"Did she ever tell you her family background did not include members of the royal family?"

"Not exactly."

"In fact, did she ever tell you about her life at all?"

"No, she never did." Sebastian laughed. "And I thought I was going to show her a whole new world. I thought she would one day be very impressed by my wealth and family background. Good God, I treated her like a child I had to train in good manners! What a fool!"

"A fool to judge people by what they have or how they live rather than by what they are."

"That was what she wanted," Sebastian said softly. "All the time, that was the mysterious question I saw in her eyes. She wanted me to accept Summer, a poor little Indian girl, before she would allow me to see Summer Storm, the lady of wealth and position. That was why she fought me so long and so hard. That was why she wouldn't say she loved me."

"Sebastian," Clay questioned gently, "did she ever say she loved you?"

Sebastian raised his eyes to meet Clay's.

"Yes, she did."

"Then that is the truth you should hold on to. If she

405

said it, she meant it." Sebastian seemed to swell with the words. His wounded heart needed such soothing balm. He thought back to the night in the barn and the next day. She had said, "I love you, Sebastian." His entire being clung to the hope that she still meant it.

"Now," Clay said firmly, "tell me of the friends she left with."

"Friends! I don't know that they were friends. I never saw them."

"You mean you let her ride away with people you knew nothing of?"

"I never saw her go. I told you. She went upstairs, and the next thing I knew she was gone."

Clay's expression was bleak as he stated, "They might not be friends at all. She could have been taken by someone. But who would know she was there?"

"Kate!" Sebastian said angrily.

"Who would have contact with—"

"Kate," Sebastian interrupted with a snarl.

"Who would want her out of the way?"

"Again Kate! Kate! Kate, damn her!"

"We cannot track any further tonight, but we can start again at dawn."

"I'm glad you're here. I'm not really good at this. Cole would have been, but I sent him back to Hawk to tell him everything was fine and that we'd be coming home to get married."

"I can track them. We'll start at daybreak."

"I never asked if you were hungry," Sebastian stated and smiled.

"I am. I didn't stop to eat. I was too eager to catch up with you."

"I guess I've got a lot to learn about living out here. I can track a little—I've learned some from Cole—but I'm not good at it."

"You were sure giving it a fine try."

"I don't think it was my ability as much as it was my need to catch up with Summer."

Sebastian offered Clay what had been left over from his supper and Clay ate.

Then they both rolled in their blankets. Clay slept, but Sebastian was not as fortunate. He couldn't find sleep. He was still shaken by how close he had come to being completely taken in by the letter he carried. He thought of Kate and new anger rushed through him. Her whole scheme became obvious now. How he had swallowed it up! He shivered with the thought of how successful Kate's plan might have been if Clay had not found him first. He might not have believed Summer, even though she would have denied his accusations, and the result would have been disastrous for them both.

Next, he began to consider whom Kate could have gotten to take Summer from him, and where they were taking her. His speculations tormented him and it was a very long time before he lapsed into uneasy sleep.

The next morning both men were awake before the sun was up. Both were silent, for their minds were on Summer, who she was with, and where they were headed. And Sebastian had recognized another concern. When Summer had been in danger before, she had mentally called out to him. Now there was no mental voice. He felt there could be only two reasons. Either Summer had not needed to call him because she had agreed to leave, or she was unable to call him. It was the last that terrified him. He didn't want to reveal these thoughts to Clay, for he knew Summer's father was worried enough.

Once they were back on the trail, Sebastian had to admire Clay's expertise in tracking. They moved much more rapidly than Sebastian had alone. And it took little effort for Clay to determine that the ones they followed had a very slim head start.

"Untie my hands, please," Sabrina begged. "Let me take care of Summer. She's hurt! What have you done to her?"

It was Three Feathers who went to her and cut through the bonds. Sabrina immediately bent over Summer and turned her gently. There was a very large and ugly bruise on her temple, but what disturbed Sabrina the most was that she had no way of knowing how long Summer had been in this condition.

Sabrina asked for water and it was provided. She tore a piece of her skirt, wet it, and placed it across Summer's forehead. Then she held Summer's hand and closed her eyes, praying that Summer was not beyond her help. It had been so long since she had seen her stepdaughter, and now to find her like this! She wished desperately that Clay were near, or that she had the power of healing Summer possessed. She felt frightened and completely helpless.

Not far from them, Carl and Toby were deep in conversation.

"Damnit, why did they hit her so hard? She ain't gonna be any use to us like that," Carl said.

"She'll be all right," Toby replied casually. "She'll come around pretty soon. We got both of them, Carl, so what's our next move?"

"Miz Gregory's got the answers to that. You get goin'. It'll take you a couple of days to get there and tell her we got 'em. She'll pay us her share for gettin' the yeller-haired one. After she does, we'll go to Miles and he'll pay us again. Then we take the women and hightail it. They'll bring another fat price from Santiago and his men. Once that's over, we'll divide up. We'll be richer than we've ever been."

408

"I best get goin' now," Toby declared. "I'll be back fast as I can get back. Meantime, you better see that gal don't die. She ain't gonna bring us a red cent if she's dead. Santiago, he likes his women lively."

"I'll take care of her; you just get goin'."

"Carl," Toby said distrustfully, "you keep your hands off the yeller-haired one. We's supposed to share her, and I ain't havin' you samplin' the goods before I gets a chance to."

"Ah, I might play with her a little, but I won't do any ridin' 'til you gets back. But you better hurry up. I got a yen to taste that pretty filly pretty quick."

"I'll be back in less than four days."

Carl nodded, but Toby was still suspicious of his intentions, for his cold and hungry gaze was still caressing Sabrina, who knelt by a still-unconscious Summer. After a short while Toby left, and Carl found a comfortable place to sit where he could keep his eyes on Sabrina.

Three Feathers too was watching close, for he had his mind set on taking Summer with him after he received his payment for abducting her.

He was worried about Summer's continued unconsciousness. He wanted her very much alive. He moved closer to the two women. Sabrina looked up and her eyes reflected a combination of protective anger and fear of the huge, dark, towering Indian. Three Feathers knelt on the opposite side of Summer. He reached out a hand and gently touched her cheek. Sabrina became even more frightened at the look of possession in his eyes.

"Leave her alone! Can't you see she's hurt?"

"Be quiet, woman," Three Feathers said sharply. "She will be mine one day. I do not intend to let her die."

"Damn you all!" Sabrina cried. "How merciless you

409

are to have done this to her!"

"What I want, I take," Three Feathers snarled. "If you do not remain silent, I shall take her to another place and you will not be able to see her again."

Sabrina closed her mouth abruptly. She did not want Summer to be taken from her now, not when the girl so desperately needed her help.

Three Feathers touched Summer again, then silently moved away. He would have her in his own time, when he was ready.

At that moment Summer stirred and moaned softly. Then her eyes fluttered open to see Sabrina bending over her.

"Sabrina"—Summer groaned painfully—"what are you doing here? Where . . . where am I? I don't remember."

"Shh, lie still, Summer. You've been injured."

"Where is Sebastian? What happened? Oh, Sabrina, my head hurts."

"Just be still, Summer. Don't try to move."

"But I don't understand. How . . ." Her eyes began to clear from their disoriented haze as memory began to flood back. It was then she turned her head and saw Three Feathers. She gave a muffled cry that signified her terror and her hand gripped Sabrina's arm.

"You," she gasped. "You are behind this. Where is Sebastian!"

"I would wish him dead, but it is not so. He is still safe with the other yellow-haired woman."

"Kate? I don't believe you. You lie. Sebastian was sending Kate away."

"When you were taken, a message was left behind for him. It did much to eliminate him from all this."

"Sebastian would not believe any message you left. He knew! He knew I would never go and just leave a message. He will come for me. He will follow you."

"I'm afraid not, little girl," Carl said in an amused tone as he approached. He had overheard their conversation. "You see, it was not a message from us. It was from you."

"He'll never believe it! Never!"

"No?" Carl chuckled. "Want me to tell ya what it said? Oh, by the way, Kate wrote it and signed your name. Seems she knew a whole lot about you and him. It made it kinda easy."

"What did she say?"

Carl went on to tell her what Kate had told him she had written. As he spoke, tears formed in Summer's eyes. After a few minutes she closed her eyes and hot tears bathed her cheeks in silvered streaks. Would Sebastian believe she had betrayed him? Would he go with Kate now? Would she ever see him again?

"Summer, don't let them do this to you," Sabrina encouraged. "Don't let them get to you! You love Sebastian?"

"Oh yes, Sabrina, I do."

"Then you must believe. You must have faith that Sebastian loves you too much to be misguided by a mere letter." She bent close to Summer to whisper, "You have something much more powerful than they could possibly imagine. You can call to him."

"Will he hear me from here? Sabrina, how far away are we?"

"I don't know," Sabrina answered helplessly. "I don't know where we are, but you must try."

"My head hurts so badly, I . . . I don't know if I can concentrate."

"What are you whispering about?" Three Feathers demanded.

"Three Feathers, get them two apart," Carl demanded, then he smiled. "Never mind." He walked toward Sabrina. "I'll take care of her."

411

Sabrina shrank back as Carl stopped beside her. He reached down and gripped her arm and yanked her to her feet. She tried to pull away from him, but her efforts were useless, and he relentlessly dragged her away from Summer. The cave was very large and Summer couldn't see them any longer from her reclining position. She tried to rise, but pain returned just as Three Feathers knelt beside her and pressed her back against the blanket. Her only hope now was to see if she could find out from someone just how far they were from Sebastian's house.

Carl pushed Sabrina roughly against the cold wall of the cave and held her there as he pressed his body against her. He chuckled as she tried to fight.

"Now, now, pretty lady. Don't get so fired up. I ain't gonna hurt ya. You give me a nice little kiss and I might think about lettin' ya go."

"Pig! Take your hands off me. Let me go to Summer. She needs my help."

"You be nice and I'll think about it."

"I would rather kiss my horse!" she gasped out as he gripped her hair and drew her head back. She struggled but his open mouth descended to hers. She struggled and gagged, but he took his time. When he released her, he was breathing heavily and she understood well the glow of lust in his eyes.

"I'm gonna have ya soon, pretty thing," he rasped, "and when I do, I'm gonna take my time and enjoy ya. For now . . ." he let his words trail off as his hands slid over her body, rubbing and squeezing until she cried out. Only then did he seem temporarily satisfied. He let her go and she sagged to the ground.

"You go near the girl again and I'll take ya right in front of her. Then I'll let my men take their turns. You stay over here. Three Feathers will take care of her." He chuckled. "Yes, Three Feathers will take real good care

412

of her."

He walked back to the fire and Sabrina wept in frustration. She didn't know what Three Feathers was planning to do to Summer. As she looked over, she saw that he still knelt beside her.

Summer looked up at Three Feathers. His dark eyes were intense as they raked over her. He reached out and laid his hand gently against her waist.

"You are very beautiful," he said in his deep, guttural voice. "I have followed you a long time. Now I wait no more. In five moons you will belong to me. I will take you to my tribe many days' ride from here. Then you will be wife to Three Feathers."

"I will never be your wife, Three Feathers, only your captive. One day I will kill you and escape."

He laughed in sincere pleasure. "You are strong, but Three Feathers is stronger. Soon you will forget all but me and where you belong."

"I will never forget Sebastian, never! He is the man I would take as husband. I want no other."

"He will be easy to kill if you try to escape. I almost killed him before."

"The first time you found us?"

"No, before that. When I burned his white man's house."

"You killed his brother and burnt his house!"

"I did not mean for any of them to live. I thought they all had died there. I do not want to take the time to return, but if you do not come, or if you try to escape, then I will go back. And this time I will make sure he is dead."

"You were the link between us. You were the one who touched both our lives. That is why I could feel the same darkness about Sebastian as I did about myself."

"I know you, Summer. I have known you a long time. We even met once as children, when Hawk

413

brought you along when he came to trade at my village. I know what you are. I will be the one to bring Summer, medicine woman, to my tribe. You will be my wife and I will be the warrior they sing about around the fire." He bent close. "You will bear my children and we will watch them grow to be chiefs."

"I will never willingly stay with you, Three Feathers. One day you will grow careless and I will be gone. I will find my way to the man I love—to Sebastian."

He shook his head but smiled. He liked her spirit. It would be amusing to tame her and she would make a magnificent mother for his children.

"You will learn," he said softly. "You will learn."

"I am strong," she replied. "I can easily travel the distance between here and Sebastian's home."

"Of course you can." He laughed. "It is only two days ride and not many miles. But my village is a long distance away, and you will not be able to do it without a horse and supplies. I shall see to it that the only time you ride is when I am with you and that you get no supplies other than what you need. Why do you not give up now and surrender to my wishes?"

Summer thought rapidly. "Three Feathers, I will think of all you have said, and of the . . . great honor you offer me, but only on one condition."

"What is that?"

"Make that white pig leave Sabrina alone until I decide."

Three Feathers looked across at Carl. He had no respect or feeling for the white man, and he was powerful enough to know that Carl and the rest of them feared him. What they did with Sabrina later didn't concern him, but for now he would give in to Summer's wishes.

"I will see they do not harm her," he said.

"Thank you."

He nodded, slid his hand gently over Summer's trembling body for a moment, then rose and left her side.

Summer closed her eyes in relief. At least she had done something to help Sabrina. Now she had to try to settle the pain in her head, restore her concentration, and try to call out to Sebastian, who she hoped was still at his house. If he had gone with Kate, she would not reach him, and in a few days it would be too late to try.

# Chapter Thirty-three

Patrick kept up with the abductors despite the fact that he was still feeling ill from the effects of the blow. He tried to let his body roll with the movements of the horse to ease the throbbing in his head, but he couldn't find much relief. Each step of the horse sent a jolt of pain through him that caused him to grit his teeth. But still he followed relentlessly.

He also marked his own trail well. He broke branches from trees or carved signs so it would be impossible for anyone to miss them.

He did not stop for meals but merely drank from his canteen of water and urged his horse on. He wanted the people who held Sabrina to be unprepared should he catch up with them.

What he would do then was still an unformed idea. His urge to kill was dominant, but he knew he would have to find a way to get Sabrina to safety first. He plodded onward ... onward, keeping his eyes on a trail that was clear to follow.

When the setting sun made it too dark to see tracks, he made his way to the highest ground he could find and searched for any sign of a campfire. There was none. It was obvious that those ahead of him did not plan to stop, and that meant one thing. Their destination must have been too close for them to have considered stopping. Where? he asked himself. This was a territory in which Patrick had trapped for over twenty-five years. He knew it like the back of his hand, but still he was puzzled. Where could they hide that they would feel secure? Then it came to him—the caves! But there was a string of at least six in the area. He would have to make a choice. Which ones would he examine first? He made his decision quickly, for he felt there was no time to waste.

He pushed his tired horse into movement and headed for the cave that would be nearest to him. When he reached it, he found it was completely empty and showed no sign of anyone having been in it.

Only with great effort did he manage to climb back on his horse. Now it was totally dark and he had to move even more slowly. But he knew the position of the next cave. With unerring accuracy, he headed toward it, still taking the time to mark the path he was taking.

He reached the area of the second cave and stopped moving. In the distance, nearly a mile from him, he could see a pale glow coming from the mouth of the cave.

He was sure they would have guards posted, and he was just as sure that he was in no condition to do anything alone. He would have to stop now and wait for the others to catch up to him. When he considered that Simon first had to make the ride to Hawk's village, he realized he would have a long wait.

He unsaddled his horse, hobbled him carefully, and sat beneath the low-hanging branches of a tree. He would have to be patient, but it would be hard, for he knew that Sabrina was inside the cave, and he had no

417

idea how many were in there with her. He would have to summon enough control to wait. He had no other choice.

Hawk, Cole, Simon, and Walking Horse covered the distance between the village and Clay's house as rapidly as they could. Still it was hours before they were anywhere near.

Once there, they had to rest the horses briefly. While they rested, Simon searched the area for Patrick's sign. He found the first mark and called out to the others.

As soon as it was possible, they were on their way again. But they met with curtailing darkness long before they found Patrick. They had no choice but to camp and wait for morning.

They built a small, smokeless fire and sat about it in worried silence. After awhile, Walking Horse and Simon rolled in their blankets and slept. Cole and Hawk sat by the fire somewhat longer. Neither wanted to sleep.

Hawk urgently urged Cole into conversation. He wanted to find out more about Sebastian and what had happened from the time Summer had followed him. Cole told him all that had occurred until the time he left for the village.

"I can hardly believe everything fell apart after I left," Cole said.

"I have the feeling that somehow this disappearance of Summer and the taking of Sabrina are connected."

"Could be, but why? It would take one or two people at the center of it to hold it together, to pay all those men. What for? What would they have to gain?"

"Who can read the hearts of evil men? They think the only way to have what they want is to take it. And they take it at anyone's expense."

"I'm glad you now believe that Sebastian is not such

418

a man."

"If Summer loves him, then I have no choice but to believe."

"I wish I knew what really happened at Sebastian's place. It's strange. When I left those two were so happy with each other. I can't understand how something could have come between them."

"We will know more when we catch up with Patrick. At least he will know where they are heading."

"So many unanswered questions."

"We'll find our answers," Hawk replied in a determined tone. "Clay will find his answers, too."

"Well, I'm going to try for some sleep," Cole said. He rose and stretched, then went to his blanket. Hawk remained alone, gazing into the fire, his mind on Sabrina and Summer and how they were faring. He also contemplated what would happen if Clay were to catch up with Sebastian now, for Hawk himself had tried to take Summer from Clay a long time ago. He hoped Clay would listen to Sebastian's story before taking action, for he believed that someone else was responsible for Summer's disappearance. In fact, he even felt sympathy for those who had actually taken her, because he knew they would eventually face his wrath if Clay didn't get to them first.

Only when the moon had risen high overhead did Hawk finally sleep. Yet he was up before the sun touched the sky again.

Now they moved rapidly, for Patrick's trail was so obvious that even an Indian child could have followed it. As Hawk continued to study Patrick's signs, he came to the conclusion that his friend had determined where Sabrina's abductors were taking her. A smile of grim satisfaction briefly altered his granite features.

Patrick gazed down on the cave mouth from his

hiding place. Men moved to and fro about it. He had made a count, for he had been watching since dawn, and as far as he could see, there were two Indians and three whites. As yet he had seen no sign of Sabrina. But he knew she would be inside.

His patience was growing thin. "Damnit," he whispered, "where the hell are Hawk and Simon?" He remained still, watching. He knew it would only be a question of time before Hawk came. And Hawk would find him; about that he had no doubt.

Patrick was so tired he could hardly move, but rest and sleep were out of the question until he knew that Sabrina was safe. Again he silently wished for Hawk's quick arrival.

He tried to move to a more comfortable position, then froze. Someone was leaving the cave with a saddled horse. Patrick watched as the man rode away.

"So," he declared aloud, "somebody else is mixed up in this. Well, maybe we had just better wait until you get back with the boss, my friend. It's good to have all the birds in one nest."

Again Patrick was jolted when he saw Sabrina being pulled out of the cave. But he soon realized she was only being taken to a small stream nearby. There she gathered a sac of water. Patrick saw her look up and speak to the man who stood guard. He nodded at something she said. Then she bent to drink. After that she washed her face and arms and tried to repair her badly torn dress. Patrick was furious, too, for he saw that the tattered garment barely covered her.

He had to grit his teeth again as the man jerked her roughly to her feet. He was pleased as she pushed herself away from him and took up the water sac, leaving the man to follow after her. Patrick looked closely at the man. In his mind he marked him for later, when he could get his hands on him.

The sun rose to its zenith and Patrick found it hard not to doze. He could not move around much, for fear someone would spot him and the alarm would make them too well prepared. As it was, it was going to be very difficult to attack men so well protected, especially with the prisoner they held inside.

He tore at his brain, trying to think of a way they would be able to get inside the cave without having any harm come to Sabrina. He was so tired that the exhaustion made it very difficult for him to think. Maybe . . . maybe when Hawk came, he told himself.


Toby rode to tell Elenora that Sabrina had been taken. He made the trip to Elenora's home faster than he ever had before. His mind was on Carl and the remote possibility that he could trust him alone with Sabrina. Toby had lost his trust in people as a child, for he had been raised among people such as Carl and his kind. He knew Carl could not be trusted beyond his sight.

Toby wanted his share of the money Santiago would pay for the women, but he wanted Sabrina almost as badly.

Instead of stopping that night as Carl had expected him to do, Toby pushed on through the night. The next day before the noon hour found Toby at the back door of Elenora's home. He knocked and the door was answered by a young maid who looked at him as if he were a dirty beggar.

"Yes?"

"Tell Miss Elenora that Toby is here." He grinned. "She'll be more'n pleased to see me. Tell her to hurry. I got important news."

The young maid's face showed her doubt that Elenora would have anything to do with this rough-

421

looking man. But she knew Elenora quite well by now and did not want to feel the brunt of her temper if the message were to prove important.

"Wait here. I'll go tell her."

Toby watched the sway of her slim hips as she walked away and he decided that the next shipment to Santiago and his band of renegades would include a young maid who had been uppity with him. He allowed thoughts of the fun he could have with her amuse him until she reappeared.

"Come with me. Miss Gregory will see you in the library."

He walked a little behind her and brushed against her as she opened the library door to let him pass. He saw the spark of anger in her eyes and that amused him too.

Elenora was seated in a large chair before a cold fireplace. He was again astounded at how beautiful she was, especially since he knew how heartless she could be. Still, he thought, having her in a nice, soft bed would not be unpleasant.

"Why did you come here in broad daylight?" was Elenora's first question as the door closed behind the maid.

"Carl said it was important that I get word to you first, before Miles. He said you wanted to see the Storm women before Miles did."

Elenora stood, and there was a bright smile on her face. "You have them?"

"Yes ma'am."

"Both of them?" Elenora exclaimed excitedly.

"Yes ma'am, mother and daughter. Only"—he laughed—"the mother sure seems to be too young and pretty to be that gal's mother."

"You like her, Toby?" Elenora smiled.

"Shore do."

"Well, you and Carl can have her, and the girl, too. Just as soon as I'm finished with them. Where are they now?"

"Carl says maybe if you was to come, then he could get word to Miles that we had 'em. The sooner we get them out of this territory and into Santiago's hands, the better and safer for us all."

"Santiago! So that's who Miles is dealing with."

"Sells 'em guns and women. Makes a good profit too."

"Well," Elenora said slowly, "maybe Santiago would like to do business with someone new, someone who might offer him just a little more profit."

"Santiago and his men"—Toby grinned—"they likes the women too. Needs 'em when times is slow. Like that pretty little maid of yours. He'd give ya a good price for her." He licked his lips. "I could take her to him."

"Toby, if I make a deal with Santiago before Miles gets here, she'll be the first, and you can take her. Right now, I want to see the two captives Santiago is going to get soon."

Elenora walked to the door. "Pour yourself a drink, Toby. I'll change and be right down. I want to leave right away."

Toby moved quickly to pour the drink she offered. Good whiskey was not his usual drink, and he enjoyed it.

In the entrance hall, Elenora stopped long enough to give orders that a horse for her and a fresh horse for Toby were to be made ready. Then she went to her room to change her clothes swiftly.

When she returned, she saw that Toby had already drunk nearly a third of the bottle of whiskey.

"I have a fresh horse for you. Let's go."

He nodded and followed her. At the stable they mounted their horses and rode away, and both were unaware of the two horsemen who sat in the shadows and watched.

"Ya see, Mr. Chandler," one said, "just like I told ya. I think that woman has talked Carl and Toby into double-dealin' ya. Toby, he come for her before he said anything to ya."

"It seems," Miles said softly, "that your suspicions have proven right, my friend. Our little Elenora is getting out of hand. I think it is time to dispose of her. Santiago will be pleased to get one like her."

"He shore will."

"Come on, let's follow and see what our little cat is up to."

They nudged their horses into motion and kept far enough behind to make sure those ahead did not know they were being followed. When Toby and Elenora stopped to rest, they did the same, keeping the same distance between them. As they grew nearer the cave, the ones on their trail already suspected their destination.

"They's goin' to the cave. I'll bet Santiago is comin' for them women and that shipment of guns and powder you got in the back."

"And our little Elenora plans on collecting, it seems."

"Whatta ya gonna do?"

Miles laughed. "Be there to give Santiago and Elenora the biggest surprise of their lives."


Summer's head throbbed painfully and she found it difficult to sit up to drink the water Sabrina had brought her. It was one of the very few times Carl and Three Feathers had allowed them to be together.

"Summer," Sabrina whispered, "have you tried to reach Sebastian, or your father?"

"I've tried, but I am so weak. It is hard to tell if I have enough strength to reach them. Maybe they are too far away."

"I don't believe that. Maybe concentrating on two is too difficult. Why don't you try to concentrate on only one."

"I will try."

"C'mon, get away from her," Carl snarled. Sabrina glared at him but moved away. She didn't want anything to happen until Summer had more time to recover and to try to reach either Clay or Sebastian.

Three Feathers had watched in silence. He knew the women had been whispering together, but that did not bother him. There was no way for the women to escape, and it would not be too long until he could take Summer and leave this place.

He went to Summer's side again and squatted down beside her. She sat resting against the cave wall. He reached out to touch the dark bruise on her temple. A low growl sounded deep within his throat.

"You are weak. You must eat. I do not want you to be losing your strength. Soon we will have a long journey ahead of us."

Summer was too weak to fight with anything but words. "Leave me alone. I will kill myself before I go with you."

His face became like stone. "Do you still believe your man will try to follow you?"

"Yes," she spat at him, "yes, I believe."

He said nothing more; he simply rose and walked away. At the mouth of the cave, he stopped near Carl.

"Where ya goin', Three Feathers? Couple of days more and we'll have our money. Then you can take the girl and go."

"I will be here," Three Feathers said gruffly. "I will return soon. There is something I must do."

425

Carl shrugged. He knew better than to question Three Feathers too closely. He was not a man to trifle with. He watched Three Feathers ride away, curious about where he was going.

Carl turned and walked back into the cave. He stood for awhile and watched Sabrina preparing food for Summer and herself. Even under these conditions she was beautiful. He turned his gaze toward Summer. As beautiful as Sabrina was, Summer was extraordinary. She sat with her eyes closed and he studied her intently. She was delicate and fine boned. Her body was slim and graceful. He began to think that maybe he would just sell Santiago the guns and powder and keep the two women with him. He was sure Three Feathers would not mind sharing.

Summer was sitting very still. In sheer desperation she was using all her strength to reach out mentally, not to her father this time, but to Sebastian. Slowly she forced all her will to focus on Sebastian. When she gathered all her concentration, she called out to him. Over and over she called out his name.

An aura seemed to penetrate the cave and Little Elk stood spellbound. He had heard strange stories of the woman they held. Little Elk was afraid of nothing—except spirits or the unknown. Most Indians were superstitious, and Little Elk was no exception. He felt a chill touch him and he fervently wished he had not taken part in this woman's kidnapping. He said nothing, but his dark gaze remained on Summer.

Carl was about to go to Sabrina and make her fix him some food, when Stace stepped inside the cave. "Someone's comin'," he said softly.

Little Elk and Carl went outside to join Stace. In the distance they could see the two riders approaching. "Toby sure as hell made a fast trip." He chuckled.

They waited until Toby and Elenora rode up.

Elenora dismounted quickly and walked to Carl. "Toby has told me you have both women. You've done a good job, Carl." She returned to her horse and took a bag from behind her saddle. Going to Carl, she handed it to him. "You've earned your money. As I agreed, here it is."

"We was supposed to get paid by Miles, too."

"As soon as I'm finished, you can tell him, if you still want to. There is something I want from them first. When I get it . . . you can do as you please, but you would be wise to listen to what I have to say first."

"What you got to say?"

"You and Santiago have been working together for a long time. You've been selling him weapons and women. Don't you realize that Miles has made all the profit? Miles and Santiago. You've been left in the middle doing all the work and getting very little pay."

"You have somethin' better to offer?"

"I do. Do you want to listen?"

"Yeah, I want to listen."

"Good. Forget Miles. We will make the same deal, only I will double what you are being paid."

"Miles wants the Storm land and the Cain land."

"So do I. I'm here, with a better bargain. What are you going to do?"

Carl contemplated Elenora's steady gaze for a long moment.

"Double the money?"

"Yes."

"And I want the Storm woman."

"Which one?"

"The yeller-haired one."

"Take her. Do we have a deal? Will Santiago listen?"

"Iffen ya have some other women to offer him. They's renegades. They need some camp women to cook and do . . . a lot of other things. Seems Santiago

427

and his men are kinda hard on women. They keep buyin' more."

Elenora laughed softly. "Fine. I can supply him."

"Then it seems like we have a bargain."

"Very good," Elenora said. "Look in the saddle bags. You will find a great deal of gold. And when I get them to write letters to their men—when I get their land—you get Sabrina."

"I gotta tell ya, that Three Feathers, he wants the Storm girl."

"Once I am done with the Storm women, I don't care what you do with them."

"All right. Come on in."

Elenora followed Carl into the cave. Summer still sat with her eyes closed, and Sabrina's back was to the cave entrance. Neither was aware yet that Elenora had come.

Elenora stood and watched Sabrina working at the fire, and all her past hatred washed over her. She would finally get the revenge she had thought about over the years. Now she would have the pleasure of destroying both Sabrina and Summer.

Elenora walked slowly toward Sabrina until she stood directly behind her. Then she spoke softly. "My, my, Sabrina, you are not the haughty lady of the manor now, are you? You're in the dirt where you belong."

Sabrina spun about, having instantly recognized the hate-filled voice.

"Elenora," she said calmly.

"Not surprised, Sabrina?"

"No, I'm not surprised. This is your kind of scheme—to prey on the helpless or to deceive and destroy. Be assured that Clay will know too."

"I am afraid you are wrong, Sabrina. You see, you are going to write a letter. For your . . . safe . . . return, Clay will sign over the deed to his land to a certain

428

company—one I own, though nobody knows it. Once I have his land"—she shrugged—"I do not need you or your half-breed daughter. Who then will be there to console Clay for the loss of his wife and daughter? Why, I, as a longtime friend, will give him the sympathy he needs."

"It will never work, Elenora. Clay does not trust you."

"Ah, well, then I shall have to settle for owning a great deal of land, being very wealthy, and being rid of you."

"Do not overestimate what you have, Elenora . . . and do not underestimate what you're going to get!" Miles suggested from the cave entrance. Elenora spun around with a cry to see a cold-eyed, smiling Miles standing before her. And Stace, Carl, and Little Elk stood beside him.

## Chapter Thirty-four

Sebastian and Clay were both awake long before dawn. In the gray light before sunrise they saddled their horses and mounted. Both were silent, for there was nothing but the grim trail to occupy their minds.

Like a soft breeze, the whisper of his name startled Sebastian. He heard it. He knew he heard it. He closed his eyes and concentrated on Summer. Everything was pushed from his mind but Summer. Then he heard it again, more clearly and stronger. It was the same as it had been before, when Summer had been in distress. Sebastian! Sebastian!

Sebastian turned to look at Clay, but it was obvious that he had heard nothing. Was it a figment of his imagination? No! He heard it again. Wherever she was, she was repeating his name over and over.

"Clay! I hear her!"

"What?"

"Summer. I hear her!"

Clay concentrated but heard nothing. "She must be close, but I hear nothing."

"I hear her! I know she's alive. We've got to keep moving."

Clay agreed, certain now of Summer's love for Sebastian, for she had called for him and he had heard.

Clay knew that this was a phenomenon that occurred only with her family . . . or with someone she loved. Now he could be confident that Sebastian had told the truth. He recognized their love as surely as if Summer had told him of it herself.

Clay tracked with skill and accuracy. They pushed on relentlessly as the sun slowly rose, but by midday, the horses were tired.

"It's best we rest the horses for a time," Clay said. "I have a feeling I know where they're headed."

"Where?"

"There's a string of caves not too far from here, maybe about a half-day's ride. Old Santiago used to use them as a hideout before he got driven west. Maybe our friends are using them for the same thing."

"You think it's possible?"

"All the tracks point to it."

"Then let's not rest too long."

"No, just long enough to give the horses a breather and a little water. There's a stream up ahead. We'll stop there. I could use a drink too."

A short time later they reached the stream and dismounted. They led the horses to the water, then both men knelt by the stream to drink. They bent forward to reach for water and found themselves in the worst possible position when the deep voice spoke from behind them. It was accompanied by the cocking of a gun.

"Do not move."

They froze.

"Throw your guns in the water," the voice demanded. Slowly they obeyed. "Now you can stand."

They stood and turned slowly about to look at their adversary. Sebastian gave a choked cry and started for him. The gun gave a harsh bark and the bullet ricocheted between Sebastian's boots, causing him to stop abruptly and glare up at the still-mounted Indian.

"You! Damn you! Are you mixed up in this?"

"In the taking of your woman?" Three Feathers laughed. "Yes, I have her. She belongs to me now. I must prove to her that you are dead. She said you would follow, so I came back to see if you would. Now I will take you to her . . . and let her see you die. Then she will know she belongs to me."

Sebastian began to speak again, caught up in his anger, but Clay placed a restraining hand on his arm. Sebastian turned to look at him.

"He," Clay said softly, "will take us to her."

Sebastian understood that their first concern was finding Summer, but it was difficult not to curse at the man who had cost him so much.

"Take your rifles from your saddles and throw them in the water, too," Three Feathers ordered sharply. They did as he told them. "Now mount and ride ahead of me. Do not try anything foolish, for I have killed before and will not be sorry to see your dead bodies on the trail."

Silently they obeyed. They rode side by side with the large and wary Indian at their back.

"Clay. . . ."

"Don't be a fool, Sebastian. Let's not get ourselves killed before we get there. He could take our dead bodies back as well, so don't give him any ideas."

"If he has done anything to Summer, I'll find a way to kill him."

"Yes, but we have to see her."

"You're right. I would give my life to have her in my arms now."

"You might be doing just that," Clay replied softly. They continued their ride toward the cave in contemplative silence.

\*    \*    \*

Patrick was numb with exhaustion, but he was startled to wakefulness when he saw the woman who returned with Toby.

"Elenora Gregory. So you're behind this." He controlled his anger only through great effort. He knew that when Hawk arrived they would find a way into that cave, and if he got his hands around Elenora's throat before Hawk, he would surely kill her.

His emotional turmoil revitalizing him, Patrick shifted position and resumed his watch. He felt now that it wouldn't be long until Hawk and Simon arrived.

His count of the occupants of the cave had grown. Now he figured there were seven men. But why seven men to guard one woman . . . unless there were more to guard than that. Something was going on in that cave that involved more than Sabrina.

He was again stunned to see three more approaching. "Good Lord, are they getting together an army down there? What the hell is goin' on?" But it was sudden recognition of one of the riders that rode ahead of the third that really shook him—Clay.

"Now damn," he muttered, "this mystery is gettin' darker by the minute."

He watched the three dismount and saw that Clay and the nameless man who rode beside him were being forced into the cave by an Indian with a gun.

His mind was so intent on what was happening at the cave, that Patrick did not hear anyone approach until Hawk spoke.

"Patrick," he said softly. Patrick turned. He was more than pleased to see the numbers they were now. Hawk, himself, Simon, and the four men who rode with him. That made it seven against seven. The only problem now was to get into the cave, and to make sure that Sabrina did not get hurt in the process.

"Hawk," Patrick whispered, "it's about time you got

here. Are ya getting old, man, to be so slow?"

Hawk grinned and motioned to the riders to dismount. They did and the group gathered while Patrick began to explain what was happening at the cave.

"Have you seen Sabrina?" Hawk questioned.

"Only once. One of them brought her out to get water."

"She was well?"

"He was kinda rough on her, but she looked all right."

"Well, now we must think of a plan to get her out of there," Hawk mused.

"Before that, I better tell you who was just brought in as prisoners."

"Who?"

"Clay and another man," Patrick answered.

"Another man?" Cole questioned. "A tall, yellow-haired man?"

"Yes."

"Sebastian!" Cole exclaimed.

"Clay seems to have found him," Hawk said. "And I will wager," he added, "that Summer is in that cave as well. Now we have a problem. We must get the four of them out safely before we can do anything else."

"And you just call that a problem?" Patrick smiled. "My friend Hawk, I look forward to your solution."

Hawk motioned to them all to gather close so they could talk quietly and try to form a plan.

"Miles!" Elenora gasped. "What . . ."

"What am I doing here, my double-dealing little bitch? I'm following you, and protecting my profit-making business. I might ask what you are doing here."

"Miles, I. . . ."

"I said I might ask, but I won't. I've been following you for weeks. I know what your little game is. But I am one step ahead of you."

"Miles," Elenora cried. She ran to him and tried to put her arms about him. He struck her sharply across the face, so sharply that she stumbled back a step and gazed at him in shock. "I was only making sure our interests are being taken care of, Miles," she said. "I was just—"

"I know what you were doing. Feathering your own bed, and this time at my expense. Elenora, I could have warned you, I'm a partner . . . I won't be a fool. This time you have gone too far. I can't afford to turn my back on you again. So"—he shrugged—"you, my dear, are expendable." Elenora's face turned gray. She began to back away from Miles.

"What . . . what are you saying?"

"I'm saying that when Santiago comes for his guns, powder, and women . . . he gets you as a personal gift."

"No!" she cried. "No!"

"Too bad, my dear. That's what being greedy will do." He motioned to Carl, Little Elk, and Stace, all of whom moved toward Elenora.

She screamed and tried to run from the cave to her horse but was caught by Little Elk before she reached the mouth of the cave. She fought wildly, but she was ineffective against three men, who soon subdued and bound her. Carl threw her down roughly on a blanket near the cave wall. Her dark hair, loosened from its pins, tumbled over her face. Her soft sobs shook her body as Miles went to her and gripped her hair, jerking her head up to him.

"You should have been more careful, my dear. You should have been satisfied with what you had. No, you had to get greedy and try to take what was mine. Now I am forced to teach you a lesson."

"Miles, please," Elenora moaned. "You can't do this to me. I thought we were . . ."

"Lovers? Elenora, you were an excellent bed partner for awhile, but you began to bore me. No, I think it's time to part company. Oh, by the way, before you go, you are going to sign a few papers for me. Where you are going, you won't need land." He laughed. "What you will need is strength. Personally, I think Santiago and his men will break you."

"No, Miles, please . . . *please!* I'll do anything you want—anything!"

"I'm afraid"—Miles sighed—"I just can't trust you, Elenora. No, I'm afraid you have nothing I want."

He rose to walk away.

"Miles! Miles, please," Elenora begged, but Miles ignored her and walked toward Carl and Little Elk. Before he reached them, they all heard the sound of approaching horses.

"Santiago?" Miles questioned.

"Too soon," Carl answered. "Maybe Three Feathers comin' back. If it is, he's got company with him."

They waited, and when the three figures filled the cave mouth, there were assorted reactions from those within. Miles smiled in utter satisfaction. Sabrina cried out Clay's name, and Summer, without a word, started toward Sebastian.

Clay had expected a lot of things, but the presence of Sabrina was not one of them. He was momentarily stunned, then he reached for her to hold her close.

No one stopped Summer as she raced to Sebastian's side. With a soft cry of his name, she was in his arms. He kissed her feverishly, and she clung to him as if desperate to be part of him. After a moment he held her away from him. His eyes raked over her, and he quickly noted the bruise on her head and the frightened look in her eyes.

436

"Summer, are you all right?"

"Yes, oh Sebastian, I was so afraid you would believe I had written that terrible letter! I thought you might hate me!" Summer cried. "I tried to call—"

"I heard you, Summer. I am ashamed. For awhile I did believe. It was your father who explained that the handwriting was not yours. Forgive me, Summer."

"Where did my father find you?"

"I was on the trail"—he smiled—"looking for you."

"You would have come, Sebastian?"

"Yes, I suppose I would have. I couldn't let go of you, even if you wanted to be free."

"I would never want to be free," she whispered.

"How very cozy." Miles laughed sarcastically. Sebastian held Summer close and turned to Miles.

"I don't know who you are or how we're involved with you, but why don't you settle whatever score you seem to have with me instead of with her. Let her go."

"Hardly possible, my friend. I need her." Miles smiled.

"What for?"

"She and her stepmother will make you and her father see some reason."

"Just what do you want from us?" demanded Clay. "You and your deceitful mistress. Elenora tried once before. She failed. I don't know what you want, but you'll never get it. Not while you hold Sabrina and Summer here."

"He's right," Sebastian interjected. "What do you want?"

"Why, Mr. Storm, Mr. Cain," he said softly, "just about everything you have."

"What do you mean?" Sebastian growled.

"I mean I have brought some papers for you to sign. I thought I would have to send them to you by messenger, but you have made it so easy."

437

"And we were to just sign them?" Sebastian inquired. "I take it it's our land you want. Well, you can just forget it."

"Mr. Cain," Miles replied in a tone that told Sebastian that what he had suspected was true, "why do you persist in making things so difficult? Must I tell you that if you do not do as I say, Summer and Sabrina will pay a very high price for your stubbornness? Why not make it easy on them?"

"Sebastian, don't listen to him," Summer said firmly. "He had no intention of setting any of us free, not even Elenora, who helped him do this. He can't be trusted."

"Listen to her, Sebastian," Sabrina responded. "She sees him clearly, just as he is, a man who is lower than a snake."

Miles chuckled tolerantly. "Mr. Cain, I am going to give you all a chance to think about your positions. We are waiting for someone—"

"Santiago!" Summer snapped. "A renegade, a thief, and a killer, to whom he sells guns, powder . . . and women."

Sebastian drew Summer a little closer. "I've heard of him," he said softly.

Miles motioned to Little Elk and Carl. "Put them in the small cave with the powder. Let them think for a few hours." He jerked his thumb toward Elenora, who still sat silently, her head bowed and her hair covering her face. "Get her out of my sight. Maybe she will be more to Santiago's taste." Elenora made a soft whimpering sound as she was dragged away.

The larger cave offered access to several smaller caves. Into one of these Elenora was pushed. Sabrina and Clay were forced into another, and to keep the two dangers of Sebastian and Clay apart, Summer and Sebastian were shoved into a third. In front of each

438

entrance a rough board door was braced.

Sebastian took Summer into his arms and held her for several moments in silence. It seemed so long since he had embraced her that he could not bear to let her go.

After a few minutes, he captured her face between his hands and his eyes burned into her. "I'm sorry, Summer. I'm sorry I got you into this."

"You don't understand, Sebastian. It was meant to be. We are linked together by this." She went on to explain that their common evil was Three Feathers and revealed how he had played a part in both their lives that connected them to each other.

"This Three Feathers," Sebastian demanded, "it's you he wants, isn't it?"

"Yes." She put her arms about his waist. "But you know I would rather die than belong to another. Sebastian"—she closed her eyes—"I can face anything as long as I am with you."

"Summer, Miles can have anything he wants, but he will have to set you free first."

"He will not do that. Miles must keep Three Feathers as a friend, for Three Feathers is Santiago's man."

"Then he can do what he will. Unless he sets you free, he gets nothing."

"Sebastian . . ."

"Shh, love," he whispered as his fingers touched her lips. "Don't you know that nothing else I have is worth one tear of yours." He smiled encouragingly. "I love you, Summer, and there is nothing more important in the world than that."

"But your land . . . your house . . ."

Sebastian laughed softly as he bound her more tightly to him. "Would you believe me, love, if I told you it doesn't exist anymore."

"Doesn't exist? I don't understand."

"I burned it."

"You what?"

"I burned it to the ground. I must say that it was the best it had ever looked."

"But Sebastian! Your house!"

"No, Summer. Kate's house. It would never be yours, and if it weren't yours, it could never be mine. I can't see me living anywhere else but with you—no matter where that happens to be."

She sighed in contentment as she rested her head against his chest and felt the security of his arms about her. She trembled with the thought that if it hadn't been for her father's chance crossing of Sebastian's path, Sebastian might still believe she had written the terrible letter. She held him close, trying not to think of what was going to happen when Santiago arrived.

"Summer, do you know anything about these caves?"

"Not much. I used to play in them when I was a child, until my father and Hawk found out. Then they forbade me to come here. They said they were dangerous."

"Dangerous? How?"

"Well, it seems they're like a honeycomb; there are many small caves. I suppose it would be possible to get lost in them."

Sebastian began to walk around the cave, examining the walls. Crates and boxes were stacked against one wall. Against the opposite one were barrels that he knew were filled with black powder, for he could see them clearly marked. Their small cave was lit by only one candle which was set high on a small, protruding shard of rock.

Unable to find anything usable except crates of supplies and powder, Sebastian stood in the center of the small cave. He felt he was missing something important.

The cave itself was just a little over fifteen feet in width and less than ten in depth. The door, though not a hinged one, proved a solid barrier. He knew if he used force on it, it would cause enough noise to have everyone on him by the time he got into the main cave.

He sat down on the floor with his back braced against the crates, which were against the far right of the entrance. Summer sat beside him and he put one arm around her to draw her comfortably close.

"I'm missing something," he said. "There has to be a way to get out of this."

"There is nothing but the main cave. We could never get past them."

"You're right there, but I still get the feeling I'm not seeing something."

He leaned his head back and let his eyes roam very slowly about the cave. Summer rested quietly in his arms. Silently she blended all her concentration with his.

The candle sputtered from a harsh draft of air. Its flame dimmed, then brightened as the air caught it. Sebastian stared at it a long time before it registered in his mind. He narrowed his eyes and watched the candle closely. Before too long it became apparent that a draft of air was doing its best to extinguish it. What made Sebastian's heart pound was the fact that the candle was sitting to the left of the door. He was elated, for he realized that the draft could not be coming from the main entrance.

He watched closely to find the direction of the air. He was rewarded as he located a darker spot amid the dark corners. It was high up, over the stacks of crates.

He stood up abruptly.

441

"Sebastian, what is it?"

"I don't know. I'm not sure yet. Stay put." He moved away from her to the stacked crates. With the silent prayer that the crates were all full and would hold his weight, he began to climb.

He tried to remain as quiet as possible. One slip, or if one crate tumbled, the game would be over and whatever slim chance they had would be gone. His shoulder brushed against one half-full crate and it began to slide. He made a grab for it and caught it just before it tipped over the edge. He was sweating with nervous tension by the time he reached the top. He could feel a very strong breeze on his face now, and he was forced to hold back a cry of success.

He tried to see through the dark but could not see far. But he was certain the emptiness was extensive, for the breeze was cool and swift.

Summer's senses were suddenly jolted and her attention was drawn from Sebastian. Someone was coming toward their stone prison.

"Sebastian," she whispered, "someone is coming."

Sebastian felt he would not have time to climb down before whoever it was pushed aside the wooden door. But he could not afford to get caught where he was.

Without another thought he jumped and nearly landed on Summer. They were standing together when the door was pushed open and Carl stood in the doorway. He held his gun pointed directly at Sebastian, but he looked at Summer.

"Come out here, girl. We wants some food cooked."

Sebastian turned to Summer, who nodded. She would buy him the time he needed.

# Chapter Thirty-five

Summer followed Carl from their small prison into the larger cave. She was determined to take as much time as possible to give Sebastian an opportunity to find an escape route.

Carl led her toward the fire, which was close to the mouth of the cave. She knelt near it and began to gather what she would need to prepare food.

No one in the cave noticed that suddenly Summer became very still, as if she were listening intently. She was, for her senses told her that Hawk was near. She knew it as if she had seen him standing before her. She opened herself to him and realized he was very close, somewhere very near the cave.

Picking up the water sac, she went to Carl.

"I must go out and get some water," she explained in a humble voice that pleased him. Three Feathers had lain on his blanket and had fallen asleep. Had he been awake, he would not have permitted Carl to take Summer to the stream. He would have done it himself. Carl knew this, and that is why he quickly grasped Summer's arm and walked with her through the cave mouth and into the bright sunlight.

Summer made no protest as he slid his arm about her

waist to walk her to the stream. She did not want to do anything to upset the flow of her thoughts. It was then that she became aware that not only Hawk was near, but with him were many others.

She moved to the stream and knelt to fill the sac, centering her mind on Hawk so strongly that she could discern almost exactly where he was.

She faced herself in that direction, placing her back to Carl, who was looking about and watching for any intruders.

Summer had no way of knowing if Hawk was close enough to understand. Her hands moved swiftly in the silent signs. She could not be sure Hawk could even see her, but while Carl's attention was elsewhere, she had to try.

She communicated the story quickly, then repeated it over and over, telling Hawk who was being held with her, how many held them, and that Santiago would come in less than two days.

Suddenly Carl's voice interrupted her conversation.

"What the hell you doin', girl?" he snarled as he came to her side and grasped her arm to spin her around.

"I . . . I was just tying the ties on my tunic."

He leered at her. "You don't hafta bother. I like 'em untied. You're too pretty to be coverin' yourself up like that." His hands reached for the ties to loosen them. Summer didn't move. She only smiled and spoke softly.

"Three Feathers will not be pleased if you put your hands on his woman."

Carl's hands froze. Summer knew immediately that she had been right. Carl was deathly afraid of Three Feathers. At the moment she counted on that for her own protection.

"I didn't touch you," he protested feebly.

"But you intended to. Three Feathers will not be

pleased when I tell him."

"You keep your mouth shut, girl," he threatened. But she could read his eyes well and knew he was shaken.

"I might."

"Might? You better shut up or I'll . . ."

"You'll what?" She laughed. "Challenge Three Feathers?"

"Hell, girl, I never laid a hand on you."

"But," Summer replied coldly, her eyes hard and unbending, "you have my mother. I tell you that if you touch her again, I will fill Three Feathers's head with a story that will make him kill you . . . very, very slowly."

Carl began to sweat. Summer's eyes were unforgiving and unbending. He knew she meant it.

"Okay, okay, I'll leave her alone. But you keep your mouth shut."

"I will . . . but only as long as you stay away from me and from Sabrina."

Carl knew she had the upper hand, and that at the moment he could do nothing about it. But he knew he would find a way to kill Three Feathers. He had friends among Santiago's men who would help him, and it would probably take more than one man to do the job. But when it was finished, he mused with suppressed fury, he would make Summer pay for the way she had talked to him.

"Get the water sac and come on. We're hungry."

Obediently she knelt and retrieved the full water sac. Silently she prayed that Hawk had gotten her message. She walked back to the cave, and smiled when she noticed that Carl was keeping his distance.

Again she knelt by the fire and as slowly as she possibly could, she began to prepare food. When it was finished, she asked Miles if she could take some food to

445

her parents.

"Yes, take them some"—he smiled at her—"but don't get any ideas."

"I won't. I want to take some food to Elenora too."

"Elenora!" He laughed. "Why do you care what happens to her? After what she has done to you and your family, I should think you would want to see her suffer."

"I don't enjoy anyone's suffering," Summer replied furiously. "She is a human being. No woman deserves what you have planned for her. At least let me give her some food."

"Take her some. I don't care."

The first thing Summer did was to prepare two plates of food for her parents. She walked to the door and Stace moved it aside so that she could enter.

Clay stood holding Sabrina close to him. He was quiet and coldly angry, but his eyes brightened when he saw Summer. They moved to her side quickly.

"Summer, are you all right?" Clay asked quickly.

"I'm fine. I only have a few minutes. You must eat, for you will need your strength." She went on to tell them what Sebastian had found. Clay quickly scanned the cave, and his face lit triumphantly when he saw dark, shadowed areas near the top of the cave wall.

"Don't do anything until Sebastian sees where they lead. He believes they are all connected and that they run outside. I'll find a way to get back to you. Maybe I can bring you another meal later."

"Summer?" Sabrina questioned. "You . . . you are really all right? They haven't hurt you?"

"No, Sabrina, I am fine. For now they won't be touching us." She went on to explain about Three Feathers and how the rest were afraid of him. "At least we are temporarily safe. I have faith that Sebastian will find a way out of this for us."

446

Clay smiled. "You do love him, Summer?"

"Yes, Father, I do." She laughed softly. "I am very grateful you didn't kill him."

"I came very close," Clay admitted. "I was certainly intent on it when I found him."

Summer came to Clay and kissed him. Beaming up at him, she whispered, "I'm glad you didn't. I wouldn't want you to harm the man who will be the father of your grandchildren some day."

Before Clay could ask the question that danced in his eyes, Stace called to Summer from the door. Summer kissed both her parents again and, with a confident smile, she left.

When Summer returned to the fire she arranged another dish of food and walked to where Elenora was being held.

Once inside the enclosure, it took her a moment to find Elenora's huddled form. She was sitting against several crates of guns that were meant for Santiago.

"Elenora?"

Elenora lifted her head and looked at Summer. Her hair was a tangled mass about her, her clothes were rumpled, and her cheeks were still wet from her tears. Her eyes were red rimmed and she blinked several times before she recognized Summer.

"You!" she said bitterly. "Are you here to gloat?"

"No, Elenora. I've brought you some food."

Elenora looked at her doubtfully until Summer went to her side and knelt to hand her the plate. "Why do you do this?" she questioned suspiciously.

"Because I thought you might be hungry," Summer replied.

Elenora began to eat and Summer took the time to quickly survey the cave. If only the empty guns and the powder and ammunition had been kept in the same place, she reflected. She looked carefully and noted that there were the same dark areas in Elenora's prison. Were they all connected? This was the question Sebastian was trying to answer.

She had no intention of telling Elenora anything for fear she would use the information to free herself. Summer had no illusions about Elenora. She could feel the wary hatred, yet she knew she could not leave Elenora to the fate Miles had planned. She could not do that to any woman.

"Try not to be so defeated, Elenora," she cautioned. "There might be some way we can get out of this."

"There is no way," Elenora said bitterly.

"Elenora, I am alive. And as long as I am alive, I will fight for my life, my honor, and for those I love and who love me. You can only defeat yourself," she stated fervently. "No one does it for you."

"Get out of here!"

Summer said nothing about Elenora's ingratitude. She simply turned and left, knowing she would still try to talk Sebastian into doing something to save Elenora. She reflected that he might not be too receptive to the idea of saving a person who had done her best to eliminate Summer and Sabrina.

Summer took a plate of food and some water, and with Stace at her side she started slowly toward the smaller cave.

Now Summer turned her thoughts to another dilemma. When they put her back in the small cave, would Sebastian be there? Would they notice anything? She held her breath as Stace pushed her back inside. Once there, she was greeted by a very dirty and disheveled but smiling Sebastian.


Sebastian had leapt into action as soon as the door had closed behind Summer. He climbed the crates until

448

he was again near the crevasse at the top. It was dark, and he had to grit his teeth when he realized he could run across any kind of creature within. Still he heaved himself up into the opening. It was about three feet in height and when he stretched out his arms to either side he could not feel anything solid, so he had no way of judging its width.

Using his arms and pushing with his knees and feet, he crawled ahead, following the scent of air. He had gone less than thirty feet when he saw the pale glow of light ahead. Was it the outside? he wondered hopefully. He studied it for a moment and realized it was not sunshine but the mellow glow of candlelight.

He edged himself ahead. The glow came from far to the left of him, so he crept closer, fearing he had only found an entrance to the main cavern.

When he reached the edge, he looked down. Below him was an area somewhat the same as the one in which he and Summer were imprisoned. Below him also stood Clay and Sabrina.

He did not have time to do anything. That would come later, when he had found some way out—if he found a way out. He knew Summer would be returning soon, and he didn't want to jeopardize her any further or their one chance to escape. He would have to get back in time, but first he would explore a little further.

He edged his way on and the passage seemed to grow even darker than before. It had also begun to slant upward. He had to grasp the rough bottom and pull himself along.

He was panting and sweating profusely by the time he saw the faint glow of daylight above him. He reached to touch the roof now and found nothing above him. Slowly, tentatively, he stood, expecting to crash into a roof at any moment. He stood to his full height and raised his arms above his head. Still he touched nothing. Satisfied, he went to the crease of light. It was nearly a slit in the rock, but he could edge his body out, and he knew the others could do the same. He estimated that he and Clay were the same size and the women were even smaller.

He knew getting out was not enough. He would have to figure out a plan that would keep them from being followed. They would be on foot and open targets for anyone who pursued them. Slowly he turned about and began to make his way back.

He went as fast as he could, realizing that if he were not back before Summer was returned, their chance would be gone and Summer might be the one to pay the harsher price. He would be killed, but Summer's punishment would be longer and much more painful that that.

As he passed Sabrina and Clay, he controlled the urge to stop. He had barely reached his destination when he heard a scuffing sound and knew someone was approaching. He had a matter of minutes. He swung down, braced himself, then jumped.

If Stace had taken the time, he would have noticed Sebastian's condition, but he simply pushed Summer inside and closed the door.

Sebastian laughed and held out his arms to Summer, who ran to him and again felt the pleasure and security his presence brought her. He crushed her to him, relieved that she was all right.

They both began to talk at once in a whisper, then Sebastian chuckled. "You go first. You seem to be excited about something. Is the cavalry coming to save us?"

"Almost," she told him and laughed.

"What are you talking about?"

"Hawk is here." She went on to explain how she had signaled him with hand signs. He did not doubt for a minute that Hawk was close. If Summer felt him, there was no question that he was there.

"Do you think he was close enough to make out the signs?"

"I don't know." She frowned. "There was no sign of him. I just knew he was there. But Hawk is quick. If it was possible, he would have moved closer and read my signs."

"Did you tell him to wait?"

"Yes. I hope to be able to go for water again at the evening meal. I wanted to talk to you first. Now, Sebastian, tell me what you found up there."

He explained rapidly, watching her eyes light with excitement as he spoke. A quick smile brightened her face when he told of seeing her parents.

"I spoke to them," she said. "They let me take them some food. I explained what you had found. Father was already looking up and debating before I was finished. He will be ready to do whatever you decide."

Sebastian drew Summer into his arms and kissed her lingeringly. She knew there were too many important things to be done, but with the touch of Sebastian's lips, she no longer cared. She also needed the courage and strength he could give her. Giving in to her yearning, she looped her arms about his neck and relaxed against him.

Their mouths merged in a kiss that devoured any fears she had and melted thoughts of all but the warmth that flowed between them.

"This is no place to make love to you," Sebastian groaned, "but I want you to know how much I love you, Summer. I still can't believe how lucky I am not to have lost you."

"Lucky? To be with me in a place like this?"

"To be with you anywhere. I would rather be with you than free and alone. We'll find a way, Summer. But

451

until we're free, until we can be together, let this tell you how much I love you." His voice was silenced as his mouth parted hers in a shattering kiss.

Both wanted more, but they were forced to contain their passion until it could be fulfilled at a sweeter time.

Sebastian held Summer a little away from him and smiled. "It would be best, love, if you sat over there while we talk and decide on some plan. Your proximity slows down my thinking to the point that I don't want to grasp anything but you. I've been too long without you, sweet. It's a most uncomfortable situation."

Summer laughed but obediently moved away.

"I have to think of a way to buy time," Sebastian began. "If we leave now, they will be on us before we get far. And if Santiago is coming tomorrow night, I would like to be able to catch him in what I have planned."

"Just what do you have planned?"

He grinned. "Not everything . . . but I sure as hell am going to blow this cave off the face of the earth. There's enough powder here to blast the place apart. It would be good to catch this group and Santiago as well."

"Everyone here?"

"Every last one," Sebastian said firmly, "because I would personally have to kill any survivors for what they've done to you."

"Sebastian," Summer said gently.

"What?"

"We can't leave Elenora here."

"We can't save her."

"We have to."

"Summer, if we told her about our escape plan, she'd sell us out just to save her own skin."

"But Sebastian, she's alone and terrified. Can't we bring her to justice some other way?"

"Summer, you know she's like a black widow spider.

452

You do something good for her and she'll reward you by biting you." But Sebastian could see the glow in Summer's eyes and he knew he was losing ground. He smiled and went to her and knelt before her. He was rewarded by her warm smile as she reached out to lay her hand against his cheek. "Lord, I love you, woman. You know damn well all you need to do is ask me for something."

"Even Elenora's life?"

"Even that." He placed his hand over hers, then turned his face to press a kiss into her palm.

"Oh, Sebastian," she murmured softly, "I do love you so very much."

"Enough to stay with me for the rest of your life?"

"For all the years I have."

"We'll get out of here, Summer," he stated firmly. "You and I have a lot of lost time to catch up on. We're going to have a lifetime together."

He bent forward and their lips met again in a promising kiss.

Summer smiled up at him. "You had better eat, my love. You must be strong to help us out of here, for I am looking forward to your keeping your word."

Sebastian laughed, but he realized the truth of her statement. They sat together and ate the food she had brought.

"Summer, you are the only one who will be taken in or out of here until Santiago comes."

"That is likely."

"Then you have to have a great deal of courage."

"What do you want me to do?"

"You have to find out just when we can expect Santiago."

"I'll try."

"It's very important that we know that, for our timing has to be just right."

453

"I will do my best. Carl and Three Feathers hate each other, but Carl is afraid of Three Feathers. Maybe I can use that to get Carl to talk about Santiago. He is very stupid."

"Don't underestimate him, Summer. He may be stupid, but he is dangerous."

"Not to me."

"Why not?"

"He is afraid of Three Feathers."

"What's that got to do with anything?"

"Three Feathers wants me. He won't let Carl touch me."

"And him?" Sebastian said angrily. "Does he think you are his possession?"

"Don't be angry, Sebastian. It is useful to us that he thinks this way. It has protected both Sabrina and me. We will use it as much as we can."

"I can't stand the idea of him touching you," Sebastian admitted angrily.

Summer went to him and put her arms about his waist.

"No one touches me, not within, like you do. He is an animal, but he is useful. Do not think that I will let him take any liberties. He wants me to journey with him to his home, which is some distance away. He wants me to be his wife. He wants the prestige of bringing a medicine woman to his tribe. All this will be useful, but he will never touch me, Sebastian. Never!"

Sebastian admired her beauty and her courage. He had never known a woman like Summer, and he vowed to keep her with him always if they were able to make it out of this together.

He kissed her again, fueling the deeper hunger that would have to remain unfed until they were free.

"After they have had an evening meal, they will settle down for the night," Sebastian speculated. "They will most likely check on us. After that, I will go to your parents and explain things."

"Oh, I wish I could go to them."

"Are you game for a crawl through a long, dark and very dirty tunnel?"

"I am ready to try anything."

"You know, woman"—he laughed softly—"we should have the damnedest kids. If the boys have one half of your courage and the girls half of your beauty, they should really be something."

"And just how many do you think we'll be having?"

"As many as you're willing to have."

"Well," she giggled, "we'll see."

"Anyway, for awhile I'd like it to be just us. I'd like to get to know you, and maybe we can find a place to be alone. We have a lot of talking to do and a lot of decisions to make."

"Decisions?"

"Yep, like . . . where are we going to live?"

"Where do you want to live, Sebastian?" she asked cautiously. Her concern was that Sebastian would ask her to leave everyone—her family, Hawk, and the people who needed her. For the first time she became shaken by the choice he might be asking her to make.

Sebastian read her thoughts with ease. He smiled and inquired, "Where do I want to live, my love? With you . . . wherever you live."

"No matter where?" she whispered.

"No matter. The important thing is that we're together. That, my dear love, is all I want."

She lifted her lips for his kiss and closed her eyes to savor her overwhelming joy.

# Chapter Thirty-six

Hawk, like a shadow, moved as close to the cave as he could without being discovered. He had to fix in his mind the nature of the terrain in order to form an effective plan. Thus far, a safe method of freeing his friends had eluded him.

He had seen men come and go through the cave entrance, but it worried him that he had seen no sign of Summer or Sabrina. It was in his mind to somehow move close enough to see inside.

He moved to within several hundred yards of the cave and saw with utter amazement that they were so self-assured they had posted only one guard at the cave mouth. He speculated that after the sun set and before the moon had a chance to rise, he could get close enough to the guard to eliminate him. Then the element of surprise could be his. He knew he would have to be quick. And his men would have to act within a matter of minutes if they were going to be successful.

He lay close to the ground and watched carefully. He was alerted when Carl brought Summer from the cave. Grasping the opportunity, he gazed at Summer's slim form intently, hoping to reach her. He let his mind open to thoughts of her and grimly held them.

Summer, his mind called, I am here . . . Summer, I am here . . . Summer, I am here.

He kept himself from crying out when he saw Summer suddenly grow still. He knew she sensed him. Slowly she turned in his direction. He watched as her hands moved in swift sign. She repeated her message over and over until the man with her seemed to become aware of her actions. He watched as the man forced her to face him. Rage filled Hawk when he saw the man reach to caress Summer. Summer did not move but said something to the man that obviously upset him, for he withdrew his hands. Then they turned and walked back into the cave.

Without rustling a bush or snapping a twig, Hawk swiftly returned to the waiting group.

"Well, Hawk," Cole said impatiently, "what did you see? Was there any chance to see any of them?"

Hawk explained rapidly that he had seen Summer and went on to discuss what had occurred.

"You mean she sent you a message?" Cole asked.

"She did. She said to wait. Late tonight they will begin to work on a plan. I will return in the morning. If it is possible, she will be by the stream again. Then we will know."

"You mean we just stay here and wait?" Cole asked incredulously. "Anything could be happening in there overnight."

"Summer was firm. We will wait," Hawk replied. "We will not endanger Summer or Sabrina unless it is absolutely necessary. We must have faith in their decision . . . and wait."

"That," Walking Horse said solemnly, "will be the most difficult thing I have ever done."

"I know, brother," Hawk replied, "but it must be. I would not be able to live in honor if I were the cause of any harm to Summer . . . or to Sabrina. We will wait," he said stolidly. Then he rose and walked away, wanting to be alone with his thoughts.

They knew they would have to camp without being discovered. They made no fire and ate no food except the dry corn they carried for just such a situation.

They were grim, silent men now, aware that if anything happened to the ones inside, they would fight to the death.


Summer was again forced to prepare the meal for the evening. It was Stace who came to get her, for, since Three Feathers was now wide awake, Carl was too wise to go near her.

Summer smiled at him, which did not please Carl. He cast a surreptitious look in Three Feathers's direction before he strategically put as much distance between him and Summer as he could.

Without warning, Summer moved to stand near Carl, who was completely unnerved by the look in Three Feathers's cold, dark eyes.

"Get away from me," he snarled softly. "Do you think I'm going to fight him over you?"

"I would not have a dog like you fight for me." She smiled pleasantly, as if Carl had said something very interesting and amusing to her. "I would even prefer a beast like Santiago to you."

"Don't worry, little girl," Carl grated. "When Santiago gets here tomorrow night, no one will fight for you. He will just take you."

"Maybe." She laughed softly, which made Carl begin to sweat. Three Feathers moved toward them. He gripped Summer's arm and shoved her away from Carl toward the fire.

"Go and finish the food," he ordered Summer before turning to Carl. "Leave my woman alone," Three

458

Feathers threatened in a voice of steel, "or I will slit your throat and throw you to the vultures so they can chew on your flesh."

"I didn't touch her," Carl protested vehemently, "and I didn't ask her to come around me. She's a devil. She's doing this just to make you all fired up."

He moved away from Three Feathers as rapidly as he could, and Three Feathers turned his gaze on Summer, who knelt by the fire preparing food.

He went to her side and looked down at her. Summer gazed up at him with an innocent, wide-eyed expression. It was probably the first time in his life that Three Feathers was unsure of anything. It puzzled him, what this small woman could do to his strength and firmness. He felt the desire to lift her in his arms and carry her away. It was a very tense moment for Summer, who read it clearly, though she held her face rigidly in control.

Three Feathers's greed won the battle. For now, he would wait. He would get his share of guns and money; then he would take her and go.

Summer again prepared plates of food for Elenora and her parents. After she gave Elenora hers, she took the two remaining plates and moved toward where her parents were being held.

Again no one came in with her. She stepped inside and rushed to Clay.

"Eat while I talk," she said rapidly. "There is very little time." She began to explain what Sebastian had found. "When they sleep, then Sebastian will come here. He will need your help."

"We will be ready," Clay said softly. "Be careful, Summer. I know you have the courage of ten men, but . . . we could not bear to lose you. Please be careful."

"I'll be careful," she answered as she put her arms

about Clay. He held her close for a minute. Then she kissed Sabrina, smiled again at both of them and left.

Once outside their door, she moved again to the fire and took food for her and Sebastian. She knew it would be the last time she would be in the main cave until the next day.

She sighed with relief when Stace closed the door behind her. She and Sebastian ate rapidly. Then they sat together and waited until they were sure the ones in the main cave were asleep for the night.

"It is a hard climb, Summer," Sebastian whispered. "Are you ready?"

Summer nodded. Sebastian told her to climb ahead of him. He watched her make her way slowly, determinedly, and very accurately to the top. Then he climbed up beside her. Her eyes were on the yawning darkness and a touch of fear of the unknown flickered momentarily in her eyes.

"It's dark and it's dirty," Sebastian said gently, "but there's nothing to be afraid of. We can go side by side; it's wide. Come on, I'll help you."

She nodded and reached for the rim of rock. Making no sound, they moved toward the dim light that signified Clay and Sabrina's place of confinement.

Clay was waiting for them. He had silently moved boxes of material to the wall so they would have no trouble getting down.

In less than an hour Summer and Sebastian were standing with Sabrina and Clay.

"Sebastian," Clay began quickly, "you have some plan to get us out of here?"

"Yes," Sebastian whispered. "You must listen very carefully. It will all be a matter of timing. Santiago gets here tomorrow night. We have to make our move at the exact moment of his arrival." He kept his voice cool and much more assured than he felt. Though the women didn't realize this, Clay did. He smiled, musing that his daughter had chosen well.

"Here is what I plan to do," Sebastian continued. All three listened in silence to a plan that was their only hope; it was so outlandish a scheme that they were quickly caught up in it.

"We must be careful not to antagonize anyone before tomorrow night. We don't want to get separated."

"We'll be careful, Sebastian." Sabrina smiled. "Is there anything else we can do?"

Sebastian chuckled. "Well, Mrs. Storm . . ."

"Sabrina." She returned his smile.

"Sabrina. Would you be so kind as to let me have your petticoat?"

"My petticoat?"

"Yes. I'm going to put it to good use. It's going to be the key to our escape, and the end of this nest of snakes."

"It will be amusing conversation later, when we try to explain to everyone that our lives were saved by my petticoat."

"Are you going to explain what you plan to do with it?" Clay grinned.

"Yes, I intend to use it to blow this entire set of caves right off the map, along with the pack of vermin that lives in it."

Without hesitation Sabrina loosened her petticoat and handed it to Sebastian, who bowed as he accepted it.

"Now, Summer and I must get back. We have work yet to do tonight."

Clay and Sabrina watched the two as they disappeared into the darkness.

"He," Clay said with a soft laugh, "is quite an innovative young man. I guess I can see how he won

461

Summer. He will be an interesting addition to our family."

Sabrina agreed wholeheartedly.


Once inside their own enclosure, Sebastian began to tear the petticoat into long strips. Without a word, Summer began to help, though she had no idea of Sebastian's purpose.

"Sebastian, what will this be?"

"If it goes as I plan, it's going to be the fuse that will set all this powder off."

"But . . ."

"Don't worry. We'll be gone . . . at least I hope we will."

"Sebastian . . . what if . . ."

"Don't even think it. This is going to work. Just keep your mind on that. Now, there's a barrel of oil over there in the corner. Dip these strips in it. After that, twist them tight. Then we'll tie them together and make a long rope."

Summer caught the idea immediately and they continued to work in silence. After an hour they had a long, coiled, black rope.

"It will burn easily," Sebastian assured her. "Now, you hide it and rest. I have another little chore to do."

"What?"

"Why, honey,"—he grinned—"I'm going out to find Hawk and tell him what we're doing. I don't want him rushing in here just as this thing goes bang."

"Do you have enough time to get out and back?"

"I'd better, or it's over. Come here and give me some good luck to take along."

She stepped into his arms and clung to him as their lips blended. She didn't want to let him go. The fear that he would be caught and killed nearly overwhelmed her.

His lips lingered against hers, for he did not have the will to let her go either. He kissed her leisurely, as if he had all the time in the world.

Reluctantly he moved her away from him. "Hold on tight, my love," he whispered. "You know I wouldn't leave you to face them alone. I'll be back in time. I promise."

She smiled through a haze of tears and nodded. Then she watched him climb to the top of the crates and disappear into the blackness beyond. She had never felt so alone in her life.

Sebastian struggled forward as rapidly as he could. He knew it was already past midnight. He did not believe the others were early risers, but he needed to be back before dawn or risk the chance that they might come in and discover him gone. He would die before leaving Summer to face that rabble alone.

As strong as he was, he was breathing raggedly by the time he reached the crevasse that led outside. He pushed the thought from his mind that Sabrina, Summer, and Elenora might not be able to make it.

It took considerable effort to wedge his broad shoulders through the small crack, but he finally succeeded. He stood for a moment to breathe the cool night air.

Looking up, he saw that the moon had already climbed high in the sky. Hours were passing too quickly, and he still had to find Hawk.

He had to move slowly, and though the loss of time was frustrating, he knew he couldn't risk being discovered outside.

Summer had given him the general idea of the area in which she had sensed Hawk, but Sebastian saw no sign of him.

After several minutes, it was Hawk who found Sebastian—and very physically. Sebastian was moving slowly, in a crouched position, when a force landed on him and sent him sprawling in the dirt. Then the soft click of a gun near his ear sent a bolt of fear streaking through him. At that moment, a rough, whispered voice sounded most welcome to his ears.

"Hawk, it's Sebastian," Cole said from nearby.

Sebastian was helped to his feet and he grunted with the effort.

"Good Lord, Hawk, you almost broke me in two."

"Fortunate." Hawk grinned. "I meant to kill you."

"Thanks for being so gentle."

"What are you doing out here without the others? Are they all right?"

"Hawk, all of you, gather around. I can't waste time. I have a lot of things to tell you."

They closed in around Sebastian, who spoke rapidly and efficiently. No one argued; they accepted the fact that this plan was the only one they had. It would have to work.

The moon hung low as Sebastian began to make his way back. He moved swiftly and dropped down into the cave to find a shaken Summer in his arms.

"Sebastian . . . oh, Sebastian, I've been so worried."

He held her tightly and rocked her against him. "It's all right, Summer. I found Hawk. It's all right, love."

He caught her face between his hands and kissed her gently. It was a calming kiss. He kissed her forehead, her eyes, her cheeks, then again the sweetness of her mouth.

"Lord, I wish we were anywhere else but here," he whispered.

Summer felt the same, but both knew that the joy of

sharing each other would be even more intense when the danger had passed.

Summer urged Sebastian to tell her how he had found Hawk and what had occurred. Quickly he explained and Summer was pleased to hear a somewhat stronger tone of confidence in Sebastian's voice.

Sebastian was tired from his nerve-racking trip to the outside and back. He wanted to sleep, but the tension had set his mind spinning and he was finding it difficult to relax.

He sat with his back braced against the cold stone wall with Summer close to him. His arm was about her and her head rested on his shoulder. With his other hand he gently caressed her hair.

"I guess for now all we can do is wait and try not to antagonize anyone," he mused.

"I do not think that will be much of a problem, at least until it becomes time for Santiago to arrive," Summer replied. "Three Feathers is keeping a close watch on them all, and most of them are afraid to cross him, especially Carl. That is at least some protection."

"Summer, I have given a lot of thought to Elenora. I don't know how I am going to get her out. She would have to be with us in here. I don't think I can manage that."

"There's no other way to get to her?"

"No. The space above this doesn't go to where she is."

"Sebastian, we must do something. She . . . she should not be left alone to die like that. I am sure she is regretting her part in this."

"Don't believe that, Summer. She's not the kind to regret anything but failure. If you get her out and turn your back on her, she'll put a knife in it. Don't be judging her by your own values; she just doesn't have any."

"But Sebastian . . ."

"I know, love"—he chuckled—"you think you can bring her to justice some other way. Well, maybe you're right. But for now, I just don't know how to get her out of there."

"Maybe, in the morning, I'll be able to think of something."

"Don't do anything that might jeopardize you or your parents," he replied firmly. "No matter how you might feel about it, you are my first concern. If I can get her out, I will, but if I can't . . . I'll still save you and your parents first."

"I know, Sebastian. It's just that I've been alone and frightened, and I know how she must feel."

"I'll try, Summer. I'll try," he promised gently. She knew he needed to sleep. She drew closer and put her arms about him. Lifting her head slightly, she kissed the steady pulse at his throat.

"That, love"—he laughed—"is in no way meant to help me rest, is it? If it is, forget it. I need very little further stimulation to make love to you here and now. I'm nearing the point where I could easily forget where we are. I'm a starving man, and ravishing you is not beyond me."

"We could—"

"No," he said with as much self-control as he could muster, "not a dirt floor in a dark cave. No, Summer. When we're free . . . well, I have my dream of that."

"Tell me," she whispered.

Sebastian was silent for some time while he let his mind lead him to his fantasy.

"It will be in the sunshine, somewhere green and warm. I want to see you, all of you, with the sunlight touching you. I want to feel your body warm in my arms. God, I can almost taste the glory of it." He tipped her head up to look into her eyes. "I want to love you until you are so much a part of me that we breathe with the same breath. I want to know you have forgotten everything but me. I want to hear you call out to me to love you." Summer watched the passion burn deep in his jade eyes and she felt the trembling of her body and the delicious sensation of melting into him. "I want to touch every inch of you, taste every inch of you. I want to make love as only we have known it, gloriously, wondrously. Do you know now, Summer, why we cannot settle for this? Do you understand, my love, why I will wait?"

By the time Sebastian finished speaking, Summer's tears were warm against her cheeks.

"I love you so much," she answered with a half sob. "It is almost more than I can bear to know that you love me as you say. I want to share that dream with you, Sebastian. Will we share it? Will there be tomorrows for us?"

"Believe in me, Summer. We will have our dream. We will walk in the sunlight. Believe in me," he whispered as he bent his head to capture her mouth.

"I do," was her soft reply as his lips touched hers.


Within their small prison, Sabrina slept in Clay's arms while he contemplated what had happened and what the next day would bring.

He refused to think of the consequences if they failed to escape. He held Sabrina closer, thinking that at least they had shared many very beautiful years together. But Summer . . . Summer and Sebastian had just found each other. He remembered so well the first time Sabrina had come to him. He prayed that Summer would have the chance to find the happiness he and Sabrina had discovered.

He thought of Sebastian and was glad Summer had chosen such a man. Then his thoughts turned to

467

Elenora, who had helped create the situation in which they now found themselves. It opened the door to memories of how Elenora had been responsible for his near loss of Sabrina.

He wondered if Sebastian were thinking that it would be better for all of them if Elenora were left to face the consequences of her deceit and treachery. Yet he knew, with a deep sense of pride, that Summer, like Sabrina, would not want that to happen. He just wondered what Sebastian would do about it; he knew what he would have done. Sighing deeply and tightening his arm about Sabrina, he too sought sleep.

Within the confines of her small prison, Elenora sat in a state of near stupor. She could not believe all her well-laid plans had met this dark defeat. In her twisted mind she directed the blame and her continuing hatred on two—Summer and Sabrina.

Like a madwoman, she allowed the slow poison of hatred to gnaw away her reason. She ground her teeth in an animallike snarl and cried, "Someway . . . somehow . . . I will kill you both. I will kill you both, damn you!" Her words turned to harsh, rasping sobs. "Damn you . . . damn you!"

# *Chapter Thirty=seven*

Hawk slept lightly, prepared at any time for something to happen. He rose early and went again to his vantage point, hoping for an opportunity to see either Summer or Sabrina.

He gazed at the cave mouth as if he could will someone to come out. But no one did. It was obvious that those inside preferred to sleep late.

After awhile, Hawk was joined by Cole.

"See anything?" Cole questioned.

"Nothing." Hawk grinned. "They are lazy, these whites. None in our tribe would keep to his mat so late."

"Late?" Cole chuckled. "Hawk, I haven't seen the sun yet."

"If I were guarding the ones they are," Hawk retorted, "I would not be able to sleep at all."

"They don't know we're here, Hawk. They have no reason to be watching."

"Come, let us go back to camp. There is much to be done. When this day ends, I want to have those men before me. Then we must teach them a severe lesson."

"If any of them get out at all."

"Yes, the ones who get out . . . I will take care

of them." Cole and Hawk walked back to their camp quickly. With rapid motions, Hawk called two warriors to him.

"Leave now," he commanded. "Move carefully. I want to know from which direction Santiago comes, when he is near, and how many men he has."

The warriors moved away like shadows. There was nothing left but to wait. It was a most difficult thing for the seven remaining men to do.

"Maybe if we watch again we will see either Sabrina or Summer," Patrick suggested. "It is obvious they are doing the cooking. Maybe Summer will come outside and she will know we are still here."

They returned to the place where they could watch. Under the newly rising sun they remained motionless, hoping for one sign that would tell them Sabrina and Summer were all right.


Summer awoke to find that Sebastian had laid her across his body so that the hard floor would not disturb her sleep. She rested against his chest, soothed by the solid and steady beat of his heart. She didn't open her eyes, but lay still, pretending she was waking in her own home, with Sebastian next to her, and with a new day ahead that they could enjoy together. She did not welcome the intrusion of reality.

The door was pushed open and Sebastian came awake immediately and pulled Summer tightly against him.

Miles stood in the doorway and smiled down at them. "I believe the men are hungry, Summer. Come out here and cook something for them."

Summer rose quickly. Today was not the day to make Miles or any of the others angry. Today was the last day they would be in this dark, dismal place. If

Sebastian's plan proved successful, they would be free tonight.

"I . . . I need some time alone," Summer said in a low, embarrassed tone.

"Of course," Miles agreed, then added, "I am sure, since you know Sebastian will pay the price if you were to try to escape, that you will do nothing foolish. You may go outside for a few moments."

Sebastian stared coldly at Miles, who was completely unruffled. Soon he would be rid of all these problems, he mused.

"Tonight, Mr. Cain, we will have your signature on the receipt of sale."

"Only if you set Summer free."

"Such stubbornness," Miles chided. "Do not worry, Mr. Cain, you will sign."

"Don't believe it, Miles," Sebastian said frostily. "Neither of us—Mr. Storm or myself—will do anything of the kind . . . unless you free the women."

"I'm afraid you are not making the rules. I am. And when Santiago and I are finished, you will sign."

He motioned to Summer to follow and he led her out of the room. Sebastian's rage was almost overpowering, but with great effort he controlled it.

"Tonight, my friend," he growled. "Tonight!"

Summer went to the stream and washed as best she could, then she made ready to return to the cave. She knew quite well that Hawk was near. It gave her an added feeling of confidence and she glanced in the direction in which she knew him to be.

"Do not look for freedom; it is not out there. It is with me." Three Feathers spoke from behind her. His voice startled her so that she spun about.

"Three Feathers!"

"Yes, I would not let you roam free, as the white man allows. I do not think he knows you as well as I do. I do

471

not believe you are not brave enough to try to escape. You are."

"I would try," she replied, "if I did not know that Three Feathers would be on my trail. I have no hope of escaping you."

"You are wise," Three Feathers said warily. "But for this day you will remain in the cave, where I can watch you."

She wanted to fight, to shout at him, to strike him, but she held back her anger. She would do nothing to rouse his wrath, for such an action might jeopardize those she loved.

Three Feathers took her arm as they walked back into the cave. Summer's nerves had been pulled taut and Three Feathers could feel her tremble, but in his arrogance he credited her reaction to desire for him.

Once inside, Summer began to prepare food. It was the same procedure all over again. First Miles and the men ate, then she carried food to her parents and to Elenora. After that she returned to Sebastian with their food. There was nothing left to do but wait until the day ended.

Miles ate while he considered methods of getting Sebastian and Clay to be more cooperative. He had been sure of himself before Sebastian, but he had now come to the conclusion that forcing those two men to do what he wanted was going to prove difficult. These thoughts brought him to Elenora, who had complicated his plans and had been responsible for his having to restructure them. It stirred a new rage in him. And the longer he sat and thought about her double-dealing, the angrier he got.

He rose and went to the door that barred her cell. He motioned Stace to him. With an evil glow in his eye, he ordered, "Close the door behind me. Come back in about an hour. I'll be ready to leave then."

Stace nodded, held the barricade aside, and closed it after him.

Miles stood in the dim candlelight and looked down at Elenora, who sat in a dejected heap against the crates of guns. Slowly her eyes lifted to his, then widened in terror as Miles walked toward her.

"Miles," she whispered as she slowly rose to face him, "please let me out of here. I swear I will do anything you ask—anything."

He reached out and caught her face in one hand. His grip was merciless and she whimpered softly.

"Anything, my love?"

"Miles . . . please."

"Maybe, just maybe, I can forgive you. But you will have to be very good to me."

She was terrified and he knew it. It gave him a great deal of pleasure to see her so, for Miles was not a forgiving man.

"What . . . what do—"

"What do I want from you?" he broke into a deadly soft voice. "Take off your clothes."

"Miles," she gasped, "don't . . . let me out of here. Let's get out of this terrible place."

"No, my dear," he said casually. "Here—on this dirt floor. Maybe, if you perform well, I might just consider letting you live. Now, take off your clothes, or, by heaven, I'll turn you over to the men now. They would enjoy spending the day with you."

Tears coursed down her cheeks and she quivered in fear as she reached for the buttons of her dress. He meant to shame her, to destroy her pride; it was a choice of facing him or facing what he promised. And she was certain now that he would keep that promise without a qualm. Her only hope was to make him want

473

to let her live a while longer, just until she could find some way to get free.

Slowly, piece by piece, she removed all her garments. She shivered in the damp cold of the cave. Without a word, he held his gaze on her body until she bowed her head and wept.

"Come over here," he demanded. Slowly she went to him. Thus began an experience that would set Elenora's mind on the edge of insanity. He was brutal, his hands hard and rough as he handled her without care. He never kissed her, but his lips tasted her flesh, biting until she moaned and cried. Then he pushed her down to the dirt and was upon her like a rutting animal. She cried out at the pain he seemed to enjoy inflicting.

Her skin was torn by the roughness of the stones beneath her and he relished hearing her gasps and moans as he thrust himself deeply within her.

Satisfied, he stood above her fastening his pants. She was a weeping, dirty, huddled mass of pain and shame.

"Now, my dear, your lessons are just beginning." He went to the door. "Stace!" he called. The door was pushed aside and Stace entered. His eyes went to Elenora, then he looked at Miles with an amused grin.

"Was she good?" he asked.

"I've had better," Miles responded coldly, "but why don't you find out for yourself? We have a whole day to waste. So, you and the men take your turns, have your pleasure and enjoy yourselves."

"No-o-o," Elenora cried and tried to rise. She saw the door close behind Miles and Stace start toward her. Feebly she rose to her feet and put out her hands to defend herself. She struck out at him, only to receive a hard slap across her face that knocked her to the floor. She cried out one more time in desperation, then Stace was upon her.

He left twenty minutes later, leaving Elenora on the

474

floor. It was only moments until the next man came . . . then the next . . . and the next. It went on and on until Elenora did not even know when another came. She did not hear anything; she only felt the pain and the terror. And finally, she felt nothing at all.

The day passed so slowly that all four of the other captives had their nerves on edge. Sabrina was forced to prepare the midday meal, but she was denied permission to take Elenora anything. She was curious but was told nothing. Maybe, she speculated, Miles and Elenora were hatching up more plans.

She told Summer and Sebastian about Elenora quickly, for she had only just handed them their food when she was told she had to leave.

"I wonder what she's up to now," Sebastian remarked. "Is there any way you can reach her, Summer? Try to find out what's happening?"

"I can try, Sebastian. It will be difficult."

"We have nothing to lose. See what you can do."

Summer sat very still and closed her eyes. With all the strength she had, she reached out for Elenora. There was nothing but a blankness, then a strange darkness. It was as if there were a barrier between them, but as if the darkness were in Elenora's own mind.

She kept trying, but still the dark blackness was there. Sebastian made her stop to rest for awhile because he could see the strain of her efforts written on her face. After an hour had passed, Summer repeated her search. This time she gasped at the pain she felt. She also felt something else, something that terrified her. This was a new kind of blackness, a blackness of the soul.

She opened her eyes to look up into Sebastian's

concerned visage.

"What is it, love? What do you see . . . what do you feel?"

"Sebastian, something is so terribly wrong. She is in pain, but . . . there is something else."

"What?"

"I . . . I think she is losing her mind. She is in a dark place. Sebastian, it's so terrible."

"What could be wrong? Do you think she's hurt?"

"Yes, but still it's . . . it's different."

"I don't know if we can do anything, Summer. Maybe Three Feathers will let you in to see if she is all right."

"Can I call to him, Sebastian? Do you think he will let me?"

"We can try. If she's sick . . ."

"I can help her."

"I know, love." He smiled gently as he caressed her hair. "And you would, wouldn't you, despite all she has done to us and to your parents."

"She is still a person, Sebastian. I cannot let her suffer if she is sick or hurt."

"Then," he added as he bent to gently brush her lips with his, "suppose we try."

Summer went to the door and pounded on it, calling out for Three Feathers. It was several minutes before he came. When he did he stood in the doorway, wary of some kind of trap, and looked at Summer curiously.

"What do you want, Summer?"

"Three Feathers, I would ask a small favor of you."

He grinned. "Come outside."

Sebastian could hardly contain the urge to leap on Three Feathers. It was only the safety of the others that stopped him. He watched the door close after them. Again, as he had many times in the past few months, he admired the woman he loved. Summer had more iron

476

nerve than any ten men he knew.

After the door closed behind her, Three Feathers drew her aside. He put one hand on her waist. "So, have you decided that you have made a mistake in the one you chose? Have you finally realized that Three Feathers is the better man?"

Summer pushed his hand away. "I did not come to ask a favor for me."

"What do you want?"

"I want to go and see Elenora. I feel she is sick or hurt. I can help her. Let me go to her, Three Feathers."

Three Feathers grinned a wolfish grin. "She is not sick."

"How do you know?"

"It is just that she has been . . . entertaining the men here."

"Entertaining! You mean . . ." Her face turned ashen. "Three Feathers! All of them? You?"

"Why should you care?" he asked in amusement. "Does it make you jealous that I thrust my seed into the body of another woman? It means nothing. She is like the dirt under our feet, useful but just as easy to dispose of."

"I . . . I can't believe this!"

"You must. And she must get used to it. When Santiago comes, his men will number more, and not be so gentle."

"Three Feathers, please, let me see her."

"Go back inside. When the men are finished with her, I will let you go see her—only to teach you what will happen to you if you disobey me. Soon I will take you from here." His eyes grew warm as he reached to touch her hair. "Then we will know each other. I have ways of making you respond to me."

She didn't want to antagonize him, for fear he would grow angry and decide to do the same to her as she knew had been done to Elenora. She was frightened.

"Will you let me see her later . . . please, Three Feathers?"

"Already you learn how to speak to one who will soon be your master," he gloated. "When the men have tired of her for the day, I will take you to her. But first . . . this," he added softly. With his two large hands about her waist, he drew her against him. His head lowered and he took her mouth in a hard and demanding kiss. She tried not to fight and, turning her mind to Sebastian, she remained still. He raised his head and his fury sparkled in his dark eyes.

"Your thoughts are not on me," he said angrily. "You must do better than that or you will not return to your prison. I will take you now."

She was truly frightened. If she kissed him back, she might ignite his passion. If she did not respond, he might do something that would ruin all their plans.

She let herself relax in his arms and lifted her lips to kiss him. She held her mind on Sebastian and clenched her hands until Three Feathers seemed satisfied that she had succumbed to his prowess.

"Later, when I take you from here," he explained softly, "we will be together. You are not like that one. Do not let it upset you that I used her. It was a convenience. For us it will be different."

She wanted nothing more than to thrust a knife between his ribs and stop his arrogant words.

"You will let me see her later?"

"Yes, later."

Reluctantly, he returned Summer to Sebastian.

"Well?" Sebastian said quickly. Summer raised haunted eyes to his. Without a word he held her close to him while she haltingly explained what had happened.

"The rotten bastards," he muttered. "That is barbaric."

"Three Feathers . . . he too . . . he said I could see her later . . . later"—she moaned softly as her arms tightened about him—"when they were . . . finished with her."

"Summer," Sebastian said gently. She lifted her face from his chest. "I love you . . . more, I think, than my own life. Hold on to that and the fact that we will soon be safe. When this is over we'll go somewhere together. We'll help each other forget all that has happened here. Let's hold on to that and to each other for now."

"I love you, Sebastian. I don't think I could have borne this without you."

"Then just keep remembering what I said."

"I will, I will." No further words were necessary, for his kiss told her all there was to know.

The hours between them and the evening meal were difficult for Summer, who could only think of what Elenora must be suffering. Any kind of suffering, by anyone, was unbearable to her.

By the time Three Feathers came for her, she was almost overcome with impatience. She prepared the evening meal as rapidly as possible. When it was done, she went immediately to Three Feathers.

"You promised, Three Feathers," she said. "You said I could see Elenora now."

"Come with me."

He led her toward the dark area in which was located the entrance to Elenora's prison. Summer was well aware of the leering gazes of the other men and of their soft, suggestive laughter. Three Feathers opened the door, pushed her inside, and closed it behind her. Stunned, Summer stared across the dimly lit cave to where Elenora lay very still.

Three Feathers was surprised when Summer pounded on the door moments later. Her eyes were wide with shock. He went to her side and spoke casually.

"Do you want to go back?"

"Yes, but I must take her with me."

"No, Miles wants you separated."

"She is harmless now." Summer told him. "She is hurt, Three Feathers—not her body, but her mind."

Three Feathers's face froze. In the Indian culture, those damaged in mind were given special treatment. It was considered ill-omened to interfere with them or cause them harm. Three Feathers was superstitious enough to believe that this had become a very serious situation.

"She is weak," he said defensively.

"She needs my help."

"Take her with you then."

"But I can't carry her alone."

His face grew impassive. He would never admit that he felt fear at the idea of lifting a madwoman into his arms, especially to Summer.

He entered with her and together they moved to Elenora's side. Summer knelt to cover her with the dress she had found nearby. Then, reluctantly, Three Feathers lifted Elenora's slight form and carried her to Summer's chamber. There he laid her down and moved away as rapidly as he could. With relief, he closed the door. He would be glad when he could take Summer away from this place. He suddenly felt a foreboding that he could not shake off.

He returned to the fire and sat contemplating this. He couldn't understand his own mind at this point, for he found himself hoping that Summer could somehow heal Elenora. He knew Elenora for what she was, but he had not expected this. He was a man who could do battle with anything—anything but the mystery of the

480

unbalanced mind.

Within their small cave, Summer and Sebastian bent over Elenora's inert form. Summer bathed her in water she had brought to the cave earlier. Then she and Sebastian dressed her again. Summer did not want Elenora to awaken to find herself in such a condition.

Elenora regained consciousness slowly. Her eyes opened and she gazed about her as if she were unsure of where she was. Summer was stricken by her eyes, which were luminous and completely unaware.

Summer had done her best to heal Elenora's body, but she could do nothing more than what she had already done. It did not seem to be enough.

At least Summer had the consolation that they might be able to get Elenora out now. Since Sebastian had had no way of getting to Elenora's prison, bringing her to them had been the only solution.

"Summer, you need to rest," Sebastian told her. "This is going to be difficult under the best conditions. If you are exhausted, it will be much harder."

"I know," she said softly. "Sebastian . . . do you think we can—"

"Get her out of here? I don't know. But we'll try."

"What a terrible thing to endure."

"She meant that, and worse, for you and Sabrina," Sebastian reminded her.

"I know. But she is the only one who has suffered from her own planning and deceit. It is just that . . . it was a terrible price to pay."

Sebastian drew Summer up and put his arms about her. "Always the gentle heart. I guess it's the thing I love about you."

"The only thing?" She smiled up at him and he chuckled.

"Hardly. I don't think I could even begin to tell you all the things I love about you. But most certainly this is one of the best," he murmured as he kissed her thoroughly.

They spent the balance of the evening sitting close and talking. It was nerve-racking to wait. The minutes seemed endless.

"Do you think we should try to explain to Elenora what she must do when the time comes?" Summer questioned.

"No, I don't think so. I don't want her upset. She might do something unpredictable," Sebastian replied.

Summer nestled close and Sebastian held her in silence. He didn't want to tell her that despite her condition, and for no accountable reason, he still did not trust Elenora not to do something to destroy their chances.

# Chapter Thirty-eight

Hawk watched as his two braves approached. "Well?" he questioned.

"Santiago rides from the west," one said. "There are only a few men with him. His main camp must be many days' ride, for they look tired."

"How many men?" Hawk asked quickly.

"Ten and Santiago himself."

"Old Santiago." Hawk smiled. "If we have any luck, we might make this Santiago's last ride." He clapped one brave on the shoulder. "How long before they get here?"

"I would say when the moon is at its height."

"Good. We will be ready. I hope Sebastian and Summer can move quickly."

"They will do what they must," Cole said. "I would count on them to pull it off."

"I kinda guess," Simon added gently, "that they have to count on us, too."

"You're right," Cole agreed. "Pretty soon all hell is going to break loose. We have to watch carefully, for at the right minute we have to move, or Sebastian and the rest won't be able to leave."

"We'll strike at the right moment," Hawk stated

firmly. "And remember, any survivors . . . I want."

"For now," Cole said, "we await Santiago's arrival. It should be interesting. He thinks he's riding in to collect."

"He'll collect." Hawk laughed. "I'll see to it he collects everything he's deserved over all the years. He's a butcher and a madman. Let's make sure his evil ends here."

They nodded. Hawk, Cole, Patrick, Simon, Walking Horse, and the three braves took up their weapons and positioned themselves at prearranged points. All they could do now was wait.

Elenora awakened from her stupor slowly. It was very dim in the cave and she saw through half-closed eyes that Summer and Sebastian sat across the cave from her. They were intent on each other only, and she lay for a long time watching.

Had she heard the word escape? Yes! She had! She wanted to escape, but she wanted even more the chance to lash out, to kill. Her mind was so confused that she did not know any longer who, or even why. She just needed to fight back from her helplessness, needed to strike out at someone—anyone.

When they saw that Elenora was waking, Summer rushed to her side.

"Elenora?" she asked softly, "can you sit up?"

Elenora nodded and Summer and Sebastian eased her into a sitting position.

"How do you feel?"

"I . . . I don't know. I'm so tired . . . I hurt. How did I get here?"

Summer explained that Three Feathers had brought her here so they could care for her. It brought a flood of remembrance. She cried out and Summer grasped her hand.

"Don't, Elenora. Lie still. You will be all right. Rest a while. Later . . ." she looked up at Sebastian, who had put a restraining hand on her arm to caution her to silence. "You had best remain still and rest."

When Elenora closed her eyes again, ostensibly to rest, Sebastian took Summer aside. "Don't tell her anything until the last minute," he whispered. "I find it hard to believe that a zebra changes its stripes. She might just call them in on us to save her life."

"Do you believe she still trusts Miles?"

"Hell no, but she doesn't have to trust him to buy her freedom."

"He would betray her too."

"Of course. But in her state of mind you could never convince her of that. Keep our secret, Summer. If it ends up all right, I'll apologize . . . but I still can't find it in my heart to believe her."

"Whatever you say, Sebastian."

"Keep that in mind, love." He grinned. The grin turned to a small laugh. "Do you know you happen to be very dirty, my sweet?"

"What a nasty thing to say!" She smiled. "Do you know, my man, that you are somewhat filthy too?"

"I wish we were somewhere where we could take a bath . . . together."

"So do I," she replied. "Shall we plan on it tomorrow?"

"Sounds like a good idea . . . tomorrow. For now, you rest. We've very little time left."


Santiago rode at the head of the group. He looked like the renegade he was. He was a large man whose strong body had begun to deteriorate from too much food and drink and other excesses.

Now he rode toward the cave where he would meet the man who kept him supplied with the guns and ammunition he needed for his force of terror.

He licked his lips as he thought of the one or two women whom Miles always managed to supply. He and the ten men he had chosen to ride with him had not had a woman to share for a long time. He looked forward to this night.

The cave was just ahead and Santiago proceeded without fear. He had been here often and had always come away with a profit. There was no reason to believe it would be different this time.

He rode past the place where Hawk and the others lay in hiding. They let him pass without a sound or a movement.

Miles had been informed that Santiago was approaching. Now he went to the mouth of the cave to meet him.

At a distance, Hawk waited. Within the small caves, the prisoners listened. All were tense and waiting.

"Your parents were to leave as soon as they heard Santiago arrive," Sebastian whispered to Summer. "They should be on their way out now. Hang on, love. It should all begin at any moment." Summer trembled with expectation but remained quiet.

They could hear the sounds of the newcomers in the main cave. They were laughing and talking among themselves. Then Sebastian saw that their door was being slowly opened.

"It's now, love," Sebastian whispered again. "Get ready." They were breathless for a long moment, then Sebastian murmured, "Come on, Hawk. Come on."

The door was open and Carl stood in the doorway.

"Come out here, girl," he said. "Santiago wants to get a taste of what he just bought."

Suddenly they heard the crack of a rifle, then

486

another and another. Carl, taken by surprise, turned from the door and disappeared. In the confusion, he left it open. Elenora chose that moment to move. She rose quickly and ran for the open door.

"Elenora!" Summer cried.

"Let her go," Sebastian said abruptly. "Come on. We've got to move fast. Get climbing."

Summer ran to the crates and clambered to the top. She looked back to see if Sebastian followed. He had broken the top of one cache of powder. In it he placed one end of his makeshift fuse. He braced it to make sure it would stay, then looped the rest over his shoulder and loosened it in a steady path behind him as he scrambled up beside Summer.

"Don't wait for me," he said quickly as he boosted her up over the rim and into the crevasse. "Get out! I'll be right behind you."

They could hear the sound of a barrage of bullets ricocheting through the main cave. It would hold the attention of their captors for awhile. Long enough, Sebastian hoped.

Summer panted as she crawled along as rapidly as she could. As she heard Sebastian moving slowly behind her, she prayed silently that her parents were out already and safe.

She reached the small opening and pushed herself through. Sebastian followed. He drew the last of the fuse with him. It had just barely made it.

Both were breathing raggedly now, but they had no time to catch their breath. Sebastian bent and struck flint to create a spark. It seemed to leap from his hand to the fuse, and a sizzle sounded as the spark disappeared within the darkness.

Their final prayer was that the fuse would not extinguish itself until it reached its destination.

"Get going, Summer," he said. "Find Hawk."

"Not without you."

"Get going," he said angrily.

"Not without you," she repeated stubbornly. "If it goes out, I know you'll go back in and try to light it. I won't leave this spot until you do. Sebastian, you must come with me."

"Damnit Summer, get out of here—now!"

"No," she cried with stubborn determination. "I will not move until you do."

He grabbed her shoulders and gave her a rough shake, but she only stiffened and stood more firmly. "Do as you please, Sebastian," she said calmly. "I won't go without you."

He glared at her for a moment, and she glared back. Suddenly he laughed and took her hand. "Okay, we go together, and hope the damn thing works."

She gripped his hand firmly as they started toward Hawk.

Elenora dashed into the main cave in time to see everyone gathered at the mouth. All had their backs to her, for their attention had been drawn to the hidden attackers. No one saw her make her way toward guns that had been left by the surprised men.

"Who the hell did you lead here, Santiago?" Miles demanded.

Santiago was enraged. He glared at Miles. "No one follows Santiago. It must be someone who has discovered you."

"No one knows where this place is," Miles shouted, "and no one followed me here."

They stood framed against the dark entrance of the cave, with the fire between them and Elenora.

She stared at Miles and her pain and madness returned. He had betrayed her. He had been the one responsible for all the darkness.

Slowly she raised the gun. She sighted very, very carefully. She wanted him to feel as much pain as possible. When she had readied the gun for its deadly task, she called out his name.

"Miles!"

Miles spun around, and the gun barked. With a wild cry, he gripped his abdomen and sagged to his knees. Slowly Elenora walked toward him with a smile on her face. She could see the agony in his eyes and it filled her with grim satisfaction.

She began to laugh—a strange, wild laugh that paralyzed everyone. They knew madness when they saw it and it chilled them. It was the last thing most of them would ever see.

The first explosion stunned everyone and shook the cave walls violently. Everyone became disoriented as a thick cloud of dust and flying debris filled the cavern. Then the second and third explosion shattered the walls and killed indiscriminately.

From outside, Hawk, Cole, and the others stood and watched the cave burst into a ball of brilliant flame.

"No one could survive that," Cole whispered.

"No," Hawk answered, "no one."

"Hawk?" Cole questioned softly. "Do . . . do you think . . ."

"Don't speak the words. They will be with us soon. They got out. In a few minutes we will see them coming."

"I hope you are right, Hawk," Simon said worriedly.

"I know I'm right."

Their eyes were turned in the direction from which they expected Summer and the others would come.

There was a fine mist of dust and thick smoke in the air, and they could barely see through it. Still, with rapidly beating hearts, they watched.

Then out of the mist stepped Clay, with Sabrina's hand in his. They were choking and dirty, but they were alive.

Hawk greeted Clay by embracing him and Sabrina. He had never felt so grateful to the gods in his lifetime.

"Clay, are Sebastian and Summer behind you?"

"They should be. Sebastian was to have been outside before he lit the fuse."

"Then they should be here," Cole said instantly. Barely breathing, they all watched the thick haze of smoke as the suspense built. One minute . . . two . . . three . . .

"Damn it, Sebastian," Cole whispered raggedly. "Where the hell are you?"

Fear tingled through all of them. Had Sebastian lit the fuse from the inside when something had kept them from escaping? No one wanted to believe that anything had happened to them, yet as time went on, there was no sign of Sebastian or Summer.

Without a word Hawk started to move in the direction from which Sebastian would come. Cole was immediately with him as were Clay and Walking Horse. The rest began to follow, all silently afraid of what they would find.

They had taken only a few steps when a shadowed form appeared.

"Sebastian!" Cole shouted.

"I'm here," came Sebastian's choked voice.

They could make him out now, and they saw with horror that he was carrying a limp Summer in his arms.


Summer and Sebastian had started to move rapidly when the first explosion struck. They were still close to the opening, and the force of the blast threw them both to the ground.

Sebastian helped Summer up, grabbed her hand, and together they started to run. The next explosion was fierce and fiery, and the ground trembled beneath their feet. Summer stumbled once, but Sebastian caught her before she fell. Flying debris was all about them now and both were barely able to defend themselves from pebbles and flying brush.

It had been a rock the size of a man's fist that had struck Summer. The blow might not have proven so disabling if it had not hit her head on very nearly the same spot in which she had been struck before. With a soft moan, she sagged to the ground.

"Summer!" Sebastian cried as fear gripped him. He knelt by her and discovered instantly what had happened.

He lifted her body and began to run. As he stepped out of the blinding haze, he was filled with relief. There before him stood Hawk with Summer's parents. They were safe.

Clay reached them first and took Summer from Sebastian's arms. Sabrina was soon beside him.

"Clay . . . is she . . . ?"

"She's all right," Sebastian assured her. "She got hit with something, but she's all right. She should be coming around soon."

"Find a place and lay her down," Hawk ordered. He turned to Simon and his warriors. "Go down and see if there are any survivors. If there are, bring them to me."

They obeyed swiftly, doubting that they would find anyone.

The smoke had not settled yet and the boulders and debris were piled high. Simon and Hawk's warriors could only move about slowly. It took them a long time, but they finally returned with the news that they could find no one alive.

"It is good that they left their horses safe outside,"

Hawk reflected. "At least our four friends will have mounts on which to return home."

"Sebastian," Clay declared, "you have our gratitude. We would never have gotten out of there without you."

Sebastian was kneeling beside a slowly recovering Summer. He smiled up at Summer's parents. "It was not all me. It was as much Summer's courage. You have a remarkable daughter, Mr. Storm."

"It seems"—Sabrina laughed—"that his very remarkable daughter has found a very remarkable man."

"Thank you." Sebastian smiled. "Is it a proper time to ask your blessing on our marriage?"

Summer had awakened and had heard the last few words. She reached up and took Sebastian's hand. He squeezed it, but his eyes remained on her parents.

"I have the feeling," Clay responded with a chuckle, "that it would not do much good for me to resist. I think you are a young man determined to get what he wants."

"Somewhat like you," Sabrina said softly to Clay. "It seems I remember a Clay Storm who would not settle for less than what he wanted, a man who spent weeks in prison with me and fought the whole legal system to have what he wanted."

"No love," Clay said gently. "To have what he needed for survival." He turned to look at Summer and Sebastian. "You have our blessing, Sebastian, and it is our sincere hope that you find the same happiness Sabrina and I have found."

"I'm sure we will," Sebastian said softly as he looked down at Summer. "I'm sure I'll find all the happiness I've ever dreamed of. Summer," he said with a quick smile, "while I have you in a helpless position, will you tell me that you're going to marry me as soon as possible, or will I have to do something drastic, like"— he laughed—"kidnapping you?"

Summer smiled up at him with tears in her eyes. "I would be so very happy to be your wife, Sebastian Cain. In fact, if you hadn't asked me now, I might have considered kidnapping *you!*"

Sebastian laughed and looked up at the friendly faces crowded around. He shrugged eloquently. "Under these circumstances, and since I know the lady is quite capable of doing whatever she treatens to do, I guess I had better give up my freedom with good grace."

Everyone was more than pleased, and Cole was the first to suggest they start back to the village. "If I have the same good luck as you, my friend," he told Sebastian, "perhaps we can make it a double wedding."

"A double wedding!" Sabrina cried. "How wonderful! Is it one of the young girls of Hawk's village?"

"No"—Cole grinned—"it's Kylie Flynn. If she'll have me."

At this, both Patrick and Simon voiced their surprise.

"Yer goin' to marry my little girl?" Patrick demanded in a voice that sounded more ferocious to Cole than Patrick had intended. Patrick had been more surprised than angry.

"I've just asked Kylie to think about it," Cole protested quickly. "It's really gone no further than that."

Simon laughed. "I'll bet that's more your fault than Kylie's. Oh, wait 'til I get back. Is she going to get repaid for all her teasin'."

"Well," Patrick responded as he eyed a sober Cole, "I'm not too sure I'm ready to give my little girl away."

"I'll make her happy, Mr. Flynn," Cole said nervously. "I can't offer much, but I'll spend my life making her happy."

"She's a clever little girl. I expect she knows a good

man when she sees one."

"She would be a very foolish woman if she didn't," Summer interjected. "I think," she added with twinkling eyes, "this will be the grandest celebration of my life."

"In that case," Hawk declared with a satisfied smile, "I think it is time we start for home, so we can begin planning this grand festivity."

Sebastian spoke up quickly. "Summer and I had better find a stream deep enough to bathe in, so we can clean some of this dirt away." He looked at Clay and Sabrina. "You two look a little dirty too."

"Sounds like a good idea to me," Clay agreed. "Besides, I'd like to put a lot of distance between us and this place as soon as possible."

There was quick agreement to his suggestion and, in a short time, they were on their way.

By the time the sun had rimmed the horizon they had run across a stream that was suitable for bathing. But it absolutely dismayed Sebastian when the women went off alone to bathe and he was forced to accompany the men. He could barely control his thoughts of Summer in his arms in a cool stream of water.

He knew one thing for certain. He wasn't going to be without Summer very much longer. The strain of his active imagination was almost too much to bear.

They stopped again at midday, but Sebastian's efforts to get a very busy Summer away from the group were thwarted at every turn. By the time they were ready to stop for the night, Sebastian had already formulated a plan.

Summer and Sabrina prepared the meat of a deer that one of Hawk's warriors had killed. When the food had been eaten and everyone had settled down for the night, Sebastian came to Summer, who was lying beneath a tree. Without a word, he bent down and

494

grasped her hand, then pulled her to her feet.

"Sebastian?"

"Shhh, love. Come with me."

He drew her with him deeper into the forest, then he turned and took her in his arms. He simply held her for a moment, enjoying the feel of her in his arms.

"Summer, Summer," he murmured. "I had to hold you. It's been so long."

"I know," she whispered. "Sebastian . . . could we take a walk . . . somewhere quiet . . . where we can be alone?"

"Being alone with you has been the only thing on my mind for hours."

They walked along through the shadows hand in hand, unaware that a sinister form was following them. As they stopped beneath the limbs of a very large tree, Sebastian muttered, "Damn, I should have brought a blanket." He took her by the shoulders and turned her to him. "Wait right here. I'll be back in a moment."

"Hurry," she whispered. After kissing her deeply, he loped through the trees to the camp, grabbed up his blanket, and disappeared back into the forest as silently as he had come.

When he reached their tree, he didn't see Summer. Softly he called her name and a muffled sound came to him. He spun about and the sight before him froze his blood. He stared at the two before him in disbelief.

Three Feathers looked as though he had risen from the dead. He was cut and bruised, and there was a great deal of dried blood covering him. His eyes were wild and he appeared beyond reason.

He held a bound Summer about the throat with one arm. In the other hand he held a long knife, the point of which was touching Summer's heart. Sebastian could see the terror in Summer's eyes.

"So," Three Feathers said in a hate-filled voice, "you

thought to leave me dead. Too bad, white one. Now you will both pay the price."

"Do what you want with me," Sebastian said, "but let her go."

"Oh no," Three Feathers said with a grim laugh, "she will pay too—longer and harder. Let me tell you what I will do with her. I will—"

"Shut up, you bastard," Sebastian snarled. "What kind of a coward are you. Face me. Let me fight you."

"I will kill you," growled Three Feathers.

His mindless hate was Sebastian's only chance. "You are not man enough. You are a coward who hides behind a woman's skirt."

Three Feathers's face blazed with rage and he loosened his arm from Summer's throat.

"Who is the coward now?" Three Feathers sneered. "I could kill her easily, but I want her to see you die first."

"I will fight you, unless you want to continue to ride behind her. Only a coward would do so rather than pit himself against a man." He paused. "Still afraid?" Sebastian taunted.

With a low growl, Three Feathers released Summer. Because her feet and hands were bound, she fell helplessly to the ground. She watched with wide-eyed fear as the two adversaries faced each other.

Sebastian slid his knife from its sheath and confronted Three Feathers with an arrogant smile. "Come on, Three Feathers. Come and taste the touch of death." With a snarl, Three Feathers leapt.

# Chapter Thirty-nine

Three Feathers was a large and very strong man. And he was filled with such rage that his strength was intensified.

The two huge men met with a crashing sound. Both were powerful, evenly matched. Sebastian gripped the wrist of the hand that held Three Feathers's knife, just as Three Feathers gripped his. With grunts of force they strained together, each attempting to get the leverage to subdue the other. Like two Goliaths, they struggled.

Suddenly Three Feathers pushed Sebastian away from him. He swung his knife and Sebastian leapt back, though he felt the point graze his skin.

Now both crouched low, arms extended, and circled each other, looking for one slip, one moment's weakness, to strike a deadly blow.

Three Feathers's knife sliced through the air, but again Sebastian moved just out of its reach. Three Feathers growled low in his throat and charged again. They fell to the ground and rolled over and over, each trying to gain control.

Three Feathers was on top of Sebastian, trying to thrust his knife into Sebastian's heart. With all the strength he possessed, Sebastian held his wrist. The knife was inches from his chest. Then Three Feathers's face lost its triumphant glow as Sebastian, with supreme effort, pushed the Indian from him.

Both leapt quickly to their feet. They were bathed in sweat and panting raggedly, but their gazes remained locked on each other. One slip would mean their lives.

Summer edged her body back from the wild confrontation. Her hands and feet were bound, but so loosely that she knew she could release herself. She only prayed she could get free before Three Feathers killed Sebastian.

She watched the battle as she worked furiously on the bindings that held her feet. The thongs on her ankles began to loosen. She was taut with fear that Sebastian would slip somehow and Three Feathers would kill him.

Frantically, she began to work on the bonds that held her wrists.

Sebastian charged Three Feathers this time, but the warrior sidestepped him neatly and Sebastian sprawled on the ground. He turned over quickly, but Three Feathers was upon him again before he could regain his feet. Three Feathers gripped Sebastian's wrist and, with mighty effort, slammed it relentlessly against a rock. Sebastian lost his hold on the knife and it skittered away. Now Three Feathers was in control.

Sebastian grasped Three Feathers's arm as it rose to strike the final blow. Three Feathers pummeled him with his free hand and Sebastian grunted for the jabs were ferocious.

Again they rolled over and over and neither could find a vantage point from which to end the conflict.

It was then that Summer freed her hands. She rose and stood for a heart-stopping moment to watch the battle Sebastian was fighting for possession of the knife. His own lay too far away for him to expect to get to it. Should she run for help? she wondered desperately. Maybe in that time Three Feathers would kill Sebastian. No! She would not leave him. She would be dead herself if anything happened to Sebastian.

She began to edge toward Sebastian's knife. Neither man saw her yet as she slowly moved forward. The battle grew in ferocity as they both began to tire and to realize that soon one would have to succeed.

Summer grew closer and closer to the knife. Just as she reached for it, Three Feathers saw her. He gave an angered roar, ripped himself from Sebastian's grasp, and headed for her. Sebastian was right after him.

It all happened at once.

Summer grabbed up the knife and turned just as Three Feathers attacked. Sebastian leapt and his weight threw Three Feathers forward into Summer's arms. The knife, which she had been holding before her, sank to the hilt into Three Feathers's chest. He gave a ragged gasp and gripped her arms. Slowly he slid to his knees, his eyes wide with shock. Then he shuddered and sank to the ground.

Summer was in a temporary state of shock. She gazed at Three Feathers as if she didn't really see him.

Sebastian was confident that the shock would wear off soon, but he felt she would recover faster if she were removed from this bloody scene. He lifted her from the ground and carried her some distance away, then he stood her on her feet and put his arms about her. It was then that she began to shake and cry. Sebastian just held her close, rocking her against him until she could find control. After awhile her tears ceased.

"I . . . I have never killed anyone before," Summer whispered weakly.

"It's not a very nice thing to experience, Summer,

but you had no choice. It was him or us. You had to do it. Now Summer, you must forget it."

She wasn't too sure it was going to be that easy. All she had ever done in her life was heal. It was the first time she had ever caused death.

"It seems," Sebastian told her with a smile as he lifted her face to him, "that every time I try to be alone with you, something happens. Look at me, woman. I'm all dirty again."

Summer tried to laugh, but the sound was forced.

"Come on, love," he said gently. "We'll go back and tell the others what happened."

He put his arm about her shoulder and they walked back to camp.

The group continued on toward the village the next morning. Summer was still finding it hard to accept what she had done. She and Sabrina spent a great deal of time talking together. Clay understood, but Sebastian wanted Summer—in every way it was possible to want a woman. He felt it was about time they started their life together. With this thought in mind, he began to devise still another plan. The only person with whom he discussed it was Sabrina, and that was only because she astutely guessed the problem and approached with a solution that was very similar to his own.

Sebastian found her awake long after the others had fallen asleep. He spoke quietly. "What's the matter, Sabrina? Can't you sleep?"

"I am awake on purpose, Sebastian. I want to talk to you. Can we go for a walk?"

"Of course."

They walked along slowly.

"Sebastian?"

"Yes."

"I think it's time you took things into your own hands."

"I don't know what you're talking about."

She stopped and turned to Sebastian and smiled. "Sebastian . . . why don't you just take Summer and go somewhere where you can be alone. She needs you just as badly as you need her."

"I can't seem to get her mind off of what happened. Maybe when we get back to the village . . ."

"No, don't wait."

"But—"

"Sebastian, take her away from here now. She is beginning to think that because she has killed, she should devote her entire life to being a healer. It has been a bad shock. She needs another shock to make her see the truth."

Sebastian grinned. "Her father and Hawk will murder me."

"No. I'll explain to Clay. Believe me, he will understand."

"You're a wonderful woman, Sabrina. I can see how Summer turned out so well. I'll take your advice. But"—he laughed—"don't forget to explain to Hawk and Clay. I don't think I could handle the two of them."

"I will . . . I will."

Sebastian bent and kissed her cheek, then they slowly walked back to the camp.

Sebastian went to where the horses were tethered and took his and one for Summer. He saddled them and packed what they would need. Then he went to Summer, who was sleeping a short distance away from the fire. As he knelt beside her, he remembered well the other time he had come to her with such great need and how she had opened her arms to him. She looked so fragile that he felt the urge to lie beside her and make love to her then and there. He reached out and gently

501

touched her. Slowly she woke.

"Sebastian," she whispered. "What is it?"

"Summer, come with me now." It was all he could say.

"Where?"

Sebastian bent and gathered her up in his arms. Determinedly he walked to the horses.

"Sebastian, what—"

"Shhh, love. Don't wake everyone. They need their sleep."

"But . . . where are we going?"

When they reached the horses, he stood her beside him. "Summer, remember when we were prisoners in that cave?"

"Yes, but—"

"I told you I had a dream of us . . . together."

"Yes," she said softly. "I remember."

"Well . . . I'm going to find it, but . . . it's just no good without you. Come with me, Summer. Let's find our dream together."

Summer lifted her arms and looped them about his neck. He kissed her tenderly. "Where will we go, Sebastian?" she questioned softly.

"To someplace green where the sunshine is warm," he replied happily.

"Yes." she sighed. "Let's go where we can find our beginning again."

He lifted her to her horse, then mounted. Together they rode away.


The next morning Clay was the first to discover that Summer and Sebastian were missing. Because of what had happened previously, he immediately assumed that there were other survivors of the explosion and that they had abducted Summer and Sebastian in the middle of the night.

He roused the rest of the men quietly but let Sabrina sleep. He had everyone prepared to search the entire area, when Sabrina woke up.

"Clay!" Sabrina cried in alarm, "what in heaven's name is going on?"

"Sabrina," Clay said urgently, "I'm leaving one of the men with you to take you back to the village. The rest of us have to leave now."

"Where? Whatever for?"

"Sabrina, I hate to tell you this . . . but Summer is gone. So is Sebastian. They must have been taken sometime during the night."

"Oh, Clay," Sabrina explained laughingly, "please tell your men it's all right."

Hawk approached at that moment and Sabrina could see that his face was creased by worry.

"Hawk," Sabrina invited, "if you and Clay will sit down, I will tell you where Summer has gone."

Clay looked at her suspiciously, then he and Hawk exchanged glances, but they sat and listened intently as Sabrina told them of her conversation with Sebastian.

"We should have known," Hawk said with a quick smile.

"Good Lord," Clay exclaimed in amusement, "I didn't even give that a thought. Well, since we're all ready to go, Sabrina, you might as well get up. It's a short ride home now."

Sabrina laughed and extended her hand and Clay pulled her into his arms and kissed her soundly.

"I should have seen the signs," he mused softly.

"Yes," Sabrina agreed devilishly, "you should still remember . . . or are you getting too old for that?"

"Old?" Clay chuckled. "Madam is offering a challenge, is she?"

"She is," Sabrina said seductively.

"Well," he whispered, "never has there been a slight against the Storm name that has gone unanswered. What do you say we go home?"

"I say," she breathed as she lifted her lips for his kiss, "that that is the best plan I have heard in weeks."

"Good. Let's get going. I don't want to waste any time." He smiled into her warm eyes. "I have a reputation to clear."

Not long after, Sabrina declared she was ready, and together they rode toward home.

As she basked in the bright sunlight, her skin seemed painted gold by the rays of the sun. Water glistened like sparkling stars over her body. Moments before, she had stepped from the water to the grassy bank, and now she stood absorbing the warmth.

Sebastian called her name softly and she turned to see him standing a few feet away. She smiled and extended her hand to him. His answering smile seemed as warm as the sun.

She watched him move toward her and felt a shiver of pleasure. He was like a god, so tall and handsome. His golden hair glowed about his head like a haze, his bronzed body was a masterpiece of controlled muscle, and he moved with animal grace.

Sebastian kept his eyes on her, for he had never seen anything quite so beautiful. She was all he had ever dreamed, all he had ever wanted. He stopped near her and they held each other's eyes with a calm, new understanding that all that they were or would be could be found within the other.

"You are so beautiful, Summer . . . and I love you so very much."

She lifted her hand and placed it against his cheek. "I know," she whispered, "and I love you, Sebastian . . . I do love you."

He reached for her and she melted into his arms. Their lips blended in a long, slow kiss that sent a quiver of sensuous need spiraling through her. Sebastian enveloped her in magic with hands that were gentle and seeking and his body so warm and hard against hers.

He let his hands skim over her sleek body as if to discover for the first time the sweet feel of her flesh. Then he swept her up into his arms and carried her to the soft grass on the bank.

He laid her down gently and stood over her. Against the deep green grass her tawny body gleamed. He drank in her beauty, framing this scene among all his visions of Summer, to remember forever.

As Summer gazed up at Sebastian, she marveled at the vulnerability she felt. He was a man of supreme strength, and his body was the flint that would always ignite the flame within her.

He knelt beside her and bent forward with one arm braced on either side of her. Slowly he bent his head to caress her mouth with his. Tenderly, gently, he touched first one corner, then the other. Her lips parted to taste his and it sent a current through him that caused a quickening in his loins.

His mouth became possessive now and his tongue, probing deeply, was answered by her own. He caught her lips with his and sucked gently, nibbling the soft skin until she felt weak and feverish. Then his lips left hers to travel the soft, smooth flesh of her throat to her shoulders. They burned a path that made her gasp, for they seemed to scorch wherever they touched.

He buried his hands in the mass of her dark hair and his hunger was hot and sweet as he sought the sensitive crests that pulsed with every heartbeat. The buds hardened and she arched to meet his questing mouth, reveling in the rough texture of his hands against her skin as he teased and taunted.

She sought more and more and yet never seemed to get enough of the exquisite pleasure he was awakening. He tasted one peak hungrily, then sought the other, teasing with his tongue, sucking gently until he could hear the soft, throaty purr that signaled her passion.

Ripple after ripple of delicious sensation coursed through her as his mouth sought other, softer places. There was no part of her over which he did not linger— the small valley between her breasts, the soft curve of her waist, the flat, taut plain of her belly.

Then he was above her again, letting his gaze absorb the abandon with which she had surrendered to his voracious lips. He was filled with an exultation that turned his blood to molten fire and set his heart pounding until he could hardly bear it. She would be his forever. The thought of it made him wild with need. But he held it in check, if only for a while longer. He was determined to have all of her, for only together could they be whole.

Now he caressed her body gently and felt her quiver with unrestrained need. His fingers found the center of this need and stroked evenly, surely, eliciting tremors of passion that aroused them both.

Summer's hands began to roam over him, touching with sensitive shyness at first, but never ceasing their quest to know him fully, as he knew her. Every inch of him would belong to her, and she was greedy for possession. Her hands slipped from hard-muscled shoulders to fur-matted chest, then down to the hard, flat belly. He was breathless from her fiery touch and filled with joy that she sought him so completely.

Her fingers were light, teasing, as they encircled his swollen shaft first gently, then firmly to begin a sensuous stroking. He closed his eyes and immersed himself in a swirling current of sensuous delight. Her lips nibbled at the buds of his fur-covered chest, and her tongue licked tormentingly until he groaned aloud. Her lips moved down, down, until a velvet-soft mouth found him, kissed softly, tasted with flicking tongue, then closed about him. His breathing grew ragged and his body tensed in unmitigated rapture. He could only moan soft words of love as she carried him beyond any pleasure he had ever known.

Hovering on the brink of urgency, he lifted her to him and proceeded to brand her flesh with heated kisses until she cried out in mindless ecstasy.

His lips moved over her flesh, leaving behind a searing path as they searched for her sweet center. Their journey left her gasping, clinging to him, and she called out his name in wonder as his tongue stroked and pressed deeply within her.

Their bodies throbbed with an almost violent passion, and gently he held her thighs apart, then drove within her to explore her molten warmth.

She could no longer breathe, but could only grasp him to her as he dove again and again. With sweet violence, he thrust harder, faster, transporting them both to a climax of shattering, swirling ecstasy that melded them together for all time.

Afterward, Summer and Sebastian remained entwined as he shifted his weight while keeping his arm about her to bind her to him. She nestled into the curve of his arm and rested her head against his broad chest. He stroked her hair gently and she closed her eyes, savoring the serene aftermath of their love.

They had shared a week of bliss. Now both were reluctant to have it end. They had unraveled their lives and had shared with each other the contents. Sebastian had explained what had finally happened to Kate, and had even admitted his moments of disbelief after he had read the letter.

They had entered into all the rooms of their minds, brightening them with light, sweeping away all the cobwebs, and illuminating all the dark corners.

Sebastian had been given insight into a Summer he had never seen before. She was a free spirit, and he found intense pleasure in her mercurial nature. She bloomed like an exotic flower and sometimes seemed a gentle child who had been overcome by the enormity of her emotions; yet she could change immediately into a knowing woman who drove him wild with the sensuous heat she exuded, which drew him like a moth to the flame.

"Summer?"

"Ummm?"

"I love you."

She sat up and looked down at him, and he saw that her eyes still smoldered from recently tasted passion. "You have said so before," she said softly, "and so very well."

"It bears repeating. I won't ever forget how close I came to losing you."

"It is over. We are safe with each other."

"I know." He grinned as he drew her back into his arms and added, "But I won't feel safe unless I hold you close—for fifty years or so."

She laughed as she put her arms about him and hugged him to her.

"Summer, I hate to leave here, but there are a lot of loose ends that have to be tied."

"Yes?"

"First of all, woman, I want you married to me. Then, after we've had the celebration I'm sure Hawk and your parents will want, I would like to go home for a short visit."

"Of course. You must see your family."

"I must tell my parents about Nathaniel. But most of all, my sweet, I want them to meet you. They've had a great loss, Summer, but you will bring the sunshine back into their lives. Will you come with me? I know how you feel about the civilized world."

"I will come, Sebastian. I want very much to meet your parents. And we shall invite them to come here . . . and, perhaps, we can promise them grandchildren."

He rose up on one elbow and cocked a questioning eyebrow.

"No," she denied with a giggle. "Not yet. But," she said as her voice took on a decidedly seductive quality, "I'm sure you will help me remedy that matter."

He put his arms about her with a joyful laugh and murmured just before their lips met, "I should love to, my sweet. I'll do my best to keep all such promises."

Again they fled to a world beyond dreams that was theirs alone . . . theirs forever.

If you enjoyed this book we have a special offer for you. Become a charter member of the ZEBRA HISTORICAL ROMANCE HOME SUBSCRIPTION SERVICE and...

# Get a
# FREE
## Zebra Historical Romance
## (A $3.95 value) No Obligation

Now that you have read a Zebra Historical Romance we're sure you'll want more of the passion and sensuality, the desire and dreams and fascinating historical settings that make these novels the favorites of so many women. So we have made arrangements for you to receive a *FREE* book ($3.95 value) and preview 4 brand new Zebra Historical Romances each month.

## *Join the Zebra*
## *Home Subscription Service —*
## Free Home Delivery

By joining our Home Subscription Service you'll never have to worry about missing a title. You'll automatically get the romance, the allure, the attraction, that make Zebra Historical Romances so special.

Each month you'll receive 4 brand new Zebra Historical Romance novels as soon as they are published. Look them over *Free* for 10 days. If you're not delighted simply return them and owe nothing. But if you enjoy them as much as we think you will, you'll pay *only* $3.50 each and save 45¢ over the cover price. (You save a total of $1.80 each month.) *There is no shipping and handling charge or other hidden charges.*

## ———— *Fill Out the Coupon*————

Start your subscription now and start saving. Fill out the coupon and mail it *today.* You'll get your **FREE** book along with your first month's books to preview.